The Big Steal

Also by Emyl Jenkins

STEALING WITH STYLE

A STERLING GLASS MYSTERY

The BIG STEAL

Emyl Jenkins

ALGONQUIN BOOKS OF CHAPEL HILL

2009

Published by
ALGONQUIN BOOKS OF CHAPEL HILL
Post Office Box 2225
Chapel Hill, North Carolina 27515-2225

a division of
WORKMAN PUBLISHING
225 Varick Street
New York, New York 10014

Excerpt on p. vii from "An Importer," *The Poetry of Robert Frost,* edited by Edward Connery Lathem. Copyright © 1947, 1969 by Henry Holt and Company. Copyright © 1975 by Lesley Frost Ballantine. Reprinted by permission of Henry Holt and Company, LLC.

Excerpt on p. 337 from "The Museum" from *Edgar Allan Poe and the Juke-Box* by Elizabeth Bishop, edited and annotated by Alice Quinn. Copyright © 2006 by Alice Helen Methfessel. Introduction copyright © 2006 by Alice Quinn. Reprinted by permission of Farrar, Straus and Giroux, LLC.

Furniture illustrations on pp. 345–49, 351 by Carol Roper, Literati Design.

Library of Congress Cataloging-in-Publication Data
Jenkins, Emyl.
     The big steal / by Emyl Jenkins. — 1st ed.
         p. cm.
     ISBN-13: 978-1-56512-446-2
     1. Women detectives — Virginia — Fiction.   2. Appraisers — Fiction.
     3. Virginia — Fiction.   4. Antiques — Fiction.   I. Title.
     PS3610.E544B54 2009
     813'.6 — dc22   2009011704

10 9 8 7 6 5 4 3 2 1
First Edition

*In memory of three gentlemen who,
like the fine antiques they loved, were priceless,*

*Sam Pennington, watchdog journalist
Robert Sack, dealer extraordinaire
Bob Volpe, art cop*

*And for my three priceless grandsons,
Benjamin, Matthew, and Levi*

Mrs. Someone's been to Asia.
What she brought back would amaze ye,
Bamboos, ivories, jades, and lacquers . . .

—ROBERT FROST, "An Importer"

The Big Steal

Chapter 1

Dear Antiques Expert: My family has always prized a green and yellow pottery Tang horse given to our grandfather by an official of the Indonesian government in the 1950s. Could it really be valuable, or is its worth just a family myth?

Ever since grave robbers and archaeologists began unearthing the colorful pottery horses buried in the tombs of imperial rulers and wealthy Chinese during the Tang Dynasty (618–907), collectors have coveted them. But reproduction Tang horses have also been around for generations. Though an expert will have to determine your horse's age and origin, if it is authentic and in good condition, then its value could be many thousands of dollars. In 2003, a pair of extraordinarily rare Tang horses sold for $1.57 million.

THERE I WAS, shivering from head to toe, searching for family pictures and records left behind by Mazie and Hoyt Wyndfield. They hadn't had any children of their own to sort through their things after their deaths several years ago, which partly explains why, in the dead of winter, I was up in the attic of this place called Wynderly, digging through their lives. Once

Wynderly had been a gracious home. Now it was a museum teetering on the edge of bankruptcy.

Unlike the stately eighteenth-century Georgian plantations Virginia is known for, Wynderly was a sprawling place, reminiscent of a French chateau crossed with an English manor house. Rooms and wings jutted out here and there, as if some tipsy architect had thrown his plans up in the air and built rooms wherever the blueprints had landed. With its peaked turrets and slanting gables, soaring towers and stone ledges, Wynderly's message was loud and clear: Look at me. This is how rich we are; how rich are you?

Its vast attic, so large it could house three families with room to spare, mirrored the helter-skelter, multilayered house beneath. Every inch was filled with furniture, garden ornaments, boxes, books, paintings, trunks. I had begun with the boxes and trunks.

The first two I opened were filled with beautiful vintage clothing, which brought to mind the question about a 1950s Christian Dior evening dress I'd recently answered in my syndicated antiques column. But there was no time to think about that now, or to finger the lace negligees and slinky satin gowns. I was searching for papers, receipts, diaries—anything that would tell me more about the opulent objects in the house below.

It had started when Matt Yardley asked if I was available to take on an appraisal in Orange County. My brain had zipped into overdrive. Orange County, California, in the middle of February? Who wouldn't jump at the chance? With my son Ketch and daughter Lily now grown, and without a husband to tend to, I could close the door and walk out with a clear conscience.

Anyway I liked being able to say yes to Matt. Ever since I'd met him when working for Babson and Michael, the New York insurance company, I had hoped he'd send another job my way. It was only after I said yes that I bothered to ask questions. That's when I learned he was speaking of Orange County, Virginia, a three-plus-hour drive down lonely back roads, instead of a five- or six-hour flight from my home in Leemont, Virginia. But it was too late. I had given my word.

There had been an unsolved burglary at Wynderly, and some items left behind had been broken during the theft. But because there were no signs of a break-in, and the police had no obvious suspects, a serious cloud hung over the whole situation. In addition, the most recent appraisal of the items at Wynderly was over twenty years old and totally out of date.

"The question is whether or not we should pay the full amount they're asking for the damaged and missing items," Matt had said. He was right to be cautious. As with stocks and bonds, the value of antiques fluctuates over time. Matt wanted me to assess the current value of the broken pieces and then to see what I could find out about the stolen objects. But it wasn't until my second day at Wynderly that I was able to escape the clutches of the museum's curator, Michelle Hendrix, for time alone in the attic.

I put the boxes of clothing aside and reached for a trunk. I was lifting out a photograph album when a picture fell from between its pages. Picking it up, I noticed faint writing on the back: "Mazie and Hoyt. Wynderly. Spring 1924."

Mazie's jet-black hair was pulled straight back at the nape of her long, pearl-white neck, which appeared even paler in the black and white picture. Hoyt Wyndfield wore a crisp linen jacket, white shoes, and fully pleated pants held up high by a shiny dark belt. Wynderly, towering behind them, had finally been completed. Hoyt and Mazie held hands, yet stood apart, as if to give the camera a wider, clearer shot of their home. Though scaffolding was still in place and muddy earth was mounded high around its foundation, I could almost feel their love for the place.

Matt Yardley had told me the Wyndfields named the house Wynderly after themselves and the windblown hills at the base of the Blue Ridge Mountains of Virginia where it was built. The name seemed perfect; it made me think of Biltmore, Stan Hewett, and San Simeon—other houses built by that rarified generation with the money, style, and taste to erect monuments to themselves. Their owners had traveled the world over and returned home with treasures to fill every high-ceilinged room.

Wynderly and its objects had survived the ravages of time, but Hoyt and Mazie's fortune had not. With the fate of the house and its objects in doubt, Matt Yardley knew to be suspicious of the validity of the insurance claim. I had been at Wynderly for only a day and a half, and I was beginning to have a few questions of my own.

Good appraisers are, by nature, detectives. I've always said it's because we see so *many* fakes and frauds—both the inanimate and the two-legged variety—that we never take anything, or anyone, at face value. Once upon a time I was as innocent as the next person. I loved antiques for all the right reasons—beauty, craftsmanship, and especially the memories our treasures hold.

Then I learned how some corrupt silversmith had fused eighteenth-century English hallmarks on the bottoms of Colonial Williamsburg reproduction silver pitchers, and how Granny's beautiful eighteenth-century console table had really been made by a sly forger in the 1920s, not Mr. Chippendale himself. It had forever changed the way I looked at everything.

During my first tour of Wynderly, a couple of pieces sent up red flags, like when I saw the Tang horses. Something about them wasn't right.

Authentic seventh- or eighth-century pottery horses made in China as tomb accessories are rare indeed, as is the pocketbook that can afford one. And over the years I'd been shown two or three dozen Tang horses thought by their owners to be the real thing worth tens, even hundreds of thousands of dollars. But instead of being several centuries old, their horses were no more than fifty or a hundred years old, and seldom worth more than a couple hundred dollars.

Wynderly's deep green horses, their heads bowed and their tails arched, had instantly given me pause. It didn't make sense. Wynderly had been open to the public for years. Every publication from *Art & Antiques* to *Southern Accents* was constantly looking for fresh material for their pages, so why was it that, outside of Virginia, few people had even heard of Wynderly?

I was beginning to suspect that those horses, along with other pieces, might teeter between truth and myth, honesty and deception. I could hardly wait to start my own investigations. Trouble was, Michelle Hendrix had been dogging my every step. And like the Tang horses, she, too, was proving to be perplexing.

I had thought that since we'd be working together, we would be helpful to each other. Instead, though Michelle never left my side, she seemed to purposely avoid answering my questions about Wynderly's antiques. I had begun to think I could learn more on my own.

I shivered, partly from the biting cold, and partly from my unexplainable, but very real, queasy feelings about the whole situation. I tried telling myself that damp, creepy old houses, especially those set back in dark country woods, can give off eerie vibes. I thought of Hansel and Gretel. Remembering my childish fright I chuckled. Why, it was nothing more than Wynderly itself that was giving me the sense that something was amiss.

Feeling better, I stared hard at the photograph of Mazie and Hoyt as if hoping it would speak to me.

We can never go back again, that much is certain, Mother had told me the day we closed up her home, some months after my father died.

Trying to make light of the heartbreaking moment, I had said, "I think Daphne du Maurier said it first, Mother. In *Rebecca*."

I tried to imagine Hoyt and Mazie's lives during that time when ladies wore picture hats to tea parties and gentlemen dressed for dinner. What dreams they must have dreamed as they watched their house rise from its stone foundation to its magnificent completion. And all the stuff in it? Chances were the Wyndfields, like scores of my clients, had simply met up with a few fast-talking antiques wheeler-dealers and fallen for their spiels.

I kept thinking about those Tang horses. Add in Michelle Hendrix's puzzling demeanor and the eerie aura surrounding the house . . . In no time, uneasy feelings had crept back into my head. What I needed was a delete button in my brain like the one on my computer.

Get a grip, Sterling, I told myself. This isn't one of those novels about art theft or jewelry heists; this is life. Real life.

I'd been bent over so long, I needed to get my circulation going again—to clear my mind, if nothing else. I stood, only to stumble over a raised beam that blended into the pine floor's shadowy grain. I lurched forward and instinctively reached out to grab something before I hit the wall in front of me. A tower of boxes moved under my momentum, and together we landed in a heap on the floor.

The plank beneath my feet had moved, or at least that's the way it felt. Instead of falling forward, my body twisted and first my hip, then my shoulder, took the impact of the fall.

The faint lightbulb dangling from the attic ceiling had flickered, then gone out when I fell. A small casement window was nearby, but afternoon clouds had settled in. Crawling forward, I mentally kicked myself for not bringing in the flashlight I kept in my car for just such situations.

No question about it. One of the wide floorboards had sunk at least half, maybe even three-quarters of an inch below the boards on each side of it. I patted the floor around me. My hand hit an obstruction. The beam I had stumbled over was definitely jutting up through the floor. It was probably part of a high-vaulted ceiling I'd seen on my tour of the house.

I pushed on the sunken board in hopes it might pop back in place. When I did, the wall I had barely avoided hitting head-on creaked ever so slightly. My hands went wet and my throat dry. I swallowed hard and pressed the board again, harder this time. There was no mistaking the connection between the movement of the displaced piece of flooring and the low creaking coming from what looked like just another wall—except it was paneled, not unfinished the way other parts of the attic were. Maybe the plan had been to build a closet or a maid's room, but they never got around to doing it.

As my eyes adjusted to the dimness, I set about restacking the fallen boxes, one of which had broken open. Strewn across the floor were sheets of dry onionskin paper held together by rusty paper clips and straight pins. Official-looking ledger pages were mixed in with handwritten receipts, as were several small books.

Enough late afternoon light was trickling through the windows so I could make out the larger lettering on some of the receipts. I gathered a handful and began sifting through them. "Société anonyme au capital de 250.000 Francs. Invoice. Nürnberg. American Consulate. Hong Kong. Customs Broker. Saaz."

That one caught my attention. Saaz? I moved the paper back and forth until I could make out the words written long ago in purple ink, but that now had faded to a light lavender.

> 1 sugar box, jeweled, 2200.
> 1 silver vessel, 600.
> 12 spoons.
> 2 little tea spoons.

I was musing over the quaint description "little," when I noticed no prices were cited for the spoons. I looked back at the stationery's letterhead. *July 1927* was scribbled at the top right hand corner. Embossed on the center of the page was a red coat of arms and, beneath that, in royal blue letters, the name Franz Bauer. A third line ran across the width of the page. Saaz—New York—Rio de Janeiro. But where was Saaz? Germany, perhaps? Poland?

Again I shifted the paper to get it in a better light when a straight pin holding a handwritten note attached to the back pricked my finger. I turned the page over and read: "To whom it may concern, these spoons are genuine antiquities and over a hundred years old and the work of Saaz handicraft and passed on in possession of families of this region of Bohemia and sold privately."

Well, that answered one question. Saaz, Bohemia, now Saaz, Czech Republic, I surmised. But the handwritten explanation struck me as peculiar. Why would a merchant have included the spoons on his list? To get them past customs was all I could think of. But no price? I came up empty.

Still, something about these papers stored—or had they been hidden?—in the attic, rather than being on file in the curator's office, seemed strange. Then again, in a house as large as this one and with so much in it, the chances were great that things would be scattered all about. I had had a gut feeling about the attic, and Michelle had been surprisingly agreeable. "Who knows what's up there," she'd said offhandedly. "Just see what you can find."

Many an attic has held great treasures. Why every four or five months there's breaking news that a heretofore unknown composition by Beethoven, a manuscript by Goethe, a long lost old master painting, or some such discovery has turned up hidden beneath often walked-by shadows. In Virginia the original eighteenth-century plans for Francis Lightfoot Lee's Menokin plantation were found in the attic of a house several miles away. I was wondering how much more might be up here.

"It's almost three thirty."

My heart leapt.

Michelle Hendrix loomed above me. She looked no different in the gloomy shadows of the attic than she had in the daylight when I had arrived at Wynderly. A tall woman probably in her mid-thirties, she had no sparkle.

"I had no idea," I said, attempting to recover, while also trying to slip the papers onto the floor without her noticing. "I didn't hear you."

"Dr. Houseman expects board meetings to start on time." Michelle crossed her arms in front of her and stepped closer. "Finding anything?" she asked.

"Board meeting?" I replied.

"Oh, did I forget to tell you yesterday? Alfred Houseman, you know, the chairman of the Wynderly Foundation board . . . anyway, he's called a meeting for this afternoon."

I struggled to my feet. Michelle Hendrix didn't budge.

"So, finding anything?" she asked again.

"Too early to be sure," I said offhandedly.

Too many questions were swimming around in my head for me to share my findings. I gave her a noncommittal shrug. "What about you? Have you had a productive afternoon?"

"Not after Houseman blew in earlier than I had expected. He has a way of doing that." She rolled her eyes. "I was back in my office when he showed up, a full half an hour early.

Didn't bother to call ahead either." She made a low growling sound. "That man thinks he owns this place."

Michelle pointed to her watch. "You'd better hurry. Houseman doesn't allow for lateness."

"Me?"

What to do? I swooped up the papers with every intention of putting them in the open box. Michelle had started toward the steps. With her back turned, did I dare slip some of them in the zip-up binder I had with me so I could take notes? Just one or two, maybe.

Opportunity makes the thief, Mother scolded. *One thief in this place is enough.*

I hesitated, but only momentarily. What's an appraiser to do?

Evidence, I thought.

Chapter 2

Dear Antiques Expert: In a recent article about a fabulous European palace museum there was mention of a pair of blackamoors, but it didn't explain what blackamoors are. Could you help me, please?

During the late 17th century, life-size statues depicting the Muslims, who had spread from Africa into Spain and Europe during medieval times, became popular household decorations in grand European homes and palaces. These were called blackamoors. (Incidentally, servants sometimes wore Moorish costumes. Remember Cary Grant in *To Catch a Thief*?) If the statue or figure held a light or torch (candle, oil lamp, or later, an electrified bulb) it was called a blackamoor torchère. But be warned. Not all the "antique" statues seen in shops are old. Reproductions come in a variety of material, sizes, quality, and prices.

I WAS STILL wrestling with my conscience when I reached the last attic step. Mother was right. One thief *was* enough. On the other hand, I rationalized, I had been sent to Wynderly to get to the truth, and that meant digging for evidence.

By the time I reached the main floor, three flights down, I

was no longer thinking about the papers I had confiscated, but the tension building between Michelle and me. Yesterday's encounter had set the tone for all that followed.

GETTING TO WYNDERLY had been no small feat. The twisty, narrow back roads would have been nerve-racking in bright sunshine. Yesterday had been gray and threatening. Only when I had brought the car to a stop in front of the mansion and tossed the directions I had clutched between my knees onto the passenger seat did I relax a little. I should have turned around right then and headed back to Leemont.

I had been reaching for the pull of the bell mounted on the front archway when Michelle Hendrix flung open the massive front door as if this were her ancestral home. Had she really been the lady of the house, surely she would have invited me to come in out of the cold and inquired about my trip. That's the polite Southern way. Instead, she had motioned me inside with a grand, sweeping gesture. "The drawing room," she had said.

My eyes had followed her arm and voice. Assuming the red velvet rope marked off the drawing room, I ventured forth. I paused at the top of the four steps leading to the sunken room beneath the vaulted ceiling. Below lay a magnificent sight.

At the far end of the room hung a Venetian mirror with a rich cobalt blue glass border. The glow of the enormous silver-plated chandelier reflected in the mirror was as dazzling as a summer sun. In contrast, the furniture was dark and elaborately carved, the sort tourists go to great expense to see in the grand castles of Europe. Ornate sterling picture frames graced every tabletop. Pairs of trumpet-shaped silver vases filled with bunches of blue and green peacock feathers adorned the twin marble mantelpieces on the side walls.

"Oh dear, I forgot to turn on the sconces," Michelle said.

It hadn't been necessary, the room was splendid enough. But when she did, my appraiser's mind instinctively kicked in: English, nineteenth century, originally intended for candles, now electrified.

As if reading my mind, Michelle said, "The sconces weren't electrified until after Hoyt died and Mazie decided it was too much to have the servants lighting and snuffing out the candles every night. Candles . . . that's how they lit the Hall of Mirrors at Versailles," she said.

Thank goodness Michelle couldn't see my frown. Despite its size and grandeur, Wynderly hardly measured up to Versailles.

"We seldom turn them on these days. Way too wasteful," she continued. "But I wanted you to get the full effect, to see the way the Wyndfields lived in Wynderly's glory days . . . when they were here, that is. They traveled all the time. And I took the sheets and coverings off the furniture especially for you."

I glanced about. In my mind's eye I could envision shrouds of white sheets and gray tarps mounding over the furnishings, turning the room into its own dreary mausoleum. Michelle turned and made another, even grander gesture, flipping her wrist and pointing ballerina-like. Assuming she meant for me to go down into the room for a closer look, I stepped forward. When I did so, Michelle announced, "No. No. *This* way. The ballroom is to the left."

She reminded me of Gloria Swanson in *Sunset Boulevard,* preparing for her grand entrance.

I followed her along the paneled corridor separating the two rooms, our echoing footsteps the only sign of life. Portrait after portrait of unsmiling people entombed in heavy gilt frames lined the oak walls. At the hallway's end, two larger-than-life wooden blackamoor torchères guarded the entrance to the ballroom. The flickering bulbs in their outstretched hands cast a golden light across the parquet floor. Only the white ceiling, a flurry of plaster loops and swirls carved to imitate fully opened rose blossoms, broke the gloomy darkness.

I know, my responsibility was to identify quality and assign a value to my client's treasures, not pass judgment on someone else's taste. But the house wasn't at all in keeping with the slightly frumpy style this part of Virginia was famous for. This was horse country. Fashions might come and go, but not the family's ancestral huntboard or threadbare Oriental rugs.

Michelle stopped to remove the roping before she almost pirouetted over to the light switch. When she turned to face me, her eyes left little doubt that not only was I expected to be impressed, I should tell her so. But gushing isn't my way.

"Hmm-humm," I mumbled noncommittally, all the while thinking that I might be more enthusiastic if I could shed my heavy coat and break away to the lady's room after such a long trip. But when Michelle flipped on the lights and I saw the life-size mural on the far wall of the room, I forgot my discomfort. So what if the scene of a masked ball replete with bejeweled women, their hair adorned with billowing plumes and feathers, flirting with men in satin britches and lacy shirts was a bit too tony for these parts. It was masterful.

"How wonderful," I said. "Venetian?"

"Oh, yes, and hand-painted," she answered.

For the first time since we'd met, Michelle Hendrix smiled a pleasant, almost warm smile. Leaning toward me as if sharing a secret, she said, "Hoyt and Mazie brought craftsmen from Italy to paint the murals. In fact, there are murals all over the house. Masons. Painters. Artists of every sort, even sculptors. The Wyndfields brought them all here. You'll see the marble statues in some of the gardens later," she added. "Mazie loved her gardens." Michelle held up her fingers as she named them. "Herb, formal, cutting, rose, even a vegetable garden, Italian, Elizabethan . . . ah . . ." She faltered. "Boxwood. And of course the maze. That's always been the public's favorite. But Mazie got tired of people always talking about Mazie's maze. Her real name was Mary Elise, you know, but everyone called her Mazie," she said. "Hoyt had it designed as a gift to her. Actually, I think the water garden might have been Mazie's favorite. It's so remote most people don't even know about it. Like the pagoda. Wynderly is a very large place, you know. Acres and acres."

I was about to make some joking comment that "large" was an understatement.

"I'd advise you not to try to wander off by yourself, though," Michelle said, her voice flat. "You'll need to stick with me. If there's anything you want, or need to see, you'll have to ask me."

With Michelle in the lead, I had dutifully followed—beneath arched doorways, in and out of wings, down long dreary passageways, around massive bookcases, through the rooms of Wynderly, each one seemingly larger and grander than the one before. Her unnecessary aggrandizing of the house and its contents was beginning to grate on my nerves. Wynderly spoke for itself. Plus, I was anxious to get down to work.

Still, I tried putting myself in her shoes. With the house closed to visitors, she had to be lonesome. What else had she to do than show me around? I'm sure she thought I needed the orientation.

On the other hand, knowing that she was a possible suspect in this unexplainable burglary was bound to have her upset. Perhaps this was her way of trying to keep control of the situation.

A few minutes later, just as Michelle was about to show me another room, I finally asked directions to the lady's powder room. *Bathroom* just didn't seem the appropriate word in these surroundings.

Michelle was waiting for me. "Isn't it a beautiful room," she said. "The faucets are gold-plated, and the mirror came from India—a gift from the maharaja. Those are real rubies and sapphires."

The opulence of the powder room had taken me aback even more than had the mural and the blackamoors.

Now remember, Sterling, you have to forget that you're in Mr. Jefferson's country, I had told myself. Stop trying to make Wynderly something it isn't. It's not Monticello.

I nodded in agreement and smiled. "It really *is* remarkable."

"But you've seen enough of the house," she said, turning away from me. "Follow me. I'll take you to the workroom."

Chapter 3

Dear Antiques Expert: When I admired a large blue and white plate at an antiques show, the dealer called it an "English Delft charger." My aunt brought back a vase from Holland that was marked "Delft." I thought all Delft came from Holland, and what exactly is a "charger"?

Delft, also called Delftware, is an earthenware pottery with a tin-glazed exterior. It originated in the 1600s in Holland when Europeans were trying to discover how to make thin porcelain like the Chinese. But because the English also produced a glaze-finished pottery, the distinction is made between Dutch and English Delft. Dutch Delft, however, has always been better known. "Charger" is the name given to large, shallow plates that we today would call platters. Incidentally, truly old Delft pieces were marked with symbols. Pieces marked with the word "Delft" are of modern manufacture.

AT LAST I could get to work. I had headed straight to the table where pieces of what had been a seventeenth-century Delft charger were spread out on a card table.

"If you're going to look at the things the thieves left behind, you're going to need these," Michelle had said, handing me a pair of gauzy white cotton museum gloves.

Though a nice piece, the large plate really didn't call for curatorial gloves, especially not in its present condition. But trying to keep a positive attitude, I told myself Michelle's offer of the gloves had been a nice gesture. Perhaps she was worried that I might nick my fingers on some sharp, jagged edge.

I laid my things on an empty chair before joining Michelle at the table. "Thank you for the offer, but I don't think I'll be needing these. I'll be careful," I said, holding out the gloves to give them back to her.

The look Michelle Hendrix cast my way told me she couldn't have cared less whether I cut myself or not. "Wynderly's house rules *require* that gloves be worn if you're going to touch anything—porcelain, crystal, furniture, silver—anything."

"I understand, but . . ."

I looked at the broken bits on the table. Frankly, I get the same sort of rush from running my fingers over wood and silver worn smooth and silky from generations of handling and polishing that a wine connoisseur gets from tasting a perfectly aged vintage wine. As for the things at Wynderly? If the house was near bankruptcy, chances were its contents would be sold at auction. I'd yet to see an auctioneer wearing museum gloves to handle his goods. Why, every piece in the house had been dusted and moved, handled and touched by human hands for decades. I guess the police had worn gloves when trying to gather fingerprints, but now what was the point? And as for this particular Delft piece, finer pieces are routinely passed from hand to hand in many an antiques shop.

But what I was *thinking,* and what I dared to *say,* were two different things. I shut up and yanked the gloves on.

So far I had only had a rushed look at a small portion Wynderly and the things in it. Though the Tang horses had genuinely bothered me, I had also noticed what appeared to be some quite fine pieces of eighteenth-century English furniture. I knew the silver I'd seen in the drawing room was good, but some garishly painted pieces of Native American pottery I had glimpsed in what Michelle called the Game Room looked more like touristy bowls and jugs. A hodgepodge. That's what the Wynderly collection was, which was also what made it so fascinating. Any appraiser will tell you, the challenge often lies not so much in discovering the real, as in uncovering the fakes, frauds, and forgeries. I had a virtual playground awaiting me. The question was, had the thieves known what they were doing?

Among the finer things I had noted in the house had been a truly valuable piece of Delft, a piece much finer than the charger I was working on. It was an exquisite blue and white water bottle, probably from the 1680s—the sort that would be estimated to sell for sixty or seventy-five thousand dollars, but might bring a cool hundred thousand or even more in the right auction venue. Why had they left *it* behind? If they didn't know what they were doing . . . Then again, the thieves who had made off with some three hundred million dollars of art from the Isabella Stewart Gardner Museum in Boston had left some of the collection's most valuable items behind, and they'd had over an hour to decide what to take. But who had said there were *thieves*?

What if Michelle Hendrix had been behind the theft? Or, what if this were an inside job, a way for the museum to get the insurance money? Then the randomness of the pieces taken, some valuable, some not, might have been purposely done as a way to throw the investigation off.

No wonder Matt Yardley had sent me on the job. "Wynderly's claim may be on the money. To the penny," he had said. "But, knowing the financial straits Wynderly's foundation is in, I want to be sure. Over the years more than one small museum has tried to wiggle its way out of financial difficulties by using its insurance payout to replenish its coffers. Not that I think that's the case here, but I have to be sure. Who knows, I may be paying you to tell me Babson and Michael owes the foundation more than they've claimed."

While Michelle peered over my shoulder, I struggled to concentrate on organizing the broken and damaged pieces. Wearing, of course, gloves.

Chapter 4

Dear Antiques Expert: My insurance agent says we need to have an appraisal made of our antiques and more valuable new pieces. How do we find a good appraiser?

Try to find an appraiser who belongs to a nationally recognized appraisal association with a strong education program and code of ethics: the American Society of Appraisers, Appraisers Association of America, or the International Society of Appraisers, for example. But if you can't, remember:

Never hire an appraiser who charges on a percentage basis or who buys the items appraised.

Because appraisers often have specialties, tell the appraiser your specific needs and the purpose of the appraisal.

Before the appraiser arrives, prepare a list and gather any receipts or pertinent information.

Finally, setting out items such as silver, china, and crystal sets will save the appraiser time and you money.

LATER, BACK AT THE antebellum bed and breakfast in town, I had phoned my dear friend Peter Donaldson, partly for company but mostly to vent my frustration.

"You can't believe how huge Wynderly is, Peter. It's much larger than it looks in pictures. And the stuff in it— There must be tons of it. Remember Xanadu, the house in *Citizen Kane,* with its storerooms filled with all those statues and trunks and stuff? That's what Wynderly reminds me of, and I haven't even seen its storerooms yet. It wouldn't be so bad except for the curator. She won't leave me alone to get my work done. First she insisted on giving me a tour of the house when I was eager to see the damage the thieves had done. Then, once we finally *did* get to the workroom, the whole time I was trying to concentrate, she babbled away, asking me questions. But when I'd ask *her* a question she'd clam up like she'd been shrink-wrapped. I hardly got a thing done all day." I paused to catch my breath.

Peter laughed. "Haven't you had anyone to talk to?"

"You wouldn't find it so funny if you were in my shoes," I said. "Michelle was nipping at my heels like a hound dog all day. There's just the two of us echoing through the hallways. The place is a *morgue.*"

"A morgue? With so much stuff around? Sounds more like King Tut's tomb."

It was my turn to laugh. "Well, I haven't stumbled over any mummies or gold caskets . . ." I hesitated, remembering Michelle's comment about removing the sheets and covers for my visit. "At least not yet." Once the image of the shrouded furnishings came to mind, somehow finding a mummy didn't seem beyond the realm of possibility.

"But that's the only thing I *haven't* seen. Most of what I've seen today is bling to the extreme, but with a 1920s and 1930s twist. I guess because I was told the house was a museum I had expected the owners to be collectors. Now don't get me wrong. It's obvious that Hoyt and Mazie Wyndfield loved the things they bought, but they weren't collectors. Not in the *true* sense, not like the duPonts or Rockefellers. Only way I can think of to describe the Wyndfields is . . . well . . . accumulators. Indiscriminate accumulators."

"You? The Queen of Stuff, complaining about too many things? Now, Sterling."

I ignored that. "Look, I'd be having a ball if left to my own devices," I said. "There are some wonderful pieces in the house, but except for seeing a broken Delft charger and some porcelain, it's been a lost day. There are more questions running around in my head than answers."

Images of the things I'd seen flashed across my mind, but it was Michelle who loomed even larger. "You should hear how she talks about the Wyndfields. She practically genuflects every time she says Mazie's name. This afternoon on our way out she stood in front of one of Mazie's portraits—there must be dozens of them." I lowered my voice to imitate Michelle's hushed awe. "And she said, 'Mazie was a princess—born and bred. And she married a *prince.*'" I stopped. "But I'm being too harsh. Actually, Michelle's admiration for the Wyndfields is rather touching."

"So tell me more. You had mentioned a Delft charger."

I grimaced. Here I was, trying to figure Michelle Hendrix out, and Peter wanted to talk about the Delft. But how like him. After all, the objects were what was really important.

Antiques had brought Peter Donaldson, a widowed and retired Episcopal priest, into my life. Sometimes it's still hard for me to believe that this old-line Virginia aristocrat runs

Leemont's Salvation Army thrift shop, where many a valuable antique has ended up, usually quite unintentionally. Naturally he *would* be more interested in the artifacts than my chatter.

"So what was it, Dutch or English Delft? What was the decoration?"

"Well it *had* been a wonderful seventeenth- or eighteenth-century Adam and Eve charger. You know, the type made in Bristol, England. One with the snake twined around the apple tree and big leaves hiding Adam and Eve's . . ." I hesitated. Then, remembering Peter's fondness for *Monty Python*, I said in my best British accent, "Their 'naughty bits.' "

I stifled a smile when I heard Peter chuckle, then turned serious and said, "But then Michelle asked me what it was *worth*. Don't you think she should have known that? And when I asked her what condition the charger was in before it was smashed, she shrugged as if she couldn't have cared less. Eventually she did say that some appraiser had said it was 'worth a lot, about two thousand dollars.' Those were her exact words. Why, years ago it would have been worth five or six thousand, even it was chipped or the paint was flaking off. Today? More like seven or eight. Maybe ten.

"What's bothering me is that I can't tell if she is really ignorant of the situation or playing dumb. Then again, it could be she's hiding something. If she's on the level, then how could she have been around these things and not have learned about them, especially since she had to take tour groups around the house? But strangest of all is the way she's so possessive of the house and the Wyndfields . . . like it all belongs to her."

"How old did you say she is?" Peter asked.

I thought for a moment.

Should I even be telling Peter all this, I suddenly wondered. Matt Yardley's unexpected entrance into my life was complicating matters—not that mentioning Matt would make any difference to Peter. Truth was, it was my own feelings I was skittish about. I'd been crazy about Peter ever since we met. From the start I'd wished I were more a part of his life, and he of mine. I probably needed to get over him. But I didn't want to let my friendship with him go.

"Sterling? Are you there?"

"Guess the line dropped out here in the boondocks," I fudged. "There's little to no cell phone service, too . . . I meant to tell you that. Let's see, you asked how old Michelle is? I'd say mid-thirties. Maybe as old as forty?"

"It could be that she's just in over her head. Seems I read something about a lot of turnover of Wynderly's personnel in some article on the back page of the paper about the theft. If this curator's only been there for a few months and the place is in trouble . . ." His voice trailed off.

"Speaking of curators," he said more spiritedly. "The *New York Times* is full of news about the Getty Museum's curator, Marion True. Not only has the Greek government confiscated some of the antiquities found in her Greek island home, it seems the Getty has to return some of the museum's finest treasures to Greece. With all this interest in the art world, if the theft at Wynderly turns out to be an inside job, you might be in the throes of a news-making scandal."

I laughed. "Oh, I hardly think Wynderly would make the *New York Times,* scandal or not. But say, keep that article for me, will you?"

"Sure. So about the Delft. Did you find out who the appraiser was—the one who said the charger was worth two thousand dollars?"

"Not yet. So far all I have is the list of broken and stolen items Matt Yardley sent to me. My task for tomorrow is to try to wrangle some paperwork from Michelle . . . if I can. And that's something else that's frustrating me. When the house was open, the hours were ten to four, which is when she left today, even though I wanted to stay later. If I could *only* get my hands on a few things in the house," I said, thinking out loud.

"Such as? What would you go for first?"

"Let's see. Hmm." The Tang horses seemed too obvious a choice. What else had I seen that I had wondered about?

"I glimpsed a terrific inlaid English gaming table that has great lines, but since nearly every British faker alive has copied that style— Who knows? And there's a copper weathervane over the fireplace in one of the less formal rooms," I said, remembering the million-dollar prices a couple of weathervanes had recently sold for. "It's of a trotting horse and has a good patina. But again, is it real? Could go either way."

"So. I can tell you're not completely miserable."

Good old Peter. His sensible, grounded ways could always rein me in.

"OK," he said, "here's my take on the situation. It's really pretty simple. Tomorrow just march into Wynderly with an air of quiet authority and very politely tell Michelle Hendrix what you have to have. Original bills of sale. Earlier appraisals, inventory, whatever."

Truth is, on the drive from Wynderly to the B and B I had already planned to do exactly what he was telling me to do.

Still, hearing Peter's advice reassured me. Like Mother's voice in my head. *You catch more flies with honey,* she would say when I was angry with one of my childhood friends and would threaten to get even.

"Peter, you're absolutely right," I said. After all, no compliment is ever wasted on a man. "I know what I'll do. I'll arrange it so she *has* to leave me alone. Then, I'll head to the attic. I've made enough appraisals to know that's where the old bills and canceled checks are stored, and *they're* what I need." I smiled to myself. "Anyway, you and I know that more often than not, that's where some *treasures* are apt to be hidden away."

Peter laughed. "Always the adventurer, aren't you? You really shouldn't be worrying so much about all this," he said. "I'm sure you have the situation well in hand. Just get the job done. Speaking of such, do you have any idea when you'll be getting back to Leemont?"

My heart stood still. Why had I even allowed myself to think about Matt? I waited to hear what Peter would say next. He didn't disappoint me.

"No? Well, take care and call me if there's anything I can do to help. I'm right here."

Chapter 5

Dear Antiques Expert: I recently bought a vase that I thought was marble in an antiques mall, but when I got it home a friend told me it was faux marble and not the real thing. Is faking marble something new in the antiques world?

Faux, or fake, finishes have been around since ancient Greeks painted wood and plaster to resemble gold and marble. During the Renaissance, faux finishes imitating marble and stone were particularly popular, especially for cathedral and palace interiors. In the 18th and 19th centuries, inexpensive woods were often painted to look like pricey rosewood and tiger maple. Today, new materials like hydroston, as well as plaster, wood, ceramics, glass, and others can be faux finished to fool the eye as jade, malachite, marble, pearl, bamboo . . . the list is endless. That's why the old advice, caveat emptor (buyer beware), should always be heeded.

BY THE MORNING of the next day, I was actually looking forward to getting back to Wynderly. I had a plan. And with my resolve to think first and speak second, and then to speak kindly, surely I'd be able to make some headway.

But the first glitch came when I overslept. I had to rush to get to Wynderly by ten o'clock. When Michelle wasn't there, I was stuck. Even if I had known how to reach her, my cell phone reception was kaput. Trying to keep a positive attitude, I took advantage of the moment to get a feel for the place without Michelle's intrusion. Looking up at the house, it was as if the attic was beckoning to me.

In truth Wynderly was a splendid structure. But reaching the diamond-shaped leaded glass windows with buckets and sponges when they needed washing, and the heights of the high-pitched slate roofs with hammers and tools when they began to leak, must have presented a challenge. Plus, securing ladders against those ragged clinker brick walls would be tricky. Scaffolding would be the only answer.

And the grounds. Summer's overgrown vines and hedges gave the place an unkempt look. Ivy, which once had defined Wynderly's striking lines, now ran rampant along its chimneys and gables, turning the house's majesty into mystery. Even its casement windows were darkened by gnarled ink green tangles. What had once been picturesque was now tomb-like. Nothing about the place felt Southern. The South of France or southern Italy, perchance, but not our antebellum South.

The gardens were in even worse state than the house. Without hands to prune the shrubs in the maze, some had spread like wildfire while others had withered into brown stumps. What would eventually become of Wynderly, I wondered as I reached down to yank up the periwinkle vine that was growing on a marble figure of Pan. Just then I heard a car approaching.

At the front door, Michelle was fumbling with the keys and alarm system. She gave me a weak smile. "I hate this thing," she said.

We shed our coats in her office, all the while speculating about the weather. It was the first time she had allowed me inside her inner sanctum. I'd left my office in disarray, but this was a rat's nest. Battered file cabinets lined every available wall space; one even blocked three-quarters of a window. Scrapbooks and yellowed boxes were piled under tables. The only way to distinguish Michelle Hendrix's desk from the other flat surfaces in the room was that she placed her pocketbook on it. Her computer had to be at least fifteen years old. When I asked Michelle about it she sighed.

"No e-mail. No spreadsheet program. Want to see the disks?"

"That's OK." I was tempted to ask her about appraisals and inventories but decided to stick to my original game plan. "If it's not too much trouble, I'd like to start the morning by seeing the other damaged pieces that were left behind," I said, keeping my vow to be nice. "That way I won't be in your way, Michelle. If you can just point me in that direction. And this afternoon I'd like to see if I can find receipts and bills of sale. Perhaps the attic would be a—"

"But you haven't even seen the second and third floors," she interrupted. "I'm going to show those to you now." Her tone was so commanding, I didn't dare suggest otherwise.

For the next two hours we roamed among lonely bedrooms and sitting rooms, dressing rooms and morning rooms, from nook to cranny, a new room at every turn. It struck me how no books or papers were lying around, no hint of a family ever having lived there. It was cold and sterile, the way most house museums are. No wonder people don't want to visit them.

These rooms were as much a jumble of styles and periods as those I'd seen downstairs. Everywhere billowing yards of elegant French silk damask, rich English toile, and heavy Italian lace competed for attention. In the ladies' bedrooms, every dressing table was skirted in layers of netting or satin, sometimes both. And every room was drowning in drapes.

As for the furniture, it was mostly what Mother always called "Gigi" furniture—gold and gilt curves and curlicues in the French and Italian styles. The exception was the occasional Oriental piece. As far as I could tell, the only reason for any of the furniture, decorations, or art to be in this part of Virginia so proud of its understated elegance was that it had caught the Wyndfields' eyes. Then again, there *were* a few gems, like the outstanding Louis XIV tortoiseshell bracket clock. But Michelle had rounded the bend of the long hall so quickly, I didn't dare hang back to examine it.

Every so often Michelle would impart a little information about Hoyt and Mazie—how wonderful they were, how grandly they entertained, how wealthy they'd been. She had said next to nothing about any of the furnishings or objects until we reached what she termed Mazie's precious stone room.

"See the doorknobs," she said. "Jade. And the mantel is malachite. And the ginger jars"—she pointed to the pair of deep blue urn-shaped jars on the green marbleized mantel—"lapis lazuli. And that chair over there . . . pure jade. The Wyndfields were far ahead of their time." Her eyes sparkled.

"Can you believe that Mazie and Hoyt had visited the Taj Mahal in the twenties?" Her chest swelled with pride like a kid boasting on the playground. "I've read that the furniture at the Taj Mahal was just inlaid with stones. Mazie and Hoyt had whole objects and pieces made of them."

I was tempted to tell Michelle about faux lapis and malachite finishes, about the do-it-yourself kits available. I wanted to tell her how glass has been made to look like jade for centuries. And as for the malachite and lapis—coat after coat of paint and varnish applied to sanded and shellacked wood followed by more shellac or varnish could be patterned to imitate those stones and fool the eye. Instead, I kept quiet.

We had begun to move through another wing of the rambling house when a cacophony of chiming clocks signaled the noon hour. After Michelle's closing up of the house at precisely four yesterday afternoon, and her arrival after ten this morning, I wasn't surprised when she announced that we would now break for lunch.

Back in Michelle's office, and over sandwiches, I tried to get some innocuous conversation going.

"So, when exactly did Wynderly close?" I asked.

"Hmm. A few months ago."

"That must have been a disappointment to the groups with tours scheduled."

"There're other places around that give tours."

"I guess you're right," I said.

Well, I had a job to do. I started by fawning over Mazie and Hoyt's things, how exceptional, wonderful, beautiful, and rare they were. I told her how, now that I had seen more of this magnificent place, I better understood how terrible it must have been for her that the burglary had taken place. "I know you must be devastated. Yet, *you're* the only one who can help me, Michelle," I said.

What I really needed to do, I explained, was roam around the attic to see what was up there. Experience had taught me that *all* the finest museums eventually found it necessary to move their archives when things got crowded. The question was where such papers might be at Wynderly. The basement, an outbuilding, or the attic.

"And I totally sympathize with your not having the time to go through everything that must have accumulated here over the years," I continued, "*plus* tend to so many other duties, and now the theft. Just the family's pictures and scrapbooks and papers . . ." I swept the room with my eyes, shaking my head in wonderment.

A great sigh came over her. "It's been crazy," she said, nodding. "There's all this, and then the bills and invoices and correspondence . . . and phone calls that come in."

"I can't imagine," I said. "Perhaps if you're not having to fuss over me, you'll have a chance to organize your files. I think that way we'll be able to keep the insurance company happy. They're eager to pay the claim as quickly as possible."

"Really?" Michelle Hendrix looked away, but I caught a faint smile on her lips.

That's how I had managed to escape Michelle's clutches and get that time alone in Wynderly's attic, which is where this story really began. As it turned out, I had had just time enough up there alone to further raise my suspicions. But at that point suspicions were all I had come up with—that and the papers

I'd absconded with. Suspicions that somewhere, in among all the furniture and papers and clothes, and heaven knows what else, there was a story waiting to be told.

DESPITE MICHELLE'S INSISTENCE that we had to hurry and not be late for the board meeting, I walked slowly to her office. In addition to fighting with my conscience about the papers I had taken, I was trying to soak up some of the warmth of the heated house, which felt good after the cold dampness of the attic.

Michelle stood behind her desk, compact in hand, fixing her hair. Behind her, one of the ancient file cabinet drawers was partially open and piles of yellowed folders and paper were spread out on the desk in front of her.

"What about you? Looks like you might have had better luck than I had up in that cold attic," I said, fishing.

"I'm getting there," she said. "I *have* found a much earlier appraisal for you, one from right after Hoyt's death in 1968. I don't think it will do you much good. I did find another one from the 1980s." She handed it to me. "But no receipts. Lot of bills marked paid, but they're for house repairs and office supplies and all paid for by the foundation. So many people have worked here since Mazie died. One filing system would be started, but when the next person came, they'd put in a new system. Redo it all. It's a mess." She threw both hands in the air. "I've been trying to straighten some of it out, but . . ."

Maybe Peter was right. It could be she was just over-whelmed.

"Oh, well," Michelle said, dejectedly. "We can talk more

after the meeting." She glanced at her watch. "Or tomorrow. Don't guess any of us know what to expect this afternoon." Her words had an ominous ring. "In fact, we need to move on."

As had become the custom, Michelle led and I followed. This time to the dining room to meet the Friends of Wynderly — whatever that meant.

Chapter 6

Dear Antiques Expert: At a local auction, I saw a large china cabinet that I really liked but the auctioneer kept calling it a breakfront. What exactly did he mean?

In the 18th century, large multipurpose cabinets were made so books and china could be displayed in the top and linens and papers stored in the bottom. The middle section (which was in the bottom part) looked like a drawer, but could be used as a desk. When it was opened, its hinged "drawer" front could be released, or "broken down," to make a writing surface. Thus the cabinet was called a *break*front. Some people call any large china cabinet a breakfront, but to be a "proper" breakfront the cabinet has to have the "break down" desk drawer.

"RIGHT ON TIME."

With an elegant motion Alfred Houseman closed the lid of the gold pocket watch in his palm and placed it on the mahogany banquet table. Rising to his feet, he motioned to me. "You'll sit here," he said, his aristocratic Virginia drawl matching his courtly manners as he pulled out the chair to his left.

Houseman wasted no time in addressing a nicely dressed, mousy woman, the type who would have the sort of handwriting perfect for note taking. "Madam Secretary, if you will call the roll, the meeting will come to order."

Clearing her throat, she began. "Mrs. Giles M. Burns. Professor Frank Fox. Dr. James Irving Langford. Mrs. Z. Harrison Powers. Miss Mary Sophie Wellington McLeod. Frederick Richmond Graham. Thomas Worth Merritt . . ."

One by one, each board member responded. "Present."

Good Lord! I hadn't heard anything so antiquated since I was in the third grade and our substitute teacher required us to answer "present" instead of "here." We mocked her for days. And all this "Mrs." stuff. Even the Junior League had dropped that pretentiousness years ago when too many first and second wives were being listed one after the other in the directory.

I tried following the roll call around the table, but there was no way I could keep everyone straight. Anyway, I was having too much fun summing up the cast of characters seated around the table to bother with their names. Whoever had appointed the board members must have first made a call to central casting. Mrs. Bulimic Bottle-Blonde sat next to Miss Corpulent Blue-Haired Matron. Dr. Ralph Lauren Casual Tweeds, more lounging than sitting, was across from a serious-looking Mr. Custom-Tailored Gray Pinstripe Suit.

Michelle was wedged in between some pudgy fellow in horn-rimmed glasses whose name I had missed, and a fidgety, squirrel-like brunette gnawing away at her bottom lip. I was wondering what was eating her when she caught me looking at her. I quickly glanced away and hoped she couldn't read minds.

I settled my gaze on the early nineteenth-century Coalport dessert set displayed in the breakfront at the end of the room. The center of each plate depicted a different English country scene. Now *that* was the sort of fine, understated antique I had expected to find in the home of a Virginia gentleman.

I looked back at the table cluttered with open notebooks and briefcases, pens and pencils strewn about. How grand this room must have been when filled with scintillating conversations and outrageous opinions served up with good food to beautiful people. Now it had come down to this—a business meeting.

Only when Dr. Houseman, whose full name I had learned from the roll call was Alfred Chittenbaum Houseman III, spoke up, did I snap back to attention.

"Now that's done, Madame Secretary, please note that, as usual—and as dictated in our bylaws—this is an *open* meeting. I'll introduce Mrs. Glass *after* we've accepted the minutes, and *before* we get on to the problem at hand."

Worth Merritt, an older gentleman whose pink oxford cloth button-down shirt, English club tie, and houndstooth jacket spoke volumes about him, was seated to my left. He leaned forward. "No money," he murmured in a stage whisper that was heard around the table. "*That's* the problem."

Houseman let out an exasperated sigh. "Yes, Worth. But"—he paused for effect—"we may just have a *solution* to that."

That got everyone's attention. Michelle's in particular. She flushed. I wondered if anyone besides me noticed, but their eyes were intent on Houseman.

Clasping his hands before him, the chairman rested them

on the edge of the table and leaned forward. "I've been approached by Tracy DuMont, Morrison Maitland's widow." Houseman waited for the optimistic murmur brought on by his announcement to subside.

Anyone familiar with America's moneyed elite knew of Tracy DuMont, the jet-setting heiress famous for her habit of buying up homes—a villa here, a hacienda there, some old antebellum plantation house in need of preserving—whatever house struck her fancy.

"She'll be joining us later. Now for the minutes, Madam Secretary."

From the looks being cast around the table, I doubted if anyone paid much attention to the minutes, or to my introduction, which Houseman took care of in short order—name, professional credentials, company working for. At least he hadn't mentioned Hank, my former husband, or elaborated on his well-known old Virginia last name, Glass. Southerners are notorious for dwelling on who you're kin to, through birth or marriage.

"She is here to . . . *verify*"—he lingered over the word—"the settlement for the lost and damaged items."

I opened my mouth to say the usual—nice to be here, looking forward to working with you—but before I could get a word out, the board had started chasing the money hinging on my appraisal.

"Well, I just don't understand the whole situation. Why can't the *bank* come through," blurted out Mrs. Giles M. Burns, who was stuck in my head as Mrs. Bulimic Bottle-Blonde. Her dark tan in the dead of winter suggested she had either just returned from the Caribbean or napped under a sunlamp.

"Frederick Graham, you're head of the trust department, surely *you* can get the money," she said, sucking her lips tight against her teeth.

Mr. Custom-Tailored Gray Pinstripe Suit answered her. "Now Lane, the bank simply *can't* put any more of our investors' money into this place." He gave her one of those there's-not-a-*thing*-I-can-do-about-it smiles that bankers must practice while shaving each morning. "The only way I got the funds *last* time was because of all the trusts Hoyt Wyndfield established at the bank way back in the twenties and thirties. In fact, if the trust department wasn't still administering those accounts, Wynderly wouldn't have gotten one red cent from the bank."

Lane Burns crossed her arms and glared back at Graham. "I still don't understand," she muttered under her breath.

"Well," Mary Sophie Wellington McLeod harrumphed. Judging from her vintage nubby wool suit and the absence of any jewels, I surmised that not only did her blue blood match her blue hair, she could undoubtedly buy and sell the entire board with her old, well-worn money. "You certainly can't expect *me* to give any more money," she said.

"Nobody's *asking* you to, Miss Mary Sophie," Dr. House-man said, a shade condescendingly, I thought.

"That's good news," she shot back. Then in a voice just loud enough for everyone to hear, she added, "Asking and expecting are two different things."

Dr. Langford made no attempt to hide his impatience. "This is ridiculous," he said. "Every meeting it's the same thing. I'm worn out with it all. And the phone calls from the press, from the TV station, from my neighbors. Why, my patients would rather talk about Wynderly than their ailments. Even the nurses on my hospital rounds."

Dr. Houseman, rapped his knuckles on the table. "This isn't getting us *any*where," he drawled. He settled back in his chair and turned slowly in the direction of a pleasant-looking gentleman who had left the scrimmaging to the others.

"Charlie Simpson, you were speaking to some powers that be. Any word on funds coming from either the county or our great Commonwealth?"

Simpson exhaled long and hard before speaking. "No. And I think our chances at both places are about as good as our chances with Miss Mary Sophie."

Miss Mary Sophie's smile rippled through her multiple chins. "Oh, good. I can sleep now, knowing *you* won't be coming around, begging for money," she said. A few chuckles echoed around the table.

"Listen here, Alfred," Langford interrupted. "You and I know there are times in the medical profession when we've done all that can be done. That's when we tell our patients they need to set their houses in order. This house has been in financial disarray for years now. Wynderly's nothing but a white elephant. An albatross. And it's time we admit it."

"Now Irv," Houseman said, "let us not forget, however, that Tracy DuMont is scheduled to join us in . . ." He picked up his gold watch, opened it, and continued. "In just a few minutes, I'd say. I don't have to tell *any*one here that she's helped rescue many an endangered home in faraway places, and Wynderly is right in her own backyard." Houseman flashed a confident smile as if the mere mention of DuMont's name set everything right. "In the meantime . . . Mrs. Glass." He looked over his shoulder toward me.

"Yes sir?" I jumped to attention.

Houseman responded with a polite nod. "You have a few words for the board?"

What to say? I sat up straight and tall. Those wretched music lessons I'd had to suffer through had at least taught me a little public poise. But I felt more like I was trapped in the witness stand than seated on a piano bench.

"Good afternoon." I smiled and nodded toward the jury. "As you probably know, Matt Yardley, one of the vice presidents of your insurer, Babson and Michael, asked me to come to Wynderly to assess the damage done to the broken pieces — most of which are beyond repair, I understand. Of course," I quickly added, "Babson and Michael is anxious that the foundation receive full compensation for Wynderly's losses — "

"That includes the *missing* items, doesn't it? We will be paid for those, as well as the broken ones I assume."

The question, not surprisingly, came from Frederick Graham. I winced. The smug look written all over his face didn't sit well with me. This was the same man who moments earlier had said his bank couldn't fork over any more money. Yet he seemed mighty anxious for the insurance company to ante up. Not yet able to figure out who among this group were the friends and who were the foes, I proceeded cautiously.

"Good question. Yes, one thing we're hoping to establish is why some items were taken and other items — "

Graham didn't wait for me to finish. "So what's the plan?"

he asked. "There's not going to be any problem with collecting is there?"

I looked straight at Michelle Hendrix who might as well not have been in the room for all the attention she had commanded from the board. Suddenly she felt like the closest thing I had to a friend in the room.

"Your curator is being most helpful," I said. "Mr. Graham, I'm here to gather *all* the information on every item in question—whether broken *or* missing. As you know, Wynderly's collection is huge." I spread my hands open for emphasis. "As I was *about* to say earlier, we are trying to establish whether or not the thief or thieves were knowledgeable, or just took random objects. That could help in the recovery—if we're lucky. In addition, Babson and Michael has to be sure that one item hasn't been confused with another. When dealing with such a large collection, it's important to proceed slowly and carefully. My purpose in being here is to guarantee that the foundation will be adequately and *fairly* compensated for each and every loss," I said, careful to keep my voice upbeat and positive, all the time silently praying no one would see the downside to my remark.

Mrs. Z. Harrison Powers, the fidgety brunette, broke in. "Excuse me, Frederick, but I want everybody here to know that Zachary and I have had our insurance with Babson and Michael for years. Remember?" She searched the room for sympathy. "Back four or five years ago we had that terr-i-ble break-in."

I tried to imagine just how terrible it had been.

"Surely you all remember it. Zachary's great-great-grand-mother's silver—"

I had a hard time keeping from staring at her. The twisted

silver and gold ropes encircling her neck and wrists belied her coquettish demeanor.

"Babson and Michael couldn't have been more helpful," she said. "I'm sure *you'll* do the right thing, too, Ms. Glass."

I met her look eye to eye. "Thank you," I said with sincere, if somewhat bemused, feelings. "I'll do my best. Let me explain, though. I'm not an employee of Babson and Michael. I'm an independent appraiser."

I angled my head so Frederick Graham would be in my direct line of speech. "I have worked with Babson and Michael on another case, though, and I, too, have found them to be helpful and cooperative. In that instance, I'd say they were even generous. They just need verification so they can do what is right for everyone involved. If, perchance, any charges, criminal or civil, have to be brought"—I paused long enough for my words to sink in—"in that case, positive identification and detailed information about each item will be essential."

I shot a glance around the room so I could observe Michelle Hendrix. If she were involved in the theft, she didn't show it. She didn't flinch.

Houseman coughed. "Well, now. Yes, indeed. I'm sure everyone here understands better now. That's why we're so glad she's, ah, *you're* here. Mrs. Glass's reputation certainly precedes her. In fact, I think some of us know her former husband's family. The Ketchington Glasses of Leemont."

Then interrupting himself, Dr. Houseman said, "Dear me." He half raised himself out of his chair for a better view of the dining room's French doors that opened into one of the house's many gardens and driveways. What he saw clearly excited him.

"Michelle, I believe I see a car has pulled up. Must be our guest. If you'd greet her and usher her in, please." He glanced toward the driveway while he spoke. "She—ah, Mrs. Glass—has assured me that everything will move along smoothly," he said to the board while Michelle dashed out. "If any of you have questions, please seek Mrs. Glass out. I'm sure she'll be most accommodating."

Figuring I had now or never to get my two cents in, I took my chances and spoke up. "May I very quickly add one thing?"

Dr. Houseman turned toward me.

"Thank you, Dr. Houseman. And the board," I said without pausing. "Please, if any of you have information, or clues, or even . . . thoughts . . . on what has happened. Or, if you know anything about the objects—those missing as well as those damaged and broken—please share that with me."

I might as well have been talking to those blackamoor torchères from the blank stares coming from the faces fixed on me. I pretended otherwise and smiled broadly. "If you go antiquing anywhere, around here, or on your travels, and you happen to see anything that even resembles items missing from Wynderly, let me know. It's amazing how often things can turn up—and where. It's happened before. Just in case you do think of something, when I'm not here at Wynderly, I'm staying at Belle Ayre."

"Well put," Houseman conceded. "Mrs. Glass, if you'd put out your cards, we'll get ready to hear from Mrs. Maitland, though Tracy tells me she prefers using her family name DuMont these days." He smiled as if to insinuate that he and Tracy DuMont Williamson Albertson Maitland were on the coziest of terms.

I was sitting back down when the sound of clicking heels broke the silence. As one, all eyes turned toward the door.

Tracy DuMont swept in, thin, fashionable, and breathless.

I'd only seen pictures of Tracy DuMont. Pictures of her with Lauren Bacall, Vanessa Getty, the Keno twins, and the like. Pictures always taken in grand places—the Met, Le Cirque, Sotheby's. She looked much better in glamorous company than she did alone and in person.

I had thought she was blonde. Today she was brunette. She wore her hair short, but cut full across her forehead and so far down over her eyebrows it skimmed the top of the sunglasses she had not taken off. Then again, considering how gray it was outside, she might have just put them on. Beneath her mink-lined sheared lamb coat she wore a short brown leather skirt and purple cashmere sweater. For a moment I thought she had her coat on inside out, but I immediately dismissed my thought as folly, born of envy.

Tracy DuMont strode across the room where she met Houseman halfway.

"I don't think *you* need any introduction, Mrs. DuMont, but perhaps you'd like to meet our board members," Alfred Houseman said, helping her off with her coat. "And Sterling Glass, the appraiser sent by Babson and Michael."

"That's OK." Tracy DuMont waved off his comment. "I know most of you already. And of course I've heard of Ms. Glass, though we haven't met." She held her hands out to me and patted mine in both of hers. "I read your column every week. How *do* you know so much? You're wonderful," she said.

She turned back to Houseman.

"What I have to say won't take long," she said. "I'll get right to the point. This whole situation is a disgrace. I don't have to tell you that Hoyt and Mazie Wyndfield left a fortune to keep Wynderly afloat. It was their wish that their home be a gift to the people of Virginia after Mazie's death. He magnanimously left this estate—his house, his land, his dearest possessions—intending for it to provide jobs and income and . . ." Tracy DuMont paused, leaned forward, and rested her palms on the table in front of her. "And inspiration," she said. "And *hope* for the people he loved, the people he never failed in his lifetime, the people who helped to make him who he was, and he helped in return. What happened to Hoyt's intentions? His *spirit*?"

She stopped abruptly. "What happened to his *money*? If I were sitting where you are right now, I'd be ashamed," she said. "What has happened— And *who* knows what has happened, *really* happened?" She finished her previous thought. "What has happened is inexcusable. None of you . . . Not you, Miss Mary Sophie. Not you, Alfred Houseman. And especially not *you*, Freddy Graham. Not one of you would handle . . . make that *mis*handle . . . your personal affairs so, so cavalierly."

I looked around the room. Only Mary Sophie Wellington McLeod, now clutching the gold knob of her walking cane, remained completely composed. She nodded in agreement.

"It's no secret that I have an interest in Wynderly. It's a gem. Just think of the luminaries who have dined in this very room—General George Marshall. Joseph Cotton. Lady Astor. Marion duPont and Randolph Scott often dropped by for drinks on their way home." Her right hand waved in some direction. "*Those* people could appreciate these fine things."

Then, gesturing toward the center of the table, she said, "This epergne is as fine as any money can buy. Just look at it. Wynderly and its things are our crown jewels. Or so I thought. Until I saw the financials, that is."

There was no doubt in my mind. What was coming next was going to be a sandbox fight.

"This place has turned into nothing but a money pit," Tracy continued. "You have carelessly and foolishly spent money you didn't even have to spend. You've been spending other people's money and now you've got to pay the price."

"Now just a minute," Alfred Houseman said. "I . . . I take exception to that statement, Mrs. Maitla—" He caught himself. "Mrs. DuMont. If we had let Wynderly fall into disrepair, the tourists would have stopped coming altogether. We had an image to maintain."

Tracy DuMont ignored him. "I'm not blaming *all* of you," she said. "Many of you are here because you love beautiful things. You revere Hoyt and Mazie's memories. But you don't know a thing about running a business. Take you, Professor Fox."

Until Tracy DuMont singled him out, I had noticed the chubby man with horn-rimmed glasses only because he was sitting next to Michelle Hendrix.

"Tell me, Professor Fox, in your department at the college, how much money are you responsible for each year?"

"How . . . ah, just how do you mean," he asked.

"Grants. Foundation gifts. Research money. You know, the kind of money that schools depend on to survive these days. The money they have to have to pay the staff, maintain the buildings. How much of that money do you bring in?"

Fox squirmed like a worm in hot ashes. "Well now. That's really not what I do, Ms. DuMont. The chairman of the department handles that, and the development people," he added. Then, drawing himself up and pulling his coat across his extended front, he said, "But I *would* say that I've been responsible for some fine contributions over the years. Not money, exactly, but in-kind contributions. Right now I'm working on a collection of rare—"

"Which proves my point," Tracy DuMont cut him off. "Collections don't pay the bills, Professor Fox. Their care and maintenance eats up the money."

Leaving Fox to stew, she swept the rest of the board members with her eyes. "There's not one of you who is involved in the day-to-day operation of this place. You don't have a clue what's involved in keeping it afloat. You meet here every few months and talk about how much you love the place. Once a year you write a nice check to the foundation. You're what I'd call a, a . . . 'do-good' board," she said. "Individually, that's admirable. Collectively, you don't know diddly-squat about running a foundation. Now that there's not enough money, you're wondering how it happened." She paused and spoke slowly now, as if to schoolchildren. "Money in. Money out. More money going out than coming *in*? You lose."

Worth Merritt, the elderly gentleman seated to my right, whispered in my ear, "Don't sugar coat it, Tracy baby. Tell it like it is."

I clamped my lips to stifle a laugh. Lord, what am I doing here? I asked myself.

I had taken the job at Wynderly for the chance to see some great things. My job was to determine the value of the antiques that had been lost or destroyed. My job was to stand up for the objects that couldn't speak for themselves. My job . . .

What *was* I doing there? The truth was I had taken this job because I was trying to ingratiate myself with Matt Yardley, and hoped to catch his eye while doing so.

I figured I had two choices. Stay or leave. My instincts said leave, run away. On the other hand, if I could keep out of the fray, the money was good. Very good. I glanced around at the cast of characters. Just who does their appraisals, I wondered.

The room was deathly quiet. Eventually Alfred Houseman took a moment to breathe deeply, then began again. "Well, we thank you, Mrs. DuMont. We will certainly look more closely at our situation. We appreciate your openness. We assume . . . We assume you are not interested in helping us. Under the circumstances."

"Let me put it like this, Alfred," the unflappable Tracy DuMont said. "I don't approve of what's happened. But I haven't slammed the door shut. Not yet. Get yourselves together and I'll revisit the situation," Tracy said.

Tracy exited as she had entered, self-assuredly and grandly, having paused just long enough to pluck one of my cards from the table.

Chapter 7

Dear Antiques Expert: I keep reading and hearing about antiques and collectibles. Aren't collectibles the same thing as antiques?

An "antique" is an item that is one hundred years old or older. The term "collectible" is used to denote younger, but still desirable (and often expensive), "old things" that have yet to reach the magical 100-year-old mark. For example, an early 19th-century Meissen figurine is an antique, but a bright red Fiesta syrup pitcher mass-produced in the 1930s is properly called a "collectible." In fact, in perfect condition and with its original lid, such a pitcher might sell for $500 or more.

ALL I HAD WANTED to do after the board meeting was get back to my quiet room at Belle Ayre. But Worth Merritt and Miss Mary Sophie McLeod had trapped me. To my surprise, Miss Mary Sophie invited me to come by for tea the next afternoon, and Mr. Merritt asked if he could take me to dinner. "Otherwise, it'll be my third Lean Cuisine this week," he said, and I accepted his offer.

We wasted little time ordering the drinks we both needed. I opted for a ladylike white wine.

"Well," Worth Merritt said, "*my* day calls for a double b and b. Maker's Mark for the bourbon and plain old branch for the water," he said. "All this stuff about bottled water is a lot of baloney."

His eyes swept the room. "I think you'll like this place. The food's not bad and the decor is, well . . . I know these aren't true antiques, but the decorations do give it a unique character," he said, alluding to the crockery and kitchenwares sitting all about. He shook his head disbelievingly. "I sure do wish my parents had kept some of the stuff they threw away. I could open a museum."

We both laughed.

"Oh, we kept the good stuff—the real antiques. It's the collectibles I'm referring to," he continued. "The prices they're bringing these days? I'm astonished every time I walk into an antiques mall or go to a neighbor's yard sale."

And so we chatted about Fiestaware and wooden coffee grinders. Once our drinks came, though, Worth Merritt dropped the small talk. Raising his glass in my direction, he said, "So, Sterling Glass. When I heard your name at the meeting, I made the connection. I once met your parents. They were older than we—Sally, my late wife, and I—were, but I remember them vividly. Your father was quiet. From New England, as I recall."

I detected a hint of pride in his voice. His message was loud and clear: I've got my wits and my memory about me even if I am old.

"Yes. Massachusetts."

"And your mother was, well— " He paused. "May I say, she was quite a fiery character. The sort you never forget."

I laughed. "I'll agree on both counts. A character and unforgettable." I hoped I had reassured him that I was comfortable with what he'd said. Worth Merritt's candor, as well as his memory, had won me over.

Worth Merritt chuckled. "It was at the Homestead. Sally and I were having a drink on the patio . . ." He raised his glass in a mock toast, then took a sip. "Your parents were at an adjoining table. You know how we Southerners are. The conversation just started. I think your parents liked our being a younger couple," he added with a sweet smile, his eyes twinkling. "Sally was still in her twenties and I was . . ." He clicked his tongue against his teeth and looked away while he did the math. "In my mid-thirties."

Judging as much from his gentlemanly manners and measured way of speaking as from his thin neck and wrinkled hands, I figured Worth must be in his late seventies.

"It was back in the seventies. You had just married your husband and your parents were— " Merritt smiled knowingly. "Let's say your parents were, well— " For the second time he halted. Then meeting my eyes straight on, his smile broadened. "Oh hell," he said, "they were *recuperating* from the event."

I almost choked when I simultaneously swallowed and laughed.

"Now don't get me wrong," Worth said while I attempted to recover my composure. "But those society weddings can be taxing, especially when the guests are old FFVs." He leaned over the table and lowered his voice the way a kid does when he's sharing a well-known secret, "Those *first families* of Virginia can be intimidating, especially the big clans."

"Oh, it's OK," I said, still laughing.

"I'm not speaking badly about the Glasses. They are good people, a good Virginia family. But you've divorced. And you've not remarried."

"No I haven't."

"Any plans?"

It was Matt Yardley whose handsome face had flashed before my eyes. I was about to speak when I realized it would hardly be appropriate to say anything about the man who had hired me for the Wynderly job. I didn't waste a moment. I waved his question away.

"Speaking of people, we certainly saw a war of the wits today, didn't we? Tracy DuMont and Houseman—" I stopped, hoping Worth Merritt would take it from there.

"Indeed," Worth said. "And by the way, don't let Peggy Powers pull the wool over your eyes," he warned. Catching my puzzled look, Worth said, "Remember. Mrs. Z. for Zachary Harrison Powers. That's Peggy. She's the one who spoke up about the settlement she and Zachary got from Babson and Michael after their burglary.

"At the time, Peggy and Zach ranted and raved over how they were shortchanged by their insurance company. Nobody pays much attention to Peggy or Zach. They didn't after their burglary, and they didn't today. The Powerses are known for leeching. Not bleeding, *leeching* the last drop of blood out of any turnip they can." Worth rubbed his thumb against his second and third fingers in that universal sign that translates into moneygrubbing.

"Then why did she say what she did?" I asked.

"You're the new kid on the block, my dear. To get in your good graces. That's Peggy Powers's way. A cunning but aging Venus flytrap, she'll court you all sweet and nice till she's got you in her clutches. She was just laying the groundwork today. Who knows, she might need you later." He lowered his eyes and wrinkled his brow. "She's not the only one who'll use that tack."

I looked at my half-empty glass. Too much information was coming at me too fast. Plus, it had been a long, tiring day. My instinct was to pick it up and drain it dry.

Much drinking, little thinking, Mother often said the morning after, quoting Jonathan Swift. I sat back in my seat and an unexpected pain between my shoulders reminded me of the tumble I'd taken in the attic. I reached for my glass. Then again, I needed a clear mind if for no reason other than to keep the people and their names straight. I swirled the wine around.

Worth Merritt obviously had the goods on everyone and showed no hesitancy—even seemed to enjoy sharing it. But why with me, a stranger? He had met and liked my parents and knew my former in-laws. To him, that was reason enough to take me into his confidence. I took a small sip of wine.

Loose lips sink ships.

This time Mother's words, though intended as a warning, served to trigger another thought. Maybe Merritt was the town gossip. Taking a chance, I forged ahead.

"What about Frederick Graham? He's the banker, head of the trust department, right? What I heard today sounded to me as if there might be some, ah, conflict of interest there. I mean, how can he direct money from the bank he *works* for into a foundation when he's on that foundation's board? Isn't that a bit— "

"Come now, Sterling," Worth Merritt said. There was no mistaking his patronizing tone. "You were married to one of those wealthy old Virginia families. *You* know how the world works. You know the influence that moneyed people in positions of authority wield," and he quickly added, "Take your former husband's family. They were, and still are, admirable in their philanthropy and leadership. *But* . . . you *have* to know the wheeling and dealing that *others* of their type do, especially those who think their birthright puts them above the law, so to speak. The higher they're born, the more money they have, the more they think they can do whatever they wish . . . and get *away* with it."

I chuckled. "Well, Hank's current matrimonial record might not be exactly *admirable*."

No more had I opened my mouth than I could have kicked myself. Why had I said that? I backtracked. "Not that Hank's a bad guy. We got on very well for twenty years. Even now we put our children's feelings and well-being first when we're together. I'll give Hank Glass this—he's always been a good and responsible father."

The puzzled look on Worth Merritt's face made me all the more sorry that I'd mentioned Hank's wandering eye.

"I spoke out of turn," I said. "Forgive me. It's just that Hank's getting married, again. Third time, and yes, to another younger woman." I shrugged. "I don't know. That's his business. This quick divorce and remarriage game seems to be a new hobby of his. He used to like boats. Always selling one, buying another. Guess he's just traded one commodity for another."

"Seems to be the way these days. Trophy wives." Worth Merritt winked. "Well, I certainly wouldn't let it bother me if I were you, my dear. Not you."

At that moment our dinner appeared. The timing was perfect.

"Another glass?" Worth asked.

I didn't wait for any objections from Mother or my own conscience. "Why not?"

"Back to your earlier question." Worth Merritt's tone turned serious again. "The one about Frederick Graham," he said between bites, adding, "And don't make the mistake of calling him anything but Frederick. His family is as well established in *these* parts of Virginia as your former husband's family is over Leemont way."

"That doesn't surprise me," I said.

When Worth Merritt put his fork down and said, "Now let's see," I knew I was in for a detailed explanation.

"Henry VII was also the Earl of Richmond. Since Frederick Graham's mother's ancestors descended from Henry VII, around here that means he and his kin are *our* royalty. Lots of our old families live on land grants from the Crown. But *direct* blood lineage? Now that's something not *every*one has. Years ago, when Prince Charles came to America, Frederick Graham's parents were invited to *all* the royal events—not just the public Williamsburg one. Can't say that for the rest of us."

Worth Merritt smiled ever so slightly. "How does all this tie in with Wynderly? Well, this is the way I see it, Sterling. This whole Wynderly thing is a mess. Especially after today." He paused as if remembering Tracy's tirade. When he spoke, it was with a heartfelt passion I had not seen in him before.

"It's not like Wynderly was Mount Vernon. Wynderly's hardly an eighteenth-century monument frozen in time, pristine and perfect. It's a huge early-twentieth-century mansion filled with a little of everything from all over the world. But in what other Virginia house museum can you find gilt French furniture and ornate boulle work like you see in the castles and palaces of Europe? Is Wynderly the greatest and grandest house in these parts? No. And it's certainly not the oldest. But, *I* think Wynderly is wonderful. And Frederick Graham's being on the board endorses its validity and importance."

"Still though," I said, "if being on the board at the same time he's head of the trust department that's responsible for Wynderly's finances means there's potential for scandal—"

"I don't think so," he said kindly but firmly.

Maybe it was the second glass of wine after such a harrowing day. Or maybe it was Worth Merritt's earnest frankness that got to me. I let go of my suspicions, at least for the moment.

"So tell me more about Hoyt and Mazie," I said cheerfully. "And Tracy DuMont," I added with a smile.

"Tracy?" He laughed. "I don't know her *terribly* well, though we're certainly friends. From the times I've been thrown with her, I'd say she was pretty true to form today. Believe it or not, she's neither mean nor vicious. She's a very bright woman. One of those who would have broken the glass ceiling . . ."

He paused and glanced away, as if calling up years of memories. "Yes, Tracy would have risen to the top even if she'd been born an orphan. She has that kind of drive. Then again, her money, her *old* money, gave her"—he smiled slyly—"a leg up. But the truth is—"

Worth Merritt turned suddenly somber. "Tracy's money has been as much a curse as a blessing. Which may explain why she acts the way she does. God knows Tracy's generous. But she's had to grow a hard, thick shell to shield herself from rascals trying to separate her from her millions. Combine her natural drive with the problems of having too much money, and well, there you have Tracy. But she isn't mean-spirited, Sterling." Worth spoke kindly, yet emphatically. "I didn't like some of the things she said today. On the other hand—" He looked long into his almost empty glass. "I can't deny the truth of any of them."

He brightened. "And if, for any reason, *you* get a chance to spend time with her, take it. It won't be time misspent."

"Oh, I doubt I'll have that opportunity," I said, secretly wondering if I would ever really *want* the opportunity.

"You might be surprised, my dear." He leaned across the table and spoke softly. "Tracy likes bright people and you certainly fit that description. She said she reads your column, remember?"

Our momentary silence was broken by sirens whizzing by.

Worth laughed. "Barney Fife to the rescue. That's what I call our deputy sheriff. Used to be this was a quiet town except on Saturday nights. These days there's a rough element on the south side that can get out of hand, even on weeknights."

I glanced at my watch, our empty drink glasses, and as discreetly as possible at my companion's plate.

"How are we on time?" I asked, still dying to know more about the Wyndfields.

"We're fine. You said you're at Belle Ayre. That's four or five minutes from here. I'm maybe two minutes from my house, in the other direction. We can even have another drink before closing."

"Oh . . . I don't think so," I was saying just when our waitress arrived.

"Going to make it your usual three, Mr. Merritt?" she asked.

I took that as a green light, sighed, and relented. "And a glass of water with lots of ice," I said.

"So . . . about the Wyndfields," I asked.

"Which ones? The public, or the private, Hoyt and Mazie Wyndfield?"

"Have we *time* to hear about both?"

Worth laughed heartily and playfully shook his finger at me. "Not in this lifetime."

Saying that, Worth turned and casually looked around the dining room. Satisfied all was secure, he leaned forward and rested his chin in his hand, his elbow on the table. "Well . . ."

Loose lips sink ships? They weren't my lips and it wasn't my ship. Full steam ahead.

Chapter 8

Dear Antiques Expert: I recently saw a nest of tables that is just right for my small den. I especially like the fact that I can keep them stacked as one table when not in use, but move the smaller tables around the room when needed. The dealer says this set dates from the 1910s or 1920s, but that nests of tables have been made since the 1800s. The concept seems very modern to me. Was she right?

Absolutely. Thomas Sheraton included an illustration of these stacked tables in his 1803 *Cabinet Directory*. Back then, though, the grouping was called "quartetto tables." That's because there were four tables in the "nest" that appeared to be only one table when the three smaller tables were slid beneath the largest one. These days some nests of tables come with only three, rather than four tables. Regardless, nesting tables (as they are sometimes called) are so serviceable they are even made for patios and decks, as well as for inside the house.

WORTH MERRITT ONCE AGAIN cast an over-the-shoulder glance around the room, which was starting to empty out. "Can't be too careful. You never know—"

Worth's cautiousness puzzled me. He had openly chatted away about Tracy and the Powerses, even Frederick Graham, all whom everyone in this small community could recognize by name, face, and reputation. Why this sudden secrecy? He leaned across the table and mouthed his words. "There *has* to be more *out there* than anyone knows."

"*Out* there? Do you mean in the house? At Wynderly?" I asked, barely speaking above a whisper myself. "Or do you mean, *out there*?" I waved my hand into the air. "You know, as in things people don't know about the Wyndfields?"

"Ah-ha! Caught me at my own game." Merritt's loud burst of laughter would have turned heads under normal circumstances. I wondered if he might have had a little more to drink than he realized. "Wynderly. The Wyndfields." A faraway look crossed his face. "Who can separate the one from the other? Hoyt and Mazie lived for their . . ." He pressed his lips together and nodded his head as he wandered back in time. "Their showplace. Their obsession. Their baronial playhouse."

Worth's eyes grew sad. "But, I think I understand. These days Sally's gone and our children scattered. I only see the grandkids every so often. Some nights I sit in our home that was once so lively, look around, and realize my old *things* have become my old friends." Worth Merritt heaved a heavy sigh and shifted about in his seat. "But enough . . . So. What do *you* know about the Wyndfields?" he asked.

"Little more than what's in the brochure," I said, reaching for my pocketbook to retrieve the out-of-print brochure I'd picked up at the tourist bureau back in Leemont. "I know the house was built over a two- or three-year span and the Wyndfields moved in around" — I checked to be sure — "1924." Trying to lighten the moment, I added, "At least they had a few years before the great crash to enjoy their great wealth."

"Now don't think that for one minute Hoyt and Mazie were affected by the Depression," Worth said. "Theirs was *tobacco* money." He straightened up and grinned. "Alcohol and tobacco. The last things a man gives up in hard times. Of course there was prohibition, but some people said that just made cigarettes all the more popular. Oh no, the Wyndfields never lost any real money during that time. In fact, their fortunes grew."

"And they just traveled about? Carefree, gathering antiques?" I pointed to the photograph of the English Regency nesting tables pictured in the brochure.

"Most of the time. Mazie and Hoyt met on one of those Mississippi River paddleboat cruises. That pretty much set the tone of their life together. Travel and romance. Hoyt was an avid traveler, but he always said he did it backwards. Said he saw the world before he visited his own country, thanks to the war. The First World War, that is."

"So you knew Hoyt fairly well?" My interest piqued. "And his family was from here," I said.

"Oh yes. Hoyt grew up a few miles from where we're sitting. Talk about highborn families and FFVs. The Wyndfields settled here about the same time Jefferson and Madison's families did." Merritt chuckled to himself. "The Wyndfield men either went down to William and Mary or over to Mr. Jefferson's University in Charlottesville. Except Hoyt. He broke the mold. Hoyt went to Virginia Tech. Passed up law or history to study farming."

I had heard enough about who Hoyt's people were. I wanted

to learn more about Hoyt. It was getting late, yet I couldn't bring myself to force the moment . . . plus I was afraid I'd break Worth's train of thought. I wasn't sure what any of this had to do with the theft at Wynderly, or the fiasco at the board meeting, but my better sense told me to listen closely. This was, after all, the South.

"According to my grandfather, it had all begun many years earlier with one of Hoyt's ancestors, Tate Wyndfield. It was one of those old Cain and Abel situations. The good brother, that was Edward Wyndfield, and the bad brother, Tate Wyndfield. Now, Tate had a wild streak in him, and after a falling out with his brother he left these parts in the middle of the night sometime, oh, in the late 1830s or so. More than a little inebriated, of course. Four days later Tate found himself a hundred miles south, down around Powersburg. He was getting ready to make camp along the James River when he came on a, ah, a . . ." He started again. "One of those . . . ah . . . one of those flat-bottomed boats they used to ship tobacco on. Not a barge," he said.

I waited a moment before speaking. "Bateau?"

"Of course. A bateau. Just wait till you're my age. You'll understand. So," he said, "Tate came upon this *bateau* partly loaded with 'bacca,' as we call it, waiting to be shipped down the James River to Richmond. There was a full moon that night. Nearby, Tate spied a tobacco sled filled with the golden leaf waiting to be loaded on the bateau at sunrise." Worth's voice grew low and whispery. "And there, huddled close by the sled, in the light of a dim fire, was a group of men playing cards." He paused to let the scene sink in.

"Tate saw his chance. In no time"—he snapped his fingers—"the sled loaded with tobacco was his." He was grinning as broadly as if *he* had been the one victorious at cards.

"But you have to put something up to get into a game. If Tate left home in a huff—"

"Remember now, Tate Wyndfield was an aristocrat from Orange and Albemarle counties. Some things never change. Rich families had a wide reputation, just the way they do today. Those Johnny-come-lately Southside farmers knew the Wyndfield name, all right. Thought they had a fancy-pants pretty boy joining their game. Little did they know." Worth Merritt laughed heartily. "Nor did they know Tate's recent break with his family and why he was a 'fur piece,' as they call it, from home."

Worth eyed his glass, picked it up and swirled the remaining ice and whiskey around. Seeing it was close to empty he put it down as if to save it. "You see, Tate's grandfather, Major Wyndfield, who, incidentally, was no saint himself, had died not too long before. It was an easy bluff. Tate just put up his share of the family land. Whether he actually had any claim . . . who knows? Little matter. Tate signed a piece of paper *saying* he did. Next morning, it was Tate Wyndfield's bacca that was headed to Richmond for auction on the bateau."

Worth slapped his knee. "Those Southside guys got what they deserved."

I gave Worth a politely impatient look. "So, did Tate come back to Orange County after that?"

"No, no. Tate had learned where the *real* money was. He sold the tobacco, took the cash, and headed straight down to Pittsylvania County. Chatham and Danville. Bought land and grew Bright Leaf. Made quite a haul over the years. Built a fine home on the Dan River. But Edward's folks stayed put, except for fighting in the War, of course."

There was no doubt which war Worth was referring to.

"Hoyt never left these parts till he went to Virginia Tech. You know," Worth said, "I don't know that Hoyt ever gambled, at least not like Tate, but there is a fine game room in Wynderly . . ."

"And Tate and Hoyt . . . what kin were they," I said, to keep Worth on track.

Worth reached in his inner coat pocket and took out a small leather bound notebook and mechanical pencil and began to write.

"See," he said, sliding the notebook to me.

The Wyndfield Brothers
1830 Tate Wyndfield (Southside) Edward Wyndfield (Orange)
1890 Whitey Wyndfield   Hoyt Wyndfield

"In 1830, it was the Wyndfield bothers, Tate and Edward. Then in 1890 you've got Tate's grandson, Whitey, and Edward's grandson, Hoyt."

I nodded.

"Now remember, too, there had been bad blood in the Wyndfield family when Tate left. The Orange County Wyndfields never had anything to do with the Southside Wyndfields. But two generations later when the cousins ended up at Tech over in Blacksburg in the 1910s, Hoyt to study animal husbandry and Whitey to study agriculture—well, having the same last name, they started up a conversation. In no time they realized they were distant cousins and became fast friends. When World War One came along, they both went overseas—Hoyt in the trenches, Whitey behind the lines in an office job. There Whitey made a simple observation. Everybody was puffing away on cigarettes, troops and civilians alike," Worth said.

"By the time Whitey was back home, he was raring to go—ready to expand his tobacco holdings. Timing couldn't have been better. Whitey got Hoyt to team up with him, and soon they were traveling the world over, piling fortune on top of fortune. When the Roaring Twenties came and glamorous women and handsome men took up the weed, the Wyndfield cousins were set for life."

"And Mazie was one of those glamorous women, I'm willing to bet," I said.

"Can't you just see them? Hoyt Wyndfield, tall and straight, polished and genteel. Mazie Bontemps, petite and lovely, sugarcane oozing out of every Cajun pore. She was as vivacious and colorful as Hoyt was handsome."

I thought I caught a hint of that same adoration for the Wyndfields I had heard from Michelle Hendrix.

"Yes, Hoyt and Mazie had it all—his old family estate, the old furniture, the old name, the old money. What they thought they needed was the *new* style." Worth laughed. "Know what was funny about that? The new style shown in all the magazines *was* the old style. But *not* the old *Virginia* style. The old *European* style—gilt chairs, etched mirrors. Wouldn't give you two cents for it, myself. Gilding the lily to my way of thinking. But Hoyt had seen it in Europe and he thought it was great. Mazie, being from Louisiana, had grown up with fancy things. It was the perfect match."

My mind began seesawing back and forth, undoubtedly helped by the wine. Hoyt and Mazie, Tracy and that whole cast of characters, Michelle, Wynderly itself, the stories Worth Merritt was telling me, the theft—like so many pieces of a puzzle, they all had to fit together. But how? That I didn't know.

Our waitress appeared tableside, scattering my thoughts like the crumbs Worth was sweeping from around his plate. "So how's it going, Mr. Merritt? Dessert anyone?" She looked at me.

Worth glanced at his watch. "Where has the time gone? It's past nine, child. Their closing time. We roll up the streets early around here," he said apologetically. "The check, Dolly."

He picked up his glass and drained it dry. He gave me a broad wink. "Her name's not really Dolly," he said.

"It's Bonnie Sue," she said with a playfully exasperated roll of her eyes.

"But I think Dolly suits her better, don't you?" Worth said.

Chapter 9

Dear Antiques Expert: When my great uncle died, he left his collection of walking canes to my husband. Actually, these were my uncle's father's and grandfathers' canes, so we figure they have to be over 100 years old. Is there a market for them?

During the 18th and 19th centuries, "walking sticks" were more than just walking aids. They were fashion accessories for men *and* women—especially ones with gold, silver, jeweled, or ivory handles. Some even concealed daggers and swords and had snuff compartments. But that was then. Today, walking sticks have generally lost their appeal. Having said that, some antique and even early 20th-century folk art canes carved as snakes, alligators, and such have sold for thousands of dollars. Hopefully you will find some folk art canes among your newly inherited collection.

WE STEPPED OUT into the cold night. Behind us, Dolly began turning off the neon "open" light in the front window. The street became even darker, the moon even brighter.

"I could go on and on about the Wyndfields," Worth said.

"And I could listen forever," I said, wondering if I'd have

another chance to hear what Paul Harvey called "the rest of the story." "But I guess we should call it a night," I said.

"I'm sure I'll see you again soon," Worth Merritt said. "Houseman was already talking about calling another 'emergency' session at Wynderly. He'll be crawling all over the place tomorrow, mark my words. He's not about to let that house permanently close down if he can help it."

"Well he won't get any help from Miss Mary Sophie McLeod," I said with a chuckle.

I made a U-turn in the middle of the block. In the rearview mirror I watched Worth turn onto a side street. The whole town was deadly quiet and it wasn't even nine thirty. Out of nowhere I had a gnawing desire to see Wynderly in the black of night. On just such a winter night years ago, I had seen Bannerman Castle. Though built a few short years before Wynderly, today only its hollow shell stands as a sad reminder of its past grandeur. But when the moon is high over New York's Hudson River and its crumbling towers and walls are silhouetted against the night, it is magnificent. I have never forgotten the romance and mystery of the moment. Tonight's moon was full and silver. Did I dare?

And then a lipstick red Nissan whipped around me and bolted into the 7-Eleven's parking lot without so much as a turn signal. I slammed on the brakes and the horn at the same time.

I proceeded on, but began thinking twice about venturing out to Wynderly, especially since I was now in the countryside, and in the dark nothing looked familiar. So much for knowing where I was. I turned into a driveway, backed out, and headed back to the 7-Eleven for directions.

I pulled into the only empty spot and had just turned off the motor when I heard a familiar voice. I was so new to Orange, I figured it could belong only to a handful of people. But at a 7-Eleven? It hardly seemed a likely place to be running into Miss Mary Sophie and her gold-knobbed cane. I glimpsed Michelle Hendrix. Of course. Who else could it have been?

Michelle was balancing a twelve-pack of Budweiser while she fumbled with the handle on the driver's side of the bright red Nissan.

"Couldn't somebody help," she snapped. Her voice sounded different, more tinny and sharp. She was obviously pissed.

The rear door on the driver's side flew open, banging into the already dented pickup truck parked beside it. A small, thin kid looking no more than maybe sixteen or seventeen from the way he was dressed, jeans billowing around his ankles and wool stocking cap, jumped out. "Hold on. I'll get it."

"What the hell're you doing? Watch the paint job."

I heard the booming male voice before I saw where it was coming from. Then a man so tall his chest towered over the roof of the car came up out of nowhere. "Damn it, Billy. Watch it."

"You two shut up. All you've done for the past half hour is bicker." Michelle's voice cut through the night air. "You want me to keep driving, or drop this right here." She heaved the bulky twelve-pack high in the air.

"She'll do it, too, Emmett," the boy said.

I ducked down, sucked in my breath, and waited for what would happen next. Husband, boyfriend, son? I hadn't noticed a ring on Michelle's finger. Figuring this was the only store open this time of night, it wasn't all that surprising she'd be here, but—

Glaring headlights from another car turning in broke my train of thought. From the engine's roar, I figured it was some sort of souped-up car—a Camero or Mustang. It had stopped immediately behind me.

A voice from the car yelled out, "Hey, Emmett. Billy. What's the plan?"

"Enough's enough." It was Michelle's voice again. "I'm going home. I've gotta go to work tomorrow. Emmett, you can get out right here and now if you want to. I don't give a flip. But you, Billy Blake, don't you even think about getting in that car with your buddies. If I have to buckle you in myself I'm taking *you home.*"

I heard the longnecks rattling against one another as Michelle tossed them into the car.

Billy slammed his door shut, muttering, "Yes, ma'am," as he did. I heard the souped-up engine rev and the wheels of the car behind mine spin as it lurched backward.

"Jeez," Emmett hollered. "Don't get so hot. OK, OK. I'll get out if that's the way you feel. Somebody I know will come along. Hold on, will you? Don't take my foot with you." He was still muttering under his breath as he walked away from the car, into the store.

If Mother had been there, she would have said Michelle drove off that lot like a bat out of hell, Billy Blake in tow. I thought she looked more like Thelma, or was it Louise, on the verge of road rage. I waited till the coast was clear before I got out of the car.

There might be two of us with a hangover at Wynderly tomorrow morning, I thought, as I walked straight back to the beer and wine section and grabbed up an overpriced bottle of

Ernest and Julio Gallo chardonnay from the display rack. It beat the Wild Irish Rose, Boone's Farm, and Thunderbird in the cooler. When I saw Emmett whatever-his-name-was hanging around the cash register, I hung back.

"Naw, I better not," Emmett was saying. "I've already dropped a butt-load of cash this week. Give me back those twenties, and I'll just get five scratchers."

The clerk handed him the lottery cards and two twenties. Emmett stuffed the bills in his pocket and went to work scratching and flicking the red specks off his Junior Ruby Red 7s cards, talking as he did. "One of these days I'm going to hit it big. Then I'll show some of these highfalutin folks."

"What happened this time?" From her bored tone, I figured the woman, whose name tag read Cindy, had heard the story before.

"You just wait and see. One day my ship's gonna come in."

"Yeah, yeah. Yours and everybody else's," Cindy said, flipping the switch on the number 4 gas pump for the car that had just pulled in. "Yeah, I used to think I'd get a break, too . . . then I wised up. When are you gonna learn there's no free lunch out there, Emmett?"

"Say, is that Jimmy's car? He'll give me a ride." Emmett grabbed up his cards and turned toward me. "You just wait and see," he said over his shoulder. "There's other ways than the lottery to turn big money."

With that, Emmett was out the door, but not before I glimpsed some company emblem on his jacket as I stepped up to take his place at the counter.

"Will that be all, honey?" Cindy asked me.

I smiled. "And some directions. No lottery tickets for me. Never bought one in my life."

"Me neither," she said. "My minister explained to me that the only one who is gonna get rich off the lottery is the person who sells the cards. We get a cut for each one we sell. And if a customer hits a big one—" Cindy smiled and counted out my change. "But these fellows around here? Some of 'em think they should have been born rich. That's not what the Bible preaches."

"Thank you," I said, wine bottle in hand. I wasn't about to stick around for a temperance lesson.

This time I hightailed it down the road myself, so fast, in fact, I missed the turnoff for Belle Ayre.

Ginny Kauffman was halfway up the winding staircase when I closed the door behind me. "Just on my way to slip a note under your door," she said. "Actually, make that two notes." She held up the while-you-were-out slips and started toward me.

"I can't imagine who'd be trying to reach me." I shifted my oversized pocketbook around and hoped my precious bottle of wine wouldn't be too conspicuous. "Don't think I've had any calls on my cell phone," I said. But before I could retrieve it, she laughed.

"Don't even bother. The reception's no better here than out at Wynderly. Totally erratic."

I met her at the bottom of the steps.

"One of these is from Frank Fox," she said, handing me the notes. "You know him? Some sort of professor." She put her free hand out, around shoulder height. "Short, chubby fellow. He hung around for a while. Seemed nice. When you didn't come in, he said he'd better start for home. This time of year whole herds of deer are out in droves. Oh, and I guess you saw there's a corkscrew in your room."

I smiled. "Thank you. So . . . till tomorrow."

I was already fiddling with the pink slips to see who the other one was from. Houseman? That wouldn't have surprised me. But Mary Sophie McLeod? What did *she* want? To remind me we were having tea, it turned out. At 4 P.M. I thought I'd explained that I didn't know exactly when I'd be able to get away. Didn't she know I was a working woman, here on a job? In the world she lived in, it probably didn't register.

I didn't bother to read Fox's note until I'd peeled off the clothes that were starting to grow to my skin. I looked for the corkscrew, found it, and then realized the bottle had a screw top. I poured a glass.

"Ms. Glass," I read. "I'd like to make an appointment with you about an appraisal. Despite Mrs. DuMont's obvious dislike for me and her disparaging and insulting remarks of today, I *do* have *some* sense and rather *good* taste."

He had underlined "do" three times, the other words only once. I could almost feel the smoke still searing the paper.

"Please call me at your earliest convenience and keep this private, please. FFox."

The second *F* had practically torn through the paper and the *x* extended halfway across the page. He obviously hadn't stopped fuming.

Between Houseman, Tracy, Michelle, and now Frank Fox, this sleepy place was smoldering.

Where the roads are paved with good intentions, Mother said.

Chapter 10

Dear Antiques Expert: My mother suggested I write to you. I was reading about the Crusades in world history, and silver and gold reliquaries were mentioned. The librarian at school helped me find information on what reliquaries are, but I'm wondering if there are museums in America where I can see these?

I'm delighted to answer your question. Many adults didn't know about reliquaries until reading *The Da Vinci Code*. Reliquaries were made to hold holy relics, usually of a martyred saint. During Romanesque and medieval times, reliquaries were works of art, often made of silver or gold and sculpted as crosses, busts, even like a hand or arm. The Cleveland Museum of Art has a remarkable silver and enamel arm reliquary that actually holds an arm bone. Reliquaries can be seen in other museums but are seldom sold other than by fine auction houses like Sotheby's and Christie's.

MORNING CAME MUCH too soon the next day. The accumulation of so many things—the board meeting, Michelle Hendrix's seeming unwillingness to help me, the 7-Eleven event—combined with not getting much work done had gnawed at me.

Every time I had tried to close my eyes, another snapshot of the day's events popped into my head. It was probably one or two o'clock before I convinced myself I should just head back home. I'd work through the day, see what I could accomplish, and then leave. The board could fight it out among themselves—whatever "it" was.

That resolved, I almost enjoyed the breakfast of homemade biscuits and ham and grits before starting for Wynderly. Once on the road I chuckled out loud, wondering what Michelle Hendrix's state of mind would be this morning. I was confident she hadn't seen me last night. But I couldn't help thinking about what would happen if it did come up.

I was lost in a pretend conversation with Michelle when Wynderly rose majestically before me. It was not a house Virginians had loved for centuries, or even generations, like many I had passed, set far back behind white fences, their names and dates on white plaques hanging between fence posts at their entranceways—names like Rolling Acres Farm, Edgefield Manor, Cottingham, and dates going back to 1815, 1796, 1807. I could well imagine that some of the residents of those stately estates had thought of Wynderly as an eyesore, perhaps even a blight on the Virginia landscape.

But today, Wynderly's bays jutting out across its front, its hipped roofline dotted with chimneys, and the quirky, intricate pattern of timbers and rocks, plum red bricks, and stucco weathered to a soft gray, looked different to me—romantic, enchanting. I chalked it up to the occasional flecks of dappled sunlight on the deep green ivy growing up its towers. I didn't allow myself to think I might be falling under Wynderly's spell, especially since I had made up my mind to wash my hands of the whole situation, even if it meant looking bad in Matt's eyes.

To my surprise, Michelle was already at the house. So the red Nissan was definitely hers. But someone else was also there. Perhaps Dr. Houseman had called an emergency session. Alfred Houseman hadn't struck me as the Jaguar type, though.

It took two pulls on the bell rope before Michelle swung open the door. Behind her stood Peggy Powers in a tweedy blazer, tailored slacks, and understated gold earrings, looking quite different from yesterday.

"My dear," she gushed over Michelle's shoulder, leading me to note that, despite her more refined look, her demeanor was the same, impatient and pushy. Then to Michelle she said, "I think Ms. Glass and I will talk in the drawing room. Will that be all right?"

"Good morning," I said to them both. "Fine with me. May I get rid of my coat and things first?"

"Oh my. I guess I'm overanxious this morning," Peggy said, her cheeks flushing.

Michelle glanced in the direction of the room. I could tell she didn't like the idea of our crossing behind the ropes, sitting in Mazie's chairs, acting as if we were guests.

"You *are* a board member," she muttered. "I guess it will be OK. Do you want me to take your things, Sterling? I'll put them in my office . . ."

"No, no. I'll do that. Mrs. Powers, would you excuse me for a moment. No reason for you to trek back and forth, Michelle."

"Then I'll be turning on some lights," Peggy Powers said cheerfully.

"So, how are *you* this morning," I asked Michelle as we walked toward the back of the house. I was thinking about last night. She turned to answer me. I searched the corners of her eyes for bloodshot telltale signs.

"Considering that Houseman called me at home last night and left a message about a meeting sometime today—he didn't say when—and then with *her* here . . . How d'you think I am?"

I dropped my thoughts of last night. "So *that's* why Mrs. Powers is here. The meeting."

"That's what I thought, too. But she said she wanted to see *you*. She didn't seem to know anything about the meeting."

"What on earth can Mrs. Powers want with *me*?" I asked. "I've got other things to do. Did she say?"

"Who knows? Who knows *anything* these days?"

"So how did you and Houseman leave it? I don't think the meeting will involve me, do you? Other than 'where's the money,' everything I heard yesterday was about the house, not anything that I'd know about."

"With *that* man? Who knows?" She shrugged. "I have to admit, though, I almost felt sorry for him yesterday. I wouldn't want Tracy DuMont working against me. What does she care about a house like this for? How many's she got? She's not even around these parts half the time. Only comes back here when she's not off to somewhere else—her penthouse in New York, her villa in Tuscany, her hacienda in Argentina, her ranch in . . ." She paused. "It's either Wyoming or New Mexico. I wouldn't know. Never been there myself."

A hint of the tough Michelle Hendrix I'd observed last night was shining through.

"But, say . . . good luck to you up there with Tinkerbell. Let me know what happens."

"Tinkerbell?"

"Yeah. All sugar and sweetness. But get in her way and you're zapped. Tinkerbell could turn on a dime. Peggy Powers can too. When I was a kid I always liked Tinkerbell, but I never trusted her."

"Thanks for the warning," I said.

Peggy Powers was seated in one of the high-backed Jacobean chairs flanking the marble fireplace. The heavily carved wood and velvet upholstery practically swallowed her. It was the first time I'd seen her close up, other than for the fleeting moment this morning. I gauged her to be in her early to mid sixties. She would have blended into any crowd of well-to-do women her age who were putting on a few more pounds than they wished.

"I could sit here for hours and do nothing but stare," Peggy Powers said as I descended the steps into the grand room.

"Indeed," I agreed, glancing around. It was my first chance to get more than a walk-through of any of the public rooms other than the dining room where the board meeting had been held.

"Of course if I were you, I'd be turning things over, looking at the wood and examining nails to see what I could find," she said, her fingers nervously rubbing the acanthus carving on the arm of her chair. "That's what appraisers do, isn't it? For me, it's just a chance to bathe in splendor."

I let her comment pass.

"When Wynderly was being built, poor people—black *and* white—would walk for miles just to see it, to thrill at its grandeur," she said.

"Even today, you should see the look of wonderment on the schoolchildren's faces when they see the sculpture Hoyt brought back from India and the swords from Japan. The masks from Bali. And the Palm Court. Have you seen it yet? No? What a shame. Just like the one at the old Plaza Hotel, or the one at Biltmore . . . marble floor and all." She sighed. "Their glory days are now a thing of the past. The Plaza, Biltmore, Wynderly. But make no mistake. Wynderly is more than just another grand house with beautifully landscaped gardens. Wynderly will always be the *world* to those of us who will never see the places Hoyt traveled to. Perhaps his journeys don't seem so extraordinary these days, not to the rich and the privileged, at least. But in the 1920s, '30s, and even '40s, why, what Hoyt did . . . it was . . ."

Peggy Powers walked over to a twelfth-century silver-gilt reliquary modeled in the shape of an arm, its cupped hand reaching heavenward. She picked it up and brought it over to me.

"Who else would have had the vision to buy such a piece and to bring it here, to this rural setting—castle though it is? Oh, I know today a place like Wynderly seems little more than folly when you can turn on your TVs and have the world in your living room or den with the click of a remote. But long ago—" Holding the reliquary close, she said, "Yes, I think what Hoyt did was noble. Thanks to him, we have the world at our *fingertips*."

I swallowed hard. Thank God Michelle hadn't been nearby to tell her to put the ancient reliquary down. Then again, as Michelle had said, Peggy Powers was a board member. I doubted Michelle would have whipped out white gloves to give to her as she had to me.

"There's no question that what the Wyndfields did was remarkable," I said. Hearing my own words, I suddenly realized that she had spoken only of Hoyt, never Mazie. I had to wonder if she had read my thoughts.

"What you just said—the Wyndfields. It's true they traveled together and did everything as one. Ultimately, though, it must have been Hoyt who did most of the buying. Thinking it over, I'm sure he did. After all, it was *his* money."

"So, all this is *his* taste," I said looking around the expansive room.

"Oh yes," she said quickly, but then paused, as if thinking things through more thoroughly. "Of course I was young when I knew Mazie. Maybe she was romanticizing her husband's memory, but *she* always spoke of all this as *Hoyt's* things. She used to say things like 'I remember how much Hoyt loved the carvings he bought at the street fair in Milano,' or some such. But that isn't what I came to talk to you about," Peggy Powers said. "I got carried away. I do that when I feel passionately about things. But I love this place so much. Maybe *too* much. Here, come sit by me."

Mrs. Powers replaced the reliquary and moved to the gilt French furniture clustered beneath a deep bay of crisscrossed leaded glass windows. Banding the top of the bay were rectangular panes and every other one was inset with a stained-glass

French heraldic medallion—coats of arms in brilliant reds, blues, and gold. It was a little shrine to all things French.

And you promised not to be so critical, Mother chastised me.

"What I'm going to say must remain between the two of us, dear," she said. "Yesterday you said if anyone had any additional information, it might help you. It's about Sandra Lee Graham."

I searched my mind for someone by that name. A former housekeeper or staff member perhaps.

"Oh, you don't know who she is?" Peggy Powers sounded crushed.

"N-no . . ."

"Dear me. I *have* spoken out of turn, haven't I?"

Oh no, Tinkerbell, I almost said.

"Not at all," I assured her. "Every bit of information is helpful. Essential, really, if we're to make the right settlement. It might even help solve the question no one seems to have the answer to: who did this terrible thing?"

She exhaled. "That makes me feel better. Here, let me explain. Sandra Lee Graham is Frederick's wife. Frederick Graham. You remember him from yesterday."

"Oh yes, of course. I guess I got stuck on the Sandra Lee part of the name."

"Second wife."

I smiled and waited.

"She's a lovely person, Sandra Lee is. It's just that she doesn't have the same, well, lineage Frederick has. She tries to make up for that by showing off what refined taste she has. Always name-dropping. And she only wears designer clothes."

As if you don't, I thought.

"I'm sure she comes from a perfectly nice family. I've never heard a bad thing said about her. But—"

Peggy looked around the room, no doubt finding courage for what she was going to say next in her surroundings. She was, after all, a board member—a steward of these things, of this place.

"The rumor is that Sandra Lee wouldn't be all that upset if Wynderly had to close. That way, when the objects are sold—" she said, a tinge of excitement creeping into her voice.

"Is that what would happen," I interrupted her, feigning innocence. "The things sold?"

"Oh, I'm quite sure it is. Zach tells me that when the bank has lent money that it can't recover, but there is personal property that can be sold, even if it's at a loss, then it's the bank's responsibility to foreclose and have a sale. Get back what money it can for the stockholders. Can you imagine anything worse than selling Hoyt's things?"

Nothing stings us so bitterly as the loss of money, I could hear Mother say.

"And you think Frederick Graham's wife would want to have some of them—" I said.

"Well, surely, the board members would get first choice. Wouldn't you think so?"

If Peggy Powers was so anxious about keeping Wynderly intact, then why was I having visions of her standing at the head of the line, waiting to get a front-row seat at some hypothetical Sale of the Century, the Property of Wynderly, the Home of Hoyt and Mazie Wyndfield?

"I wouldn't know about that," I said, "but to sell them off . . . You think that's what would happen?"

"What else can the board do? If Frederick Graham isn't going to give us any more money and demands we pay the bank back what they've already loaned us, what else *can* we do?"

"Are things that bad? If Babson and Michael makes an insurance settlement—"

Peggy Powers moved closer to me. "Do you think there's really a chance they will?" she asked.

"Tell me, Mrs. Powers, what do *you* think happened? All I know is hearsay. There was a burglary. Some things were stolen. Some things were broken. I've been told no evidence was left, things like broken locks or forced entry, but *no* one seems to be under suspicion, at least I haven't heard any one specifically named. I'm really in the dark. But those of you who *live* around here, who know the situation . . ."

Her lips made a thin line. "I just can't *stand* being a gossip," she said, looking toward the doorway. "Some people are saying we should keep an eye on Michelle Hendrix, but the police questioned her." She ended her sentence on a high note, turning it into a question. "I don't think her name has been brought up recently. The board certainly hasn't seen any reason to let her go." She frowned. "But why *should* she do such a thing? What would she have to gain? She'd be the first to fall under suspicion wouldn't she, having access to the house and being free to come and go?"

"And there's never been a night guard?"

"Used to be, but not for a while now. We've been working on a terribly tight budget. That's why the bank loan was needed to begin with. It's like Zach says, 'insufficient funds.'"

"So when did Wynderly's financial trouble start?" I asked.

"Oh, I don't know," she said. "Probably sometime before we found an earlier curator with his hand in the till. Looking back, I imagine he took more than money—but we didn't look any further. At the time the cash didn't seem like that much of a loss. He cashed a couple of contribution checks and skimmed a little money off the top during our busy Christmas and spring garden tour seasons. But he was having some personal problems, so nobody wanted to cause a big row. Maybe we should have. It seems that things have gone downhill since then."

"When was all this?"

"Seven, eight, maybe nine years ago?"

"*That* long? How long have you been on the board?"

"This is my fourth term. It's more or less a lifetime appointment. Of course some people resign. Move away. Get bored. Get tired of asking for money—or *giving* money. Then again, it used to be fun when Miss Mary Sophie was giving a couple hundred thousand a year." Peggy Powers laughed.

That reminded me, I needed to call Miss Mary Sophie about tea this afternoon.

"And what happened to him, the curator?" I asked.

Peggy Powers looked shamefaced. "Nothing. You know how it is. We Southerners, particularly Virginians in *these* parts, we're still trying to act like our English ancestors—with stiff upper lips. We go along pretending everything is just fine. We'd *never* let on we're responsible for any indiscretions that one of us makes under the other's watch. We knew we were to blame, but we kept quiet. That was the honorable thing to do. What difference did it make? Dr. Landerley found another position right away. Oh, dear." Her hand flew to her mouth so fast I thought she was swatting a fly. "I do hope you don't know him."

I let her comment pass, but remembered what Worth Merritt had said the night before when I mentioned that something untoward might eventually happen to Wynderly. "I don't think that's a worry, Sterling," he had said. How like Virginians to turn their heads the other way or, ostrich-like, to bury their heads in the sand as if nothing had happened.

"But didn't he have to have letters of recommendation to get the other position?" I asked.

"I said, we did the honorable thing," Peggy Powers replied. "We kept quiet. We had trusted him. Landerley had been a guest in our homes. He had become one of us."

Strange that she mentioned his name a second time after the dramatics of a moment ago, I thought.

"Now we're talking about it," she said, "I realize how much the board has, well, gone down over the years."

"Gone down?"

"Once all the really fine people were on the board. The ones with money and old names. People who were in a position of power, who could make decisions and ante up when money was needed. Then one by one, they seemed to drop off after their terms, or resign, or whatever. Soon we were left with trying to *find* people to ask to serve. People like, well, there's that nice man Professor Fox. I'm sure he's well intended, but—and I don't mean this in a bad way, my dear—but just who *is* he? And as far as having money goes? I've never heard of him having any personal wealth and . . ." Her voice trailed off.

"So, what Tracy DuMont said yesterday about the board being at fault—"

"We haven't faced that yet," she said before I could finish my sentence. "Guess we'll have to come to grips with it though." She paused. "Eventually." She looked at me with wistful eyes.

I could return her look only with a wary one of my own.

Chapter 11

Dear Antiques Expert: After much agonizing, my brother and I are selling our grandmother's living room furniture. It's French and very ornate and just isn't right for our houses. To our surprise, the auctioneer has told us the upholstery on the pieces is older and more valuable than the furniture itself. How is this possible?

During the 1910s and '20s, "old world" tapestries depicting Gothic, biblical, and mythological scenes were quite the rage. So was elaborately carved French and Italian furniture. Believe it or not, even though new tapestries were being loomed, many 17th- and 18th-century tapestries were cut up and used to upholster brand new reproductions of 18th- and 19th-century furniture. Had the antique tapestries been left uncut, today they might sell for tens, even hundreds of thousands of dollars.

MICHELLE HENDRIX WAS standing in the entranceway. I hadn't any idea how long she'd been standing there, or why I hadn't heard her approach. With its high, plastered ceilings, bare floors—some wooden, some marble—and with no one around, Wynderly was a virtual echo chamber. Trying surreptitiously to catch Peggy Powers's attention, I simultaneously tipped my head toward the door and slithered my fingers along the eighteenth-century French tapestry upholstery toward her.

"If it does come to selling things—" she was saying, oblivious to my signals.

That's when I said, "Oh, Michelle. Won't you come join us?"

Peggy Powers started, only to instantly recover. "Yes, Michelle. Please do."

"Aren't *you* the popular one today," Michelle said, addressing me.

I pointed to myself. "Me?" I hadn't the vaguest idea what she was alluding to.

"First Mrs. Powers, and *now*, Miss Mary Sophie. She wants you to call her."

Damn, I thought. Before I could respond, the doorbell rang. Michelle let Frank Fox in.

"Good morning, everyone," he said in his fidgety way. "I know I'm early for the meeting, but, well, I was hoping I'd find you here, Ms. Glass, and that maybe I'd be able to have a few minutes of your time. But I'm afraid I'm interrupting something aren't I? Oh dear. Am I? I *do* hope not."

My mind was on Miss Mary Sophie. I should have called her. No doubt she had assumed that either I had no manners or I was avoiding her.

I looked from Peggy Powers to Frank Fox to Michelle Hendrix. Peggy Powers flushed. Too much was happening too fast for my liking.

"Dr. Fox, would you excuse me for a moment first, please. Mrs. Powers? I do apologize, but there's a phone call I *must* make. Michelle, I, ah—"

I looked to her in hopes of finding some way of escaping what I saw as a potential uncomfortable situation. I thought fast. She wouldn't dare show an uncooperative side in front of two board members.

"I really hate to disturb you, Michelle, but you do have Miss Mary Sophie's number, haven't you? It's so embarrassing to be such a bother," I said, casting Dr. Fox and Peggy Powers an apologetic look. "And to make matters worse, my cell phone doesn't work out here—"

"We understand, dear." Peggy, all sweet and nice, spoke up. "Michelle, you help Sterling. Dr. Fox and I have plenty to chat about I'm sure. Right, Frank?" No one would guess she had just spoken of him in less than complimentary terms.

Michelle and I had taken only a step or two into the hall when, once again, the doorbell rang. "Her number's on my desk," Michelle said and turned on her heel.

I made the call to Mary Sophie in blessed privacy. It turned out she wasn't coming to the meeting Houseman had called. We agreed on tea at four thirty instead of four.

By the time I returned to the front of the house, Dr. Houseman and a handful of the other board members from yesterday had arrived, including Frederick Graham and Worth Merritt. With Houseman calling the shots, there wasn't time for conversation. In what seemed to be a replay of yesterday, Houseman pulled out his pocket watch, checked the time, and led his troops down the hall. Frank Fox and Peggy Powers hung back.

"We'll talk later," Fox mouthed nervously before scurrying off to catch up with the others.

"Since I was already here, Alfred invited me to the meeting, too," Peggy said. "I think he was a little embarrassed that he hadn't called me. Who knows, it might have been an oversight."

I couldn't tell if she was amused by the whole situation or was trying to save face.

"And Michelle's going to the meeting, too?" I asked.

"I assume so. Alfred told her to get a notebook and join them. In fact, I'd better toodle-oo off myself," she said gleefully, adding, "We'll talk later."

"Oh, I'll be around," I said casually.

For half a second I thought about going back to further examine the broken items. That had been my intention hadn't it? I threw that thought away. With no one paying me any mind, I was on my own. I was ecstatic. Thank you, Lord, I said, casting my eyes heavenward, which was also in the direction of the attic.

My next thought wasn't quite so pious. Damn. I needed a flashlight.

Surely I couldn't ask to borrow one, or snoop around in hopes of finding one. And where would I look in this huge maze of a place? I had only so much time. My only choice was to retrieve mine from my car.

It only took a minute. I slipped back in and, tiptoeing to keep the heels of my shoes from clopping, started down the hall to the stairs leading to the attic.

I had no more than glanced at the few sheets of paper I had absconded with the day before. Between dinner with Worth Merritt and the unsettling episode at the 7-Eleven, my mindset hadn't been such that I could deal with much else. But what I *had* seen was enough to make me eager to dig further, to find more. My gut feelings told me more was to be found in those boxes. That's what comes from being an appraiser. You get this eerie feeling—some people call it a sixth sense—that something is right or wrong, even before the evidence is spread out before you. That sense had drawn me to the shoe box at the flea market a couple of weeks ago where I found the Tiffany sterling silver candy bowl marked fifty cents. And the same sense had told me the Oriental figurine with the five-hundred-dollar price tag was plastic, not ivory. Rarely had this feeling led me astray.

Plus there were all those other things up in the attic—the statues and lamps, the bedposts and stacks of chairs I had seen. Their call—like the call of the boxes and cartons—was as strong and compelling as that of Ulysses' alluring sirens. There was no turning back. I tested the batteries in my flashlight. The bulb flickered, then shone. Though it was little more than a penlight, it would have to do. I tucked the briefcase under my arm and started up the steps.

Chapter 12

Dear Antiques Expert: At a recent estate sale I saw a prayer bench that looked like it belonged in a Catholic church, but the auctioneer said it was a family piece. It resembled a low chair with a high back. Did families really own such a piece, and what would be its value?

Individual prayer or kneeling benches, known as prie-dieux, usually are considered liturgical furniture. However they were also made for home use, and highly carved 19th-century prie-dieux made for European houses and castles can sell for thousands of dollars in shops and at auction. Less elaborate antique prie-dieux usually sell in the low to mid hundreds, as do most reproductions.

So there I stood, right where my gut feeling had told me I wanted to be. In my nervous state, the attic seemed even larger and darker than before, the sort of space where you could get lost forever. If Michelle hadn't heard my fall before . . .

But now was not the time to think such thoughts. I needed to figure out where I had been yesterday—but with so many objects and boxes piled on top of, and in front of, one another,

I hadn't a clue where to start retracing my steps. I turned slowly, making a full circle, all the while casting my feeble light from side to side, up and down. The ceilings in the attic had to be nine, twelve, even fourteen feet high where the roof peaked. Such vastness defused the light to the point that it was next to useless.

Venturing blindly forth, I looked about for some object to use as a benchmark to help me find my way back to the steps. It needed to be large. A mirror tilting forward at a catawampus angle caught the dim rays from my flashlight and cast them back. There, reflected in the mirror, I saw the tower of boxes I had toppled over and haphazardly restacked.

I swept away the curtain of cobwebs tangled around a marble statue of some mythological creature for a better look. No more than two feet tall, the statue was a dancing faun like the type found in Pompeii. What I couldn't tell in this light was whether it was truly old, or a replica. Little matter. With ribbons of water cascading from a pouch tucked away under one arm it would be charming. And valuable. Wonder why *it* was in the attic, and those fake Tang horses were downstairs? Lord, I hoped I'd get the chance to do an appraisal of the whole place. I needed to talk to Matt about that. I smiled, wondering just how familiar he was with our Southern homes and plantations. He'd surely find Wynderly fascinating.

I reached the boxes I was itching to get to. Working quickly, I removed them, one from on top of the other, until they were in a row on the floor. I yanked at the top of the box closest to me. Only then did I notice it was securely taped on all four sides.

Slow down, I told myself. I cleared a space on the floor

where I could sit. That's when my sixth sense kicked into over-drive.

The day before, I had noted the paneled wall in the attic and thought it strange, but dismissed it as part of a closet or maid's room that had never been completed. But with the boxes moved, and by my scant light, combined with what sunlight could slip through the casement windows, my curiosity was piqued.

Remembering yesterday, I figured I was safer crawling than walking. I dropped to my knees and edged along the floor. Despite the thick dust and grime all around, from this vantage point I also had a clearer view of how far the wall extended. At eye level, the furniture and boxes stashed sometimes two and three thick obscured anything behind them.

I inched along, shining my flashlight ahead of me as best I could. The light from the French window on the opposite wall helped, but only slightly. When an upright steamer trunk blocked my way, I struggled to a half-standing position to get around it. The further I ventured, the more sinister the attic felt. Beads of sweat broke out on my palms like gum on tree bark.

After what seemed like hours, but probably had been no more than a few minutes, I came to a break in the stacks of boxes and furniture. Surely this was the end of the wall. I wrapped my fingers around the corner edge of the paneling. My hunch had been right. This partition had to be some sort of room or storage space. But how to get into it.

I stood up and inched around the corner. I was now facing the third wall of this strange room that jutted out into the attic. This wall, too, was obscured by things stacked in front of it.

I retraced my path to where I had begun, the first wall that had started my exploration. I edged myself around the things piled in front of it and leaned in, gently tapping in hopes of finding some sort of opening.

It was nothing but solid wall. A wave of frustration washed over me. I had no idea how long I'd been sneaking around, or what time it was. Precious minutes I could have spent foraging through papers and documents were gone. Still, I pushed on. But now, I literally *pushed* on.

The summer I had turned eight or nine, my parents must have decided I needed to see every historic house in Virginia. From Woodrow Wilson's home in Staunton to the Last Capitol of the Confederacy in Danville, we trudged through them, one by one. My favorites had been those with ghost stories, especially when they had secret rooms and passages. At Virginia House in Richmond, I learned the owner had built a hidden staircase leading from the library to his bedroom. I could still see guides pushing against the paneled walls in those rooms. It had been thrilling.

Many years later, Hank and I had taken our children on similar trips. At the forty-two-room Hermitage House in Norfolk, the curators told us they were still looking for secret hiding places they had heard or read about, but whose location had been lost track of over the years.

But I wasn't eight or nine anymore, and I wasn't taking a house tour. I wasn't Nancy Drew and Wynderly definitely was not Twin Elms. This was the real thing, not *The Hidden Staircase*. Still, it was worth a try.

Since my flashlight wasn't doing much good, I turned it off. As an appraiser, I long ago had learned to trust my sense of touch. Many were the times my fingers had shown me what my eyes had missed.

Like the time I felt the ripples along the top of a newly painted chest—telltale signs that the board had been hand-planed and was much older than it appeared to be. Seems the conniving daughter had slapped a coat of paint on a Hepplewhite chest to disguise it when her stepsister came to town to claim her share of the family's antiques.

And back in the 1970s, when silver reached fifty dollars an ounce and silver thieves were rampant, often the thieves would remove or rub out a monogram or coat of arms to make the stolen silver service or set of goblets easier to front in an antiques mall or flea market. What the eye couldn't see at first, the fingers could feel. If the surface of the silver felt wavy, or the thickness of silver grew thinner, you knew to look closer.

I felt my way, inch by inch, wall by wall, until I reached the last wall—the one I had just found, the one furthest away from the steps.

You never would give up, would you Sterling, Mother used to say.

If this box-shaped protrusion was some sort of *secret* room—and what else *could* it be with paneled walls—the opening would be on the most distant wall where it would be more concealed.

I wiggled in between the old upright steamer trunk and the tall chest of drawers. I fought the temptation to stop what I was doing and dig into the trunk in hopes of finding some great treasure. Instead, I laid my flashlight on top of it, and with both hands began feeling along the wall. I felt something off to the right. I grabbed the flashlight. There, slightly above my shoulder, was a stubby wooden knob. In the narrow opening, I could barely reach the knob with my fingertips. I tried turning it, but it wouldn't budge. I leaned against the paneling, trying to figure out what to do next.

I don't know what happened first—if I heard the moaning creak of the wood, or felt the wall give way. What appeared to be a loose board had begun moving, then stopped. I pressed against the wall, cautiously at first, then harder. A board of the paneling groaned, giving way to a black hole and a dank, heavy smell.

There was no way I was going in there.

In truth, the darkness was a letdown. After all that time and trouble it appeared that the space was just that—a dark, empty space. I glanced back over my right shoulder to get my bearings, or was it to be sure I had a quick escape route? Then I held the flashlight in front of me and stepped forward.

In the blackness the room seemed smaller, much smaller than I had imagined it would be when I had been crawling around its exterior walls. I cast the light about for clues. It wasn't cedar lined, and no coat hangers were lying about—both of which I would have expected had it been a closet. Without a window of any sort, it certainly couldn't have been a maid's room. I was coming up empty when my stomach jumped into my throat with such force I gasped to find some air.

In the far right corner, leaning against the wall was something thick and lump-like. I shone the light directly into the corner. Was it a burlap sack with a body? I crept forward.

What I feared was a body in a bag was an upholstered seat attached to a tall rectangular wooden frame. The object now appeared to be a low, boudoir-type chair. But along the top of the frame was a horizontal railing. It, too, was padded and upholstered. Jutting out the way it did would have made it impossible to sit on the low seat and lean back. But you weren't supposed to because it wasn't a chair; it was a prie-dieu, a prayer bench, the sort pictured in religious paintings and woodcuts. You were meant to kneel on the low cushioned section, and to use the railing to hold a prayer book or Bible, or to lean on as you prayed.

Then I knew what this was: a secret room, sometimes called a prie-dieu like the kneeling bench, but also known as a priest hole.

In sixteenth-century Protestant England it had been treasonous to hide a Catholic priest in your home, but there were still many devout Catholics in the land. A "priest hole" or hidden room, usually in the attic, provided a safe place for holding sacred rites. I had seen such rooms in castles and stately homes in the British Isles—the type Wynderly had been modeled after. Knowing Hoyt and Mazie Wyndfield's passion for all things European, and the depths of their pockets, of course they'd add this little touch for greater authenticity. And Mazie had been from Louisiana. She was probably Catholic.

My equilibrium restored, it was time to get back to more serious business. Oh well, the episode would make a good story, great cocktail party conversation. Then I noticed something different about the wall I was standing by. Lower than the other three walls, it was little more than six feet tall. Suddenly the space felt closed in—but, of course, that was because of the slanting roofline. What was strange, though, was that the wall was tilted slightly outward, rather than being straight up and down. It felt like one of those wonderfully evocative illustrations of the rooms in the misshapen castles and towers in *Grimm's Fairy Tales*.

I was turning to leave when I realized I was looking into a pair of tiny orange eyes. I screamed as some critter darted toward me and then ran between my legs. I must have jumped a foot off the floor. The flashlight flew out of my hand, and I careened into the tilting wall. I looked up to see it moving toward me like a drawbridge.

Chapter 13

Dear Antiques Expert: On a tour of historic homes in Louisiana our guide pointed out a bird print by James Audubon in almost every house. Are his prints terribly rare or expensive?

John James Audubon, whose lavishly illustrated *Birds of America* is a classic, was born in Haiti and lived in France. But it was Louisiana's unspoiled and exotic wildlife that Audubon found captivating, which explains the popularity of Audubon's prints in that region. Today, because of their rarity, original 19th-century Audubon prints sell for many tens of thousands of dollars each. Reproductions of Audubon's prints can range from a few dollars to a couple thousand dollars, depending on quality. "Antique" Audubon prints should be purchased only from a highly reputable dealer to avoid buying a replica or fake.

"DOGS." MISS MARY SOPHIE held her teacup halfway between her lap and her lips. Her multiple chins shook as she nodded her head. " 'Dogs.' That was Mazie Wyndfield's dying last word. Not what you would expect from a woman who hated dogs."

We were seated in the library at Oakcliffe, Miss Mary Sophie's ancestral home. It was a large, handsome room with leather bound books on the shelves and English hunting prints on the wall. A fire warmed the room and high above the walnut mantelpiece a stately gentleman painted in oils lorded over it all. There was no doubt the room was lived in. Books were everywhere, opened on the tables, stacked on the floor, even balanced on the library steps leaning against one of the top shelves. The room had an air of timeless elegance that no *Elle Decor* or *Architectural Digest* center spread could duplicate. Miss Mary Sophie, who had been reading the *Wall Street Journal* when I walked in, provided the perfect finishing touch in her English tweeds.

After my attic experience at Wynderly, I had been hoping for a stronger beverage. Even sherry, the old ladies' drink, would have been fine. Instead, I settled for tea when Miss Mary Sophie's maid, Nora, brought it.

"So you knew Mazie well, too," I said. "Like Worth Merritt."

"Quite well, even though Mazie was my senior by twenty years." Miss Mary Sophie placed her teacup on the coffee table. "Around here, at least back in the old days, everyone knew everyone, either socially or through the community—doing work on the farms or running into one another through the natural course of the day. The mailman, the grocer, everyone. My father and Hoyt were contemporaries. In fact, Hoyt often sat in that very chair." She nodded toward a leather lounging chair across the room. "My father was best man at Hoyt and Mazie's wedding. Would you like to see a picture?"

Miss Mary Sophie rose without waiting for my reply. "Hoyt

and Daddy were thirty-one or two and Mazie was twenty-two, if I remember correctly," she said as she crossed the room, slowly—she had left her cane propped against her chair—rather regally, I noted. I had no doubt that Miss Mary Sophie remembered *everything* correctly.

She picked up a black and white photograph in a silver frame from among several on the table, but another picture, now visible, caught my eye. I wondered who was the handsome uniformed man wearing his officer's hat at a rakish tilt.

"Quite lovely, aren't they, the three of them," Miss Mary Sophie said, handing me the picture in her hand. "Of course I remember how old Mazie was when she married. How could I forget? That's how old I was when I married."

She knew she had surprised me. I felt her eyes on me, watching for my reaction.

"Thought I was an old maid, didn't you, dear? Oh no."

Her "Oh no" and its accompanying smile left little doubt that Miss Mary Sophie Wellington McLeod had relished the married life.

"Eric and I were married quickly, impulsively. Our love was blind, the way it ought to be. It was 1941. That's him, over there," she said, pointing toward the table.

My heart sank. Hearing the date, I knew what was bound to come next.

"He had just graduated from college—the University, of course. I had finished Sweet Briar the year before. We were both from Virginia, but we met in Philadelphia of all places. We had barely known one another for two weeks when Pearl Harbor came. Naturally my family insisted I come home, as they should have. But I wasn't about to leave him. It was the only time in my life I defied my parents. We married ten days later. A year and ten months to the day I was widowed." Her voice trailed away. "Oh, I had other suitors. But no one could ever take Eric's place."

Then, turning back to me, her voice lighter, more spirited, her face radiant, she said, "I don't have to tell you that over the years as I grew older the children at church and around town were told to call poor, poor Mrs. McLeod 'Miss Mary Sophie.'" She chuckled. "It's never bothered me. I've had a comfortable life." She gestured to the things around her. "My father saw to that, and his father before him. With Eric, I'd had much more happiness in a short time than many people have in a lifetime."

I struggled to see Miss Mary Sophie young and carefree, wearing the look of love. Was I seeing myself in years to come? As hard as I tried to silence it, Mother's voice rang out in my head: *I feel it, when I sorrow most; / 'Tis better to have loved and lost / Than never to have loved at all.* I swallowed back a lump in my throat and felt sorry for myself.

"Probably even Mazie," Miss Mary Sophie said so softly I hardly heard her.

"Oh?" That roused me out of my pitiful reverie. "Mazie?" I said. "But, I thought she and Hoyt lived a *charmed* life."

Miss Mary Sophie folded her arms in front of her and lowered her eyes. "Too many secrets. Too many lies to live," she said.

"Tell me, Miss Mar—" I stopped myself.

She smiled. "That's OK, dear. That's what I like to be called. It fits."

"Yes, ma'am," I said out of habit and training. "Was Mazie Catholic?" I asked.

"What an interesting question." Miss Mary Sophie paused and leaned forward, picked up her teacup, then put it back without drinking from it. Her puzzled eyes met mine. "She never went to Mass that I know of. She and Hoyt attended the little Episcopal church down the way on occasion. Certainly not regularly. They traveled so much. And partied." She broke into a mischievous smile. "Mazie did pray a lot, though," she said reflectively. "Up in the attic there is supposed to be a secret place. Well, actually, I *know* there was one at one time, but whether it is still there?" She shrugged and looked aside, as if she were keeping from saying more. "So many changes have taken place. Much has been lost track of. The foundation board has gone through staff changes every few months for who knows how many years now. Disgusting, really. And this Michelle—" The corners of her mouth turned down in distaste.

"I shouldn't have said that," she said. "I'm sure the young woman is well intended, it's just . . . Well, I remember the time I overheard her say to a school group, 'Mazie was like a princess living in an ivory tower.' *Really* now. Many people lived, and continue to live, *much* grander lives than the Wyndfields—and without so much show. Princely? That's hardly the image *or* the legacy the old families around here would have wanted to pass on. Frankly, I'm not sure the young woman is well suited for the job. She lacks poise. Polish. Of course her title means nothing. She hasn't a background in art and antiques. Why, she's little more than a guide. A hostess.

What does she do other than show strangers around, which should be done more graciously. Yes, I find her edges a little too rough— " Miss Mary Sophie heaved, her heavy chest falling on her stomach.

"Then again, maybe all that bragging about the Wyndfields is just to cover up what she doesn't know," she said as if re-thinking her remarks. "Whatever the reason, I'm afraid I find her unsuitable."

"Then why was she given the responsible job?"

"We had drained the well dry long ago," she said. "Over the years the board brought in people with degrees and pedigrees. But these days they're nothing but a greedy bunch. Either passing through . . . what do they call it, on a career path? Or looking to pilfer what they can while everyone else's back is turned. Yes, we've had our share of those."

Who besides Dr. Landerley, I wondered.

"Such a shame that it can't be like the old days when there were respected professions and honorable careers. Librarians, museum people, professors, schoolteachers . . . oh, the teachers. They didn't make much money, but they were admired and revered. They shaped us and the people around us, and in so doing made our lives richer. It's all changed so much. Too much." She shook her head sadly.

"Although, Michelle's being there is partly my fault," she added. "Though in my defense, when I voted to take the young woman on I thought she'd have a deeper appreciation for what Wynderly stands for. After all, her family came to these parts when Wynderly was being built. From Louisiana. Like Mazie. In fact, Mazie brought them here."

"Really? How did that happen?"

"They came to work there. Hoyt spared no expense on any-thing. There were plenty of brick masons and wood-carvers in these parts. Georgian and Federal are our traditions, you know. But Wynderly called for craftsmen who could work with marble and stucco and paint cupids on the ceilings." She wrinkled her mouth up in distaste. "So, Hoyt brought them from Europe. And when Mazie said she missed the food from home, dear Hoyt, in his accommodating way, brought in the Fortiers . . . Daphne and Jacques. They were Michelle's, let's see, grand—no, *great*-grandparents, I do believe. Daphne cooked and Jacques gardened and painted, especially flow-ers and birds. His birds were magnificent. Someone up here started a ridiculous rumor that Jacques Fortier had descended from the Audubon line back when Audubon was painting the birds down in Louisiana," she said. "There was no truth in that, of course, but, you see, Audubon was illegitimate, so people just assumed *he* . . ." She broke off.

"You know. Guess that's what made it easy for the rumor to get started." Without missing a beat, she added, "Isn't it *ter-rible* how the past stays with you. The sins of the father, and all that stuff . . . and it's not even your fault. I ask you, what does it matter who Jacques Fortier was kin too?"

Hardly the words I expected to come from Miss Mary Sophie, especially on the heels of her judgmental remarks con-cerning Michelle. I was mystified. Might I have misheard her, this woman whom I was sure had never in her life missed a meeting of the Colonial Dames, Daughters of the American Revolution, or United Daughters of the Confederacy? I was tempted to ask Miss Mary Sophie to repeat her last sentence, but she had already moved on.

"Obviously Jacques Fortier was quite talented. His murals are outstanding, and the gardens he designed and planted were magnificent—even if they were more, well, shall we say *flamboyant* than the English gardens we Virginians prefer. But they're mostly gone now—overgrown and dreary. None of it is what it used to be—the house, the gardens. The people."

Miss Mary Sophie pulled herself out of her self-imposed gloom. "Anyway, the Fortiers had a daughter who came with them. Babette. I guess it goes without saying that Babette was a little wild. All that French blood and a name like that. She left home early . . . only fifteen or so. A short time thereafter she returned with a little girl, but no husband. Now what *was* that child's name?" Miss Mary Sophie paused to think.

"Actually, Babette's daughter turned out to be quite solid. She married a nice boy from over near Crozet. Michelle Hendrix is *her* daughter, Babette's granddaughter. Mazie and Hoyt left some sort of trust to look after the Fortiers."

The old woman paused and looked straight at me. Her face took on a graveness I had not seen before. "In these parts, my dear, we still believe noblesse oblige is part of our responsibility. Looking after our own is, well, it's our *custodial* obligation. It's as much a part of our tradition as honoring our heritage. Hoyt's family always looked after the colored people, even after the War. It was a *tradition* that the Wyndfields remembered their servants, black or white, in their wills."

Miss Mary Sophie stopped abruptly. She picked up her cane, then put it down with an angry thud. "It's such a shame we had to have that little disagreement with the Yankees, isn't it? They never *did* understand how we took care of our slaves."

I almost choked on my tea. Miss Mary Sophie, so proper and judgmental one minute and forgiving the next, was no more concerned with the propriety of what she had said than if she had asked the time of day.

"Nothing we can do about it now," she said. "As far as the arrangements Hoyt made for Fortiers' heirs . . ." Her voice trailed off. "Of course I wouldn't know the details," she continued, "but Frederick Graham would, *if* you could pry the information out of him, which I doubt. This much I *do* know, though. There was money for Michelle to go to college. I doubt if she even knew how she came by it. I'm not sure what she did between the time she graduated and when she came back here, but about the time she returned, the position for curator came open, *again*. By then it wasn't as if we were looking for a *real* curator. Just a warm body, and she was here." Miss Mary Sophie shrugged. "Michelle has been a . . . well, I'd call her a temporary fix."

I was still recovering from Miss Mary Sophie's casual dismissal of the War. But I had to say something.

"Michelle doesn't strike me as being terribly knowledgeable about the house, other than about Mazie, that is. She seems to idolize Mazie and the house itself. But as far as knowing the antiques — "

"Well, we can't all be to the manor born, or with a silver spoon in our mouths." Miss Mary Sophie looked me straight in the eye. "I'm told I'm harsh and expect too much, *but*, with education, *anyone* can learn."

Was this the same woman who had just bemoaned the loss of her family's slaves? What had begun as a cordial teatime was turning into a fiasco. But I wasn't about to cut our time short, for as a police officer once told me, DNA may put the bad guy away, but through conversation you'll learn who the bad guy is.

"And I'm learning much from you," I said as sweetly as I could. "You've been immensely helpful. I do have one question, though." I laughed to further soften the moment. "Actually I have *loads* of questions, but one in particular about Wynderly. With Hoyt's old Virginia ties and the conservative architecture and traditions of this whole region, how *did* he come to build a place like Wynderly? Was it Mazie's influence?"

"Even before they met, Hoyt loved to travel. He'd seen a lot of the world during the war and by the time he and Mazie married, mock French châteaus had become quite fashionable in America. Between Biltmore and Graylyn in North Carolina and the show places in Connecticut and Newport, Rhode Island, the second generation of robber barons were all trying to outbuild one another."

"Mr. Merritt told me how Hoyt's tobacco business took him all over the world," I said.

"Yes. I'd say his travels certainly made an impression on him. But there was another influence. A family down Richmond way. Great friends of Hoyt's grandfather."

"Oh?"

Miss Mary Sophie leaned far back in her chair and laughed. "Everything in Virginia seems to harken back to our grandfathers doesn't it? This time it was the Valentines. Hoyt's grandfather Edward was great friends with Mann Valentine down in Richmond. Seems the Valentines were enthralled by archaeology and anthropology . . . you know the kind of things, arrowheads, shards from old vessels and plates, bone fragments and tools. It was quite the fashion to make a show of your learning in your own home. Sir John Soanes had done it in London; Thomas Jefferson did it at Monticello. I remember, when I was a child, my grandfather told me that visiting the Valentines was better than going to the Smithsonian. He could *touch* the things at the Valentines' house." She smiled. "Oh, it must have been wonderful."

Once again Miss Mary Sophie thumped her cane hard on the lovely old Heriz carpet I had been secretly admiring. "Listen to how I *do* go on. Of *course* you know about the Valentine collection now that it's been turned into a museum." She made no attempt to stifle a heavy sigh. "I used to get *so* irritated when old people would tell you their stories over and over, especially stories about their dead ancestors. It bored me to tears. I thought they were bragging about their legacy, showing off. Now I'm old, I understand. It's not that at all. Those recollections of people and events from the past are concrete and real and *dear*."

The wistful look in her eyes was touching. And when she chuckled and said, "These days, *I'm* the one who is boring, boring *you* to tears," I felt a tinge of remorse. Perhaps I had been harsh in my judgment of her.

"Oh no, Miss Mary Sophie," I insisted. "Yes, I know about the Valentine Museum, but"—I smiled and reached across the years to pat her hand—"*but,* I can't say that I've ever heard anyone tell of a family member who saw the collection before it became a museum. I find that thrilling. Now I'll be able to tell others. The story will live on."

"You're kind." She clasped my hand. "But enough of that,"

she said. "Back to the point I was meaning to make—*hours*
ago. Hoyt was trying to bring the fruits of his journeys and
experiences home with him to share with all. Mazie added an
extra touch of the exotic with her Louisiana ways and French
and Spanish, and who knows what other blood running in her
veins. And, Hoyt loved her. He gave her anything and everything she wanted."

"But from what you said earlier, I'm assuming no dogs," I
said.

Miss Mary Sophie let out a howl of her own. "No sir. Mazie
Wyndfield was scared to death of dogs, which was most un-
fortunate. As you know, *every* Virginia gentleman, at least
those in the countryside, has his dogs." She pointed to the portrait above the mantel. "That's Brandy with my grandfather.
A King Charles spaniel. You probably saw Colin when you
came in. I've lost track of what generation he is, but his papers
go back to Brandy. Poor Hoyt. He had to keep his springers
in the kennel."

I couldn't help thinking about the rows and rows of porcelain dogs I'd found up in the attic. Why had Mazie put them
there? How did *they* fit into what I was hearing?

Chapter 14

Dear Antiques Expert: My great-great-grandmother's pair of red and white china spaniels sat on my grandmother's living room mantel for as long as I can remember. They had wide eyes and big noses and a collar with a chain and I loved them, but my uncle has inherited them. I want a pair myself, but need to know how much they will cost. Can you help?

Your grandmother's English Staffordshire spaniels, also known as "comforter dogs," were made in the last half of the 19th century. Staffordshire potters made many sizes, styles, and colors of various breeds of dogs for use as mantel decorations. Spaniels, then hounds and poodles were the most popular styles. Today a fine pair of Staffordshire spaniels standing about ten inches are usually priced between $500 and $800. But beware. Reproductions abound, and have for years. Be sure you purchase your dogs from a reputable dealer who guarantees that they date from the 19th century.

IT WAS AFTER six o'clock when I pulled out of the front gates of Oakcliffe and started toward the main road at the end of the estate's private driveway. I remembered how Mother often spoke of the *quaint* old homes that dotted the Virginia countryside. There had been nothing quaint about either Oakcliffe or the woman who lived in it. Oakcliffe was old and grand. Miss Mary Sophie, old and formidable. They seemed uniquely well suited.

Thoughts of the strong-willed Miss Mary Sophie took me back to my childhood. Mother and I had gotten into the typical mother-daughter row about something. Who knows what, now? My father had taken me out to the backyard under the guise of punishing me for being disrespectful to Mother. But instead of giving me a tongue-lashing—my gentle New England born-and-bred father would never have spanked me—Daddy said to me, "Sterling, I could *try* to explain your mother to you if I had a lifetime, but I don't. Suffice it to say, *never* try to understand a Southerner, at least one of her generation." Boy was he right.

I was getting hungry, but knew that if I stopped for supper and had a glass of wine I'd be done for the day. I had told Frank Fox that we'd get together, though I hadn't the vaguest idea what he wanted, nor, right now, did I give a damn. But he was as tenacious as a candidate chasing votes on Election Day. It was bad enough that Fox had tracked me down at Belle Ayre and Wynderly. When I had left to go to Miss Mary Sophie's, I found a note tucked beneath my windshield wiper insisting that I call him ASAP. He had included a string of numbers where he could be reached, and a p.s. Like before, he had underlined to make his point: "*No* time is too late. Try my *cell phone* first. I'll find something to do in Orange in *hopes* that *I'll hear from you*. I won't start home till 9:30 or 10 P.M."

What was really bothering me, though, was knowing I needed to call Matt. But tell him what?

Taking the day as a whole, I had little concrete information on the hard dollar-and-cent value of the stolen and broken items, or on the theft itself. Truth was, more questions had been raised than answered. So what news had I? The secret rooms up in the attic? I could practically hear Matt Yardley laughing in his Madison Avenue corner office about the Southern bimbo he'd hired.

This place, these people, their lives, those hidden rooms . . . the strange way things had unfolded when I ventured back up into the attic. Never would I have imagined the roof could have extended so far, or that the room hidden behind the priest hole could have been so large.

SPIDERWEBS HAD ENVELOPED the room's single crystal chandelier. Yet, when I tried the wall switch, two bulbs still burned.

Gradually, my eyes had adjusted to the dimness. There, on shelves running along the wall, were rows of Staffordshire china dogs. On the bottom shelf, one by one the figures grew larger, one, then another, larger and larger, on and on. Then, one by one, they grew smaller. In among red and white spaniels was the occasional curly-haired poodle and long-nosed hound. On another shelf were dogs with cats, dogs with Scottish lads and lassies, dogs with tunic-clad Romans.

It was like being in a haunted toy store.

Beneath the shelves, old magazines and books were stacked high on worktables, but my eye had been drawn to a lady's desk—small and elegant. It had a flat writing surface and a narrow raised shelf at the back. On the desk, as if arranged for a photograph, had been a brass candlestick and an open book. A gold-tipped mother-of-pearl fountain pen lay across the pages. To the far side of the desk was a crumpled sheet of paper speckled with yellowish brown, like so many liver spots brought on by the years.

I slipped my fingers beneath the cobwebs just far enough to remove the wadded up page. Moving closer to the window to catch more of the winter's day low light, I half blew, half shook away the grime covering the fine vellum. The page's thickness had helped preserve it. I folded back the corners and smoothed them out. The writing was large and legible, though where the paper had been creased for so long, some words were distorted. I began to read.

Mrs. Hoyt Thompson Wyndfield, wife of Hoyt Wyndfield, died suddenly at ten o'clock last night at Wynderly, her home in Orange County, Virginia. She was born at Apulosa Planta-tion, Louisiana, the daughter of Colonel Claudius Adolphe Bontemps. An accomplished woman, she had attended school in Nazareth, Kentucky, and later, the Peabody Conservatory of Music. Surviving is her husband.

That was all. Thinking I might have missed something, I rotated the page back and forth in the light when, at the bottom right hand side, I saw some small numbers: "12/25/55." Christmas Day 1955.

It was all too weird. Mazie hadn't died until 1985. Had Hoyt had another wife? Of course not. He couldn't have. Hoyt and Mazie had married in 1922. Even if there had been an-other wife, she certainly would not have come from Louisiana like Mazie, and had the same last name. I reread it to be sure I hadn't missed the name. I hadn't. And whose handwriting was it? It was too feminine to be Hoyt's.

Running my fingers across the roughness I had realized that what I had thought was part of the wrinkles and creases was a deeply embossed monogram. *MWE*. Mary Elise Wyndfield . . . Mary Elise Wyndfield.

Somehow, I had enough wits about me, or was it just plain nerve, to gather a few papers and books to examine later. Yes, it must have been nerve, because I had also done something I had never done before, but then I'd never been in such a situation before. Whatever the reason, I had grabbed up one of the figures—a medium-size spaniel, maybe eight, nine inches tall, sitting on a raised white base with a single gold line painted on it. I slipped the dog next to it over a bit; with so many dogs lined up like ducks in a shooting gallery, one would hardly be missed. In doing so, I stirred up the dust and left an uneven trail. That bothered me. Then again, would anyone else ever find this godforsaken place? What if *I* were never found?

That ghastly thought had about done me in. I had come upon this room completely by accident. It had been by chance that the wall had moved. If the wall had closed behind me, entombing me in the room with no air, no light, no—

Present fears are less than horrible imaginings, Mother had said years and years ago, using my childish dread of going to the dentist as an excuse to spout a line from *Macbeth*.

I headed straight to the opening and stepped back into the priest hole. The slanted wall had remained ajar. I didn't dare touch it.

Thank God the door between the priest hole and the attic

had not closed. What *had* I been thinking, blindly stepping into first one black hole, and then another? Alice in Wonderland hadn't had anything on me when she fell down the rabbit hole. Like her, I had never once considered how I was going to get out again.

With my small flashlight, I was able to find the small knob on the attic side that had gotten me into trouble in the first place. In the priest's secret room, instead of a knob, there was a single round hole, an inch across at the most. In the darkness anyone might have mistaken it for a simple knot in the wood. I slipped my finger into it to be sure I could move the door if, just if, it ever closed on me. If, just if, I ever came back and got trapped. I grabbed the door ledge with my thumb and crooked my pointer finger into the opening. It was when I pressed my fingers against the door itself that I felt a deeply embedded line running vertically down from the hole. I looked more closely. There was a second line running horizontially. A cross. Of course. Even in total darkness, the mark of the cross would have shown a priest or those in the room with him, the way out.

I closed the door behind me and found my way back to the attic proper. I tucked a few more items from the boxes into my briefcase. Once downstairs, I had slipped back to my car, dropped off my booty, and then headed to the room where the broken pieces from the theft had been stored—the place I was supposed to be from the very beginning.

Now, SITTING SAFELY in my car at the end of Oakcliffe's driveway, I realized that I had done something for Babson and Michael, after all. Once I had deposited the objects in my car and was safely back inside Wynderly I had gotten right to work figuring out the values of items that had been broken and left behind.

I had matched up what once had been a circa 1890 Art Nouveau blue tinted glass vase with sterling silver overlay with its entry on the earlier appraisal that Michelle had given me. Today the vase would be worth perhaps six or seven thousand. On the old appraisal—which I now knew had been made in 1986—it was valued at ten thousand dollars, a greatly inflated value at the time of the appraisal; back then, two, maybe three thousand dollars would have been a top price.

And an exquisite late Meissen mythological figure, now missing its arms and head, had been appraised at almost five thousand dollars—again, outrageously high for the 1980s. Eight hundred or a thousand would have been closer to the mark. Some of the missing items had been valued at fifty thousand and above. Babson and Michael had been right to double-check the claim that had been submitted to them.

My intention had been to ask Michelle a few questions—not that I figured she would have the answers, but it was the right thing to do. Though she was in her office, her door had been closed. When I heard her voice, I had knocked a couple of times. She seemed to be talking to someone on the phone. When she didn't respond and I realized what time it was, I had slipped a note under her door saying I would see her in the morning, and had left for Miss Mary Sophie's home.

NOW, SOME TWO-PLUS hours later, I was so absorbed in replaying each minute detail as the day had unfolded that when headlights from an oncoming car shone through the night, I literally had to think twice to get my bearings. Jarred back to the here and now, I turned on to the main road and headed back toward town. On my right, a tall, castle-shaped sign came into view.

WYNDERLY — TREASURES OF THE WORLD

OPEN TUESDAY THROUGH SUNDAY, 10 AM TO 4 PM

Dangling from one hook beneath it, a straight board swayed in the wind. CLOSED, it read.

Several times during my conversation with Miss Mary Sophie I had almost asked her about the secret rooms, then stopped. Now I was second-guessing my decision. Then again, maybe it was better that I hadn't asked; no telling what secrets I had stumbled upon. Nor could I be sure that Miss Mary Sophie wouldn't tell another board member of my findings. Until I had time to sort through it all, a pack of watchdogs hovering over my every move at the house was the last thing I wanted. Michelle was warden enough.

But what to do now? Food. Had there been any lunch? Oh yes. One of the stale Snickers at the bottom of my briefcase. No wonder my stomach was growling almost as loudly as my brain was churning.

Up ahead I spied Kentucky's most famous colonel beckoning to me from under the red and white awning. I swung into the drive-through lane and placed my order. Perfect. I was going to be set for the night.

Or so I thought until I pulled into Belle Ayre.

There, in front of the front door, was Michelle Hendrix's red Nissan.

Chapter 15

Dear Antiques Expert: In my grandparents' home there's a Victorian armchair. I've heard it called both a lady's chair and a gentleman's chair. How do you tell the difference between the two?

Victorians glorified the family as personified by Queen Victoria and Prince Albert and their children. Nowhere was this idealized family image more evident than in the Victorian parlor with its two chairs, one for the father—a sturdy "gentleman's" armchair with a high back, and one for the mother—a smaller proportioned "lady's" chair that was lower to the floor and often had only partial, or demi arms. Over the years many of these pairs have been separated, and now any smaller Victorian armchair is generically referred to as a lady's chair, while larger chairs are called gentleman's chairs.

DRESSED IN JEANS and a bulky sweater, Michelle looked woefully out of place seated in the high-backed Victorian gentleman's armchair.

"I'm desperate," she said, nervously wiping her hands on her jeans. "Otherwise I wouldn't be bothering you."

From the moment I'd seen her car parked there, I had felt pretty nervous myself. I had made a quick decision to take only my handbag and coat with me, leaving the Wynderly items in the car.

Now here Michelle and I sat, both of us acting awkward.

"In that meeting today Dr. Houseman as much as accused me of stealing the things missing from Wynderly and breaking the others to cover my tracks," she said.

I didn't find that news particularly shocking. "What did you tell him?"

She gave me a puzzled look. "What *could* I tell him? Nothing. I didn't do it." Her tone was emphatic.

"Why would he bring that up now . . . at this late date?" I asked, hoping to draw her out while begging a little time to think the situation through. I felt like I had dozed off in the middle of a movie and missed a few scenes. Something must have happened while I was having my own little drama up in the attic.

"The papers. Didn't you see today's newspaper?" Michelle asked.

"No. I haven't seen a paper since I got here . . . two, three days ago." I had noticed Houseman had a copy under his arm when he arrived at Wynderly, but that was as close as I'd come.

"Well, they said terrible things about Wynderly and even some of the board members."

"Did the article mention *you*?"

"Not directly, but it said Wynderly had been mismanaged, and since the thieves hadn't left any signs of entry, the obvious conclusion was that it was an inside job. They might as well have put my name in the headlines. Everybody knows I work there. But the thing is, the police questioned me right after the theft. Dr. Houseman knew that. So why'd he have to start in on it all over again?"

"But you said you weren't named specifically. Right?" I said, attempting to calm her. "OK. Then let's try to think this thing through, Michelle. First, the mismanaging part. Did they cite anyone in particular? Board members, past staff members, anyone?"

"No."

"So they didn't actually imply that *you* had mismanaged the funds," I said, putting a positive spin on the situation. "How could they? You can't spend any money without getting the board's approval can you?"

"Right. The checks have to have two signatures. But the point is, even if the paper didn't name names, the article got everyone talking about what's happening at Wynderly all over again. Why else would Houseman have put me through the third degree the way he did?"

I wished I had read the article. Hearing about it secondhand from Michelle wasn't much help.

"They even mentioned your being here," she said.

Damn.

"They said you had been sent to investigate the break-in."

Where had they gotten that?

"It made you sound like some kind of PI or policeman," Michelle said. "You aren't, are you? Or are you? I thought you were just an appraiser."

So that was it. Michelle Hendrix was afraid I was some strong arm of the law. I almost laughed at the thought until last night's scene at the 7-Eleven flashed across my mind. Oh dear. I spoke slowly and deliberately.

"Let me assure you, I am *not* an investigator, and I don't have anything to do with the police," I said. "Babson and Michael sent me here to help with the insurance claim. They could have sent someone else, another appraiser, but they're in New York and I'm in Leemont . . . much closer." I laughed self-consciously. "All I'm supposed to do is sort out the value of the broken items and do the same for the things that were stolen . . . as best I can, that is. There's a lot of money involved. Babson and Michael doesn't want to overpay or underpay. It's the way insurance companies do business. That's all."

I looked at Michelle for some hint that I was getting through to her. "Look, my asking so many questions isn't being nosy. They're necessary. I'm trying to establish where the values the foundation sent to the insurance company came from. That's why having both the appraisal made not too long after Hoyt's death *and* the one made in 1986 is so helpful. The 1986 one is the one I was using this afternoon."

"I realize that," she said.

She sounded impatient with my detailed explanation, but I wanted to be sure we understood each other. Then, as if a light had gone on in her head, she said, "Yeah, that appraisal would be important. That's probably where the board got its values. It's the one the bank had made right after Mazie died and the foundation was being established," she said. "That's when they took over ownership of the things. At least that's what somebody told me when I took the job, I don't remember who."

I balked. "Whoa. Back up for a moment, please. *Who* took

over ownership? The foundation owned the property. You mean the *bank* took possession of some of the things? You didn't mention the bank taking ownership of any of Wynderly's things. What's that about?"

"Oh they didn't *take* anything, not out of the house." A frown crossed Michelle's face. "At least I don't think so. I'm not sure of all the details, but as best I know . . . See, the Wyndfields left plenty of money, but certain portions of it were designated to different purposes, various trusts and charities. The Y built a new wing and named it for them. Things like that. Anyway, some of the board members had big ideas about publishing coffee table books and putting on seminars, but the foundation didn't have the funds to pay for all that. Somehow, though, the bank and the foundation worked it so there would be more money. That's how the bank ended up owning some of Wynderly's antiques."

That was interesting. Most banks weren't in the business of owning antiques. They wouldn't even give loans on personal property other than cars and real estate. Something sounded fishy. I'd have to give that some more thought, but Michelle didn't need to know what was going on inside my head.

"I guess that makes what Tracy DuMont said all the more true. Money in, money out," I said. "You've got to have the money coming in before you can pay it out. And as far as my being here, Michelle . . . You see with that appraisal being, what, twenty-some years old, it's totally out of date. If there had been a more recent appraisal, made, say four or five years ago, I probably wouldn't even be here."

Michelle just looked at me. As we sat in silence I found my-self reassessing my opinion of her. I hadn't come to Wynderly expecting or wanting to dislike this woman I had never met before. Yet from the moment she had opened the door, the way she had been so bossy, her unwillingness to help me . . . she had put me off. Now, though, she seemed so genuinely distressed that part of me wanted to reach out and reassure her—and send her home. I was getting awfully tired.

On the other hand, the newspaper article had clearly unnerved her. What if she was just playing against my sympathy?

I remembered her questions about the Delft charger. Then there was the much finer Delft water vessel I had noticed. Why one piece of Delft would be broken and the other left untouched had puzzled me. What Michelle knew about antiques couldn't fill a postcard. What if she *were* the thief and had just taken things at random because she liked them, or perhaps she had overheard other people talking about various objects' values. That could have influenced her choices. I needed to know more.

If she really thought I was a threat, wouldn't it be more likely that she would keep her suspicions to herself and continue dogging my every move? "But why have you come to see *me,* other than to be sure I'm not working for the police," I asked.

"Remember earlier today when you were in the room looking at the broken things, and Houseman called the meeting . . . Well, I told you he took to interrogating me, first in front of those board members and then later by himself. It was like he was trying to break me down—you know, the way they do it on *Law and Order.*"

Her words were music; she hadn't mentioned the attic. No

one seemed to have noticed I wasn't where I was supposed to be . . . at least part of the time.

Michelle bit her lip and glanced at the floor. Her eyes shifted from side to side before she returned my gaze.

"That's when it dawned on me that you might come up with some evidence that would help me out, that would point to who *really* did it. That's why I came here. I need your help to prove I didn't do it. No matter *what* anybody thinks."

I had to feel sorry for her. "Look, Michelle, I've already told you I'm not here to investigate the *crime*. I'm investigating the *things*. If, along the way, I happen to pick up some . . ." I felt out of my element. How should I put what I was thinking? "Some, well, *clues* about the theft, then of course I'd tell Babson and Michael. What they would do, I don't know. That would be up to them. But listen to me . . . I haven't been thinking in those terms. I haven't reported *any*thing to anyone — not to Houseman, not to Babson and Michael — not to anyone, not anything." I didn't add, "because I don't have anything to report."

Michelle smiled weakly. "I wasn't sure, but I thought *you* might have told Houseman I'd done it."

She got up and walked over to the fireplace and looked into the fire. "Oh, I don't even know why I took this job." Her voice was close to breaking. "I only did it to be helpful. And, well, I guess I thought it was what my grandmother would have wanted me to do." Michelle brightened at the mention of her grandmother. "Babette. She was my grandmother. Doesn't the name almost dance when you say it? I wish they'd named me that."

I couched my words carefully. "Was she from here?"

"Yes and no. Her parents came from Louisiana to work for Mazie. Jacques and Daphne Fortier. Some of the old people around here still remember them, but I never knew them. They were my great-grandparents and my mother was in her late thirties before I was born. But my grandmother, Babette . . . She's why I love this place so much. She's how I got to know Mazie." Michelle smiled, showing a sweet side of her I'd not seen before. "You see, my whole family worked for the Wyndfields. When I was a little girl I heard Mazie calling her Babette. When I tried to say it, Babby came out." Her smile broadened. "It just stuck. Anyway, when I came back here and was asked to oversee Wynderly—why, it was like I had *arrived*. I thought I was bettering myself and honoring my family." She gave a little laugh, but quickly the corners of her mouth turned down.

"Looks like the joke's on me. All I end up doing is ruining my name and bringing disgrace on my family's memory. How's that for irony?"

I forgot my resolve to hang tough. My heart went out to her. "Michelle, what's behind all this? What do *you* think happened? Who did it?"

I thought I detected a ray of hope in her eyes before she looked away and said dishearteningly, "I don't know. I've been gone from here for a long time. It's not like I went down the road to UVA to college and kept up with things at home. I knew I wouldn't fit in over there in Charlottesville. The kids who go to Virginia from around here live in the big houses. I had some friends from around town who went there, but they'd gone to Woodberry Forest or St. Margaret's for prep school. I wasn't one of them. The way they acted. The way they dressed—

"Anyway, I wanted a new start, something different. So, I did the next best thing. I went to the University of Maryland. Nobody knew me, and I was just another face in the crowd. No big deal. I hardly bothered to come home for vacations, and I got a job waitressing up on the Cape in the summers. I pretty much lost contact with this whole area. I mean, I was young."

"But you must have had good grades. And the out-of-state tuition at Maryland couldn't have been cheap."

"Oh, I did well in high school. Really well. I knew I didn't want to live my whole life here. The bank gave a scholarship that year and I won it. I pretty much had a free ride through school."

Ah . . . I remembered what Mary Sophie had said about the Wyndfields setting up a trust for the Fortiers. Miss Mary Sophie had been right. Michelle hadn't any idea the scholarship had come from the Wyndfields' trust. It was the sort of deal a small town bank could work, especially if they had other uses for the Wyndfields' money. They didn't want inquires into how they were managing the trust's funds.

"And after college?" I asked.

"Well, that's another story." Michelle pressed her lips together and took a long breath before speaking again. "I'd always been sort of a loner, and then I met this guy in college who swept me off my feet. To make a long story short, I married him and went home with him . . . to Saudi Arabia."

I must have shown my surprise.

"Yep. That's what I did. Well, it didn't take me long to realize that had been a *big* mistake. Then again," she said, shrugging nonchalantly, "maybe somebody was looking after me. Turned out I was barren." She looked at me to see my reaction.

I was surprised, not at what she had said, but at her choice of the word *barren*. It must have been the word her husband and his family had used.

"How did your family feel about your marriage?" I asked, going back a step.

"What would it have mattered at the time? My husband was handsome, and the thought of marrying him was like something out of the *Arabian Nights*. And his manners. Compared to the guys I'd known in high school, even the ones I met in college—"

Again Michelle spread her hands for lack of words. "A lot of the girls were jealous, and they let me know it. See, the American guys all wanted to go on Dutch dates. Haadhir paid for everything. Babby didn't object at all. She said that people would understand . . . that no one had objected when an American girl had married the king of Jordan and become Queen Noor, or when Grace Kelly married Prince Rainier—not that he was Muslim, but he was sort of foreign-looking. Babby must have thought all Saudi men were princes, and I was going to be a celebrity or something." Michelle laughed. "Looking back, I think all the tales my grandmother heard from Mazie and Hoyt about their travels and seeing the rich people who came to Wynderly . . .

"I don't know . . . probably being around all those things in the house from all over the world . . . Well, it must have warped Babby's view of life," she said. "Anyway, I came back to the States and knocked around here and there for a few years. I wasn't about to come back home. Then both Babby and Mother died, and when my father got sick, well, I didn't think I had much choice."

She took a deep breath and straightened her back. "So here I am. Not that I intend to stay. Certainly not *now*."

Unless they put you in jail, I thought. Taken at face value, Michelle's story sounded fine. But a kernel of doubt kept nagging at me. I didn't know whether to chalk it up to being a suspicious appraiser, or if that trusty sixth sense was kicking in again.

Chapter 16

Dear Antiques Expert: When going through some boxes packed away from my great-grandparents' house, I found a pretty porcelain mantel clock. Taped to the back was a picture of it sitting on their living room mantel. There are no markings on either the clockworks or the porcelain case. It does have a key to wind it up, though. I'm wondering if it is valuable and worth repairing?

At the end and turn of the 19th century, Austrian and German factories made a wide variety of porcelain cases—from small and simple, to large and elaborately decorated—to hold clockworks. Today a simple porcelain mantel clock from that era usually sells for around a hundred dollars, but fine, large porcelain clocks by factories such as Meissen can soar into the thousands. A clock specialist can estimate the repair costs, but regardless of the clock's value, the photograph shows how much your ancestors treasured their clock. I would keep it, working or not.

MORE THAN FOUR HUNDRED years ago Shakespeare had written that discretion was the better part of valor. If some subversive plot was brewing on the Wynderly battlefield, there was no way I was going to be part of it. Forget the valor. *Discretion* was the word to live by.

I had stood on the front porch until the taillights on Michelle's car faded. Only then did I venture out to my own car to grab both briefcases and take them back to my room. Once inside, I slung my bag and coat over my shoulder, called out a cheery thanks to Ginny, who was rustling about in the kitchen, and headed straight to my room.

Little matter that the chicken thigh I was calling dinner was cold and the glass of chardonnay I poured was warm. I wolfed them both down. I was licking the last crunchy crumbs of batter off my fingertips when there was a knock on the door.

"Sterling?"

I opened the door and Ginny Kauffman wedged her head and shoulder inside. "You sure are popular," she whispered.

It was the second time I had heard that comment, and I didn't like it any better now than I had the first time.

"Professor Fox." She motioned toward downstairs.

"Damn."

Ginny Kauffman winked. Then, holding the door with one hand to steady it, she rapped on it with her other. Turning her head in the direction of the stairwell, again she said, this time louder, "Sterling." And to me she mouthed, "Want me to tell him you're not here, or in the shower?"

I shook my head no. "Thank you, but tell him I'll be down in a minute."

It had been tempting to avoid him. I was chomping at the bit to get to the papers in my briefcase, even though I was dead tired and emotionally exhausted. But with Fox so intent on cornering me sooner or later, I decided to get it over with.

THIS TIME I SAT in the Victorian gentleman's chair. Frank Fox, all tittery and twitchy, chose the sofa where he spread himself out.

"I knew I was taking a chance on catching you, but—" he began.

"No, no. It was my fault," I apologized. Like Michelle had said about Peggy Powers, he was, after all, a board member. "*I* should have called *you,* and I would have, but my time hasn't been my own tonight, and my cell phone doesn't work at all."

Fox cut to the chase. "I don't know how much you know about my research."

"Nothing, I'm afraid." My voice sounded flat, even to my own ears, but I was becoming tired of pretending to be excited, or upset, or ignorant, as the situation demanded. At least I was being truthful this time.

Fox beamed. "Actually, the hydrosphere is quite exciting."

"Hydrosphere?"

"Why, yes. Universities teach several courses dealing with the importance and evolution of water's role in the universe."

"I see."

"I happen to have a few papers I've written about vessels with me." The sofa creaked as he leaned over the arm to get his briefcase.

"Vessels?" I knew I was tired, but what *was* he talking about?

"Well, not just *any* old vessels. Ancient vessels," he said, handing me a manila envelope.

When, for the second time that night, I remembered the seventeenth-century Delft water bottle that I had figured was worth seventy-five thousand dollars or more, I got a queasy feeling. I decided it was in everyone's best interest if I feigned as much enthusiasm as I could. "Oh, of course, *water* vessels."

"I knew you'd be excited," he said, edging so close to the edge of the sofa I was afraid it might tilt over. "I got the idea while watching a National Geographic special," he began. "*And,* from being on the Wynderly Foundation board, of course. What an honor that is. Hoyt was interested in these things, too, you know. There are several fine vessels in the collection."

"So," I said in an attempt to shift the conversation back to Fox, "you're at the University of Virginia."

"Well, no, I mean, not *yet* . . . not at *the* University. I teach at a small college not too far from there."

In truth, I'd already figured that out. One of the traditions at the University of Virginia is the addressing of professors as Mister, rather than Doctor or Professor, part of Jefferson's rules of equality, at least for men. But to be polite, and certain, I had given Professor Fox the benefit of the doubt.

"And you'll have to forgive me if I'm not really familiar with what you do," I said. "You say it's the hydro . . ."

"Hydrosphere," he said.

"Living over in Leemont and meeting so many new people here . . . well, I'm struggling to simply remember names and keep everyone straight."

"Of course you are. But I have to tell you, when I saw you come into the board meeting yesterday, I thought I was dreaming. I've cut out practically every column you've ever written."

"Why, thank you," I said slowly.

He jumped right in, emphasizing his words the same way he had underlined them in his notes.

"Since I'm such a big fan of yours, do you think—I mean, would you possibly have enough time while you're here to see my collection. Well, it's not really *my* collection. I mean it *is* a gift that *I'm* responsible for, so in that way it *is* my collection, but it's going to the college." He stopped and beamed with pride. "But I'd like for it go to *the* University. More people would see it that way. That's why I need you. Someone with your reputation would be an, an *endorsement* of just how fine a collection it is. I'm sure it would draw a lot more attention with *your* name associated with it."

I forced a smile. My bet was that Frank Fox was thinking that if the University of Virginia accepted the collection, he'd be the natural pick to be its curator. I had the uncomfortable feeling I was being set up.

"Professor Fox, I, well, you see, I'm here on this one specific job and my time is limited. I'm not sure Babson and Michael would approve of my taking time away from the Wynderly investigation to . . ."

A wry smile crept across Fox's face. "Investigation? So *that's* what it is after all."

"No, no. That's not what I meant to say. *Appraisal.* It's not an investigation, it's an appraisal. But you have to *look* at the pieces, investigate them, when you're doing an appraisal."

Fox shifted his cumbersome weight forward in a way that a body language expert would have labeled confrontational. "There's certainly nothing to *investigate* as far as Wynderly goes," he said. "You couldn't have taken what Tracy DuMont said seriously. She's a real *trouble*maker. She could write a check to help the board get through this . . ." He hesitated long enough to choose his word carefully—more carefully than I had chosen mine. "This *difficulty,* and not even miss it. I don't know *why* she's being so selfish. Not with all her tens, maybe even hundreds of millions."

"No. No," I had begun saying during his brief pause.

"Well, good," he said, vigorously bobbing his head in rhythm with his words. "I'm glad to see you aren't falling for all that trash in the paper about the foundation."

"About the collection, *your* collection, of water vessels. It certainly sounds interesting. You said it was a gift?"

Keeping Frank Fox happy had suddenly been added near the top of my lengthening job description. All I needed was for him to start some rumor that I was there to *investigate* the Wynderly theft, truth though it was.

He shuffled about and relaxed against the back of the sofa. I ignored the groaning wood.

"Yes," he said. "I met Victor Shafer at a party in Palm Beach. I like to vacation there, it's so cultured and sophisticated. Victor and I no more than met when we immediately connected. We are both interested in the environment. I told him about my dream—to create a living history of how water is essential to mankind. Do you realize that the quest for pure drinking water is as ancient as man is? That night Victor and I talked way into the wee hours, and that very next day my dream began to become a reality."

I wondered how anyone could get that excited about water, essential though it is. Then the light went on in my head. His memories of meeting Victor were what had him so animated.

"We, Victor and I, decided right then and there that our

chance meeting had to have been in the stars. I had the knowledge. Victor had the money and he *loves* antiques. We agreed
that he would put together a magnificent collection of vessels
through the centuries—or anything related to water. Pottery
jugs from Greece and Rome, copper vessels from Persia and
Damascus and Brazil, holy water vessels from Provence, urns
from Azerbaijan and Turkey, even old pewter tankards from
England." He paused to draw a deep breath before exclaim-
ing, "And guess what business Victor is in?"

I tried to censor my thoughts, but my answer came tumbling out of my mouth. "The travel business?"

"Almost. Even better though." His eyes settled on mine.
"The *import* business. That's what he was doing at the party.
He lives in South Florida."

I exhaled my answer. "Oh. How convenient. So he has access to—"

"Yes, *yes*," Fox said. "He not only knows the exporters in
all those places, he *goes* to them himself. He had visited all
the museums." Frank Fox literally glowed. "Now *I* know just
how Hoyt Wyndfield felt when he was collecting his treasures
for Wynderly."

What was I to do? Tracy DuMont had laid into Fox at the
board meeting, openly humiliating him. Now it almost hurt
me to look into his eyes. They were so shamelessly trusting.
Clearly Fox idealized Hoyt Wyndfield and Wynderly. The sadness of the situation went beyond the moment.

This Victor Shafer—I didn't have any proof that Fox was
being used by him, but my gut instinct told me some sort of
deal was being cut. The question was how Fox fit into it all.
From the beginning I had found his persistence annoying, but

now he seemed pitiful, little more than a gullible babe, trudging blindly into deep, uncharted . . . did I dare think . . . waters. Then again, Fox obviously was working his *own* scheme, asking me to anoint "his" collection. There were wheels turning inside wheels, and I didn't have a clue what was going on.

I glanced at the ornate Victorian porcelain mantel clock to check the time. Though it had been in my line of vision through my conversations with both Michelle and Fox, I had barely noticed the elaborately modeled satyrs and cupids dancing atop it—an indication that I was dead tired and distracted. It deserved a closer look. Meissen, perhaps?

"Look, Dr. Fox, it's really late and I've had a terribly long day. I want to hear more about your plans—"

"Museum," he interjected.

"Yes, that's what I meant—plans for your museum," I said. "And I want to hear all about the collection you and Victor have. It sounds interesting indeed. My first obligation though, as you understand, is to Wynderly.

"If I can make good headway tomorrow"—without too many interruptions, I thought—"then maybe we'll have some time before I head back to Leemont."

Fox grabbed my hand and pumped it like he was trying to get water. "Oh, that would be wonderful. Almost as wonderful as my chance meeting with Victor."

Fox gushed on about heaven knows what as we walked to the door. As we stepped out on the columned porch a cold wind brushed by, the sort that burns your skin and smells like dry ice. The temperature must have dropped ten degrees. Still I stood, watching in the dimness of the porch light, as Fox took his time going down the steps and into the parking lot.

He paused by my car, almost identical to his. For a moment I thought he was going to try to get into it. Then he moved on a couple of cars down to his own old dark blue Mercedes.

I gazed into the black night as he pulled out of the driveway and thought, Dear Professor Fox, look not to the stars but to yourself.

Chapter 17

Dear Antiques Expert: Among my family's books and papers is my great-great-grandfather's 16-year diary from 1890 to 1905. Most of it relates to family events, but in 1903 he tells of hearing about the Wright Brothers' first flight in Kitty Hawk, North Carolina. Pasted in the book is the local newspaper report of the event. Would this information make the diary valuable?

For diaries, photographs, or other family papers to be valuable there has to be something distinctive about them. For example, a daguerreotype depicting a person posing for the picture is standard fare. But, if the subject is a black man in a Confederate uniform, then the image becomes historically important, and valuable. While your great-great-grandfather's telling of hearing about the flight is interesting, for his diary to be really valuable, the account would have to be his own firsthand seeing of the actual event.

IN THE SANCTUARY of my room, I leaned against the closed door and ran my hands through my hair and left them there. At last I was alone. Finally I could get down to the business at hand, the reason I was here. Frank Fox was already far from my thoughts. It was Hoyt and Mazie's world I was about to enter.

Reaching into my briefcase, I ever so carefully took out the Staffordshire dog, opened one of the lower drawers and tucked the figure in among my lingerie. I spread out the rest of the contents of my briefcase across the bed, leaving bits of yellowed paper like Hansel and Gretel's trail of bread crumbs. Photographs, receipts, papers, books. The photographs beckoned, but they could wait.

I settled in the middle of the bed where I heaped the pillows up against the high headboard. I gave the stack of papers closest to me a glance. Sales receipts, ledger pages. "Get organized before you start," I told myself. "Papers in one pile, photos in another, books over here."

I reached for the dark red leather book teetering so near the edge of the bed I was afraid it might fall off. Worn letters were embossed in gold across the front: "Mazie Wyndfield." I opened it to the first page. There, written in the same hand I had seen earlier, the hand that had penned the strange obituary, I read, "Mazie Wyndfield, My Diary."

I never had forgotten my disappointment upon discovering my grandfather's diary had been more a daily account of the weather than of his life. The typical entry had read something like, "Thursday, March 19. A much chillier day than yesterday. I had to wear a sweater under my vest. I took it off when I got to the bank." I chuckled at the memory.

As I randomly flipped Mazie's book open to someplace midway through it, the pages, some so loose they almost fell out, flopped over by themselves. I let the book fall open where it would. Then I began to read.

Wednesday, April 23, 1930. With Hoyt away, these days all blend into one. If only he knew how very much I miss him, would he go away and so far . . . and so often? I wonder. Why <u>*must*</u> *he have the heart of an adventurer? I shouldn't complain. I know, I know. But it is lonesome in this big place, beautiful though it be, and I still grow lonely even after all this time, even with Daphne and Jacques living here now. Hoyt says when he returns from Brazil we'll plan another cruise. That gives me hope, but it doesn't help the endless minutes of the days or the nights pass. It isn't that I haven't enough to do with decorating and planning for our upcoming party when our friends from the last cruise come to visit, but I hunger for my husband's kisses, his caresses, and when night falls I remember the joy of lying with him, in his arms.*

I turned my head. I felt a little embarrassed, as if I had peeped through a keyhole. My mind scattered in a million directions. I had assumed the diary would be like my grandfather's—filled with facts about the things Mazie and Hoyt had bought over the years, all about their travels, where they had gathered their treasures, even mentions of parties and how they entertained . . . anything that would shed light on Wynderly and the objects in it. But these were the words of a passionate young woman, twenty-nine, maybe thirty years old. It was 1930. Mazie had been married for eight years by then. And she still loved her husband. She even held a deep passion for him. I smiled, partly in wonderment, partly in jealousy.

I glanced back at the page. Mazie's words were so intimate, so innocent and heartfelt, that on my second reading it was as if I had accidentally pushed open the door and beheld Hoyt and Mazie in a loving embrace.

To break the spell, I got up and checked the lock on my bedroom door. Of course doing that was unnecessary, but it helped to banish the unwelcome melancholy that had swept over me. To add to my misery, I was suddenly struck by the possible consequences of my actions. The responsibilities of discovering the priest hole and that other inner sanctuary, whatever it was, and now reading Mazie's innermost thoughts enveloped me like a shroud. It was as if I had entered Mazie's chambered catacomb.

Miss Mary Sophie had made mention of . . . what had she called it, a secret place. In my own worries of not having much to report to Matt, I had had a passing thought of telling him I'd discovered a couple of secret rooms in the attic. But how to explain having absconded with the papers if, just if, I *did* find some hard facts in them, or by chance discovered answers to the questions I had about the things in the house and their authenticity and value? I'd have to say where I'd found the papers, wouldn't I?

I returned to my bed and continued to read.

Chapter 18

Dear Antiques Expert: My aunt used to travel extensively in South America. She was very proud of the santos she gathered in the various countries. Would these have much value these days?

South and Central American countries are famous for their figurines of the saints, called "santos." These range greatly in style and quality, from naïve wooden folk carvings to exquisitely molded and painted sculptures. Because every town and even household has its patron saint to protect its members, tourists have long purchased santos as mementos—usually at markets or bazaars, but sometimes from antiques shops. (Unfortunately, santos purported to be "old" have sometimes been falsely aged.) While truly old—18th- and 19th-century and older—handcrafted santos can be valuable, mass-produced touristy, 20th-century ones seldom sell for more than $50 or $100.

Hoyt totally surprised me today. I think we need a teahouse, he said. Or maybe a pagoda. Some cozy place where we can get away. I can't imagine why we would need to get away from Wynderly, other than our trips to see the world, of course. Dear, dear man, he has so much energy! He always needs a project. I know the perfect place, he said. And then I realized he wanted to build it just beyond the house, over past the rose garden. I really don't see any reason to disturb that land. Wild turkeys live in the thickets and the deer are quite lovely when they come there to graze. I'm quite sure a family of red foxes lives nearby. If it stretched out flat instead of rising and rolling, that patch of land would remind me of home. I miss Louisiana, but not so much now that it is summer as I do in March when I'm ready for spring . . . and instead . . . it snows!

There was a sweetness about the way Mazie expressed herself with exclamation points that reminded me of a schoolgirl's outpourings. And in its own way, this page, dated June 17, 1930, was as loving and passionate, and as wistful, as the entry written three months earlier when Hoyt was away.

I turned through the pages, fast-forwarding the years of Mazie's life.

November 2, 1932. Today I defied Hoyt. I cut my hair. It's not that I hadn't cut it before, but now it is a <u>real</u> bob. Little by little I've had it shortened, but never have I done anything this drastic. I know how much he loves my long hair. But with the new hat fashions fitting so close, there's no room to tuck all my tresses up and under, and anyway I like the waves around my face. Hoyt wasn't very pleased, but he soon forgave me when I explained that he didn't want me to look like an old fuddy-duddy, especially with the holiday party season about to begin. He does like all the new fashions. He said he guessed it was an old Virginia way not to like change. But *when I pointed out that there is absolutely nothing "old Virginia" about Wynderly, he relented. I reminded him that people drive here just to see our fancy "French" house. Of course England was the Mother Country of Virginia, but she wasn't anyone's mother down in my part of the world. Our papas were French and Spanish and Italian, which is why Hoyt tells everyone he built this home, to make me feel at home.*

I almost heard Mazie sigh when I read the next line.

Oh, if only he knew what was hidden away in my heart. I remember the first time I saw Hoyt. So straight and tall, so refined, not at all like those willful, boring boys I was used to being with—half bent-over from spending endless hours at the gambling table, still reeking of smoke and whiskey hours later. He reminded me of Dominique. I still remember the thrill I would get when I'd see Domi in the summertime when he returned home from college in Charlottesville. Each year he would be changed, quieter and more serious. He didn't swear like his boyhood friends, and I remember how he would hang back, apart, when in a crowd. But then the war came along—

Finding Hoyt was like a miracle. What was there not to love about him? He was a gentleman. He was perfect. I wanted to be like him. To lead his kind of life. To be a Virginia lady.

Mazie had drawn a thin fountain pen line through her last sentence. Rewritten, it read, "To be a lady from Virginia." It did sound much more elegant.

Now I *was* puzzled. Hadn't Mazie been born a lady? Of course she had, it was obvious from her writings. My mind raced back to what I had heard about Mazie Wyndfield. That first night Worth Merritt, speaking of Hoyt and Mazie's differences, he called Mazie vivacious and lovely. The sweet ramblings of Mazie's diary were certainly consistent with his description. What was the distinction between being a lady, and being a lady from Virginia? I guess it had to do with refinement. Why Miss Mary Sophie had just bemoaned the loss of refinement in today's world. Gentility, poise, grace—those characteristics that define refinement—these were all part of the image of the early mistresses of the Virginia plantations. But that didn't mean a lady couldn't be lively and captivating. What was that quote about Virginia women? Ah . . . "The Virginia women are tall, and slender, and have much more personality than other American Women." That's how the Frenchman Ferdinand Bayard had described Virginia ladies back in the eighteenth century.

I recalled that Miss Mary Sophie had also said that Mazie and Hoyt had lived a life filled with too many lies. Perhaps because Miss Mary Sophie had spoken so kindly of Hoyt, yet said little about Mazie, I had taken her remark to be about Mazie.

But had anyone ever said anything *really* disparaging about Mazie? Where had I gotten the impression that Wynderly was all *her* doing? When Worth had said that sugarcane oozed out of Mazie's very pores, he hadn't said it in a critical way. It had made her sound fetching.

Really, the strongest image I had of Mazie had come from Michelle Hendrix. "A princess," Michelle had called her, "a princess—born and bred." Laboring under my less than favorable early impression of Michelle, I had naturally put the worst spin on her words. That must have been the source of my negative impression of Mazie. How wrong I had been.

Or, perhaps knowing Mazie was from Louisiana, a place so very different from Virginia, had led me to that impression. Or might it have been Wynderly itself?

Why Hoyt wants to turn his back on his Virginia ways is beyond me. I love Wynderly, but not for its showiness and flamboyance, because that is what it is, a place to show off where we've been and what we've bought. I love Wynderly because it is our home and Hoyt loves it so. I would be quite content if we never went to another place or bought another thing, but I wouldn't tell him so. He has his pride. I would have been so happy to have a less pretentious place, one of the lovely stately brick homes all around us. That had been my dream. But then, not all of our dreams can come true.

There, at the end of the page, Mazie's entry stopped. To my disappointment, the next few pages were totally unlike the others I had read. She wrote of upcoming trips and rearranging the furniture in the breakfast room to accommodate a new set of chairs, which I had paused over, hoping to learn more about the chairs themselves. Instead, I read,

I am trying to be better about my record-keeping. Hoyt is so meticulous in his bookkeeping. He spends hours at night bent over figures the way a gambler does over a card hand. He says that every time he buys something new for the house he makes note of it, how much it cost, and checks it against how much the old one had cost. I can't imagine being interested in such things! Thank goodness he takes care of the finances. But I'm going to start keeping track of the gardens. That should please him.

The following pages were filled with notes about some new species of trees and roses and an exquisite description of seeing three sprays of orchids simultaneously in full bloom in the greenhouse. One entry about selecting an artist to paint Mazie's portrait did catch my attention, but no artists were named so I moved on.

As I neared the back of the book, a sense of dread fell over me. Was I going to have to make yet another trip up into the attic, retrace my steps into that forlorn black pit and literally pray that I would find other, later volumes? Mazie's world had so mesmerized me that I had forgotten about all else. Only two or three more diaries remained among the papers and photographs spread out around me on the bed. I grabbed one up.

May 14, 1955. Hoyt hasn't been feeling well for the past few days. I do hope it isn't anything serious. He tells me that if his heart gives out it will be because he has used it up loving me. I tell him that if his heart gives out it is because he is racing around too much for a man of sixty-five.

I've never seen a man hate to slow down as much as he does. When we came back from Europe the last time, I told him it wasn't necessary to book another trip, but oh, no. We were no more home than the conversation was the same old thing, all over again. Why we must go back to Vichy and on to Thiers and then on to Lyon, I do not understand. Nor do I know why he must continue his trips to Brazil alone. Now that Whitey's son has taken over the tobacco business it really isn't necessary for Hoyt to make these trips. Yet he has one planned for this fall. Every time he comes back from Brazil, once he is rested, then it is off to New York or London, but that's fun because I usually go with him to those places. And oh! that surprise piece of jewelry I always find under my pillow while we are there delights me. I would enjoy it if he would take me to Tiffany's, or Asprey's when we're in London, but Hoyt always says he knows where there are better deals. I don't dare complain.

I'm still hoping he will bring his Brazilian friend Felipe to see us. Whenever Hoyt talks about him, all I can imagine is Errol Flynn. Felipe must have been quite a swashbuckler when he was young. Imagine finding whole pockets of precious gemstones in the mountains of Brazil! He must be very rich. Of course Hoyt loves Brazil with so many friends and memories.

But ah, when I raise the question of why the need for all these trips now that he is older, Hoyt laughs and says he has to keep up with me. That's foolishness. He knows I am never happier than when we are home at Wynderly, and Lord knows I have never looked at another man since first laying eyes on him.

In the secret chambers of my own heart I sometimes wonder if he is wearing out, not from loving me, not even from insisting on continuing to race through life, but for the life he has lived.

I stopped dead in my tracks. 1955. We forget in these days of longevity that sixty-five years old was much older then than now, especially for those with heart conditions. That thought aside, I turned back to Mazie's words. "But for the life he has lived," I read over and over.

What had transpired in the thirty years between the young Mazie's romantic musings and these much darker, more solemn words? There was little question of Mazie's genuine and lasting love for her husband. How sad that they had never had any children, I thought offhandedly. I stuck a Post-it on the page, laid the book to one side, and picked up another one in hopes that it would fill in the gaps of those other years. I clasped the unopened book in my hands and pressed it hard, as if it could magically speak to me, surrendering the mysteries of so many years. As suddenly as I had grasped Mazie's book, I released it.

Where was this all leading? Why was I bothering, and what, dear Lord, did this have to do with why I was here in the first place? The corner of a single piece of paper caught my eye as the book fell onto my lap. It was way past midnight. No wonder my patience was running short and my eyes were beginning to cross. I needed to get some sleep before becoming more frustrated by the hints and morsels. I picked the book back up and opened it to slip the paper back in place. I also made the mistake of glancing at it:

"Edouardo Ziegler. Ouro Preto, Brasil."

Ouro Preto had been one of my favorite places ever since Hank and I had gone there, two, no, three times when we had gone to Brazil with his family on combination business and pleasure trips in the late 1980s. Ouro Preto had once been a favorite resort for European travelers, but these days few people have even heard of the charming village tucked away in the mountain region of Minas Gerais. As suddenly as my tiredness had come upon me, it faded. And when I saw the page was a listing of English Staffordshire dog figurines, I bolted straight up. Gemstones, santos and crucifixes, soapstone carvings—those you found in Ouro Preto, Brazil. Not nineteenth-century English Staffordshire dogs.

Chapter 19

Dear Antiques Expert: When we were in Europe I noticed many grand houses had fireplace benches in them, but I can't recall seeing these in Colonial homes in America even though the early homes were warmed with fireplaces. Why would this be?

What a perceptive observation. Though our finest 18th-century American homes were quite grand, they couldn't compare to Europe and England's majestic homes with huge banquet halls and reception rooms. In Colonial America, usually a table that could be used for tea, card games, or even business, was placed in front of the fireplace, rather than a bench where just one or two people could sit. Eventually, when America's "castles" copying the European style—homes such as Biltmore, the Breakers, and San Simeon—were built at the turn of the century, fireplace benches became fashionable over here.

THE SPLITTING HEADACHE I had the next morning was a reminder that I should not have stayed up so late reading Mazie's diary. Or at least that's what I told myself driving to Wynderly half an hour later than I should have. I didn't even try to rush to get there on time. In fact, when I turned into the driveway leading up to the mansion, I slowed down.

What if, at the end of the lane, instead of rambling high-walled turrets and castle-like towers there had been built a house in the Colonial tradition, restrained and elegant, with perfectly balanced proportions—the house Mazie had spoken of wanting? Would it have been more welcoming, less off-putting than Wynderly, I wondered. But she had also said she was never happier than when she and Hoyt were at home, at Wynderly—

Only when a squirrel ran across my path, did I realize I had slowed to a crawl. I veered as far to the right as I could without brushing against the undergrowth then sped up.

There, lining the driveway in front of Wynderly were parked so many long black cars that I thought either the antiques big boys had finally arrived, or someone must have died. The smell of money was in the air.

Michelle Hendrix rushed out the door toward me. "Thank God you're here," she said. She was wringing her hands the way I remembered my grandmother doing, and like my grandmother, Michelle looked old beyond her years. "They didn't even call first," she said.

"Who?" I asked, closing the car door.

"*Them*. The men from the bank. And Dr. Houseman isn't with them."

"Why are *they* here? Is, ah . . ." I couldn't remember the banker's name I'd met at the board meeting. I could see him in his gray, custom-tailored banker's suit, but his name? "You know, the board member from the bank. Is he with them?"

"Graham. Frederick Graham. He's the ringleader."

Taken aback, I asked, "So, what does *he* say," all the while rushing to keep up with Michelle's long strides toward the house. It had begun to spit something, sleet maybe, or a little snow. Michelle was muttering something about packing things up, which made no sense.

It was too late. Graham, himself, opened the door.

He quickly nodded in my direction. "Look," he said, addressing Michelle, his voice brusque. "The bank's held out on collecting on the loan long enough. It's time we take possession of what's rightfully ours." I had the feeling he was finishing a conversation that had been interrupted when she'd run out to intercept me.

I tried frantically to recall exactly the discussion at the board meeting about the bank not giving the foundation any more money. As best I could remember, nothing had been said that jibed with Graham's comment about things at Wynderly being "rightfully ours." But it fit like a glove around Michelle's comments of last night.

"If you could give me a minute to take off my coat, Mr. Graham—"

"Call me Frederick. And forgive me, I didn't mean to ignore you. I've got a conference call coming in later this morning, but it seemed important to move on this matter now. That's why we're here and in such a rush." He helped me with my coat, folded it over his arm, and gestured toward the drawing room. "Not sure how comfortable the chairs are, but . . ." he said more calmly as he ushered me across the hallway and into the room.

After having read Mazie's diary, it was as if I had never walked these halls before. I entered the room and saw it through different eyes. In the silver gilt mirror above the mantel I glimpsed Mazie's image. She was smoothing her long hair. Or was she fluffing her bob after it was cut? She glowed in the reflected light cast from the twin chandeliers as she waited for Hoyt to join her before their guests arrived. Wynderly no longer seemed so distastefully over the top. As if by magic, the house had become lively and vibrant, and I seemed to have fallen under its spell. But now was not the time for such thoughts.

Graham laid my coat across the needlepoint fireplace bench. I seated myself, pulled myself together, and spoke.

"I totally understand about your morning, and I'll try not to take up much time, but what you said . . . well, it sounded as if you'll be taking things from the house." I hesitated. "It seems to me, Mr. Graham, that Babson and Michael has a vested interest in these items, too, at least some of them. I'm not sure what the legalities are, but I need to know what's going on. What pieces are you talking about? I need time to finish the appraisal. In fact, I'm not at all sure I can complete the appraisal if things are taken away."

Seated across from me, the banker flashed a smile. "Please," he broke in. "Frederick, not Mr. Graham. Actually, Ms. Glass, I doubt if your services will be needed any further here. I think between the foundation board and the bank, we'll have everything *well* under control."

His words hit with a thud. Not needed? *He* couldn't fire me. And his tone of voice. For a moment, he reminded me of Alfred Houseman—scornfully solicitous.

Frederick Graham stood and turned his back to me. Apparently to his mind, our conversation had ended.

"Mr. Graham," I said, "I didn't just *appear* at Wynderly's doorstep. If I'm not mistaken, the *foundation* contacted Babson and Michael. You're on the board. *You're* the ones who submitted the claim. I'm here at the request of the insurance company. It would hardly be proper for me to walk off the job because you now say I am no longer needed." I felt my face flush.

He turned and looked down at me. His was a self-satisfied grin if ever I'd seen one. "Now, Sterling," he said, "I'm sure you'll be compensated for your time."

"That's not the point," I said, struggling not to tag on, "and don't you dare speak to me in that manner."

"The point of my being here, Mr. Graham, is to put money in the foundation's coffers. What I'd like to know is *how,* without my report, Babson and Michael will be able to" — I glanced around the opulent room — "cut the check for the foundation, which, I do believe, will then go to the bank." I cast him a puzzled look. "Now, it would seem to me that with your being on the foundation board *and* in the trust department at the bank — "

"Who I am and what positions I hold are hardly your concern."

"But aren't you the treasurer of the foundation *and* the head trust officer at the bank, Mr. Graham?" I asked.

Frederick Graham's back stiffened. "Ms. Glass, I'm here on orders from the bank. My position with the foundation board has nothing to do with my taking things out of Wynderly."

"I would think your position on the board, especially as treasurer, has *everything* to do with your *not* allowing things to go out of Wynderly. Of course I could be mistaken, but if *you're* not going to protect the foundation's assets, who is?"

Frederick Graham thrust his hands into his pants' pockets and rocked back on his heels. Clearly he was as uncomfortable with this conversation as I was.

"Freddy. There you are."

Tracy DuMont stood at the top of the steps, hands on hips. Behind her trailed Michelle Hendrix.

"What the hell's going on here? And what are all those minions doing dragging in boxes and rolls of tape?"

"Now Tracy, no reason to get excited." Graham stepped forward, his voice all silky and affable.

Tracy turned, removed her sunglasses, and addressed me. "Is this *your* doing?"

I knew how a deer in headlights felt. My hand went to my heart.

"Well, I can see it isn't," she said before I could say a word.

"Mr. Graham was already here when I got here," Michelle said, eyes locked with Tracy's. "Them, too." With her thumb she pointed like a hitchhiker over her shoulder toward the entrance hall where Frederick Graham's minions, as Tracy had called them, were scurrying about.

"So, it's back to you, Freddy. Which, by the way, is why I'm here. I stopped by the bank earlier. When I asked for you, Laurie said you weren't in. When it turned out Clarence and Jerry were gone too, I asked who was minding the store. When Laurie told me everyone had gone to Wynderly—"

Tracy DuMont stopped, waiting for an answer. When no

one said anything in response, she turned to Michelle. "Seems you're the only one willing to speak up." Tracy reached into the Chanel pocketbook slung over her shoulder, then stopped. "My cell phone's not worth a damn out here. Get House-man on the house phone. Tell him to get over here right now. Meanwhile, those men out there . . . what do they know about packing china and silver? Freddy, stop them right this minute before they do more damage than they've probably done al-ready. Then you and I have some talking to do."

She looked and sounded adamant. But when, I wondered, had Tracy Dumont not looked and sounded adamant?

I HAD BEGUN to gather my belongings when Michelle Hendrix reappeared.

"Matt Yardley's trying to get in touch with you," she said, handing me a slip of paper. "He left this number and asked for you to return his call ASAP. Said something about only being in the office a short time then having to leave. I told him you'd call him right back."

My face obviously had said more than I would have wished. "When—"

"Just now. Say, this Matt fellow, he's the big shot at the in-surance company, isn't he? Not that Houseman confided in me before you got here"—Michelle rolled her eyes in that sarcas-tic is-the-pope-Catholic sort of way—"but his name sounds kind of familiar."

"Matt Yardley? Ah . . . yes. That's him. Babson and Michael," I said.

"He sounded sorta sexy . . . in a highbrow way," she said.

How, with everything that had just transpired, could she be thinking about some man on the phone she didn't even know? But then there was a lot about Michelle that, from the beginning, I hadn't understood.

"Oh?" I said.

She gave me a wry smile. "Yeah," she said.

Chapter 20

Dear Antiques Expert: After a friend took me to an estate sale I became interested in antiques. But she also told me that a lot of things being sold as antiques really aren't that old. Do I really need to worry about being sold a fake? How can I avoid it?

Unfortunately, crooks know when there's money to be made. For over a century, English and Continental pieces have been made with the express purpose of being sold as 18th-century antiques. Those are fakes. But don't confuse fakes with reproductions. Fakes are *intended* to deceive; reproductions are honest re-creations of the old style, though old reproductions are sometimes mistaken as original antiques. To avoid being taken, read and study. Countless books and classes show how to distinguish the real from the fake or reproduction. Be assured, wonderful antiques are still available; you just have to know how to identify them.

I PERCHED ON the side of the desk and punched in the numbers, apparently just in time.

"Sterling. Caught me halfway out the door."

I pictured Matt the way I'd seen him in his tastefully ap-pointed Madison Avenue office, looking and acting like the New York executive he is—tall and dark-haired and charming to the point of distraction. Michelle was right, he did sound sexy.

"I've only got a second," he said apologetically. Then in a more leisurely way he asked, "But, how *are* you? I half ex-pected you to call yesterday. I'm anxious to hear how things are going at Wynderly. Any clues as to what happened? But more to the point right now, I'm on my way down to D.C. A problem came up late yesterday that I need to take care of firsthand. You're not that far away once I'm in Washington, right? What would you say if I pop down and check things out? I'd get there tomorrow . . . probably late in the day."

"You have no idea how glad I'd be to see you," I said. "This place is a snake pit. You wouldn't believe what just happened. Frederick Graham . . . he's the treasurer of the foundation, and he's also . . . You *really* aren't going to believe this. He's the trust officer at the bank. Anyway, he just fired me."

"What? Fired you? He . . . he can't do that. What did you *do,* Sterling?" He sounded nonplussed, totally unlike his usual self, or maybe he was just amused.

"Nothing."

"He can't *fire* you. You're working for us. What's going on? Are you about finished up?"

"I wish. I'm embarrassed to tell you how little I've been able to do," I said, then added, "I told you, this place is a snake pit."

"Look. Just ignore what . . . whatever his name is . . . ."

"Frederick Graham."

". . . what Frederick Graham said. Tell whoever you need to that I'm in meetings in Washington today and half of tomorrow but I'm on my way down. Sounds as if this trip of mine is fortuitous. I'll be in touch with you tonight, OK? I'll call you on my cell phone."

"Just don't try *my* cell. It's next to useless out here. Call . . . Hold on. Let me give you the number at Belle Ayre. I should be there after supper."

While I was digging out the number, Matt said it would be late. He'd be in a business dinner and wouldn't call till maybe eleven. "Meanwhile, just do what you can today, but be sure to tell them I'm coming. I'm sorry this has turned into such a disaster. I had no idea."

"Me either," I muttered.

"Hang in there and I'll ring you up tonight."

I DIDN'T KNOW when my headache had gone away. But who had time for a headache? Heartache? Now that was a different matter.

The prospect of Matt's appearing on the scene had sent me in a tailspin. I slumped into Michelle's desk chair. Today was Wednesday, wasn't it? No. It was Thursday. It seemed I'd spent weeks at Wynderly. And damn . . . Fox was expecting me to take a look at his stuff. Right now the task at hand was to get something done to show for the time I'd spent here other than hearing about my own parents and Hoyt's great-grandparents from Worth Merritt, listening to tales of Wynderly's bygone days and Michelle's lineage from Miss Mary Sophie, learning about the hydrosphere from Fox, watching Tracy DuMont's antics, nosing through secret rooms and diaries, and last, but not least—getting fired.

I made my resolve. I wasn't P. D. James delving into deep-seated psychological motivations, or Colin Dexter playing around with Inspector Morse's idiosyncratic approach to a crime. I was Sterling Glass, an antiques appraiser who had been hired to give fair settlement values.

In the hall I bumped into Michelle Hendrix.

"I think Tracy snuffed out Frederick Graham's fuse, at least for the time being," Michelle said. "Houseman's on his way. We'll see what happens next. So? What did Mr. Insuranceman have to say?"

"Mr. Yardley will be here tomorrow afternoon, and we'd better have the information he needs or we're both going to be up the proverbial creek."

Her eyes widened.

"Yes. Between the board meeting and Houseman's showing up here yesterday, plus the time I've spent ferreting around in the attic, I've hardly seen a thing. Look, I'm not blaming you," I said, thinking I'd better soften my words, "you've been tied up too. But, if any money's going to be forthcoming to try to save this place, then it's imperative that I get good, solid information about the things on the list Babson and Michael gave me. That's what I'm here for. To do that, you and I have to go over the stolen things with a fine-tooth comb. Without interruptions," I added.

Michelle hadn't blinked an eye since I began to speak. Finally I broke the awkward silence that ensued and said in as offhanded a way as I could, "The way I see it, anything you can add, help me with, show me, point me towards . . . anything will be helpful. There's also the matter of clearing you of any responsibility in the theft."

The muscles in her face tensed. Michelle set her mouth in a straight line. "Come with me," she said.

I didn't make any attempt at small talk. I just followed along until Michelle stopped and motioned me inside a room. When I saw the hodgepodge of things gathered from around the world I instantly remembered having passed by it on my first day at Wynderly. The Game Room, she had called it, and come to think of it, Worth Merritt had mentioned it during our dinnertime conversation.

Following me in, Michelle closed the door behind her. I glanced about the room. Unlike the overfurnished Continental-style drawing room and bedrooms, or the formal dining room and hallways, this room, with its well-worn oak trestle table and high-backed Windsor chairs, was rather homey in that comfortable English-cottage style. At the stone fireplace were large andirons and a simple black firescreen. The mantel was bare except for tall brass pricket candlesticks that had once sat on the altar of some Irish chapel, as was obvious from the ringed cross and IHS motif engraved on their bases. I liked this room. Had Mazie and Hoyt sat here on gray winter days like this day, warmed by the fire, chatting while reading or planning their trips or playing Scrabble, or chess perhaps? Had it been the heart of the house, I wondered. That was the idyllic image it evoked. For a moment I forgot I was in Wynderly and stepped toward the hearth for a closer look at the verse etched into the stone: "Here time is slow and gracious. A companion, not a master."

Michelle had walked over to a row of built-in bookcases. She stopped in front of a section of shelves where photographs taken of Hoyt and Mazie on their trips to Africa and Asia, Europe and Russia were mixed in with the books. She reached up and began running her hand along the vertical support. Midway down she stopped. "How do I know I can trust you?" she asked.

I knew why, but how to answer her?

"Let me put it this way," I said, "who else around here *can* you trust?"

"Give me a hand, will you? I'm going to push here." Then, pointing to the end board of the section she said, "And you go over there and push when I tell you to."

I did as she said.

"Push now. Harder. Push harder."

I felt the paneled section give slightly, just as the attic wall had.

"Hold it there."

Michelle joined me. Standing on tiptoes, she reached above me and grabbed the upright board. "On the count of three." Together we pushed. The photographs quivered as the bookcase shifted back.

"You can move back now," she said.

I watched as Michelle placed both hands beneath the middle shelf of the recessed section and slid that portion of the bookcase to the right, making a wide entranceway. Behind it there was a room.

I caught my breath in surprise. "Another one?"

"Another what?" Michelle said.

"Oh . . . just another one of those sliding walls and hidden rooms. Secret passageways. They're not only in the pages of books, you know." I was trying to hide the rush of nervousness and surprise running through me like cold water. "These old mansions are full of them," I said.

"Really? I never thought much about it. Come to think of it, though, there's a house down the way with a secret room in the portico over the front door."

I hung back before joining her as she stepped into the room. "When did you find this . . . room?" I asked, my hand still holding onto the wall as if to anchor me in the real world.

"I've always known about it. It was Mazie's secret room. Babby showed it to me when I was little, but she made me promise to seal my lips forever." She placed her forefinger over her lips.

"Did you?"

She seemed surprised. "Of course. Until now, that is."

The room was an orderly place, though filled with books and papers. And wonderful antiques. In one corner was a fine walnut corner cupboard, a plain piece except for the elegant line inlay that accented its pure lines. Pembroke tables with delicately scalloped leaves at the side flanked a Federal sofa made sometime around 1790 and upholstered in red and gold damask.

But the pièce de résistance was the American secretary-bookcase. Most such pieces have a simple molded cornice. This one had a bold, curved swan neck pediment, made even more stunning by its delicate pierced lattice-like work. I wanted to drop to my knees and examine its ball-and-claw feet. It would have taken a true craftsman, someone like John Shaw of Annapolis, Maryland, to execute a piece of such superior quality and workmanship.

Even more amazing was that, except for the Federal sofa, which likely was from Philadelphia or New York, these were all Southern pieces—the sort collectors would pay tens, even hundreds of thousands of dollars to possess. And they were hidden away in this room. I was speechless.

Michelle was oblivious to my enthrallment. "I guess I should have told you about this earlier," she was saying. "I didn't mean to do anything I shouldn't. Looking back, I realize it was wrong to keep any secrets from you. It's just that I love Wynderly so much, I didn't want anything to hurt its reputation." She spoke softly, reverently.

"I know," I said. "And these are magnificent, finer than the majority of pieces in the house. May I have a moment to . . . look more closely at them?" I didn't dare use the word *examine*. But that's what I needed to do to be sure I was seeing true eighteenth- and early nineteenth-century period pieces and not the work of some shrewd faker. I felt reasonably positive they were the real thing. The market for Southern antiques had soared only in the last ten years or so. Until then, it hadn't been worth the time and effort needed to fake a Southern piece.

But New England antiques? That was a different matter. They had always sold for high prices. Since the end of the nineteenth century many a dishonest cabinetmaker had made a fine living by faking grand eighteenth-century Boston, Philadelphia, and Newport, Rhode Island, furniture. Why just a few weeks ago I had dashed a family's dreams when I had to tell them the lady's writing desk they thought had been made in Boston in the early 1800s by John Seymour was one of many such fakes made in the barn behind a well-known antique dealer's shop in the 1930s. I hate days like that.

While I was crawling around checking for (and thankfully finding) the telltale signs of age, Michelle had taken a book down from one of the bookcases in the room.

"And you'll want to see this," she said, holding the book in front of her. "I would have thought some of the people working here before me would have found it, but no one has ever mentioned it. It was in one of the file cabinets in my office. Actually, at the back of one of the bottom drawers, behind a lot of other papers. Mostly old newspaper clippings, I think. I can't remember . . . not exactly. The only thing I can figure is no one else ever dug down far enough to find it. But then there have been times when I've wondered if maybe somebody put it there on purpose. I brought it in here to be sure no one else found it. Anyway, when I started reading and comparing it to what I had been told and to some of the later appraisals, like that one I gave you, well, I didn't know who to believe. It's all so confusing."

I took the book from her and sat down on the sofa I had so admired seconds before. Michelle stood above me.

"What does it mean?" she asked.

Chapter 21

Dear Antiques Expert: I see the term "giltwood" used a lot to describe very fancy antique European pieces that are also usually very expensive. What exactly does the term mean?

Giltwood means that a thin layer of gold leaf or gold foil has been applied onto the exposed wood. Pieces highlighted with a gold wash have been found as far back as in the tombs of pharaohs dating from 1700 BC. Over the years, different techniques used to apply the gilt have evolved, but the process of gilding the wood has always been expensive and time-consuming. Giltwood pieces were especially fashionable in Europe throughout the 17th and 18th centuries. You're right, antique giltwood pieces in good condition *are* expensive—the finest examples often sport five- and six-figure price tags.

"AND YOU FOUND this in your office," I said.

That was understandable. It's not unheard of for valuable information to lie untouched and unnoticed for years, even centuries, in some of world's finest museums, to say nothing of a disorganized place like Wynderly. Nonetheless, my head was swimming with questions.

"So, just how well *did* you know Mazie?" I asked offhandedly, the book still closed.

"She was already old when I was born. Probably seventy, maybe seventy-two. But I do remember her," she said, adding, "though sometimes I wonder if my memories come more from Babby's stories about Mazie than from the Mazie I *really* knew and the things that really happened." She cocked her head as if pondering her own statement. Then after a chuckle Michelle said, "Of course, I remember her. Mazie didn't die until I was oh, fourteen or fifteen. But why do you ask?"

"I'm just trying to get everything straight in my head. There's so much going on around here."

"If it helps any—I saw less and less of her as I got older. That explains why my own memories are fuzzy, I guess. Mazie was sick for a long time. Dementia, my grandmother said. Whether or not it was Alzheimer's or just old age, who knows? One thing though," Michelle said, walking over to the secretary-bookcase, "from the time I was a little girl Babby always told me that Mrs. Wyndfield had a collection of china dogs that she wanted me to have. That's how I happened to see this room. One afternoon when Mazie was out, Babby brought me here to see the dogs."

As she talked she turned the key, unlocking the glass door in the upper bookcase section.

"They were in the secretary, on these shelves," she said.

I put the unopened book to one side and joined her. Surely I would have noticed any dogs, though it might have been possible that I had been so enthralled by the secretary-bookcase's beauty that I had had blinders on.

"Oh, they aren't there now," she said. "And I've never found them anywhere in the house. Just another one of life's little promises broken." Her sigh left little doubt how disappointed she was, even now, many years later. "But just knowing that Mazie Wyndfield even thought of me . . . that's special."

On the shelves Chinese Export bowls were stacked on top of one another. Brass candlesticks were concealed behind vases and pitchers. With so many things crammed into the bookcase top of the secretary, anything could have been in there. "Have you looked really carefully?" I asked.

"I didn't open any drawers or shift things around," she said. "I guess I was always afraid I'd be caught, even if, as far as I know, I'm the only person who knows this place exists."

Our eyes locked. We both realized the implications of what she had said.

I grabbed the book from the sofa. "I'll take this with me," I said, glancing back at the room and thinking how Mazie's old things had become her old friends, too.

Only when we were in the sanctity of the back workroom did I dare open the book—and then with trepidation. Though I would have preferred to be alone, without Michelle looking over my shoulder, what choice did I have?

The book was a bound appraisal made by Eugene Kirklander in 1955. On the cover, in gold lettering, was the single word WYNDERLY. Inside, on the title page I read, "Wynderly— Its Contents." The next page was a letter to Hoyt from Mr. Kirklander written on his letterhead and signed in a scrawly hand. His Manhattan Upper East Side address made perfect sense. In the days before values skyrocketed and thieves emptied out whole housefuls of antiques while the owners were vacationing or just out for dinner, appraisers were seldom found outside metropolitan areas, and certainly not in the Virginia countryside.

Kirklander's appraisal read the way a good appraisal should. There was a description of each article, its date and condition, any other pertinent information, and finally its value. I read at random.

> *French gold snuff-box formed as a bouquet of flowers, 18th century. 3-3/8 inches long. Deaccessioned from the collection of Mr. and Mrs. Augustus Cruikshank. $540.*
>
> *Louis XV oak cabinet in the provincial style, with garland decorated glass upper portion above a solid-doored cabinet base with ball feet. Mid-18th century. Repairs to the upper portion. $2,500.*
>
> *George II giltwood side table, circa 1740–50, with marble top. The elaborate S-scrolled legs and paw feet and the shell motif at the apron testify to its exceptional quality. Purchased in London, 1933. The marble appears to be of more recent date than the base. $7,000.*

Oddly, the entry for the George II giltwood side table had been marked through. Across it, in red pencil, was written, "Sold. 1951. $7,500."

Wait a minute. 1951? I looked back at the cover page. The appraisal had been made in 1955. How could an appraisal be made in 1955 for something that had been sold four years earlier?

"Michelle. This 'sold' notation. Whose handwriting is this?"

"Hoyt's. And just you wait . . ."

I turned the page. Laid into the book was an invoice from Ewan Antiques in Baltimore. It, too, was dated 1951. "Giltwood side table in the George II style. $550. Marble top. $60. Total $610. Paid in full. Thank you for your order."

Kirklander had been right about the new marble top. Old marble tops are easily broken or cracked and often replaced. What he had *missed* was that the table itself was also new. Eugene Kirklander had been an appraiser of some note in his day. For him to think the table was a mid-eighteenth-century George II giltwood side table after thoroughly examining it, the table was obviously meant to masquerade as an antique.

I didn't blame Kirklander for his mistake. There isn't an appraiser, museum curator, auctioneer, or dealer alive who hasn't been fooled by some expert craftsman who has used old materials and tools to make new "old" pieces. Newspapers and antiques publications are filled with stories of some prized piece being pulled from a museum collection or auction sale upon learning it is a reproduction or a fake. In the trade we say that any professional who won't admit to being fooled is ignorant, lying, or too embarrassed to fess up to having been duped.

The person I blamed was Hoyt. He had sold the original George II table in 1951 and replaced it with a fake.

I flipped over two or three pages. When I saw another entry scratched through, I paused.

Kashmiri bronze figure of Lokesvara. 6-1/2 inches high. Dating from the 10th century. Extraordinarily rare. $3,000.

Once again, and in the same hand that I had just seen, was written "Sold. 1957. $2,500." And beneath that, "Sold. 1958. $2,800." And beneath that, "2 figures. Sold. $5,000."

Again I asked Michelle, "And this? Hoyt's writing?"

"Yes."

I turned the page. There, as I had found behind the gilt-wood table listing, a page was laid into the bound book. Only a few words were in English. "Objects of Art. Kobe. Kyoto. Mr. Hoyt Wyndfield, Virginia, USA, 1928. Lokesvara." Beneath, rows of neat columns ran up and down the page in what must have been Japanese. I hadn't a clue whether they were words or numbers.

Paper-clipped to this was a letter.

Dear Mr. Wyndfield, As you ask me to, I go to the shop asking when the Lokesvara figures be ready. I go more than 15 time. Mr. Nomura always say the figures not good enough. Hoping you understand that I do my best. Mr. Nomura now finish them. He call me and I get them for you. I have your ancient figure and the five new ones. You not be able to tell them apart. Enclosed are all documents for shipping of your purchases. Kindly send draft sum of Y 38.55, payable at our Kyoto office. P. Yas ka. December, 1928.

Between the *s* and *k*, only a faint portion of the upper part of the letter had come through. It might have been an *a,* or maybe an *o.* An *e* perhaps? But considering the long-ago year, what did it matter? Whoever P. Yas ka was, surely he was dead by now.

"Michelle, that figure of Lokesvara. It was on the list of stolen items, right?"

"I . . . think. But which one is that again?"

"Lokesvara. It's a figure with multiple arms—four, I think it is." I smiled when I realized I was waving my arms around, palms outward, in imitation of the figure's usual pose. "A Buddha god. You've seen all sorts of representations of him. Anybody who ever visited a Buddhist country has probably brought one home, like santos from Catholic countries. They're sold in every bazaar and souvenir shop in Tibet and Nepal, Japan—everywhere. You can even get them on Fifth Avenue in those shops that have been going out of business ever since they opened."

"Oh, I know the statue you mean. About this tall?" She held one hand above the other. "You're right. One of the figures was stolen. There were two of them, you see. I thought maybe they were a pair, but they were kept in different places. Guess that's why they didn't take both of them. I'll go get the one they didn't take."

I kept turning the pages. I was sinking deeper and deeper into the murky hole Eugene Kirklander's appraisal and Hoyt Wyndfield's notations had opened up. Items sold. Copies made. And always the money. Not that there's anything wrong with making a profit. What was getting to me were the questions those receipts and correspondences were raising. It was starting to look like a fair number of Wynderly's pieces that could be copied or faked had been sold and replaced with—yes, a fake.

But why would Hoyt have put the evidence of what he was doing in with the appraisal? One would have thought that he would have destroyed, or at least hidden away, the damning information. Compiling it and putting it with the appraisal made no sense. I was totally befuddled until I remembered a passage in Mazie's diary.

It was just before she began listing plantings and details about the gardens. She had complained, though gently, that Hoyt was a meticulous record-keeper. Apparently, so obsessive was he that he wanted all the records kept together to keep track of exactly how much money he was spending and making. I remembered how Thomas Jefferson had kept detailed records of every debt he incurred as he spent himself into bankruptcy.

But why the wheeling and dealing at all? What dishonest streak was running through Hoyt's psyche? Yes, I had a lot of thinking to do.

I turned to the list of stolen and damaged items Matt had provided and began searching through it. I found what I was looking for, "Ancient bronze figure of Lokesvara. 6-1/2 inches high. Circa AD 900. Extraordinarily rare. $8,000," just as Michelle returned.

She held the Lokesvara figure out to me.

"In a moment," I said. "Right now, I'm trying to sort out facts and dates. You can be a big help, if you would, please. To start with, where did the values Wynderly turned in to Babson and Michael come from?" I counted with my fingers. "We're now dealing with what . . . three different appraisals? This one by Kirklander, which no one knows about. The one from after Hoyt died in the late sixties. And then, the one after Mazie died two decades later in the mid-1980s. That's the one that the bank had made . . . the one you gave me. Which is why I'm here . . . because it's so outdated."

Michelle nodded.

I did the hypothetical math. While I talked, Michelle jotted down the figures.

"The real Lokesvara that Hoyt purchased in the 1920s on their trip to Koyoto was appraised at an accurate three thousand dollars in 1955. In 1928 Hoyt had paid a few yen to get a group of fake figures made. He later sold them, one by one, all but one of the five fakes, passed off for the real thing, for a couple of thousand each—enough below the appraisal value of the real one to make the sale look really sweet. He made quite a profit from his investment of a few yen, around ten thousand dollars. A nice sum for the 1950s."

"What about the appraisal from the sixties, after Hoyt's death?"

"In this instance, we don't really need that one," I explained. "By the 1980s, when the bank had their appraisal made, the value of the real figure had increased to eight thousand dollars. Now that would be OK . . . *if* it *was* the real figure."

"And the value of the fakes?"

"In the eighties? Twenty-five, fifty dollars perhaps."

This wasn't the first time I'd seen an antiques flimflam job. And from the get-go I'd had my suspicions when I saw those Tang horses. Other pieces had added to my skepticism. But this scam was bigger than I ever would have imagined. No longer did it appear that a couple of antiquing amateurs had been taken by some shrewd or shifty dealers out to make a quick buck. Hoyt obviously knew what he was doing. Did Mazie know? And the secret rooms . . .

Michelle picked up the Lokesvara she had placed on the table and looked at it. Her face said it all.

I laughed. "I'm wondering the same thing you are," I said. "I don't know either. It'll take an Oriental antiquities specialist to determine if this one's real or not, someone much more knowledgeable in that field than I am."

Chapter 22

Dear Antiques Expert: Hester Bateman is frequently mentioned in articles about 18th-century English silversmiths. What made her work so outstanding?

Hester Bateman was probably a more innovative businesswoman than she was a great silversmith. In 1760, after her husband's death, she began using new technology that made silver items such as cream pitchers and spoons less expensive, thereby expanding the family's business. (Her sons and daughter-in-law worked with her.) Whether Hester actually made any silver is debated, though pieces bearing her mark do exist. These, however, don't compare in craftsmanship to pieces made by some of her contemporary silversmiths. Still, with so much written about her (she's been called the Queen of Silversmiths), silver marked Hester Bateman brings top prices.

I WAS BEGINNING to understand how the stories Babby had told Michelle about Mazie, and Michelle's own experiences with Mazie could blur. I, too, was having difficulty distinguishing events that had actually transpired over the last couple of days from the impressions I had formed based on what I had read, been told, or surmised. "Life is not what one lived," Gabriel García Márquez wrote, "but what one remembers and how one remembers it in order to recount it."

Concentrating on the work at hand was next to impossible. My mind kept circling back to Mazie and Hoyt and the horde of secrets their lives must have held. I was tempted to ask Michelle if she knew about the rooms I had discovered in the attic.

I had begun to adjust my perception of Michelle. She had seemed so genuinely touched that Mazie had wanted her to have her china dog collection. And in retrospect, Michelle's love for Wynderly seemed sincere, if sometimes displayed dramatically. Then there was the fact that she had shown me Mazie's secret room and Kirklander's book. Those actions spoke volumes in her favor. Yes, I was beginning to warm up to Michelle Hendrix the same way I had unexpectedly found myself warming up to Wynderly. Still I couldn't bring myself to take her into my total confidence.

For one thing, she didn't know antiques well enough to be of much help. I was in dire need of someone disinterested, but trusty, who could help me winnow through Wynderly's tangled web of stories and the endless accumulation of stuff. I kept thinking of Peter. Together, we could surely get to the root of it all.

But boy oh boy, was the foundation's board going to go through the roof when they learned that several of the big dollar items weren't what they were cracked up to be. I moaned to myself. One thing was for sure. Hoyt's records, though helpful evidence, were going to greatly upset those who revered the Wyndfield name. What Hoyt had needed was a Rose Mary

Woods. If she'd erase Nixon's tapes, surely she would have burned Hoyt's receipts. Wonder why *Mazie* hadn't destroyed them?

"Michelle. Let's you and me take a step or two backwards," I said. "This book . . . this appraisal made by Kirklander. You say you found it, then hid it away again. How long have you known about it? And you're sure, really positive, no one else knows about all this?"

"It happened by accident. Right after I took the job. You think the office is a mess now? You should have seen it then. Anyway, the house was still open for some tours that had been booked before Wynderly was officially closed. I knew the closing was inevitable, but the board hadn't announced it publicly yet. One day I got this call from Frederick Graham. He said he needed a copy of the agreement that the board had signed with the bank. I turned the place upside down looking for it. And I did find it, but I also found lots of other stuff, including Kirklander's book in the bottom of one of the drawers. Well actually, it was in a *box* in the bottom of one of the drawers. Like I told you, it was underneath old papers and clippings—articles about parties and, well, nothing that seemed to have any relevance or importance."

"So, why did you pay any attention to it?"

"I was being diligent. I came across lots of things that I might have overlooked if Graham hadn't been so insistent that I find that specific paper. I wasn't about to have him come search the place and find I'd overlooked it. That's partly why the office is the wreck it is now. I started to organize at least some of the important things." She laughed. "Then, after it was announced in the newspaper that the house was going to be shut down, well, I figured, why bother? What difference did it make if the place was going to go to rack and ruin anyway. But that book—" Michelle covered her mouth and chin with her hand in an attempt to hide her emotions, but tears had already begun to well up in her eyes. "I just couldn't let it be found. I hid it."

"But why, Michelle? Why didn't you tell someone?"

"I don't know how to explain it." She crossed the room and sank into one of the straight-backed chairs lined up against the wall. She sat and said nothing for a while.

"Look, I love this place," she finally said. "There's no other way to put it. When I was a little girl, I practically had free rein of Wynderly. To me it was like a dream out of a fairy tale. I'd come with Babby, then when I'd go home, I'd lie in my bed and remember all the things I'd seen. All night long I'd dream I lived here, especially if Babby had sung her special song to me."

Michelle began to hum, then sing. "I dreamt that I dwel-t in mar-ble halls, with vassals and serfs at my side, And of all who assem-bled with-in those walls, That I was the hope and the pride."

I hadn't thought of that song in a hundred years, and probably never would have thought of it again without Michelle's prodding. "I know that song," I said. "It's the, the . . ."

"The Gypsy Girl's Song."

"Yes, yes. My mother used to sing it, too. Her father had sung it to her."

"For me, that's what Wynderly was," she said. "Marble halls. Long, beautiful marble halls. I dreamed I could live here. That Wynderly could be mine, or even if I couldn't live in Wynderly, that at least I, too, could live in a grand house filled with beautiful things." She wiped the corners of her eyes and laughed. "I didn't have a clue what vassals and serfs were, but I knew I wanted them. So you have to understand, when I realized what Hoyt was doing, it was as if my dreams had been shattered," she said. "I wasn't going to let him do that to others. If I could keep it all secret, then Wynderly would remain as it had been for me, as magical and wonderful as the pages of a big, beautiful pop-up book. I would leave the real world of my life. I was transported into a fairyland, but it was a *real* fairyland. Here *I* could be a princess like Mazie," she said, her face glowing.

"Don't you see, if something happens to Wynderly, we'll all have lost something special, something none of the old plantations and horse farms around here can begin to provide. Everybody needs dreams." Her smile had turned sad. "You know, when the house was still open, every time I would take a school group through the house I'd see some little girl just like me—stars in her eyes, seeing beautiful things she would never have seen if it hadn't been for Hoyt and Mazie. I'd watch her eyes grow larger and brighter, as if I was rubbing Aladdin's lamp when I'd tell her this was from Italy or that was from India. She could travel the world over right here in these marble halls, the same way I used to do.

"Then I found Kirklander's appraisal. At first it didn't make sense to me. You know I don't know much about antiques—not like you do. But you don't have to know squat about antiques to figure out when a scam's going on."

Her eyes searched mine as if hoping to find some understanding. "I'd never been so disappointed. That's why I hid the book," she said. "But what I don't understand is *why* Hoyt would have done it? All that cheating and stealing was bad enough, but what he did . . . Why, he *lied* to us. He made us believe these things were real. You don't build people's dreams and hopes and then destroy them."

I was at a loss for words—an unusual situation for me. When I remained silent she continued.

"And Mazie. Poor, poor Mazie. How could he have betrayed her so? She loved Hoyt. Tell me, what's going to happen to Wynderly *now*?"

"If only I knew," was the best I could come up with.

Michelle took a deep, unhappy breath. "Oh well, I guess what's done is done. What Hoyt didn't destroy, looks like the bank will," she said walking back to the table where we had spread out the papers alongside the bits of broken china left behind after the theft. She picked up one of the pieces that had once been part of the Delft charger.

"Isn't it weird how you don't think of something for years and then, when the idea hits you, it's as if you had known it all along," she said thoughtfully. "I just realized that Wynderly is probably one of the reasons why I married Haadhir."

She ran her fingers along the jagged edge of the fragment. "No wonder I had wanderlust. For a little girl to be surrounded by the stories all these beautiful things held . . . It sounds silly now, but back then, thanks to Wynderly, I could dream of a better world." Michelle cast her eyes downward. When she looked up, her eyes had a bittersweet look.

"You asked why I didn't tell anyone about the book after I found it," she said. "I didn't want to destroy the myth. I couldn't be the one to dash other people's dreams and hopes.

And, I guess I didn't want to hurt Mazie's memory. Too late for that now, right? I mean, with the bank wanting to pack things up and take them away. Oh, what are we going to do?"

"If only I knew," I said.

I checked several more pieces on the Babson and Michael list against the Kirklander appraisal. The boat-shaped, covered tureen made by Hester Bateman in London in 1786 that had been valued at $1,500 on the Kirklander appraisal had lept in value over the decades to $10,000 on the 1980s appraisal. That seemed an exorbitant increase, but I had just read where a collection of contemporary Chinese art purchased for $25,000 in 1995 had sold for four million in 2007. These days Hester Bateman silver is so hot that I upped the $10,000 to $25,000 on the Babson and Michael claim. Wynderly would pick up a nice piece of change on that piece. I circled and initialed the listing. But I put an X by the next item—an Egyptian stone sculpture.

Even before reading the full description of the piece in Kirklander's appraisal, I had known I would find a receipt for a forgery or two laid into the pages. Egyptian antiquities have been faked for centuries. What unsuspecting layman mesmerized by the mysterious history of an exotic Egyptian figure would ever think to ask for a chemical analysis of a figure's stone to determine if it had come from an ancient, or a modern, Egyptian quarry?

Sure enough, a receipt for multiple copies of the figure was right where I had expected to find it. Once he had sold them, Hoyt had made several thousand dollars on the deal.

Remembering Sydney Greenstreet and Peter Lorre in *The Maltese Falcon* and stories of the ever-changing two-bit players on eBay, I considered telling Michelle that antiques con men were nothing new, that Hoyt Wyndfield belonged on that list. It had been easy for him. He had possessed all the trappings of a successful charlatan (the word seemed to suit him better than *swindler* or *snake oil salesman*) — aristocratic charm, courtly manners, a golden tongue, and a self-confidence that can hoodwink the gullible every time.

Add in Hoyt's restless, adventuresome spirit. According to the tale Worth Merritt had taken great delight recounting, the Wyndfields had had a wild streak in their blood for generations. Little matter that Hoyt hadn't needed the money. I was willing to bet that Hoyt's schemes had been done for no reason other than the rush he got from making a deal. I'd read enough to know that the thrill of the kill is real, and a kill doesn't have to be a murder.

It could have been that. Or it might have been just plain greed. It's one of life's ironies that those who have it all will risk it all, be it at the poker table, the boardroom, the battlefield, or the bedroom.

By the end of the day, Michelle and I figured that perhaps as many as half of the stolen and broken items had been counterfeits, and we had the proof. What we still didn't know was who had committed the physical theft at Wynderly, and why. Would the thieves have even bothered with some of the pieces if they had known they were taking *fakes*? I hardly thought so. It's a cardinal rule that you better know what you've stolen before you try to fence it.

Chapter 23

Dear Antiques Expert: What does it mean when an antiques dealer refers to "smalls"? I have a friend who says she's going to take a space at an antiques mall and will specialize in smalls. I hate to appear ignorant.

"Smalls" is a term that antiques dealers use for items that don't take up much space—little things. Porcelains, ivory carvings, sewing and smoking accessories, jewelry, medals, beadwork, dressing table items—just about anything that can be easily transported, especially put in a shopping bag or pocketbook, is termed a "small." Since doodads, knick-knacks, and bric-a-brac were especially popular during the Victorian era, some dealers even specialize in what they term "Victorian smalls."

MICHELLE AND I had worked past the usual four o'clock quitting time before realizing how late it was. Though neither one of us mentioned it, we both had assumed the other people in the house had left some time earlier, or I certainly had. Foolish me. I should have known it was folly to assume anything around this place.

"Oh Michelle. Sterling? Anyone back here?" Tracy DuMont's clicking heels and throaty voice were unmistakable.

I motioned toward the door. While Michelle went out into the hall, I slid Kirklander's appraisal in the bottom of my briefcase. By the time Tracy had stepped over the threshold, sunglasses perched atop her head, I was casually gathering up the other papers.

"I cannot thank you enough for coming along when you did," I said. "If Mr. Graham had had his way, I'd be back in Leemont by now."

"Oh that Freddy. He makes me so damn mad I could choke him. Nobody around here who knows Freddy pays him any heed. Only reason he was picking on you is because you're new blood."

New blood? Where had I heard that before? Ah . . . Worth had said something like that when explaining why Peggy Powers was being so nice to me. "The new kid on the block." How nice to know that everyone was finding me so gullible and amusing.

"One thing's for sure," Tracy was saying, "I wouldn't put him in charge of anything I care about—not with that superior attitude of his. Pompous. That should be his middle name and the initials after his name. Freddy P. Graham, P.A.—Pompous Ass. Sometimes we have to show these men around here who's the boss. Like Alfred Houseman. He's another one. Michelle, remind me to give you some lessons on how to handle him."

Tracy flipped her hand in the air, reminding me of the old description of a knife cutting through butter. "Piece of cake," she said.

I didn't know if it was Tracy's frenzied good humor, the late hour at the end of a trying day, or the fact that Michelle and I had our secret, but the air in that back room had turned as sweet as a Southern summer breeze. We were like three girl-friends having fun.

"What if I call home and have Yves fix us a little supper," Tracy asked.

Michelle froze.

Tracy laughed out loud. "I don't bite. Is that a yes or a no?"

"Oh, I wish I could, Ms. DuMont. I just can't."

Tracy didn't push her. "Sterling?"

What had Worth Merritt said at dinner? "If, for any reason, you get a chance to spend any time with her, take it. It won't be time misspent."

"That's awfully nice of you. Are you sure it isn't too much trouble?"

"Trouble? For whom? Certainly not for me. Yves? That's what I pay him for."

I thought I caught a tinge of regret cross Michelle's face.

"So, you'll lock up, Michelle."

WE HAD AGREED that I would be at Terena, Tracy's estate—no other word would describe it—a little past six. We neither one wanted a late night, and I really needed to run by Belle Ayre. Uppermost in my mind was being sure Kirklander's book was safe and secure. I had the harebrained thought that if I hid it away I wouldn't be tempted to tell Tracy about it. Back at Belle Ayre, I put the book between the mattress and box spring of the bed. If that weren't foolish enough, I *sat* on the bed, as if to seal its hiding place.

I was putting on fresh lipstick when a wave of loneliness swept over me. I wished I'd never even heard of Wynderly. It had such an invasive sadness about it. But who had time for such thoughts now. Certainly not anyone who had been invited to Tracy DuMont's for dinner. Still, that thought didn't sweep away the clouds in my head. I'd call Peter. He'd cheer me up.

Deep down, I suppose I had hoped this trip away from Leemont might make Peter miss me. During my recent jaunt to New York where I had met Matt and as I began working for Babson and Michael, Peter had been as attentive as a pup—calling to check on me and then coming around once I got back to Leemont. But once things had leveled out, so had Peter's attentiveness. It was back to politeness and courtesy.

I played over in my head special moments Peter and I had had together. Not that they provided anything concrete for me to pin my hopes on: Peter's hand brushing mine, whether intentionally or accidentally, a tone of concern in his voice when he told me to be careful and to keep in touch with him while I was away, the time he had hugged me and held me closer and longer than I thought he would.

That's a pretty sad state of affairs, if I do say so, Mother declared, interrupting my moment of painful pleasure as I dwelled on those memories. *Finding pleasure in a touch rather than a kiss, a tone of voice rather than a declaration of passion, a mere hug? Live a little, Sterling. For God's sake, live!*

I picked up the phone and prayed Peter would be at home.

Our conversation was so pained that you would have thought we'd both just gotten Christmas cards from one another after a decade of silence. We chatted about everything from the new bypass around Leemont to pros and cons of the candidate who had just announced he was running for mayor. Finally I could stand it no longer. I blurted out, "I wish you were here to help me with this appraisal."

"Actually, Sterling, there's a great estate sale going on not too far from there this weekend. What are your plans?"

I fought back my initial enthusiasm. With Matt coming down . . . Then again, for all I knew, Matt would breeze in, look over the situation, and breeze back out.

"You're awfully quiet, Sterling."

"It all goes back to these lunatics. The one from the bank fired me today. So, you'd think I'd be packing up to come home, but . . ." I hesitated. No reason to tell Peter that Matt was coming down at this stage of the game. "Well, I got a reprieve, but at the moment, I really don't know if I'll be here through the weekend or not."

"Fired you?"

"It's too long a story to go into, really. Right now I'm on my way to Tracy DuMont's."

"*The* Tracy DuMont?"

"I certainly hope there's only one of them." I laughed. "Takes no prisoners, that's for sure. How about I call you later tonight? Would that be OK? I've got to scram in a minute, but tell me about the estate sale."

"Haven't you seen notices about it? It's been in all the papers around here. From what I can tell, apparently it's not too far from Wynderly. Milton, that's the name of the estate. Ever heard of it?"

"The house? No. And about the sale, I haven't so much as *seen* a paper or a TV, and I've only heard the radio a time or two when driving between Belle Ayre and Wynderly, and then it's mostly country music stations. The world could have ended, and I wouldn't know about it."

"The sale sounds good," Peter said. "My bet is that the big pieces will go well—the ones with a Virginia history, that is. But there are some Victorian smalls that I doubt if anyone will be too interested in. Anyway, if you're able to get away, we can go together."

My heart leapt.

"Give me a call when you get back from Madame Du-Mont's." He laughed. "Take a look around Terena for me, will you."

I was surprised. "You know the name of her house."

"Doesn't everyone? So, let me know your plans, Sterling, and have fun. Give me a call if you can."

The call had ended abruptly and, to my mind, as awkwardly as it had begun.

On my way out to Terena, only a streak of daylight remained on the horizon before total darkness settled in. The gloaming, as Mother used to call those twilight hours. I always hated it when she used that word, it was so old-fashioned and foreboding, but it sure fit the moment and my mood. My heart was as threadbare as the tires on my car. The whiff of burning wood didn't help cheer me up either. I blinked hard to black out the romantic scene of a fireplace.

I came to the country store set back in the V in the road and drove right by the turnoff Tracy had told me to be sure not to miss. Turning the car around I remembered what she had said. "Terena is set far off the secondary roads. And without cell

phone service, when you're lost, you're lost . . . so pay attention." I *had* paid attention then. The problem was now.

In the far distance a row of lights flickered against the horizon. If I get too lost I'll just head over that way, I concluded,
not giving any thought to how I would get there in this wil-
derness of curvy, rough roads that splintered off like so many
arms on an octopus. Between my state of mind, the dark of
the night, and the shadowy countryside, I was beginning to
feel as if I was in a time warp. Was I skirting on the edge of the
world, about to tumble off at any minute?

Finally, I saw the sign: TERENA, CIRCA 1789.

I drove along the gravel road flanked by towering cedars
of Lebanon, slowly rising and falling with the lay of the land.
Even in the night I could sense the setting's majestic beauty.
Eventually the rolling pathway leveled off, giving way to
a deep, swelling incline. There, rising before me, in its full
beauty was Terena.

Compared with Wynderly, Terena was almost austere. A
late Georgian brick house, it had a square, two-story center
section. Set back on each side were perfectly matching wings,
added at a later date I surmised. A portico supported by
round columns provided a protective covering over the front
entranceway. Other than that, the only really sophisticated
touch to the house were the tall chimneys that rose above
the slate roof. They gave it a certain timeless elegance. The
house was grand in an understated way, which hardly fit Tracy
DuMont's reputation or her personality.

The Tracy who answered the door didn't look a bit like the
Tracy DuMont who had burst into the board meeting with
such flair. Wearing a simple moss green cashmere sweater set

and navy blue slacks, her only jewelry was a floral spray pin set with emeralds and sapphires. I immediately recognized it as a mid-twentieth-century Tiffany piece. She greeted me in a down home sort of way. "Oh good, you made it. Hope you didn't have too much trouble getting here."

That was just the beginning of the surprises the night would hold.

Chapter 24

Dear Antiques Expert: I've become very interested in early American antiques. When I read about them, the region or even a specific place where they were made often is given great importance. Why is this?

Early American craftsmen had to use the materials at hand. Though furniture makers in cities with good seaports could buy imported mahogany, craftsmen further inland mostly relied on wood cut from nearby forests. Location also influenced a region's lifestyle. Thus in sophisticated Philadelphia, furniture makers carved mahogany piecrust tables, so called because of their fancy ruffled or crimped edge. But in the Shenandoah Valley, craftsmen made simpler, more utilitarian cherry dropleaf tables for their clients. Since many collectors prefer locally made pieces, scholars and dealers try to identify a piece's origin based on its woods, style, design, and techniques used.

ON FIRST GLANCE, like its exterior, Terena's interior was deceptively simple. Structurally, it was what is called a two-by-two, or a four-over-four house. Off the front section of center hallway, there was one room to the left, one to the right.

Behind those, also opening off the hallway were two more rooms. Midway down the hall, a staircase led to the second floor. Upstairs, four more rooms were arranged in the same unpretentious pattern.

But to call the walnut paneled entrance a hall hardly did it justice. It was large enough to hold a coach and four, and its arched doorways leading into the rooms off of it were flanked by impressive reeded columns. Around the ceilings, the carved molding depicted trailing vines so lifelike you wanted to reach up and touch them. The chair rail in the dining room was a deeply carved Greek key banding. And the marble mantels depicting different scenes from Greek mythology were so detailed you could see each gracefully poised goddess's fingernails. Yet nothing about the house was overdone or flashy. It was simply grand.

And the furniture: four acanthus-carved Chippendale chairs surrounded the New York gaming table, a rare Boston chinoiserie Queen Anne chair was drawn up to a shell-carved Connecticut slant front desk, and between a pair of Baltimore Pembroke tables inlaid with bellflower drops was a camelback sofa upholstered in bright crimson damask. But the piece that grabbed my attention was the Philadelphia mahogany piecrust tea table with ball-and-claw feet—the sort that could soar to a million dollars *plus* at auction.

I made no attempt to hide my astonishment. "Wow."

"I like it," Tracy said casually.

"I guess you *do*. And, to tell you the truth, it's quite refreshing after Wynderly. It's not that Wynderly is in bad taste. It has its own charm," I quickly added, fearing I'd spoken too frankly and hastily. "But *this* is what a truly grand *Virginia* estate is supposed to look like."

Tracy laughed. "Don't worry. I know what you mean about Wynderly. I couldn't live there. When I come home, I need order and stability, not glitz and glitter." She heaved a deep sigh. "I know some people would call Terena stuffy. I call it calming. I grew up here. To me it's home. But let's have a glass of wine. I'll take you on a tour upstairs later. You've had a long day and getting here is no small feat till you know the roads. I've had Yves prepare something light for us to eat. He and his family live in the gatehouse you passed when you turned in, but I don't want to keep him here too late. I told him we'd eat early and visit over supper. Is that OK?"

"Sounds wonderful," I said. "Where would you like for me to sit?" I half expected there to be neatly folded, white "Do Not Sit" cards on the museum-quality chairs and sofa.

"Oh, just anywhere. Make yourself comfortable."

While I stood debating between the sofa and the circa 1780 Philadelphia wingback chair, Tracy disappeared into the hallway.

She returned with two glasses, not the cut Waterford, fine Steuben, or Baccarat crystal people of her status usually have, but simple etched eighteenth-century wineglasses. The chilled bottle of white wine was resting in a wooden-bottomed old Sheffield silver wine coaster, its copper base showing through.

"Hope you don't mind, but I couldn't resist." Tracy turned the bottle of Sterling Vineyards chardonnay so I could see the label and laughed. "Now. Tell me about *you*, Sterling Glass," Tracy said, handing me the glass she had just poured.

"Oh, there's not much to tell. You know why I'm here. Babson and Michael wanted to get the values of the Wynderly pieces resolved before they paid the claim."

"So, tell me, what *are* you finding over there?"

I found myself squirming. I should've been better prepared for Tracy's inevitable questions about Wynderly. But since I wasn't, I tried skirting the issue. "Speaking of Wynderly, I cannot thank you enough for coming to my rescue this afternoon."

"That Freddy. Give a man a little power and watch your back. 'Absolute power corrupts absolutely.' Thing is, Freddy *is* the trust department," she said. "Therein lies his power. Trust department? That's a joke. I wouldn't *trust* that bunch of jokers at the bank as far as I can spit."

For a second I wondered why Tracy was being so forthcoming with me, whom she hardly knew. Then again, speaking her mind was Tracy's way. But Tracy's comment about the bank? I took a lesson in boldness from my hostess's book and spoke right up. "I thought you'd gone to the bank looking for Mr. Graham, or at least that was the impression I got back at Wynderly," I said. "If you don't trus—"

"Look. I'm not going to totally alienate myself around here. I keep enough money in the bank so they *have* to be nice to me. There are times when I need favors too. As long as the bank guys have the local yokels in their pockets, I *have* to be nice to them so *they* will be nice to *me*."

"Then I'm not speaking out of school in assuming one of those yokels the bank has in its pocket is Alfred Houseman?"

"You've got it."

"And you do know that Alfred Houseman as much as told

the board that you were going to step in and save Wynderly," I said. "Now I'm here in your home, I'm wondering why he said that. Wynderly is so totally different from what you have here at Terena. Would you, I mean, *are* you *really* interested in—"

"That's the impression Alfred would give. Am I interested in saving the place?" She frowned. "You put it well earlier. Wynderly doesn't fit in around here. Montpelier's the big tourist draw, yet I've been told there are days in the dead of winter when it's almost empty. The same is true at Monticello, according to some of the guides. Thinking that tourists will flock to Wynderly is a pipe dream. But I *do* hate to see the place turned into . . . who knows what? A resort golf club? The grounds would be suited to that, but it would destroy the gardens. A bed and breakfast? We've got enough of those. Anyway, between the house and the acreage, Wynderly's far too big for one family to keep up without having a whole staff the way the Wyndfields had. And as far as all that stuff in it? Why, half of it is—" She stopped in mid-sentence. "Well, you tell me. You're the appraiser."

I dropped my eyes and fiddled with the stem of my now empty wineglass. What should I say? I would appear ignorant if I *didn't* acknowledge the fakes and reproductions in the house, especially after the suggestive hint she'd just dropped. But if I *did* acknowledge them, I would be betraying my client's confidentiality. I sat, hoping that she'd say something. All the while, the silence, as they say, hung.

"Good girl!" Tracy suddenly blurted with such gusto that she startled me. "Your silence tells me what I've figured for years. It's all a sham. Just like Hoyt himself."

"I . . . I . . ."

"My daddy never *did* trust that man. It wasn't like you could put your finger on anything wrong he was doing, so everybody just looked the other way and whispered under their breath." She stopped as abruptly as she had begun.

"I'm a fine one to talk," she said. "That harangue I delivered at the board meeting glorifying Hoyt?" She shook her head. "I didn't believe a word of it . . . the part about Hoyt, that is. But with Peggy Powers and Miss Mary Sophie and others perpetuating Hoyt Wyndfield's name and reputation, the only way I can get their attention is to play along with them. Wynderly's worth saving, of that I'm sure. And you can't just sweep a romantic family story aside. That's why tourists visit old homes, to see how other people lived, especially rich people. But we *can* stop *glorifying* Hoyt. The house will be the same. The architecture, the objects—even the spurious ones—have their own stories to tell."

I was expecting Tracy to launch into one such story. Instead she said, "Yes, Hoyt's ways really bothered Daddy. The whole thing . . . the house, some of the people who visited there—it was a real mystery. But what's a mystery without a dead body? It takes a corpse to get the action started, to get to the truth, or, if not a corpse, a scandal. And we didn't have either one at Wynderly. At least not one we'd make public in this tight-lipped society where 'Thou shalt not tell thy neighbors' secrets' is the eleventh commandment. Daddy wasn't the only one who felt something was amiss, but without anything to pin on Hoyt, everybody rolled over and played possum." She laughed.

"Now about *you*. I've read your columns and heard your name in the antiques world, but of course we know all about heresay. If *half* the stuff written about me were true—" She muttered an exasperated "aghh."

"Me? Well, there's not much to tell. I live in Leemont."

"Divorced, right?"

"Three, four years. I'm not counting."

"Good for you. So, is there a man in your life?"

"Well . . ."

"Listen honey, there's no 'well' about it."

I grimaced. Tracy DuMont was starting to sound a lot like my mother, despite the fact that Tracy was probably in her early sixties, only ten or twelve years older than I. But when someone has lived life as fully as Tracy DuMont, she should be listened to.

"There either *is* or there *isn't*," Tracy said.

I smiled to myself. The emphatic Tracy of the board meeting couldn't stay hidden for long. Still, Tracy DuMont trouncing through my love life was not part of the bargain. In an attempt to end the conversation, I shrugged and said, "Put that way . . . no, there isn't."

Little did I know I was throwing out the bait she was waiting for. "Why *not*? You're an attractive woman."

"Thank you, but it's not like there's an eligible man my age on every street corner," I said.

"You travel. You don't think I've met my husbands hanging around *here* do you? Who would I hook up with?" Tracy exploded with laughter. "Frank Fox? I call him Light-in-the-Loafers Fox. Can you *believe* he has a *son*? Worth Merritt?" Her attitude changed. "Now there's a real gentleman for you. If he were only about twenty, maybe twenty-five years younger—"

"But you do travel to a lot more exotic places that I do."
I held out my hands like Blind Justice holding scales. "Rome,
Roanoke? Venice, Virginia Beach?"

"You'd be surprised. I met my last husband in Des Moines.
So. You're telling me that every man in Leemont is either married, dead, or gay?"

I found comfort and courage in the wine she had poured.
"Well, actually, there is one . . ."

How to describe Peter?

"I don't know how interested he is in me. One minute he's
all attentive, and the next I seem to be just a good friend. Not
that anything has been said, or anything . . . well, romantic
has taken place . . ."

Hearing myself stumbling over my words and realizing that
I couldn't define our relationship gave me pause. This was not
good.

"Well, who *is* he? Divorced? Not a married man is he?" She
raised her eyebrows in her worldly way.

"Oh no." I threw up my hand and gave a protesting laugh.
"He's widowed. Several years now. A retired Episcopal
priest—early retirement. He's about my age. Actually, it's
rather interesting. He moved to Leemont just because he liked
it. He hasn't any family there. In fact he runs the Salvation
Army's secondhand store and has turned it into quite an antiques shop. He has a boyish way about him."

"So," Tracy said with great finality. "What's holding him
back? Seems you'd have a lot in common."

I shrugged. "Wish I knew."

The wine and Tracy's unrelenting way, plus my own unsettling feeling about Peter spurred me on.

"Well, there's also Matt Yardley, the Babson and Michael executive who hired me for this job. He's quite charming. Actually, he has a more, well, sophisticated manner than Peter." I couldn't help telling her, "In fact, Matt said he's going to drop by tomorrow. He's in D.C. right now and since he's so close . . ."

"Aha. Now *that* sounds more like it," Tracy said. "That minister fellow, Peter whoever, I'd say that dog won't hunt."

I laughed. "We'll see what happens. Oh, but that reminds me. I've heard there's an estate sale somewhere around here this weekend. Do you know anything about it?"

"The one at Milton? That's the old Trumbull place, ten or twelve miles west of here, in Madison County. Just a stone's throw. It's been sitting empty for a good two, three years now. Family dispute. Thank God they're finally emptying it out. It's a miracle there hasn't been a fire or robbery. As a matter of fact, there's a Queen Anne dropleaf table that I'm interested in. Whether I'll get it is a different matter. I'll send Yves to bid on it for me. I have it on good authority that some New York dealers are coming down for the sale. It's got some fine pieces in it," she added, then laughed and said, "Shame we can't interest those fellows in some of the stuff at Wynderly while they're here."

Chapter 25

Dear Antiques Expert: I have found the perfect mirror to go in my entrance hall, but the glass needs replacing. When I asked the dealer if he could have a new one put in, he said that since it was an 18th-century mirror with its original glass that I'd be hurting its value. How could this be since the glass that's in it is so dark and crackled you can hardly see your own reflection?

In the 18th century it was difficult to cut a large piece of glass without breaking it. Thus, mirrors, especially ones with beautiful frames, were expensive. Over the years, when the "looking glass" (as the mirror was called) broke, cracked, or became cloudy, it was replaced. American-made all-original mirrors are rare. A record $242,000 was paid for a labeled, museum-quality Philadelphia mirror some years back. So, should you find a genuine early mirror retaining its old glass, it is wise to place a new glass in front of the old (separated by mylar), thereby keeping the original mirror intact.

I SLIPPED INTO the bathroom to wash my hands before dinner. How different it was from Wynderly's powder room with its bejeweled mirror and gold-plated faucets. Terena's simple fixtures dated from the 1920s, about the time the room was added to the house, I figured. Above the lavatory hung an eighteenth-century Chippendale mirror still fitted with its original glass. I peered around its cloudy and flaked portions to find a spot where I could see my reflection well enough to apply a fresh coat of lipstick.

I recalled that oft-quoted biblical verse, "For now we see through a glass, darkly; but then face to face." If only it were *then,* not *now,* and I *could* see the truth face to face, for everywhere I turned, everywhere I looked, all—Hoyt, Mazie, Wynderly itself—was becoming darker by the moment, especially after Tracy's most recent comments.

Truth never hurts the teller, Mother had drilled into me. Thing was, the truth was becoming as fuzzy and distorted as my own image in the mirror.

My only comfort was that I had *not* come across any dead bodies up in the priest hole or its adjoining room. The strange, and apparently unfulfilled, false obituary note I had found there had been unsettling enough. Thinking back, it struck me as funny how I'd been so disturbed by it at the time, only to have it slip to the back of my mind until now.

I stood, staring in the mirror. What *was* the date of that handwritten obituary—1954, '55? If it was 1955, and I thought it was, that was the same year the Kirklander appraisal had been made. And Hoyt's notes indicating that he had begun selling replicas dated back to, when was it . . . The earliest date I recalled was 1951.

Tracy had more than hinted about things at Wynderly being amiss, but my fears were beginning to run much deeper.

Something more cruel than the faking of a few antiques had surely happened those many years ago.

My thoughts went back to Tracy's recollection of her father's comments. She had left me with little doubt that Hoyt had been up to no good. But would the proof of his notations in the appraisal be sufficient? And would it be possible to track down the people he had sold the fakes to? He hadn't mentioned names that I had noticed. And the companies that had made them: surely they were out of business, or, like the one in Kyoto, out of reach. I didn't want to think what was going to happen when Babson and Michael, the bank, and the Wynderly Foundation board got hold of the information only Michelle and I held. As I'd learned long ago, money invariably brings out the worst in everyone.

YVES HAD PREPARED a scrumptious supper of traditional Virginia foods—creamy peanut soup accompanied by ham biscuits made the way they're supposed to be, with country ham piled half an inch thick on hot buttered biscuits no larger than a fifty-cent piece.

"Have antiques always been your passion?" I asked. "Everywhere I look, another treasure. This is a real treat for me."

Tracy put her soup spoon down and laughed. "I was born with the gene. Some are born scientists or mathematicians. My father loved antiques, as did his father, and on and on . . . though of course these things weren't *always* antique." She gestured with her wineglass. "That huntboard over there goes back to Orange's halcyon days. I remember the day my father decided to bring it in from the outbuilding where it had been stored for years and put it right there under that picture."

Above the huntboard hung a handsome oil painting of blue-blooded, red-coated huntsmen, thoroughbred horses, and kennel-bred dogs. In the background stood Terena. I couldn't help wondering who had painted it and what sort of money it would bring in these parts where people vie with horses for the title "thoroughbred."

"Daddy told me how *his* grandfather and his friends used to ride around to the back of the house after the hunt," she said. "The servants would have laid out a whole spread of food and drink on that very huntboard so the men didn't have to dismount, wash up, and go inside to eat. They'd just lean over and grab a biscuit."

She picked up her own ham biscuit and tipped it as if saluting toward the picture, the huntboard, and, of course, her ancestors. "Why, it was nothing more than an outdoor picnic table to them then. Now it's a prized antique worth tens of thousands. How times *do* change. But not the biscuits."

"You just made me think of something my mother used to say," I said. "Mother would see a fine antique and say, 'Time's been a friend to you, you're an antique.' Then she'd say, 'Too bad time can't be that kind to people.'"

"I'm with your mom," Tracy said. "Time's a lot nicer to things than it is to most people. Sounds like you had a good mother," she added. "I never had any children. Wasn't about to burden any poor child with having *me* for a mother. Never have regretted it either. I guess I never really loved any of my husbands deeply enough to want them to be my child's father." She paused. "You know, if Mazie and Hoyt had had children, this whole mess over at Wynderly probably wouldn't have come to be."

"Actually," I said, "I've wondered who—which one of them, Mazie or Hoyt—decided to turn the house over to the foundation and make it a museum. I know Mazie outlived Hoyt by years, but was it *his* idea, or was it she who—"

"Miss Mary Sophie would be the one to know that," Tracy said. "She's much older and knew the Wyndfields fairly well. Yes, quite well. There might have even been some distant kinship between Hoyt and her father. I'm not sure, though that would certainly explain why she's been so generous in her gifts to Wynderly in the past, especially considering that Miss Mary Sophie is quite shrewd and sees right through things. But to your question—I would think that Hoyt and Mazie both would have agreed to it, then again, I really don't know.

"Like I said, my father never had much time for Hoyt Wyndfield. Back when Hoyt was alive, I was a young girl and much more interested in horses and boys than I was hearing about stuffy old neighbors who lived miles away. Anyway I got shipped off to school pretty young—eighth grade—and before that it was camp every summer or trips to Europe. My mother died when I was seven. I just wasn't around a lot, plus . . . Well, truth is, I didn't much like it here—not then. It was hard for me to fit in. There weren't many other kids, and the ones there were, well, they weren't like me. The families that owned the big houses tended to be older. Sometimes their grandchildren visited, but I never really got to know them. Most of the kids my age were from families that worked the farms or had businesses in town or clerked in the stores around here. Back in those days, we didn't associate that much with people who weren't like us. It's a better world these days. Soccer. Science camps. All those activities kids have now. They can get together and play and learn about each other. We didn't do it back in the fifties, especially when we lived such distances apart. Wasn't like you could run over to your neighbor's house."

Tracy's eyes, usually feisty or lively or both, took on a melancholy gaze. She looked her age. "Funny how the hurts of our youth stay with us, and they cut so much deeper than later hurts. It's like they become embedded within us, grow, and harden our hearts. Who knows? Maybe that's why the later hurts aren't as bad. They haven't lived as long."

It was easy to envision Tracy as a solitary little rich girl longing for what she couldn't have at any price—a childhood.

"Of course, I eventually put that all behind me," she said, much brighter. "Still, for many years I stayed away, coming back to Virginia only when I had to. But I guess the land and this house had a strong pull after all." She shook her head in disgust. "Listen to me. I sound like Scarlett don't I?"

"Speaking of Tara," I said, laughing along with her, "where did the name Terena come from? It's not exactly a Virginia or English name."

"Hardly."

"Italian, maybe?"

She shook her head. "That's what you'd expect. After all, Mr. Jefferson named his house Monticello. But Terena is Portuguese. Actually, I don't know exactly when the house became Terena. Years and years ago—sometime during the nineteenth century. Before that there are some old mentions of it being called Helmsley after the region in England where the family originated. But somewhere along the way, someone went to Portugal on the 'grand tour,' fell in love with Terena, came back and gave this very sedate Georgian house a totally inappropriate romantic name." With her fingers she put quotes around *romantic.*

I must have looked puzzled.

"You know, Terena, the cork and wine country, near the Spanish border. Have you been there?"

I shook my head. No.

"Oh, It's lovely. It's the sort of off-the-beaten-track place that Hoyt and Mazie adored. The countryside is rolling and hilly, like around here. But there the similarities cease. Thank goodness *my* ancestors had enough sense to only change the name of the house and not bring back trunkloads of souvenirs and antiques to junk up the place. Can't you just see this house done over with terracotta floors and heavy dark furniture and hanging baskets of bougainvillea suspended from sky hooks?" Tracy's look said it all.

"Now don't get me wrong, it looks great in Portugal," she said. "I love it. But bringing Portugal to Virginia makes about as much sense as taking New Mexico to Russia." She shook her head in disgust. "Some people don't get it, though. Never will forget my friend who moved to Vegas for the climate. Trouble was, she got homesick so she built a Williamsburg-style house. It stuck out like tits on a bull."

While Tracy refilled my wineglass I asked, "What about Hoyt's family's home. I'm assuming they had a fine place somewhere around here."

"Well yes . . . and no. There were two branches of Wynd-fields."

"Oh yes, I know. Worth Merritt told me about them."

"I will tell you this. Hoyt's family had what my father called the gambler's curse. To Daddy, a Wyndfield moving down to Southside Virginia back when tobacco money changed hands under the table was like an alcoholic going to a bar. 'Honest thieving' Daddy called the tobacco-growing business. He said that those Southside people didn't understand an honest day's pay for an honest day's work any more than a carnival man selling snake oil. My daddy said the tobacco field hands lived the whole year off of just half a year's work, and the 'big men' lived off the poor men's sweat. He didn't think any of it was right. Daddy didn't trust anyone who made a living from cashing in on other's people's sins. Tobacco. Whiskey. Casinos. Daddy felt so strongly about such things he didn't even buy Coca-Cola stock cause of the cocaine that was in it way back in the early days. My father was a man of high ideals."

Glancing away, she said, "I wish I had inherited more of his principles." Then she met my eyes. "Anyway, as best I can tell, Daddy considered Hoyt unprincipled. Was he right? I don't know. I think I mentioned that my father was a lawyer. There was much that was never discussed, client confidentiality and all that. But I've often wondered what was really going on behind Wynderly's high towers and long shadows. Even back when I was a girl I could imagine all sorts of wild things going on in the pagoda and summerhouse. Once I got lost in Mazie's maze and it scared me to death. After that I didn't go over there for years. I hadn't been in the big house until recently, but I do know it changed over time."

Tracy leaned back in her chair. I sensed she had something important to say from the look on her face. "When you asked about my passion for antiques I told you it was in my blood. I always loved going in the houses around here and seeing what other people had. Ours were usually as fine, or finer," she said as an aside. "Anyway, I do remember my father commenting on all the 'new things' at Wynderly at some point in time. French and English things, the things there now. Apparently there had once been some very fine American pieces at Wynderly, back in the 1920s and '30s."

Tracy drummed her fingers on the table and squinted as if trying to bring pictures in her mind into focus. "I do remember some conversation about those things though. It must have been when . . . when . . . Yes. It was either when Frank Horton was here from the Museum of Early Southern Decorative Arts, or someone from the National Trust came down to gather information about these houses and their furnishings." Satisfied, she put her hand back in her lap.

"You know, I don't think I ever thought about the possibility of good things having been at Wynderly until this fiasco came up. But now I *do* wonder what happened to the other pieces. Hmm. I guess there's the chance they went into storage . . . and if things are going to be sold . . ."

She had spoken her last words quietly, more to herself than to me. Then turning her full attention to me she asked, "You haven't come across them have you?"

I didn't say a thing. I just moved my head ever so slightly in a noncommittal way and hoped I had kept my body language under control while trying to block out images of the grand American pieces in Mazie's secret room.

"I wouldn't have thought so," she said. "But about the furniture over there . . ."

All the while Tracy had been talking, half my brain had been thinking about the secret rooms and the appraisal stashed between the mattress and box spring of my bed. Now I was wondering how we'd gotten back on the furniture at Wynderly. I had consciously dodged the subject first go-round. Tracy had even praised me for not saying anything. Was it a coincidence that our conversation had come full circle, or had that been her intention all along? A glass or two of wine. A little cozy conversation about men. A couple of harmless confessions about her personal life to put me at ease . . .

I do wish I wasn't so suspicious *all* the time. But that's part of being an appraiser.

Casting my Southern manners to the wind, I leaned forward and rested my elbows on the table. "I think I know how your father felt being a lawyer," I said. "There must have been many times when he wanted to talk about a case, get it off his chest, but couldn't. Client confidentiality can be a real burden. That's what I'm struggling with right now. You see, before I can say anything about what I've found . . . or *haven't* found at Wynderly, I really *do* have to talk to Matt Yardley. Then, if he gives me permission to . . . But meanwhile, my loyalty has to be to the insurance company," I stuttered. "Until then . . . I can't even discuss the situation with the board . . . not till I've talked to Matt. I'm sorry."

I had watched Tracy DuMont as best I could while trying to find my words.

"Sterling Glass, I'll give it to you. You are a rare person. I've seen men of influence crumble in this setting, knowing the power my name and money hold. You didn't. My daddy would have liked you."

I wished Peter Donaldson could have heard her words. Matt Yardley, too.

She crossed her heart like a kid. "I promise not to bring up Wynderly again, how's that? Let's have some decadent dessert. Chocolate."

"But we can talk about *your* things, can't we?" I said.

"Oh yes. My favorite topic." Tracy pushed the silent buzzer on the floor beneath her feet. Yves appeared.

"We'll take dessert now. And tea," she said. "Now, I told you about the huntboard. These chairs . . ."

AFTER THE PROMISED TOUR of Terena, as we stood at the door saying our good-byes, Tracy said, "Are you sure you know how to get back to Belle Ayre?"

I dismissed the cautiousness in her voice with a laugh. "Oh yes, I think so. I have directions. I'm going to turn them around, read them backwards, and see what happens."

Opening the drawer of the Pembroke table, Tracy said, "You do have a gun, don't you?"

"Gun?" I could hardly get the word out of my throat. "Gun? No, I haven't."

"Here, take this one." She took out a .38 Smith and Wesson revolver, checked the cylinder, and handed it to me, butt first. "It's fully loaded."

My hand leapt to my heart.

"Or would you feel better with a semiautomatic? I've plenty of nine millimeters around. They can be temperamental, though, hard to control. I find a good old revolver more foolproof."

Even though I'd taken the Leemont Citizens' Police Academy and handled a semiautomatic pretty well, I'd also learned it wasn't wise to be toting around a concealed weapon. "Thank you, but I really don't think I'll need it. I don't have a permit and I don't—"

"How about some mace, then?"

When she saw the look on my face, Tracy shrugged. "Guess not." She glanced at her watch. "You're right. It is early yet. You should be fine."

Tracy put the weapon back where she'd gotten it. "But do be careful." Then smiling, she reached out and gave me a warm hug. "It's been a delightful visit, and it won't be our last."

Another typical Tracy DuMont over-the-top moment, I thought, and waved to her while unlocking the car. "Thanks again for everything," I called to her.

"OK, but *do* be careful, and watch out for the deer and foxes," she called back.

Chapter 26

Dear Antiques Expert: When going through some family things we found a pistol. Accompanying it was a note reading "9 mm WW I German Luger taken off a Nazi officer." My great-grandfather served in WW I, and my grandfather in WW II. Could this information be true, and what would the gun's value be?

Interestingly, the manufacture of the Luger changed from Jewish control to the Nazis in the early 1940s. Because Lugers were issued to ranking German officers during both world wars, the information could be accurate. However, if the gun bears the stamp "Germany," it would have been among those made for export to America, of which there were many. A weapons expert can identify the age of the gun by its marking—the serial and model numbers—and give you its value according to its type, condition, etc. It could possibly be worth a thousand dollars or more.

THOUGH I HAD made every effort to sound confident, once I closed the door and started the engine, I threw up a little prayer. Dark nights and strange places with no houses, stores, or streetlights around are not within my comfort zone. I stopped at the end of Tracy's driveway and fumbled with the wrinkled page of directions, turning it first this way, then that. The dim reading light in the car was next to no help. I fished around in the glove compartment till I found my flashlight, but even with the extra light, the more I looked at my directions, the more confused I got. Why had I let Tracy pour that last glass of wine? In frustration I flipped the flashlight off, looked at the road in front of me. Which way was I supposed to turn at the gate? Left. Right. Which way had I turned when I was coming to the house?

It was only a little past nine. If I went the wrong way, I'd surely figure it out eventually, then turn around and go the other way. I turned to the right, looking for anything familiar that I had seen a couple of hours earlier. But in the black of night, who can tell one stand of dark trees from another? Even with my brights on, I had a hard time reading the names of houses and watching for blind curves at the same time.

Trying to get my mind on something less worrisome, I flipped on the radio, but the twangy voices singing country and western music dominating the airwaves didn't do anything for me, especially after the elegance of Tracy's home. My mind wandered back to Terena.

Worth Merritt had been right when he'd sworn that any time spent with Tracy DuMont would be time well spent. Mother often said that every woman has two faces—one she shows to the world, and one she shows to the man she loves. I'd learned that Miss Mary Sophie was certainly living proof of that old saw. It was clear that Tracy, too, had a public and a private face. I was glad I'd had a chance to see them both—the one entertaining and domineering, the other, though strong at times, surprisingly endearing.

I was midway through a long twisting curve when a bolt of light from a vehicle flashed in my side mirror. Startled, I grasped the steering wheel so tightly that I accidentally veered into the other lane, or what normally would be the other lane, except these back roads had no center lines.

At the same instant, lights of an oncoming car practically blinded me as it swung onto the narrow strip of grass on the roadside, missing me by no more than a foot or two, its horn blaring as it did so. By the time I had steered my car back into my lane I was a wreck. And the vehicle behind me was still on my bumper.

I slowed down to see the next curve and allow the fool behind me to pass. By now, I realized it wasn't a car, or even an SUV tailing me, but a pickup truck. The driver was undoubtedly from around these parts and knew the road. Of course he wanted to go fast.

Up ahead four or five deer were grazing a few feet from the road. Again I clicked on my brights. One of the deer turned and ambled away. The others ignored the whole situation. Thank you, Lord, I said, thankful none had bounded across the road. I reached to open the driver's window so I could motion to the truck to pass me. When I touched the brake lightly, my car lurched forward as the truck hit me, not hard, but with too much force to be accidental. I threw my hands up in the air and strained to get a better look in my rearview mirror.

Sitting high and laughing hard were two guys in the lighted cab of the truck. Its bumper couldn't have been more than an inch or two off my rear. Maybe if they were drinking they hadn't meant to ram me.

I crept along until I got to what looked to be an even patch of ground, pulled onto the shoulder, and eased to a stop. But instead of zooming past, the truck stayed glued to me.

At least I hadn't been forced into a low ditch or sent tumbling down a hillside. Surely someone would come along. It wasn't like it was midnight.

I heard the truck doors slam.

The seconds that passed seemed an eternity. The guy in the passenger seat had disappeared behind the truck, probably to take a leak. The driver stood by his door shuffling his feet, bull-like, snuffing out the remains of a cigarette. My instincts told me to gun it and get the hell out of there, but I knew that they could outrun me cold.

The one who'd gone around the truck reappeared. He was tall and wore a baseball cap. Together they sauntered up to my side of the car. The one who'd been driving peered in my window.

"Pro fess or Fox," he called out in a singsongy falsetto voice.

I grabbed my flashlight and clutched it as tightly as I would have a World War I German Luger and shone it straight in his eyes.

He jerked back in surprise. I could hear the men's cussing through the glass. The tall guy in the baseball cap kicked the side of my car.

"Damn it, Emmett. Don't get him mad."

The one who'd spoken banged his fist on my window. "Open up, Fox."

I didn't point the flashlight this time. I just listened to my own heart beating above their commotion. The one named Emmett leaned over the hood of my car so he could see in.

As he did so, the moon slid out from behind clouds, and I caught a clear glimpse of his face—the same face I'd seen at the 7-Eleven a couple of nights earlier. I turned to see who the other man was. It wasn't the boy who had been with Michelle and Emmett. This man was middle-aged and with a sallow, pockmarked complexion.

"Emmett, this ain't Fox. It's a . . . a woman. It's a lady."

Emmett cupped his hands and face against the windshield so he could see inside my car, distorting his features as he did so. Shrinking back even further, I pressed my hands hard against the steering wheel as if that would create some invisible barrier between his looming presence and me. Only when he jumped back, cursing and yelling, did I realize I was hitting the horn. I jerked my hands off the wheel.

"Honest lady. We didn't mean to scare you," the older man yelled. "Open the window." He was making a wide rolling motion with his hand.

I cracked the window no more than an inch. He put his lips up to the opening. A burst of sour whiskey and cigarettes exploded with his words. "Honest. I'm real sorry. You OK? My buddy Emmett and me, we thought you was somebody else." He laughed a fake laugh. "We was just having a little fun. Guy thing, you know."

By now Emmett had joined him. "Why'd you have to lay on your horn like that for? Huh?"

"Hold up, Emmett. I'm sure she didn't mean to," he said.

I could feel the panic of the moment passing. I cracked the window a little more. For half a second I thought about apologizing for scaring him. Instead I said, "You guys scared the living crap out of me. My God, don't you know you could have killed me back there. I thought you wanted to *pass* me. Who'd you say you thought I was anyway?"

"Fox," the one blurted out before Emmett boxed him on the side of the head.

"Shut the crap up, Joe," Emmett mumbled between clinched teeth. "Nobody," he said to me. "Just some old guy we like to mess with. No harm intended, lady." Emmett made a half effort to tip the rim of his John Deere cap in my direction.

Fox. I'd heard right the first time. I did my best to laugh like I didn't think any harm had been intended, and they turned to leave.

"Did you hurt yourself when you kicked my car?" I called after them.

"Huh?" Joe turned and stopped.

Emmett shook his head and kept walking back to the truck.

"Him. Your buddy, Emmett. He kicked my car door," I said. "Did he break his toe? Dent my car?"

"Naw. Your car's not hurt. Them Germans, they built these old Mercedes like they built their panzers. That's what started it. Your car's just like the one—" Joe stopped. "Yeah, it sure looks like our buddy's. Most Mercedes in these parts is *new*. Say, you live around here? Wouldn't want to make the same mistake twice."

"Just passing through." I shook my head and heaved a heavy sigh. With genuine feeling I said, "Trust me, I can't say I'd want to run into you guys again. But hey, before you go . . . I think you owe me something."

I saw Joe reach into his jeans pocket. "How about helping me out after scaring me to death. Is this the way to Orange and on up to Culpepper?" I purposely made it sound like I was heading somewhere else.

"No, ma'am," Joe said. "Orange is back that a way." He swayed slightly as he pointed with his thumb over his shoulder. "Going straight down this road will end you up in Uno and carry you on to Rochelle. You need to turn around and go for, about, oh, I dun't know . . . two, three miles. When you come to the V in the road, go left. Pretty soon you'll see a sign pointing you toward the highway. Once you get on it there's signs into Orange." He paused and scratched his head. "Hell, you *are* lost, lady."

Slapping the side of his thigh, laughing and coughing, he said, "Maybe it's a good thing we stopped you, otherwise you'd of ended up down in one of them hollows with the wild dogs and black bears."

I didn't say a thing.

Chapter 27

Dear Antiques Expert: My grandmother always raved about her John Belter slipper chair. To me it's just an uncomfortable low chair. Is it tremendously valuable?

John Henry Belter, a 19th-century New York furniture maker, is well known for his high-style laminated and carved rosewood furniture. Belter's pieces are included in many museum collections of American furniture makers, and fine examples of his craftsmanship have sold in the mid-five-figure range. But unlike a sofa or armchair, a slipper chair's low seat limits its use and desirability and thus its value. I'd estimate that a documented Belter slipper chair could be expected to sell for six to eight thousand dollars at auction.

I HADN'T THE VAGUEST idea how I got back to Belle Ayre. I hardly knew I was there until I cut the car's motor. That's when I realized my fingers had clutched the steering wheel, hanging on for dear life. I sat frozen, thinking, trying to forget what had happened. But my mind wouldn't let go of the fear I had felt. Not one car had passed while I'd been waylaid by those guys, and I must have driven another two or three miles before house lights came into view.

It took raw determination to drag my body up the long flight of stairs to my room. With every step another what-if scenario popped into my head—each more troubling and disturbing than the last.

Inside my room, I reached beneath the mattress until my fingers touched the spine of the book I'd hidden there. I slid it out and began to read again the pages I had tagged with Post-its—those pages having Hoyt's notes on them. It was as I had remembered. The dates he had penciled and inked in were all in the early and mid-1950s.

I dug through the stash of papers I had taken from the attic until I found the haunting announcement Mazie had written of her own death. 1955. I took it and the appraisal book over to the slipper chair by the fireplace, but it was next to impossible to hold anything in my lap the way my legs slanted downward. I moved to the bed, and settled in between the piles I had stacked there. Despite my resolve to forge ahead, a wave of tiredness swept over me. Maybe it was too late at night for deciphering scribbled notes or trying to match the items in the appraisal book with their original receipts. But there were the photos. Now that was manageable.

Photo after photo chronicled Mazie and Hoyt's lives through the places they had visited and the things they had done in the 1920s and '30s—elephant rides in Nepal, skiing in Saint Moritz, wild game hunting in Africa, visiting the Amazon, on and on. It was like flipping through an old travel magazine. After that were several pictures of Wynderly. Someone had dated each picture in the sort of precise hand people used to have and arranged them in chronological order, as if planning to put them into a scrapbook or photograph album.

I smiled to myself. I wondered if Mazie had done this as part of her vow to herself to get better organized.

The first few pictures progressed from Wynderly's ground-breaking to its completion—1922 to 1924. These were followed by photographs of the house's various gardens in their differing stages of completion. Finally, there was a group of interior shots held together by a rusty paperclip.

Looking closely, I recognized the arched doorway and steps leading into the drawing room, but other than that . . .

I looked again. The chandelier was the same, but there was no Venetian mirror. The furniture, rather than being in the European taste, was distinctly fine eighteenth-century American furniture. The same beautiful silver accessories that had caught my eye that first day were present, but so were Chinese Export porcelain bowls and teapots, the sort that affluent colonists bought from eighteenth-century seagoing merchants when they returned from the Orient. None of these furnishings were there now. Had I not known I was looking at Wynderly's drawing room, I might have thought the picture was of Tracy DuMont's living room. These must be the items that Tracy's father mentioned being at Wynderly some fifty years earlier. Though lovely, they definitely were not the ones I had seen in Mazie's secret room.

I turned the photograph over. There, in a hand I had come to recognize as Mazie's, was written "Wynderly, June, 1932."

I put that picture to the side, then tugged a second photo loose from the clip. This was of one of the bedrooms, but which one? I'd not seen one with lovely American Federal pieces—a canopy bed, cherry chest of drawers, brass inlaid work table, and convex mirror. Some architectural detail, a mantelpiece or arrangement of the windows, would identify the room. But I couldn't do it from the quick walk-through I'd had of the house.

The quality of the antiques was unquestionable. I moved the piles to make a new space for the photos when an envelope caught my eye. It was yellow, the sort that photographs and negatives used to come back from the developer in. I placed it in the picture pile, but on second thought decided to take a quick peek. Here were pictures that had been taken in the late 1940s or '50s. I could pick out the occasional American antique, but mostly the rooms were now furnished with much fancier, showier pieces from abroad. I felt as if I had finally found the pieces needed to finish a huge jigsaw puzzle. I was getting closer, but I still had to fit them all together to see the big picture.

"Too many secrets. Too many lies to live," Miss Mary Sophie had said.

"Hoyt and Mazie lived for their showplace. Their obsession. Their baronial playhouse," Worth Merritt had told me over dinner.

And Fred Graham, what had he said? "The only way I got the funds last time was because of all the trusts Hoyt Wyndfield established at the bank way back in the twenties and thirties. If the trust department wasn't still administering those accounts, Wynderly wouldn't have gotten one red cent from the bank."

And Mazie. She had wanted "To be a lady from Virginia." She'd also been frustrated: "Why Hoyt wants to turn his back on his Virginia ways is beyond me. I love Wynderly, but not for its showiness and flamboyance, because *that* is what it is, a place to show off where we've been and what we've bought. I love Wynderly because it is our *home* and Hoyt loves it so."

Hoyt's was the absent voice. Then again, the notations he had written in the appraisal book—didn't they say it all? The receipts for the fakes . . . The letter from Kyoto . . .

That was it. Pure and simple. Worth Merritt had said it, as had Tracy's father: thieving blood had run in Hoyt's veins.

Thieving? Oh my God. Matt was coming tomorrow. I still didn't have a clue how the things from Wynderly had been stolen. But that wasn't what I'd been hired to do. Still, I had hoped to have answers.

Why hadn't Matt called tonight the way he had said he would? Then again, maybe he had. If he'd called, surely a note would have been slipped under my door. Nothing was there. Surely he wouldn't call now, not at midnight.

And Peter. How had we resolved *his* trip? I couldn't remember.

I went to bed without so much as brushing my teeth. I might as well have taken the time to do it, though, for once my head hit the pillow I was fully awake. No telling how long I tossed and turned, and once I did drift off, my dreams were as unsettling as my wide-awake thoughts had been.

BACK IN LEEMONT there's a town character known as Bagman. He's perfectly harmless, but people cross the street to avoid his bare feet and burlap bag. It's the bag that frightens them. Rumors have it that he's toting around everything from Confederate gold to homemade bombs.

Over time Peter has gotten to know Bagman, as you would

expect when a retired priest is doing good deeds. Which is how I know that Bagman carries nothing more than a couple of cans of tuna or beanie-weenies and whatever book he's reading. Sustenance for the body and the mind, he says. And invariably, when I'm in the middle of an appraisal and stumped, Bagman romps through my dreams.

When I finally drifted off, I dreamed I was a prisoner in the priest hole, rather much like the mad wife in *Jane Eyre*. But Bagman wasn't Rochester. Bagman was a thief who would bring me treasures for safekeeping. Soon the priest hole was piled to the ceiling with the pieces I had seen in the interior photographs from Wynderly's early days—the beautiful worktable, a banquet-size Federal dining table set, a bow-front cherry chest of drawers, chairs of every style and period.

In my dream, Bagman stuffed the furniture into his bag, then loaded it in the back of a pickup truck. He then drove the truck several flights up to the attic the way actors used to drive cars up and down steps in old silent movies. To make space for the new load, I dragged chairs and tables over to the wall leading to the secret room off the priest hole. Before I could push on it, though, Michelle would swing the wall open. There I'd be greeted by barking English spaniels. But when Michelle would tell them to sit, they'd hop up on the shelves and become figurines.

While Michelle stood by, I heaved furniture out the window to Frederick Graham, but instead of arms he had vulture-like wings. Once, while tossing out a huge four-poster bed, I overthrew the mark. Graham chased after it and disappeared into Mazie's maze, but Peggy Powers appeared, flapped her wings, soared into the air, and caught it. At least I think that's who it was. I never saw her face, but she was decked out in heavy gold jewelry.

Like most dreams, mine made no sense whatsoever.

Like most dreams, it made perfect sense.

Chapter 28

Dear Antiques Expert: I recently attended a large antiques show and was particularly attracted to one dealer's display of majolica. When I looked the term up on the Internet there were so many definitions of it I became confused. Can you give me a simple definition?

Those definitions can be confusing indeed. But generally when people speak of "majolica" they are referring to the 19th- and early 20th-century colorful tin-glazed earthenware made in Italy, Spain, England, and America. This type of majolica is highly recognizable by its raised decoration, with fruits, vegetables, flowers, and sea life being particularly popular motifs. Majolica kitchenwares included pitchers, oyster plates, sardine boxes, covered cheese dishes, and biscotti jars. No fashionable Victorian home was complete without some majolica and originally it was very affordable. Today rare majolica pieces can sell for thousands of dollars and even the more usual piece can cost hundreds.

IT'S NO WONDER I awakened long before I would have liked to. I sat up in bed. What now? With an hour or so to spare before having to get ready to go to Wynderly, once again I stacked some of the purloined books on the bed. I reached for Mazie's diary from the twenties. If I could only find some documentation telling exactly when the transition of Wynderly's furnishings had begun.

Reading the entries before, I hadn't paid much attention to where Mazie had been while writing them. There was the one written at Wynderly when Hoyt was away. I thumbed through the pages. Again, luck was with me, or perhaps Mazie was willing it to be, but I quickly found it—1926. Turning several pages over I read, "Spring, 1927. Kyoto."

That was the place where Hoyt had purchased the Lokesvara figures. I marked the page, scrambled out of bed, found Kirklander's appraisal, and the letter from Mr. P. Yas ka, the one where he had apologized for the delay in filling Hoyt's order. It was dated 1928, not too long after their visit. I turned back to Mazie's diary.

April 9, 1927. We took rickshaws for sightseeing. The cherry blossoms are exquisite! Imagine being in Japan when the cherry blossoms are blooming. Hoyt thinks of everything. And the temples and shrines! They are everywhere. Today we even saw a shrine to the god of the silkworms. How busy those silkworms must be, too, for the kimonos are beautiful. Hoyt tells me the finest ones are made for the geishas. Tomorrow we will go to the ancient palace of the emperors, then shopping and to Mr. Yasaka's house. I can't wait. I know his home will be very beautiful and have a garden. Everything is light and airy in Kyoto—like the cherry blossoms themselves— so very different from Wynderly with its tall towers and dark paneling.

Hoyt has already met with Mr. Yasaka, both yesterday and today. When he comes back from these meetings he is like a kid, all excited and happy. He tells me he has found a treasure trove and we will soon be even richer. I don't dare interfere with his business dealings. He loves to tell me all about them, but then turns impatient and agitated if I ask him questions so I leave it at that.

What I needed now was a volume from the 1930s or '40s—something with a specific mention of what happened to the furniture that had been removed. A postcard stuck out from the pages of one volume.

Your shipments from Japan and Brazil have arrived and been forwarded on to Richmond. Because of the holidays you may wish to have your agent collect these. Otherwise it will be after the New Year before we can forward them on to your residence at Orange via the Chesapeake & Ohio RR. Mr. Elliott is expecting to hear from you. They are stored at the Bonded Warehouse in the usual place. James B. Heyward, Customs Broker.

It was stamped December 12, 1955. There was that year again.

I opened the diary to the page where the postcard had been inserted.

December 15, 1955. Why, why did I do it? I know why. I thought I would surprise Hoyt. Instead I have ruined my life. Not that I haven't suspected something for years and years, but suspecting and knowing are two different things. Now it has all come clear to me. What Hoyt has done is wrong. Could

*I have stopped him? I don't know. It isn't as if we needed the
money . . . at least I don't think we did. But even if we had, to
have cheated other people . . . to have lied and deceived them.
Why, why did he do it? Would he say he did it for me? I never
wanted all the things . . . HE was the one who was obsessed
with them. But he told people I had fancy tastes and I let him.
I stood by and let him have his way. That's what made him
happy. Oh, why did I? Why did I?*

The question mark and last words were smeared, undoubtedly from Mazie's tears. It was easy to picture Mazie hidden
away in the attic with no one to confide in. "I only wanted to
surprise him," she had written, repeating herself in her outpourings, the way we do when trying to explain or rationalize
our actions.

*Hoyt won't be back from Atlanta until the 20th. I had thought
to myself how wonderful to have his packages waiting for
him. And then . . . Oh why didn't the notice say that the packages were damaged? If I hadn't had to sign the insurance papers and verify the damage! To have to stand there to claim
them when I realized what they were. I thought I was going to
die. When I saw those Tang horses from Japan I felt sick. But
it was the dogs. All those horrid Staffordshire dogs. It was
when I saw their beady little black eyes staring at me that I
knew something was wrong. Really wrong. Hoyt would never
have bought dogs knowing how frightened I am of them. It
was as if my heart stopped beating. And the men were so nice.
They didn't know. Now what am I to do?*

*I am worn out from thinking and worrying. I can do only
one thing. Ask for guidance. I will do what I have done so*

*many times. I will pray to the Blessed Mother. Forgive us all
that is past.*

There her entry stopped. I could envision Mazie going into
the priest hole to pray. My own hand was trembling as I replaced the postcard and put the book down.

Hoyt had long ago learned about importing goods from his
ventures in the tobacco market with his cousin. As rich Americans, they had had access to every aspect of foreign trade. Between Hoyt's love for things and contacts in places like Kyoto,
having little objects like the bronze figures and pottery horses
made and shipped to him was simple. With Hoyt's aristocratic
background and gentlemanly ways, selling them as precious
antiquities was equally simple. Some antiques dealers have
long been notorious for selling fake wares to overly eager, un-
knowing clients. Undoubtedly Hoyt dealt with dealers, indi-
viduals, anyone whose money was real, and whose knowledge
was slim.

As for the furniture he was having copied, European things
were extremely fashionable between the wars. Newly rich
Americans had traveled abroad and wanted the pieces they
had seen in stately homes and palaces for themselves. As early
as 1931, Herbert Cescinsky had warned his readers that more
"antique" furniture existed than could ever have been made.
In *The Gentle Art of Faking Furniture* he had written that
eighteenth-century English furniture alone "has equipped
most of the millionaires' houses and apartments from New
York to the Pacific Coast, to say nothing of the huge stocks
in the hands of American dealers and department stores . . . .

What has been left has to be divided into what remains *in situ* and the residue left to reinforce English dealers' stocks."

With Hoyt's international connections he could buy well-crafted fakes and easily pass them off to the gullible public as genuine—making a pretty penny along the way. Or, as in the instance of the giltwood table, have a masterful fake of the real thing made here, sell the valuable piece, pocket the money and pass the bogus one off at Wynderly as an original antique. It would have been his own private joke.

Mazie seemed so pliable, so willing to please her husband, Hoyt only had to say that he had found something he liked better and move an old piece out. Who knows, he might have said he was just changing things around, putting some piece up in the attic, or bringing one down. With so much stuff crammed up there . . .

But the Staffordshire dogs . . . and coming from Brazil? There I was stumped.

Lots of fakes and scammers have come out of South America, including Eduardo de Valfierno who had arranged back in 1911 for the *Mona Lisa* to be stolen so he could sell forgeries of da Vinci's masterpiece. Talk about a notorious scheme. But de Valfierno stood to make a fortune—several times over. Prissy little Staffordshire dogs? That was a different matter altogether.

There was no money to be made from selling Staffordshire dogs in the United States. You could buy them by the container load in England for only a few pounds each in the 1950s. What was I missing?

I went to the drawer and retrieved the dog I had taken from

the attic. I turned it over and over in my hands looking for something about it that would be wrong. It wasn't a fake, I was sure of that. It had all the earmarks of dating from around 1850 or 1860. The coloring was right: the hand-painted patches of the dog's coat were orangey red, not crimson like so many of the repros, and the gold was muted and only on the dog's chain and padlock. That passed muster. Shiny gold is a telltale sign of the fakes made in Czechoslovakia and Japan.

I placed the dog on the chest and stared at him. It made no sense. English Staffordshire pooches weren't even on the Brazilian radar screen, not in that land of bossa novas and sun-kissed beaches. How had they gotten there in the first place?

I had read about how families who had fled Europe and England during the world wars and landed in Brazil and Argentina had taken with them only what they could.

How many times when making an appraisal had I been shown a fragile piece of porcelain, only to be told the same story by some dear old lady. The piece of Meissen or Wedgwood or other treasured china had traveled across the ocean with her grandparents or great-grandparents to their new country. And always the teapot or figurine, or whatever it was, held more than memories of the home and life left behind. It was a symbol of hope, the fulfillment of dreams. If something as fragile as the china could arrive safely, so could they.

I'd seen museum-quality pieces of majolica and Wedgwood and other European and British porcelains in the antiques shops in Rio. Where you find majolica and Wedgwood, you will find Staffordshire. That took care of how the Staffordshire dogs would have ended up in Brazil. But why ship a box of nineteenth-century Staffordshire dogs from Brazil to America?

It wasn't as if every magazine was featuring Staffordshire figures as a must-have accessory. Then again, a pair of spaniels, or "flatbacks" as they were often called, since they sat flat against the chimney wall, would look nice on the mantel. They did have cute little faces and floppy ears and rounded fronts and— Rounded fronts. Ah . . .

The winter morning sun beginning to trickle in through the window was considerably brighter than that of the bedside lamp. I smiled. For the first day since my arrival, it promised to be a bright sunny day. I took that as a good omen.

"Come on, pooch," I said and made a beeline over to the window where I could get a better look at him.

When my eyes couldn't detect anything wrong, I did what good appraisers learn to do early in their careers. I ran my fingertips over every inch of the dog, from his head to his toes to the tip of his tail wrapped around his hindquarters, feeling for any sort of irregularity—the slightest difference in hardness, a crack in the finish, a variation in how the surface felt—that would indicate some sort of repair. My fingers slid along until I came to the area where the spaniel was seated on the raised base. As my fingernail snagged on the tiniest indentation I paused. And then I felt a barely perceptible difference in texture.

I got out my magnifying glass. I could see the variation of the porcelain finish. No wonder I hadn't seen it: it was on the back of the figure and no larger than an inch square. But magnified, it was as clear as the day breaking outside. The porcelain surrounding that spot was a rich white, made even whiter with the sun shining on it. The small, repaired surface had an ivory tinge and a dull finish. The naked eye would never have picked up the difference, especially if you weren't looking for it. But once detected, it couldn't be missed. Now I knew exactly what *else* to look for.

I held the dog in one hand. Did it feel a little heavy—or was that my imagination? I held it up to my ear and shook it. I couldn't hear or feel anything moving around inside. I turned the figure upside down. In the base was a tiny hole no larger than a ten-penny nail head, further evidence of the figure's mid-nineteenth-century age; without a small space for air and gas to escape during the firing process, the figure would have broken.

I laid the dog down on the bed while I searched for some small object to stick into the hole. A simple straight pin or needle, even a safety pin, would do, but it wasn't an item I usually kept with me. The bathroom. There, on the radiator cover, along with the tissues and toiletries was a mending kit.

Holding the spaniel in one hand, I inserted a needle into the hole. The tip went no deeper than half an inch before hitting something soft. I could feel it giving, but not much.

The dog wasn't mine. I had stolen it. Did anyone know the Staffordshire figures existed? Would anyone ever miss one—that is if the other Staffordshire dogs were ever discovered. Surely eventually they would be. In fact, I probably would end up telling someone about the whole room, but would anyone suspect that I'd taken one of the dogs?

I stared long and hard at the spaniel. Chances were it would never be missed. But if I found something hidden inside, and it held the key to this puzzle, then how would I explain that I knew about it?

The harder my mind worked, the more tangled my thoughts became. One thing I *was* sure of, though. I was in too deep to turn back.

I picked up the spaniel in one hand and one of my shoes in the other. I walked back into the bathroom, placed a towel in the sink, laid the figure on the towel, covered it with the washcloth, and in one swift blow with my shoe, broke the dog open.

When I lifted the washcloth, the towel was covered in red.

Chapter 29

Dear Antiques Expert: I've found a platter I like, but it is marked "as is." How do I decide if it is a good buy?

Begin by asking why you want the piece: for investment, to use, or to enjoy looking at. If for investment, remember, serious collectors seek items in perfect condition, though a truly rare piece may be bought if damaged or repaired. If you plan to use the platter, ask if its condition will affect its use. If for display, can the damage be hidden? I suggest you find out what pieces like, or similar to this one, are selling for in perfect condition. Knowing that, and how you will use it, you can then make a wise decision.

MY MARRIAGE TO Hank Glass might have ended, but I owed him a lot. When we'd been in England some years back he had wanted to buy me a lovely ruby and diamond ring. I had liked a sapphire pin better. We had chatted on and on about them . . . which one I'd wear more, which one was the better buy, which one was prettier. Finally the saleswoman, whether being helpful or just trying to move on, pulled us aside. "About the ring," she had said in her British way. What came next was a lesson on rubies I'd never forgotten.

From inside the case she took out a whole tray of what I would have said were ruby and diamond rings. "Aren't they pretty? Stunning, actually. Sophisticated. Pure Art Deco. They loved rubies in the 1930s and '40s," she said while removing one and putting it on her finger. "Everyone wanted them back then." Moving her hand back and forth so the oval-cut center stone caught the light she said, "See the deep, almost fiery pigeon blood red color."

She had our attention for sure. Then, watching us she said, "Rubellite. That's right. Rubellite. Pretty as a ruby. It would fool anyone except an expert. And the diamonds—"

Once again she turned her hand until the diamonds encircling the rubellite sparkled brightly. "Not only do the diamonds make it glisten all the more, they, well, let's say they give the"—she paused, no doubt to avoid calling it a ruby—"the center stone *credence*. With all those beautiful diamonds, the usual customer presumes it's a—" She ended her sentence with a smile.

"So, where do rubellites come from?" Hank asked.

"Brazil. A gemologist would explain that rubellites are really a variety of tourmaline. But few women care. It's the look, the romance. To be fair, most men don't bother to ask either." She smiled at Hank. "*You* hadn't. If you had asked about the center stone, I could easily have told you it was a Brazilian ruby without blinking an eye."

She glanced around to ensure our privacy. "That's what many people call them, even some salespeople. *Brazilian ruby.*

It's rather like an inside joke. There are very few rubies found in Brazil." Then she said, "Yet, I've seen several 'ruby' rings . . ."

She didn't have to say another thing. Hank bought the pin. Now I remembered that ring.

I put the remnants of the dog to one side and moved the stones on the towel around with my fingers. That many red stones that color and that large? And these were in only one dog. If all the dogs I'd left untouched on those shelves concealed rubies of this size and brilliance . . . No. That just wouldn't be possible. But *rubellites,* that was a different story.

Hoyt and his cousin's tobacco business had taken them to Brazil. Mazie had mentioned their trips there. From the notations in the appraisal book I had proof that Hoyt ordered counterfeit antiques and antiquities and sold them as the real things. So how did gem trafficking fit into the picture?

I stopped dead in my tracks. That reference in Mazie's diary to, oh, what was his name? The one who had found a gemstone mine. Felipe. How on earth had I remembered that, I wondered. I thought hard, trying to remember what she had written. From what I could recall, Hoyt had known him for a long time. It was totally possible that Hoyt had bought stones from him.

I put myself into Hoyt's mind, which I now knew was the mind of a gamesman and a crook—a gentleman rogue. What could be more of a challenge than to figure out how to smuggle large quantities of gemstones out of Brazil and into America? Add in the rush that comes with the risk . . .

My mind bounced back and forth between Felipe and the saleslady in the English jewelry store. Using the Staffordshire spaniels as the vessels to carry them in had been a brilliant idea. Hoyt would have bought the figures in a secondhand shop for a pittance after they'd been cast off by some of the immigrant families who had moved to Brazil in the early twentieth century.

Brazilian customs officers wouldn't have had any interest in a box of figurines described as "ornamental pottery dogs, circa 1850–60; country of origin, England" leaving the country. Brazilians have never paid a lot of attention to their *own* national heritage, let alone another county's.

On one of my trips to Rio de Janeiro, when I asked Francisco, my driver, to take me to a museum that I'd carefully researched, he had said, "Who needs a museum? We Brazilians have no memory. *We* live for today." I had insisted, only to find it was closed. "Gone to the beach," the note tacked to the door read. With that, we had headed for Ipanema.

If Rio's customs people had even bothered to look at the figurines they would undoubtedly have thought they were ghastly. Yes, using the Staffordshire spaniels to smuggle stones out of the country was brilliant. Or it *would* have been if the stones had been rubies. But why go to the trouble to smuggle out something that wasn't so valuable? The export duty couldn't have cost that much, not in those days.

Then again, exporting a few stones was one thing. Exporting them in quantity might have posed problems. Or perhaps bringing them into the U.S. was the problem. Who knew? I'd have to check with someone who knew more about customs laws than I did. And what would Hoyt do with the stones once he got them here? I was stumped.

I stopped my pacing and sat down on the bed. I stared at the diaries and papers and photographs as if the answer would pop out at me. "What did he do, Mazie?" I said aloud.

Mazie. That was it. Dear, innocent Mazie had written how they would go to New York or London after returning from Brazil. She had wanted to go shopping at Tiffany and Asprey. Instead, Hoyt would bring her a present from "where there were better deals," as she had put it.

That had to be it. Bringing Staffordshire figures into the U.S. wouldn't have posed any problem, and taking them back to England, where they were prized, was a perfect cover. By hiding the rubelittes inside the dogs, no one could trace how the stones had gotten into either country once they were in the hands of unscrupulous gem dealers who then passed them off as rubies either on the legitimate or black market.

It was all coming together in my mind. Gem smuggling had been a big deal back in those days, the old black and white movies testified to that. The scheme fit right in with Hoyt Wyndfield's thrill of living on the edge. Though he probably got a cut from the sale of the stones, so what if someone else was making the really big bucks off the deal? Hoyt was having fun.

My imagination went wild. And if some truly valuable stones were in the mix—diamonds, emeralds, sapphires . . . After all, I'd taken only the one dog.

But how had Hoyt gotten the stones *inside* the Staffordshire figurines? Ironically, that was the easy part.

The dogs had been molded in two parts—a front and a back. These parts had then been stuck together when the clay was fired, which meant the two sides could also be separated. It took only a careful sharp whack with a punch tool that fit into the figure's base for the front and the back to separate. The stones, wrapped in cotton, could then be stuffed into the cavity between the two parts, and the dog glued back together.

Even if the base had splintered in the process, or a section of the figure had cracked away, a good restorer could repair it with glue, plaster of paris, and a little enamel that only an expert would detect. Who would be looking for repairs anyway? Not the customs or import people. The figures would be closely examined only if they were going to be sold in a high-end antiques shop or auction, and these plentiful and inexpensive dogs would never have reached that market.

It all made perfect sense, at least to me. But I had no *proof* of Hoyt's intentions or actions. I thought of who might possibly help me out. Of all the people I had met, Miss Mary Sophie was the only one who had seemed to really know the Wyndfields.

I returned to the bathroom, carefully folded the towel around the stones and glanced at the clock. Where had the time gone? I had been so preoccupied that it wasn't until I was in the shower that I remembered that Matt was coming.

Downstairs I had a quick bite, all the while thinking how to arrange the day so I could somehow get back into the attic and work in a visit to Miss Mary Sophie. I would have been happy to spend the day holed up at Belle Ayre reading and sorting through the pictures and papers and books. I probably could have justified doing it—after all the insurance settlement would be based on the true value of the items. Chances were, Babson and Michael wasn't going to have to pay tens of thousands of dollars for the bronze figure of Lokesvara. The one Michelle had brought to me was heavy, the way bronze should be, though, as I had told her, it would take an antiquities expert to know for sure. Yet, I felt reasonably sure that the one left behind was the real figure, and the stolen one was the tourist repro made of spelter, worth less than a hundred dollars.

The Delft charger was a different matter. It was worth far more than the two thousand cited on the most current appraisal. What I couldn't yet know was if all the values would even out in the long run.

I was pouring a second cup of tea when Ginny Kauffman burst into the room. "I'm so glad I caught you before you got away. You got a phone call last night, but it was late. You'd come in, but I thought you might have retired for the night. Anyway the caller, Matt . . . but you know his last name . . . said it wasn't urgent, and I'd already undressed." She pulled the chair across from me out, asked "May I?" and without waiting for an answer Ginny sat down and handed me a folded piece of paper.

"I gave him directions. He'll probably be here around four or five, depending on traffic and when he gets away." She began nervously fiddling with the place setting in front of her. "And well, I didn't want to pass on the other news to you, but it's probably better you hear it now."

I was much more interested in the message Matt had left. But the tone of her voice caught my attention.

"News?"

"Yes. It seems there was a rather bad wreck last night. Dr. Fox came to see you, so I know you know him. Anyway, it's really tragic. Despite these curvy dark roads, we haven't had a terrible wreck in a long time. I don't think he was drinking. Maybe he just fell asleep — "

"Frank Fox? In a wreck? He's all right isn't he?" I fought to control my voice and my thoughts.

She shook her head sadly. "Unfortunately . . ."

"He's not dead is he?" I blurted out before she could finish.

"No, but he was unconscious when he was taken to the hospital. The last I heard, it was touch and go."

Chapter 30

Dear Antiques Expert: I love the excitement of an auction. The trouble is, sometimes I get carried away when bidding. Recently I saw a piece in an antiques shop that was priced less than what I had paid for one very similar to it at an auction just a week before. What's your advice on how to keep from overbidding—other than not going to the auction?

You're not alone, even experienced auction goers can overbid. But here are some tips to help you bid "responsibly." First, attend the auction preview and inspect the pieces you're interested in for condition and quality and set your own price limit. Then, to better establish a reliable top price, visit antiques shops, check out price guides, even eBay auctions prior to the auction, to know what the pieces you're interested in are selling for. Third, learn who the dealers attending the auction are. A good "rule" is to go one bid above what a dealer will pay for something. Good luck!

IT'S A MIRACLE I didn't faint dead away. Instead, a cold calm came over me.

"What time was it?" I asked. "The wreck."

"It must have been sometime around ten? We got the call right after your friend called, so I'm sure you were already here. Dan's a volunteer fireman. That's how we knew. The call came in. But I said that, didn't I?" She tried to smile. "You didn't hear Dan leave? He tried to be quiet even though your room's on the other side of the house."

"Do they know what happened?" I asked, ignoring Ginny's nervous small talk.

"No, at least not yet. The Wilsons down the way were coming back from Charlottesville when they saw something burning, like a little brush fire. You know how bad our cell phone service is around here, so they stopped at the nearest house and called the fire department and then started calling all the volunteers around this area. Nobody knows exactly what happened and obviously Dr. Fox can't say anything."

"But surely somebody must have seen something," I said, despite my memories of nothing but black pavement stretching out in front of my headlights. "What about the police? Have they said anything?"

"I haven't heard a word," she said. "It barely made the newspaper. Dan said that it was way too dark to tell much last night even with the searchlights. Who knows? It could have been a deer bounding across the road. That happens all the time." She gave a helpless shrug. "I sure am glad you got back safely. You didn't stay at Wynderly *that* late did you? Were you able to get a nice dinner?"

I could tell she was trying her best to be nice. "Oh, everything was fine," I said.

"That's good. And your friend . . . He said he'd be staying the night."

Coming on the heels of the news of Frank Fox's accident, frankly I couldn't have cared less. My only thought was what *I* should do in light of the accident, and Matt wasn't the one to ask.

"Before I leave for Wynderly, I'm going to need to make some calls," I said, probably more abruptly than I should have. "Is that OK? I don't want to tie up your lines."

"No, go ahead," she said. "It'll be fine."

"And tell me, would you have Miss Mary Sophie McLeod's number, or know how I can get it? With her being a single lady, I'm not sure if it's listed."

"It's probably not in the phone book, but it'll be in the church directory," Ginny said, getting out of her chair. "I'll get it. And can I get you anything else? You've hardly touched your breakfast."

"No, thank you. I'm fine," I said. "Guess the news just took my appetite."

BACK IN MY ROOM I took a chance that Miss Mary Sophie would be up and called her first. She was having her hair done at ten thirty, but she would be home and have had lunch by one. Then I called Peter and told him what Tracy DuMont had said about the big boys coming down from New York for the auction. But my tone of voice must have given him a clue that more than that was on my mind.

"Sterling, is everything OK there?" he said.

My voice cracked and I broke into tears—something I never do. I walked Peter through what had happened, beginning with leaving Tracy's house and ending with what Ginny Kauffman had told me. "Oh Peter, this really isn't like me, but what *should* I do? Go to the police? Keep quiet? What if those men come looking for me? I know you have to get to work. I'm sorry. It's . . . it's just that I don't have anyone to turn to, anyone to advise me. I've never been in a situation like this." I made an attempt to laugh. "And I don't like it very much."

A silence followed. Then Peter laughed quietly. "Me either."

We both fell quiet. I spoke first.

"I've gone over and over it, as best I can. Ginny Kauffman said it might have been a deer. It could have been, don't you think?"

Peter's silence wasn't one bit reassuring.

"Or maybe Dr. Fox just ran off the road," I continued. "I almost did once on the way up here. It was foggy and the road's so curvy and if you so much as take your eyes off it . . . Or he could have fallen asleep," I said. "Or the guys who stopped me could have just . . ." My heart leapt into my throat.

"Look, you're absolutely right," Peter said. "It might have been any one of those possibilities. And as far as the guys who stopped you, maybe it *wasn't* them, Sterling. Maybe Fox was drinking. You don't know. He could have been on medication or drugs. You don't want to jump to hasty conclusions. I know you're concerned about the men, but you told them you were just driving through. They wouldn't know any differently. Besides, over the years I've learned that oftentimes what we *think* is the obvious answer—in this case that the same guys who stopped you ran Fox off the road—isn't necessarily the *right* answer. How much do you know about Fox anyway?"

"Not a lot, and what I do know is as much from what I've been told as from what I've observed. The one time I talked to him for any length I found him a little boorish and braggy, but he's not *that* bad. Mostly he was"—I looked for the right word—"overeager, like he was trying to be a big shot."

"Trust me," Peter said. "Until the cause of the accident is known and the police report comes out in the newspaper—"

"But don't you understand? That's why I'm so upset. Who knows *when* that'll be. And what if he *dies*? Oh Lord, why did I bring that up? Don't you think I should go to the police *now* and tell them about Emmett and the other man Joe, just in case?" The panic I'd fought hard to shake off was coming back with a vengeance. "Oh, I don't know what to do. What would *you* do?"

Peter's voice was calm and firm. "For now Sterling, don't do anything, not until I can get there. What I advise you to do is to go back to Wynderly. Isn't there's something you can do there that would be productive? At least that way you can get your mind on something else. That's going to do you more good than anything else at the moment."

"Oh, but Peter, you don't have to come."

"Look, I was planning on coming to the auction on Saturday anyway. LaTisha works today. She's completely capable of running the shop. What I'll do is drop by the store, tell her I'm taking the day off, then I'll head on over your way. Anyway I'd like to see Wynderly after hearing so much about it. This might be my only chance."

"Well, that's true," I agreed.

"I know you're worried, Sterling, and it's admirable that you're concerned about doing the right thing. But from what you've told me, I can honestly say I don't know *what* the right thing is. If Fox really did hit a deer, let's say, or if it was a freak accident and there's no evidence of foul play, then the last thing you'd want is to be needlessly drawn into the incident. Once you start implicating other people, no telling what might happen, especially if they're innocent. Accusations, lawsuits."

"Oh my God, I never thought of that."

"So. What you should do right now is continue your life as best you can for the next few hours. It's what, about nine o'clock. I should get there by, oh, two or three. Maybe later."

"That's when I'm going to meet Miss Mary Sophie about—but that's *another* story, and now's not the time to go into all that. Thing is, I don't know how long I'll be with her."

"Don't worry about that. I'll get away from here when I can. Can you make a reservation for me at Belle Ayre or should I call them?"

"I'll do it . . . No, wait, you'd better do it," I said. "They've been pretty empty, except for me, all week. But on a weekend they may fill up. If so, Ginny, she's the owner, can tell you where else to call. But honest, Peter. Don't rush. I don't have any idea what time I'll get free this afternoon and I've papers to get ready for M—"

That's when it hit me. Peter. Matt. And me. We three. All here together.

Chapter 31

Dear Antiques Expert: Could you tell me the name of the Russian antique I keep seeing at antiques shows? It is usually boat- or saucer-shaped and has a curved-under handle. It looks as if it might have been a sauceboat or even ladle of some kind.

What you have seen is a kovsh. Originally, these ancient Russian vessels were made to hold a mild alcoholic drink. During the 19th century, its attractive form was much admired and many kovsh were made as purely decorative pieces intended to be admired for their beauty and craftsmanship. Even Fabergé made beautiful silver-gilt enameled and jeweled kovsh. But a word of caution: many lesser craftsmen also made souvenir-quality kovsh, and fake kovsh with bogus hallmarks have been identified.

THOUGH TEMPTED, I REFRAINED from asking Ginny where the wreck had happened. If I came upon the site on my way to Wynderly, so be it, but at the moment I wanted to distance myself as far from what had happened as possible. Peter had said not to worry, but in truth, he had frightened, rather than comforted, me. Telling me to do nothing, though, had made a lot of sense. My intention was to make myself invisible. There was no way I was going to chance running into Emmett and his buddy by stopping to get gas or a Diet Pepsi. And once I got to Wynderly, if anything was said about the incident, or Frank Fox for that matter, I would listen. But I was not going to volunteer anything to anyone.

It was a little before ten when I turned onto the grounds at Wynderly. As usual Michelle was running late. I needed to calm down. I decided to take a stroll around the gardens, flawed though they were. Michelle would find me soon enough.

I passed a pair of stone columns beginning to crumble beneath the English ivy and Virginia creeper coiled snake-like around them. Following an overgrown path I came upon an opening where only half an iron gate still clung to its post. Beyond that was a small flagstone patio far enough away from the house to be totally private. It must have been lovely once upon a time.

I looked across the distant fields, then turned back toward Wynderly just as a splash of reddish orange light burst along the bottom ledge of one of the towers. It was only the sunlight shining on a strip of guttering. I was thinking how the sunshine was helping to improve my mood when I realized— That's odd. Copper oxidizes to a lovely gray-green almost instantly once it is exposed to the elements, and on a house of Wynderly's age, for copper to be that bright and shiny, it would have to be brand new. Now *that* didn't make any sense.

I shaded my eyes and looked at the sun to get my bearings. I was on the northeast side. The front of the house faced west. With Wynderly's many towers and turrets and zigzagging rooflines, I had no way of knowing where the room off the priest hole might be.

Damn. If only I had my camera. But it was in the briefcase in my car, I was pretty sure. To be positive, though, I double-checked my pocketbook, pulling out my wallet and cell phone, which hadn't done me one bit of good this entire trip. Which made me realize I could take a picture with my phone. I'd only done it once or twice before. I turned it on and snapped away.

Feeling quite proud of myself, I paused for one last look before starting back toward the house. Climbing up there to work on that roof was not a job for me. I felt dizzy just thinking about it. Yes, I sure was glad *I* didn't have to crawl along that passageway between the attic windows and the outer ledge of the roof. It was probably only a couple of feet wide. Couldn't have a fat roofer or gutter repairman working up there.

I chuckled to myself. That had been some dream I'd had last night or this morning, whenever it was. Hauling furniture across the room and tossing it out the window the way I had done in my dream? You couldn't heave anything of size through those narrow casement windows.

That's when sweat erupted on my palms and my legs went tingly. With every step my brain turned over bits of information about the objects, those stolen and those broken.

All the broken pieces had been very delicate—pieces like that Delft plate. And there had been the other porcelain pieces, an ivory figurine or two, and a beautiful engraved glass trumpet-shaped vase, now nothing but splinters of glass. On the other hand, the pieces listed as stolen had been bronze and silver and brass and a couple of small, very fine silk prayer rugs. Why hadn't I realized this before?

In my mind's eye I raced down the list of missing items. There was the fake bronze figure of Lokesvara, of course, and a circa 1850 Kyoto pierced bronze flower vase. I was naturally skittish of anything listed as Kyoto. I had figured it to be worth around three thousand if it was the real McCoy, but even if it wasn't, an attractive flower vase like that would still have a decorative value of about a thousand. I would let Matt fret over that one.

And then there was a late nineteenth-century Russian silver and enamel kovsh. It was surely worth five thousand, but maybe seven or eight or more. I'd noted it needed more research. Among the other missing silver items, two particularly valuable ones were an American coin silver teapot made in the early or mid-seventeen hundreds, and a heavily embossed English sterling silver sugar bowl dating from the 1830s.

Yes, every one of the items that had actually left the premises in the theft had been sufficiently durable to survive intact if handled reasonably well (or dropped), whereas the objects that had been broken and left in the house were all fragile—items that would have required extremely careful handling to avoid being broken or damaged.

I had followed a pebbled path back to Wynderly, straight up to a terrace with French doors that led into the house itself. I peered through the lace curtains. As best I could tell, it was Mazie's bedroom. Then going over to the edge of the doorframe, I ran my hands across the bricks.

Years back, after an out-of-town soccer game, Hank and I, our son Ketch and a couple of his friends, had stopped for lunch at an old stone mill that had been converted into a lunch-room. After lunch, the boys had run ahead and gone outside. They were probably twelve or thirteen, so we weren't worried that they would career down the rocky drop-off behind the restaurant. What we weren't prepared for, though, was finding those rascals on top of the roof when we came out. They had climbed up the side of the old stone building the same way climbers scale mountains and cliffs. Using the stones that jutted out from the craggy building as steps, those wiry kids had shinnied right up the wall. Of course getting down was more difficult.

Wynderly's irregularly laid clinker bricks would have been easy to scale; the very feature that made Wynderly's brickwork so handsome was its undoing. A willowy kid with a small foot could shinny up those bricks in nothing flat. But all the way to the ledge along the roofline? Now that was questionable. Also how could something be dropped from so high a distance, even when securely tied to a rope, without it swinging loose and banging against the building, or landing too hard and breaking?

But what if someone brave enough to go out on the ledge could ease a package down a story or so? Especially if, at that point, someone who had climbed midway up the wall could intercept the bundle, or even guide it safely down to the ground for a soft landing. The old cat burglar trick.

Still, there was the matter of the items that had been broken and left inside the house. Perhaps an attempt to throw everyone off, that's pretty commonplace. Or vandalism born of meanness. Red herring or pure meanness—thieves had been known to do both.

Then again, what if the burglars had *tried* to lower down a couple of plates or bowls or whatever, only to have them caught by a stiff breeze or simply break on impact. Though they would have wrapped the goods before dropping them, it would have taken much longer to carefully pack a piece of china than a piece of bronze or brass. Time might have been of the essence.

But suppose a piece of hastily wrapped china had broken when it was being lifted down, wouldn't there be some evidence left on the ground? Not if it had been put in a sack or a bag. Chances were, even if it had broken and spilled out, the ivy and periwinkle and other vines around the house were so thick the pieces would have been lost in the bramble. In fact, the growth around the foundation would have hidden any footprints.

But why, I wondered now, hadn't the alarm gone off?

Chapter 32

Dear Antiques Expert: I recently read that an early American teapot made by Jacob Hurd sold for over $40,000 at an auction. What made it so special?

One reason this 18th-century coin silver teapot brought such a high price is its maker, Jacob Hurd. At a time when most wealthy colonists still imported their silver from England, Hurd became one of America's first silversmiths recognized for his craftsmanship and beautiful work. The teapot you read about was rare, in excellent condition, and had a spotless provenance (or history of ownership). Since then, though, another Jacob Hurd teapot sold for $81,200.

MICHELLE FOUND ME as I approached the house. I wasted no time in pointing out the patch of new guttering to her.

"Oh, that?" She made no attempt to disguise the disgust in her voice or on her face. "Talk about a row. You should have heard the goings-on at the board meeting. And all over three or four thousand dollars. You would have thought it was three hundred thousand. Why, their behavior made the U.S. Congress look like a meeting of Quaker brothers. What I don't get is why, if they were letting the place go to wrack and ruin, they even bothered with repairing the gutter?"

"What happened? Why did it need repairing in the first place," I said.

"That's it." She shrugged. "Who knows? Squirrels, the ice storm earlier this winter, strong winds, nobody seemed to know *when* it happened. The gardens haven't been tended for over a year so nobody was out here to notice when it happened. Last summer some of the docent ladies cut some flowers and the Friends of Wynderly had a couple of cleanup days when volunteers came and weeded, but without the garden staff nobody was around that side of the house on a regular basis. Apparently one day somebody happened to notice a piece just hanging there, flapping away. It was right about the time the decision was made to close the house to the public."

"No one had heard it? Seems it might have banged around."

"Who *would* have heard it? Once the place was closed, all those faithful Wynderly supporters left this place like rats abandoning a sinking ship. I was the only person here for days at a time."

"It is *big*," I said smiling. But I was thinking: and in that time when you were all alone, you could have done anything.

"Aren't you cold?" Michelle asked abruptly.

"I was so glad to see the sun shining, I forgot about the temperature. But now you mention it, yes."

While Michelle fumbled with the door and then the security system, as usual, I realized that after traipsing around on the wet grounds my feet really had become chilled.

"I hate this thing," she declared, just as she had the other morning.

"Don't we all," I said. "Half the time I don't even bother to turn my alarm on at home, especially during the daytime."

"Can you imagine the thrashing I would have gotten from Alfred Houseman if the alarm hadn't been on when the burglary happened? I'd a been drawn and quartered."

"About that day—I think you and I need to go over everything that happened before Matt Yardley gets here. I'm sure he's going to have questions for both of us. I don't want to be suddenly surprised by hearing something new."

"He's the sexy-sounding guy who called you yesterday, right," she asked.

I flushed. "Yes, but more importantly, he's the vice president of Babson and Michael," I said. "Since he's in D.C. on another case anyway, it made sense for him to come look this situation over. There's a lot at stake here . . . for everybody."

Michelle tossed her coat over the back of a chair. I sat down in another. "Let's start from the beginning," I said.

"It was a Tuesday, oh, two . . . no, three weeks ago now. I'd come in for work as usual. Ever since the place was officially closed and I didn't have to be concerned about phone calls and inquiries from tour groups, I'd been trying to make some progress in organizing this mess. Usually on Mondays I would make a check of the whole house—well, most of the whole house—to make sure everything was OK. I started doing it on Monday since nobody had been in the house over the weekend with it being closed and all. I mean, with whole wings closed off, why bother? Plus, I couldn't hear the phone or the door or anything when I was in the other parts of the house. But that Monday I'd had a dentist appointment so I didn't get to work till almost eleven. And then this car full of ladies showed up.

They didn't know the house was closed, so I had to go through all that."

"Didn't they see the sign?"

Michelle laughed. "I'm sure they were chatting too much to notice something like a sign."

"Did you turn them away?" I asked.

"No. They were real nice and they'd made an effort to get here all the way from Waynesboro. They seemed really sad about the closing, and it turned out that one of them was visiting from out in Wyoming or Montana, or somewhere out there. I mean, what else could I do? I only showed them around the front rooms, but it still took a lot of time. Then one of them wanted to go to the ladies' room."

Michelle let out a sigh and a moan. "I couldn't say no, but maybe I should have. After she went, the toilet wouldn't stop running, so I had to call the plumber and before I knew it, the whole day was gone. That's how come it was Tuesday before I got a chance to check on things."

"And you set the alarm Monday night after the plumber left."

"Of course I did," she said resentfully. "And *no*, I didn't leave the plumber alone, and *no*, he didn't roam around the house by himself."

I could tell she'd gone over all this many times already.

"And he only went out to his truck a couple of times, and I saw him both times, and he didn't have anything with him. Anyway some of the things that were stolen, or broken, were from the back of the house and upstairs. Not everything was from the front rooms. He couldn't *possibly* have gotten into those parts of the house."

"And you didn't notice anything missing from the front rooms when you were showing the ladies around?" I asked.

"Are you kidding? With them chattering and asking questions and the house having been closed up since Friday and them not even supposed to be here?"

"I was just thinking that maybe something like the very valuable *missing* Jacob Hurd eighteenth-century coin silver teapot might have been in the parlor, or dining room," I said. If I owned that seventy-five- or eighty-thousand-dollar piece of American history, I wouldn't bother to put anything else out, other than maybe a table to set it on and a chair to sit in so I could stare at it.

"It was in Mazie's bedroom," Michelle said casually. "Anyway, it wasn't very big, maybe only . . ." She held her hands one above the other, then adjusted her upper hand down. "Maybe only four or five inches tall. With so much stuff sitting around, it would hardly be missed."

Her comment reinforced my strong opinion that Michelle had a long way to go before she became a serious antiques connoisseur. But more importantly, the mention that the teapot had been in Mazie's bedroom pulled at my heartstrings. At least Mazie had this one treasure she could openly enjoy and admire without having to slip into some secret place.

"That's true," I said, reluctantly agreeing with Michelle. "So then what happened?"

"OK. On Tuesday I finally got the chance to get into the east wing. Anyway, I checked the morning room first. They called it that because it's where the morning sun comes in."

I refrained from adding that in the English tradition, the morning room was also where the lady of the house often gave her servants instructions for the day. I wondered if Mazie had used it for that purpose.

"Well, I no more than opened the door, and I got that sick feeling you get when you know something is wrong. The rug was rumpled under in one corner, which struck me as strange. Then I noticed the lampshade on the floor lamp all catawampus like somebody had bumped into it. Then I saw that Delft plate lying on the hearth all broken up. At first I thought maybe a squirrel or a bird had gotten in through the chimney. That happens, you know," she said. "I looked all around, but nothing else was disturbed. Then when I got up to the room right above—" She pointed upward, and said, "That's one of the French rooms, but I always called it the blue room because of all the blue upholstery."

"I think you showed me that room," I said. That was the room drowning in drapes.

She nodded. "It had been one of the docent's favorite rooms, and she always kept flowers in the vase on the dressing table. It had been knocked off and was in a thousand pieces. So was one of the figurines—you saw it on the table with the Delft charger, the figurine, that is. The vase was smashed to smithereens. There was nothing I could do with it but sweep up the pieces. That's when I called Houseman. He called the police."

"And you're sure the alarm was working," I said for no reason other than to hear the words from Michelle Hendrix's mouth.

"I have answered that question so many times I'm *sick* of it," she said impatiently. "Yes. If you don't believe me, just ask Houseman. He'd even had the security people out a week or so earlier to upgrade the system when the board had voted to close the house. They were trying to save money so there was some talk about cutting off the service, but that didn't make any sense."

"And the alarm system would have been even more essential then than ever, without anybody here, especially on the weekends," I said thinking aloud. "But then again . . . Michelle, just how close is the nearest house? Would anyone even have *heard* the alarm if it had been triggered?"

"Not likely. It used to be that if it went off, the call went to Jake Nichols's house."

"And who is he?" I asked.

"You mean who *was* he. In the old days the Wyndfields didn't have any guards or security. Once the house became public, though, Jake Nichols was hired on for security, but he was more than that. Jake was from these parts and he knew everything that was going on. If the housekeepers were gone or the gardeners were on break, Jake stepped right up and did what was needed. Everyone loved him. You see, after the Wyndfields died and the foundation took over, eventually all of the staff left. A few of them stayed on for a while, but then the old folks like my mother and grandmother retired or died. Soon it was all new people holding down the jobs. They didn't feel any particular loyalty to Wynderly. A lot of them probably figured it was only a matter of time before the place folded anyway. Naturally the board thought Wynderly needed more security. Who can blame them?"

"And Jake Nichols. How did he come into the picture?"

"Well, he'd retired from his construction job, and since he lived right down the road, he was perfect for the security job. He tried the job for a while, but finally gave up. I mean wouldn't you? Each time one curator left or got fired, another one would come in from up north or out west or somewhere. Every few months Jake had a different highfalutin boss telling him how to do his job, and he'd lived in these parts his whole life. How would *you* like that? By the time I got here, Jake was the only person left, him and Patsy Jones, the housekeeper. Now it's just me."

"Does the alarm still signal his house, even though he no longer works here?"

"No, that's part of the problem. Now it goes off in the security company's headquarters, but the company didn't have any record of a call coming in. But why *would* they when the alarm wasn't triggered? There *wasn't* any forcible entry," she said wearily. "How many times do I have to tell people? The doors were all locked and latched. And the windows—"

"They're casement windows anyway," I broke in. "I noted that as soon as I got here. There's not much way for anyone to crawl in and out of those. Sideways maybe, if you were really small, and could wedge yourself between the outer frame and the center bar, but even that would be difficult. Plus you could only crawl *out*. There's no way you could open these old casement windows from the outside to crawl *in* when there's no outside latch or handle."

I walked over to the casement window behind Michelle's desk. I placed my palm against a single windowpane and spread my fingers. Its panes were the usual rectangular sort, measuring about four and a half or five inches wide by about eight inches high, and banded on all sides by metal stripping.

I turned back to face Michelle. "And many of the windows

in other rooms have leaded diamond panes that were never intended to be opened," I said.

She nodded in agreement.

"But let's just pretend that somebody opened one of these windows and managed to crawl out . . . then how would he close it? The cranks are inside."

"I pointed that out to the police," Michelle said shaking her head. "They sent a bunch of young guys over here after it happened. When I said something about the casement windows they looked blank. I'm not sure they had even seen casement windows. Around here all the houses have those Colonial-type double-hung, up and down windows," she said. "I've never noticed any casement windows other than at Wynderly. I even walked the guys around the house and showed them how the windows had gotten painted shut over the years."

"True," I said. "On a house this old and with, what, way over a hundred windows, you can be guaranteed the painters would slap a couple of coats over the outside windowsills onto the casing. There's no way they'd bother to open each window to paint every part separately. Yep, every time Wynderly's been painted, the windows have become more theftproof."

"So that's how we ended up with no suspects," Michelle said, giving me a half-questioning, half-resolved look. "Except me."

"That's not exactly the case," I said hesitatingly. "The security company . . . Any chance you know any of the people who work there?"

"Are you kidding," she asked. "It's Luck Security—the same company everybody around here uses. My cousin Emmett's worked for them for years. He says he doesn't know why people even bother to put the alarms in, though— *nobody* ever breaks in around *here*."

I swallowed hard and took a deep breath. "A guy about, oh, about fortysomething, kind of gruff-looking and with real crooked teeth?"

"You *know* him?"

"Not personally," I said. "But Michelle, I think it's time for you and me to have a real heart-to-heart."

Chapter 33

Dear Antiques Expert: Among my grandmother's things we have found a beautiful ivory crucifix. It still has its paper sticker from France where she visited in the 1930s. I know there is a lot of fake ivory on the market, so how do we tell if this one is real or not?

You're right, ivory has long been counterfeited. Most fake ivory objects are made of plastic or resin, and some have even been soaked in coffee or tea to make them appear antique. To test your piece, start by holding it against your cheek. It if is cold, it may be ivory. Next, heat a pin to red hot and on a hidden surface try to pierce the object. The hot pin will go into plastic, but not ivory. If the crucifix passes these tests, it may be real and should be authenticated by an expert.

MISS MARY SOPHIE'S MAID greeted me at the door. "Mrs. McLeod will see you in the library. She's by the fire."

It was the first time since the foundation's board meeting that I'd heard Miss Mary Sophie's last name. It sounded strange.

"Don't you look pretty," I said, for indeed, dressed in a

cornflower blue sweater and gray tweed suit and with her hair just done she looked quite nice.

"Thank you, my dear, and it's good to see you again," Miss Mary Sophie said, putting the day's mail to one side. She pointed to the same chair where I had sat before. "It's too early for tea or sherry. Can Nora get you something else?"

"Miss Mary Sophie, to tell you the truth, I'm famished," I said. "Even a glass of water sounds good."

"What have we, Nora? Some chicken salad left from yesterday? How does that sound? Just fix a plate, Nora, and . . ." She turned to me, looked over the top of her glasses, and said, "*Ice* tea, of course, this time of day."

I didn't even care if it was sweetened or not. "That would be lovely. Thank you, Nora."

We exchanged small talk about the weather, how spring would soon be here, and other meaningless topics. If she knew of Dr. Fox's accident, she didn't mention it, nor did I. Nora had come and gone and I'd downed half the sandwich and tea before Miss Mary Sophie asked, "So, Sterling, what brings you back to see me?"

In the car from Wynderly to Oakcliffe, I'd rehearsed what I would say. The way I had it figured, I would be leaving sometime tomorrow. Matt and I would discuss things tonight, and then tomorrow morning we'd spend time at Wynderly looking over the premises. I'd probably join Peter at Milton for the afternoon session of the auction, and then we'd drive back to Leemont. In other words, come Saturday night I'd be out of here. What people around here thought of me once I was gone was of little consequence. Still, I had to be cautious. Eventually the foundation would learn of Hoyt's deception and the fakes—I hoped from Matt—but it would still be my word against what the community had been told for decades. Because dreams were going to be dashed, it was important that I not go blindly forward, spouting false accusations based on erroneous suppositions. It was imperative that I have some backing from a knowledgeable source. Miss Mary Sophie seemed my only hope, though what she would, or could tell me, I didn't know. That had been my long-winded reasoning. But now facing Miss Mary Sophie, I felt terribly awkward. I began gingerly.

"Since I've been here, everyone has been lovely to me. Dr. Houseman has left me to my job, and though Michelle Hendrix and I had our rough moments at first, we've ironed those out. Thanks to Worth Merritt I've had a chance to learn more about the Wyndfields. Even Tracy DuMont has been helpful."

Miss Mary Sophie spoke up quickly and emphatically. "Tracy didn't know them well. Her father never did like Hoyt, and I doubt if he ever knew Mazie other than to say hello."

"And Ms. DuMont told me as much," I replied, "which is exactly why I'm here. You're the only one who seems to have known Mazie well."

"Ah, so it's Mazie who has your attention." Miss Mary Sophie's eyes turned from reprimanding to interested. She settled back in her chair and knitted her hands together over her stomach. "And so you've come to see *me*. May I ask what exactly has prompted this? Have you found something?"

"Yes, I have." I hesitated. In the silence that followed I heard what I thought sounded like a chuckle.

"No reason for us to play games, my dear," said Miss Mary Sophie as she removed her glasses and put them with the mail. She smiled, then quietly said, "So you found the priest hole, did you? There's much I almost mentioned when you were here before, then thought better of it."

"Yes, ma'am, I did. And the room beyond."

"Oh?" That seemed to take her aback. A frown flashed across her brow. "So you saw the dogs?"

"Yes, ma'am. And I saw what was in them."

She caught her breath.

"It was quite by accident, I assure you. I came upon the priest hole and the other room totally by surprise. I wasn't looking or expecting—"

"Oh, it's all right, Sterling," she said kindly. "Sooner or later someone would have come upon them. But tell me about the dogs and what you found."

Despite Miss Mary Sophie's reassurance, my composure was shot. "I hate to admit this, but I was so startled by the room and the books and papers I found there . . . Well, I'd already found some other papers in the attic—but again, totally by accident. You see, when Michelle didn't seem to have much to offer I went up into the attic on a hunch, thinking I might find receipts for some of the things lost in the burglary. It was when I knocked over some boxes . . ." I gave Miss Mary Sophie an imploring look.

"You came to Wynderly to do a job," she said. "If you found what you needed, through whatever means, it sounds as if you did it well. You're to be commended."

Her response, though well intended, did little to assuage

me. I felt no better than a grave robber digging up peoples' secrets that should have stayed buried. I took a deep breath and continued.

"I didn't come upon the priest hole that first time in the attic. It was the next day. And when I discovered the other room, I, well, in addition to taking some papers that I thought might relate to the objects, when I saw the dogs— "

"You took one of them." She finished my sentence.

"Yes, ma'am. But only one."

"I doubt if one will ever be missed, and you know it's inevitable that someone will find them," she said.

"Yes, but you see, I also found some of Mazie's diaries."

"My, you *have* been a busy girl." Miss Mary Sophie laughed aloud.

I could feel the neon red glow of my cheeks.

Miss Mary Sophie inched forward in her chair, gathered her cane and walked to the table of photographs. "Do you know who is smiling down from heaven right now? Mazie Wyndfield.

"I'll never forget the day Mazie came to see me," she continued. "It was a few days before Christmas. I was decorating the dining room when the door rang. Jacques Fortier always chauffeured her about, or Hoyt. This day, though, Mazie drove herself. She looked dreadful, something hardly possible for one so beautiful. She told me that, the day before, Jacques had driven her to Richmond to pick up some packages for Hoyt at a warehouse. She had planned to surprise her husband by having them at the house when he returned home from wherever he was. But, Mazie said, the packages had been damaged in transit and before they could be released she had to inspect them. It was at that point she burst into tears."

Speaking softly she said, "She loved that man so much. Of that I'm very sure. Mazie never stopped loving Hoyt, even . . ."

She raised her head and looked straight as me. "The damage was minimum, mostly to the outer wrappings. But *all* the boxes had to be opened, and when Mazie saw the four Tang horses . . ." Miss Mary Sophie let out a long, labored sigh. "You see, back when they had visited Kyoto in the 1920s Mazie had admired a beautiful Chinese terra cotta Tang horse statue. It was a reproduction, of course, and made in Japan, not China, but Mazie loved it."

Miss Mary Sophie paused, then said, "Isn't it amazing how the Asian people can make anything?"

Her remark came as a relief from the building tension of the story. Though I was eager to learn anything that might provide insight into Wynderly and the Wyndfields, a strong sense of dread had begun to hang over Miss Mary Sophie's every word.

"Actually, I'm amused when I hear people talking about all the things being imported from the Orient these days as if globalization is something new," I said. "The Japanese tea set I played with as a child had been my mother's. And all the items I've appraised that are stamped"—I held up my fingers to make quotation marks—"'Occupied Japan' . . . There've been more than I can count."

Miss Mary Sophie smiled patiently. "Anyway," she continued, "because Mazie loved the statue, Hoyt bought it for her. Everything would have been fine, except one day some years later, something strange happened. Upon returning from one of their extended trips Mazie noticed that the horse seemed somehow, well, *different*."

Miss Mary Sophie frowned. "Now you know Wynderly well. Things are everywhere. And the attic is a storehouse. When you're surrounded by so many things and have so many rooms and, on top of that, you spend month after month away traveling, well, I can see how Mazie might have thought she was mistaken in thinking the horse seemed different. Remember, too, Mazie had never cared that the statue wasn't the real thing. To her it was a gift from Hoyt, bought for her as a memento of their time in Kyoto. So, she put the idea out of her mind. But *then,* shortly thereafter, the same thing happened, only this time it was an ivory crucifix that they had bought in France. Mazie was a devout Catholic, you know."

"Yes, I do know that now," I said, remembering how Miss Mary Sophie had skirted my question about Mazie's religion on our first visit. But she had also said something else. She had spoken of a secret place that *used* to be there. Now I understood. That had been Miss Mary Sophie's way of dropping a hint about the priest hole. Might she have been trying to encourage me to explore more, I wondered.

Yes, Miss Mary Sophie, I thought, you're a sly old bird.

"It seems that one day when Mazie went to the vitrine to get her crucifix, it wasn't there. She thought maybe she'd put it elsewhere. The help knew nothing about its disappearance, and since Hoyt was in Spain or France or some such, she couldn't ask him. Not long after he returned, though, Mazie noticed an ivory crucifix, similar, but not the same, right where she had looked for hers. That's how, little by little, Mazie grew suspicious of her husband, but it wasn't until the damaged shipment incident that she confronted him."

My head was spinning with thoughts and questions. I'd seen a crucifix the day Peggy Powers had made such a big deal over the reliquary. I would check it out when I got to Wynderly. Chances were it would be plastic, not ivory. I needed to bring our conversation back to the reason why I was there, to find out what had happened to the American antiques I'd seen in the old photographs, yet Miss Mary Sophie had raised questions that went far beyond the realm of things.

How, I wondered, could Mazie have continued to love her husband who was so obviously dishonest? Why hadn't she left him? He had died first . . . why hadn't she gotten rid of everything then? Why had she allowed Wynderly to be turned into a museum? If she knew the truth, wasn't it as if she were an accessory to a crime in perpetuating the myth? I pushed my thoughts aside for later.

"Mazie told me how Hoyt would buy something and bring it home," Miss Mary Sophie was saying. "Then, weeks, even years later, it would have to go out for repair or Hoyt would find another one like it and replace the old one . . . She said things were always being shuffled about. Boxes and crates taken to the attic; things brought down from the attic." Miss Mary Sophie looked as puzzled as Mazie must have felt when this began happening.

"Then, that day in the warehouse, and in front of those people, when she saw the horses it all came clear to her. Hoyt was counterfeiting antiques, just as people counterfeit money. It must have been terrible for her, poor dear. The warehouse people didn't know, of course. They probably just thought Hoyt had ordered a lot of doodads to give as Christmas gifts."

"But the dogs," I said cautiously.

Miss Mary Sophie shook her head. "Ah, yes. The dogs. They were Hoyt's undoing. There Mazie had him, what's the saying, by the short hairs?

"As I remember her telling it, that shipment from Brazil arrived the same time as the horses. That crate wasn't badly damaged, so they only pried it open partway. But when Mazie got home and opened it further, a couple of the dogs had been broken after all. You know how it is with china. Sometimes it's an inside piece that gets broken. Well, that's exactly what happened. When she lifted the figurine out of the box, the dog fell to pieces in her hands and the stones that had been concealed inside tumbled to her feet."

Miss Mary Sophie looked to me for my reaction.

"The rubellites," I said.

"Oh! So they aren't real rubies?"

Miss Mary Sophie fell silent. Then, recovered, she said, "Oh dear. I don't know if Mazie knew they were fake." She looked close to tears. "I do hope *she* didn't know. You see, Hoyt gave Mazie a beautiful ruby and diamond ring at their engagement. When I was a young girl, Daddy told me that, just as the diamond symbolizes enduring love, the ruby symbolizes mutual love. Love given and love returned. To know the rubies were fake, that would have killed her."

"My mother used to tell me, 'Trust not him that once hath broken faith,' " I said.

Miss Mary Sophie smiled sadly. "And how appropriate

those words are. What I *do* know is that, after that day, Mazie never trusted Hoyt."

"Yet she never stopped loving him—"

"Don't you know about love, my dear?"

I dropped my eyes to avoid hers.

Miss Mary Sophie didn't give me a chance to respond. Staring off into the distance, an even sadder smile crossed her lips. "Thomas Moore said it best. 'The heart that has truly loved never forgets, but as truly loves on to the close.' That is the kind of love Mazie's generation grew up with. It was a different time, my dear. Mazie might have been a woman of the 1950s, but she had been a *child* of the teens—a full century ago, now. It was a time of gallantry and undying devotion. Mazie would never have done anything to disgrace Hoyt."

Her voice broke. "You know how we Southerners are. We are loyal to our own. Even to the death. At least that's how we used to be."

When she turned back to face me, Miss Mary Sophie's smile had faded. She said, "But Mazie also knew right from wrong. She couldn't undo Hoyt's wrongs, but she could try to prevent more from happening. I'm sure in today's world, things between them would have ended quite differently. Your generation is a different breed. *You* wouldn't turn a blind eye. The truth is, I questioned Mazie's reaction even back then." Miss Mary Sophie drew herself up as if reclaiming some years of her life. "I was still young. Thirty-five. Mazie was fifty-five, so there was considerable age difference between us."

"Were you *that* close as friends?"

She began to speak, hesitated, then said, "I don't know how

to answer that. Remember this is a rural area . . . it's not like we had next-door neighbors. And then, the Wyndfields were gone so much. Even when Hoyt was off on his trips, I don't think she had the opportunity to make a lot of friends."

"But all the entertaining they did— "

"Their lavish parties were more for visitors to the area than for their neighbors. Their guests were usually people they would meet on trips who would be in the vicinity visiting Washington or even Charlottesville or Richmond. Who from California or Maine or Europe, for that matter, would pass up a chance to visit a Virginia plantation house—not that Wynderly was one, but it was a fine house, there's no denying that. No, we weren't close, but we were certainly friends. I think there were two reasons why she reached out to me.

"The obvious one," she continued, "was my father's friend-ship with Hoyt. Not everyone liked Hoyt Wyndfield. Many people were jealous of him, but he and Daddy had been child-hood friends. Our families had been friends for generations. There was some kinship through a distant cousin's marriage, but the wife died in childbirth. The other reason . . ."

Miss Mary Sophie glanced wistfully at the picture of her husband across the room. "I was widowed, but my love for my husband was no secret." She frowned thoughtfully. "I am sure that Mazie recognized the depth of my love and devotion, and that made her feel comfortable with me. I think she knew that I, better than anyone perhaps, would understand both her dilemma *and* her loyalty. I have never forgotten the exact words she said to me that day."

Chapter 34

Dear Antiques Expert: In a lot of historic houses I've heard the docents call a needlepoint picture atop a tall pole standing in front of the fireplace a "fire screen." Why is it called that? It couldn't possibly keep the embers from jumping out and catching something on fire.

The pole-type fire screen once had a very practical purpose, though, as you said, it wasn't to keep the room safe, the way mesh fire screens do today. They were intended to defray the heat and glare of the fire, and even to keep a lady's makeup from "melting" under the fire's intense heat. These screens also provided the perfect place for displaying needlework. Today such screens are purely decorative pieces, and those having antique needlework are highly prized. Their prices range widely, from hundreds to thousands of dollars, depending on quality, style, and age.

"I HAD JUST FINISHED decorating the mantel with magnolia boughs and holly for the holidays. Mazie stood in that very spot," Miss Mary Sophie said, pointing toward the now fading flame with her cane. "She told me that in Louisiana a family's pride and its property came first, and at all cost. 'I was raised to live by the rule of pride, property, and then—only then—people,' Mazie said." Miss Mary Sophie rested her cane by her chair.

"I don't think this code of honor was exclusive to the Deep South," she said, "but Mazie felt it more deeply than other people, and she lived by it. In her mind, if she had exposed Hoyt to the world, the damage would have been to his pride, and as his wife, her pride—*their* family pride would have been destroyed by scandal."

Miss Mary Sophie smiled sadly. "Sounds old-fashioned now, doesn't it? I know Mazie grappled with her decision, for this is what she said to me . . . and this, too, I have never forgotten. 'I love my husband,' she said, 'and I vowed to obey him when we married. My problem is with myself. How can I obey him in light of what I know and still respect myself? It is my self-respect I must hold on to.'"

Miss Mary Sophie made no apology when her voice cracked. "Yes, Mazie was what my generation would have called a woman of substance."

I barely heard Miss Mary Sophie's last words. I was transported back to the night of Christmas 1955. Mazie was in the room off the priest hole, seated at her desk, pen in hand. I must have blanched. Miss Mary Sophie gave me a questioning look.

"Oh, nothing. Just something I remembered. Not important. Not now."

But I couldn't erase the image. It had been on Christmas, that day of hope and renewed life, that Mazie had written her own obituary. So *that* was how Mazie thought she could solve the problem. She would remove herself from the situation. Being Catholic, though, she couldn't do it. Suicide would have meant eternal damnation for her soul. Instead, she sealed the secret in her heart and lived with it by perpetuating the myth. But at least she had kept the stones hidden away.

"How hard it must have been for her to harbor all she knew," I said.

"Oh, there have always been strong women, my dear. It is how they choose to show their strength that says so much about them."

"And Hoyt, how old was he then?" I asked.

"Well, he was about sixty-five at the time . . ."

"And when did he die?" I asked. "She didn't kill him, did she?" I said jokingly. "I might have, you see."

Miss Mary Sophie joined my caustic laughter. "Tell you the truth, I would have been tempted if Hoyt had been *my* husband. But not Mazie. It did seem as if she aged overnight, though. She became quite reclusive. And," she said, "never once did she mention her visit to me. I know I wasn't any help to her. All I did that day was listen. I didn't know what else to do." She turned melancholy. "I've relived that day a million times," Miss Mary Sophie said, only to suddenly perk up. "Tell me, dear, did you ever read any of Ellen Glasgow's books?"

I shook my head guiltily. "Mother did," I said.

Miss Mary Sophie glanced toward the books lining the walls. "Oh, Glasgow was a remarkable woman, lived her whole life in Richmond, you know. I have little doubt that Ellen Glasgow wrote through her problems through the characters in her books. Most of us aren't fortunate enough to be so talented. But even that didn't seem to be enough. Probably because she was a spinster and kept her life bottled up inside her. She wrote an autobiography, but didn't allow it to be published until nine or ten years after her death. I'm telling you all this, my dear, because there's one line in that book . . . If you'll bring it to me, please. It's *The Woman Within*. It's over there, on the third shelf from the top. There. No a little further in toward the fireplace."

I took the book from the shelf, careful not to tear the cover further than its constant handling had caused, and gave it to her. Miss Mary Sophie held it in her hands until I was settled. When she relaxed her hands, the book fell open to the very page she had known it would. In a slow steady voice she read. " 'I, who was winged for flying, should be wounded and caged.' "

Closing the book, Miss Mary Sophie folded her hands across it. "Ellen Glasgow became increasingly deaf during her twenties. That is what wounded and trapped her. But when I read that passage it was as if *Mazie* was speaking to me from the grave. Mazie had once been winged, poised to fly. Hoyt wounded her, Wynderly became her cage." Miss Mary Sophie sighed.

"No wonder eventually Mazie's mind began to go. She was quite senile when she died. Whether or not she ever intended to tell anyone about the dogs, or Hoyt, we'll never know."

Without realizing it until Miss Mary Sophie asked, "What is it, dear?" I had begun rubbing my head, trying to sort out what I learned.

Mazie had promised to give the dogs to Michelle—the sort of gift a young girl would have delighted in. If Mazie had thought the gems were real, that might have been a way of trying to pass on some of the Wyndfields' wealth to her as a member of Jacques and Daphne's family. Yet, at some point, Mazie had hidden the dogs away deep in the attic.

And, on my first visit to Oakcliffe, Miss Mary Sophie had said "dogs" had been Mazie Wyndfield's dying word. I wondered how she might have known that until I realized the nurses attending Mazie had surely talked.

Miss Mary Sophie was right—fretting over issues that Mazie took to her grave was getting me nowhere. I smiled self-consciously and drew my hand from my head.

"Oh, I was just thinking," I said, "it would seem that no matter what her intentions, Mazie could never let go the hurt the dogs had brought into her life—for how many years was it?"

Miss Mary Sophie did the numbers on her fingers. "That was Christmas 1955. Mazie died in 1985. Thirty years. A long time."

"Miss Mary Sophie, I don't mean to ply you with questions, but I have to ask. Why do you think Hoyt did all the things he did?"

"Hmm." She rested her chin in her hand and thought for a moment. "Pure and simple show. Hoyt liked showy things, and he liked to stand out in a crowd. I guess, in his own way, he was our F. Scott Fitzgerald. Drop-dead handsome. And flashy. Flashy in the way only handsome aristocratic Southern men who have it all can be." Her mouth curled in an ironic twist in a way unlike her. "Trouble is, sometimes those fellows who have it all never feel that they have enough. Soon they're bored and restless. They drink and gamble. They go to war. They take chances. All the while thinking—no, make that *believing*—they're impervious to harm, to rules, to the law."

Miss Mary Sophie cast a glance over at her husband's picture on the table, and I wondered what secrets were in *her* past.

"I was always amused at the board meetings when people like Peggy Powers would go on about Hoyt's noble reasons for bringing treasure to these backwoods to share with those who would never travel to foreign lands," she said. "Hogwash. Hoyt bought them for show and brought them here to gloat. He really should have been a riverboat gambler."

Miss Mary Sophie smiled. "You're young, my dear. At least to me you are," she said when I started to protest. "It's taken me years, but I finally realized Hoyt's hold on us. We all yearn to be a little villainous in some way. What *we* can't be, we like our men to be." She chuckled. "Think of it this way. Scarlett may have loved Ashley, but her passion was for Rhett."

There was truth in her words. "Still, I can't imagine what it must have been like to be in Mazie's shoes," I said. "To have your own morals and ethics at conflict with those of the man you love . . . One last thing, though, Miss Mary Sophie, and please, *please* understand that I've been fighting my own private war this last day or so. You see, I've never done anything like I did at Wynderly when I took the papers. Most of them were receipts . . . but there were Mazie's diaries, too, and some personal things . . . and the dog. That damn dog. I still feel terrible about it."

"Well don't," Miss Mary Sophie said emphatically. Then turning thoughtful she said, "Frankly, dear, I'm glad this will all come out while I'm still alive. No one else knows what I have told you. After you've had some time to think about it, you'll know what to do. I'm quite confident that you can couch what you tell the board in terms of the antiques."

She leaned her body into her words and held out her hand to me as if to encourage me to think seriously about what she was saying. "Just tell them how you became suspicious about some pieces. How far you go in your explanations, only you can decide, Sterling. Don't worry. I'll stand behind you. And as far as your *guilt* goes, my dear, *I've* been as guilt-ridden for years as you've been for the past day or so." She let out a long sigh. "Yes, I think we're *both* going to feel better now. But there is one thing I would ask," she said. "Please be kind to Mazie. She was so misunderstood. That often happens when good people are caught in a bad world."

My eyes locked with Miss Mary Sophie's now tear-rimmed eyes. "When we first talked, you told me that Hoyt and Mazie had lived lives filled with too many lies. I didn't know what you meant then. But now— " I had to clear my throat before I could continue. "A few minutes ago when you said what you did about Mazie smiling down on us . . . that helped soothe my conscience. Thank you."

"I meant it, Sterling. From the way Mazie changed after that day, I know that keeping those secrets took a tremendous toll on her. But the truth is, Mazie was too proud for her own good. Shakespeare said, 'He that is proud eats up himself.' Mazie's secrets eventually consumed her. Maybe if the truth about Hoyt comes out, Mazie can rest more peacefully. At least in my mind she will." Miss Mary Sophie crossed herself.

"I don't usually do that, my dear, and certainly not in public, but it seemed the right thing to do," she said, smiling peacefully. "For Mazie."

"Miss Mary Sophie, do you think Hoyt ever felt any guilt?"

"That's something else I've grappled with," she said. "He, too, began failing shortly thereafter. I've often wondered if it was because he had been found out, or simply because he could never play the game again. Knowing his type, and I've known lots of rascals, I honestly think Hoyt's shenanigans were an amusement, a way to entertain himself. I doubt if he ever gave any thought to the wrong he was doing." She stared into the fire. "We'll never know. But no need to dwell on that."

But I couldn't let go of the thought. "I wonder what Hoyt said when Mazie confronted him," I said.

Again Miss Mary Sophie cast her old eyes toward her husband's photograph. "That, too, we will never know. But this I *do* know. No one knows what goes on between two people but those two people."

Miss Mary Sophie straightened herself up and looked my way. "So," she said, almost cheerfully, "any *more* questions for me?"

I laughed. "Actually, yes. One I almost forgot to ask. In early photographs of Wynderly's rooms there are lovely antiques, American pieces. Whatever happened to them?"

Miss Mary Sophie smiled. "Look around."

"Around?"

Her head turned and she nodded. "There. And there. And the fire screen, of course. It still has the old needlework. It's one of my favorites. Yes, my father bought a lot of them. And in the living room—" Miss Mary Sophie grasped her cane as she rose from the chair. "After Hoyt's death, Mazie bought some fine Southern pieces," she said. "Have you—"

But before I could answer Miss Mary Sophie said, "Oh, Nora. I didn't see you there."

"Yes, ma'am. I'm sorry to interrupt," Nora said from the doorway. "I said you couldn't be disturbed, but Ms. Hendrix at Wynderly said the police were on their way over there, and she insisted that she speak to Ms. Glass."

Chapter 35

Dear Antiques Expert: A friend of mine has a collection of 18th- and 19th-century stirrup cups. I know the old ones are rare, but they would make a nice gift for gentlemen who are hard to buy things for. Are reproductions being made?

Originally stirrup cups, like flasks, were designed to hold liquid and thus had either a hinged or screwed top to keep the contents from spilling. Today jiggers are being made that replicate antique fox and stag motif stirrup cups, but since jiggers are intended for pouring, they are open-ended and often have a handle at one side. These stirrup cup kinds of jiggers are made in silverplate, pewter, and sterling silver, and usually are sold in boutiques and jewelry stores in horse country regions where thoroughbreds are raised, especially Virginia, Tennessee, Florida, and of course, Kentucky.

OF ALL THE THINGS Miss Mary Sophie had said, one rang in my head the entire drive back to Wynderly. "Don't you know about love, my dear?" she had asked me.

"I must not," I said aloud as I turned off the highway toward the house. I had been wondering how my own love story would play out until I saw the police car. That jarred me out of my melancholy.

Before I could even get out of the car, Michelle had opened the front door. And as soon as I reached the top step she started talking. "You need to hear what they have to say," she said, adding, "It's about the burglary."

I swallowed hard. "Do they know who did it?"

She didn't answer my question. Instead, we started down the steps toward the officers huddled together in the drawing room. "This is Sterling Glass," Michelle said, "the woman I was telling you about. The one from the insurance company."

I extended my hand and said, "You are—"

"Officer Cash, ma'am. Johnny Cash." I didn't have to say a word. "Yes, ma'am, that's right. My mother named me after him," he said. I smiled.

The other officer stepped forward. "And Sergeant Terry. Ron Terry. Good to see you, ma'am. Sorry we had to pull you away from your meeting but Miss Hendrix here said you're the person in charge."

"Won't you have a seat, officers," I said, motioning to the area where Peggy Powers and I had chatted a day or so earlier. "There's room for all of us there." I turned to Michelle. "Have you called Dr. Houseman?"

"I thought about it," she said, "but it seemed to me with the insurance man coming this afternoon that you were more important than Houseman."

"Ah, excuse me, ma'am, but we don't have a lot of time," the younger officer spoke up. "We've been waiting for you and—"

"That's fine. I understand. Michelle, my briefcase is in the car, do we have some paper to write down any of the details we might need later?" I took advantage of the moment to remove my coat and collect my thoughts. "Here's my card," I said, handing one to each of them and taking theirs in exchange. "I'll be going back to Leemont, but I'm easily reachable, and I may have some additional questions when I'm making out my report for the insurance company."

"Yes ma'am," they said in unison.

"So, just what has happened?" I asked.

Sergeant Terry referred to the notebook in his hand and began to read. "On the night of Thursday, February twenty-third, Emmett Cheatham was a customer at Do-Drop Inn on Oglesby Road. Also present was one Cary Walker and his companion Pamela Bass. Ms. Bass later reported that she became suspicious when Mr. Cheatham started bragging about owning a lot of valuable antiques, but she didn't say anything at the time. Around midnight when it got close to closing time, Mr. Cheatham began to cause a disturbance. Pop Dinder, the proprietor of said establishment, refused to continue serving Mr. Cheatham when it became obvious that he was inebriated. When Mr. Cheatham began making inappropriate comments to Ms. Bass, Mr. Cheatham and Mr. Walker got into an altercation and the police were called. While taking statements from the parties involved, Ms. Bass told Officer Cash that Mr. Cheatham had been bragging about antiques. Ms. Bass had not been drinking. Ms. Bass said she remembered there had been a burglary at Wynderly. When Mr. Cheatham offered to show her some of his 'fine things' in his truck she got suspicious."

Terry turned to Cash. "You can fill her in on those details."

"Well, ma'am, since most everybody around had read about the theft, after we'd arrested Mr. Cheatham for public drunkenness and disorderly conduct, it seemed appropriate to ask Mr. Cheatham what he'd meant about the antiques. Of course he denied having said anything, but Mr. Walker had heard it too, and so had Pop. Pop had started listening real close when he saw things were getting heated up over there. With so many people having heard it, we felt we had due cause to search his truck. In the glove compartment there was this ah, little statue of one of them gods with lots of arms. It was all wrapped up in paper like he didn't want anything to happen to it."

I looked at Michelle. Her eyes burning with anger. "That—" she started.

I raised my index finger to quiet her.

"That's one of the items missing," I said quickly. "A bronze figure about, oh, so high." I held out both hands. "It's Lokesvara, a Buddhist god."

"Yes, ma'am. Maybe if you could spell that for me, I could put it in my report."

I told him I'd write it out for him, and that there might be other things he'd want me to write out as well.

"Well, once we found that," he said, "it was easy to get a search warrant for Mr. Cheatham's house. We incarcerated him on public drunkenness and disorderly conduct, like I said. This morning we got the warrant, conducted the search, and found other things."

"Officer Cash." I smiled weakly. It was all I could do to keep standing, much less keep my wits about me. "Officer Cash and Sergeant Terry, wh . . . when did Mr. Cheatham get to the bar? Do you have a time on that?"

Terry looked through his notes. "About ten o'clock, ma'am. He was there a long time. Seemed to have been drinking before he got there, too, Pop said. That was one reason why Pop had his eyes on him so careful."

"Was there anyone with him?"

Michelle jerked her head toward me. She was obviously as mystified as she was upset. I shot her a look to silence her.

"No, ma'am. He said Joe Boggs had been with him earlier, but he'd dropped him off. Mr. Boggs confirmed that. He'd gotten home around nine thirty, he'd said. You're not from around here, are you?"

"No. I'm from Leemont."

"Well you see, Mr. Boggs's house is about five minutes from the Do-Drop Inn over the other side of Route 20. That's how Emmett Cheatham happened to stop by there. It was the closest beer joint around."

"I see." My head was pounding. Nine thirty? That pretty much eliminated him from being responsible for Frank Fox's accident, didn't it? "Ah, one more question before we get back to the Wynderly things. In the paper this morning I saw about Dr. Fox's accident," I fibbed. "He's on the board here at Wynderly. I was ah, well, just thinking, ah, if Mr. Cheatham was driving drunk, is there any chance—"

"Mr. Cheatham wasn't anywhere near that wreck, ma'am. It was way across the other side of town."

"Oh. Just wondering. You're right. I don't know these parts well. You see, I was on some road around here last night and well, I kind of got lost, and I was just wondering where I'd been." I gave a half laugh.

Again Cash looked at his watch. "How about if we leave

this list of what we found at Cheatham's house with you?" He held out a piece of paper and looking sheepish said, "We hope you aren't going to grade us on what we call things. It's as best we could do. Like that silver thing . . . it really stumped us."

He glanced sideways at Terry. "It was real funny-looking, like an old dog's face with its ears laying flat against its head. It was about . . . oh . . . about this big and shaped like this." Cash held his left hand out as if he was making a shadow image. With his right hand he made a twisting motion. "And it had a screw top." He looked bewildered. "We didn't know what it was."

When I laughed, they joined in. "That would be a stirrup cup," I said.

"What's that?"

"Let's put it like this, it's something like a small flask, though a very fancy, sterling silver flask. It's what English gentlemen who were 'in the stirrup,' or mounted on their horses, would drink from—usually sherry or port, or whiskey. Kind of like a toast before or after the hunt."

"I told you it looked like a hound dog," Cash said to Terry.

"Well, that particular one was probably a rabbit's head," I said, "but with its ears back I can see why you'd think it was a hound. They made them to look like foxes and deer, too. Want to take a guess of how old it is and what it's worth?" I asked. "No takers?"

I watched them when I said, "It's over two hundred years old and worth about eight thousand dollars."

The policemen just looked at me. I could only imagine what they were thinking.

"And I have one more question," I said. "I don't know why

I didn't ask earlier. Has Cheatham said anything about how he stole the things?"

"No, ma'am. He's got a lawyer, so he's not talking. But he hasn't been able to make bail yet . . . or he hadn't about three o'clock when we left to come over here. We do know where he's employed, though," Terry said with a knowing smirk. "Luck Security."

Michelle suddenly spoke up. "So, this lets me off the hook, right?"

Cash and Terry glanced at each other.

My heart, which unfortunately oftentimes jumps in before my mind has a chance to think, said yes. But in this instance my good sense took over.

"Sergeant, did Mr. Cheatham say anything that would involve Ms. Hendrix in his theft of the antiques," I asked.

"No, ma'am. In fact, we don't know much about Mr. Cheatham's modus operandi. We're waiting for him to give a full confession. If he doesn't, we'll start an investigation. This case has just been opened. Right, Officer Cash?"

"Yes, sir. The first charges were about his disorderly conduct. Now we're looking into the theft."

"He's my cousin," Michelle said out of nowhere.

Officer Cash spoke up. "Isn't everybody related around here somehow? Those Cheathams are kin to just about anybody who's breathing." He laughed.

I wished Michelle hadn't mentioned that she was kin to Emmett, but it certainly hadn't seemed to make much impression on the police.

"So I don't see anything for you to worry about, Michelle.

Do you, fellows?" I asked in an attempt to console her and absolve myself of my lingering doubts about her.

"No, ma'am. And I'm sure we'll learn more about those antiques soon. Mr. Cheatham's lawyer will advise him to come clean. Judges always dole out lighter sentences when they hear a full confession. Well, guess we'd better be going. If you've any questions . . ." Sergeant Terry grinned. "And about that list. Yeah, we'da never known what that stirrup cup was if you hadn't told us," he said as they started toward the door. "Imagine we'll learn about a whole lot of stuff before this case is over."

Michelle was still sitting, statue-like, when I closed the door behind them. When the phone rang, I didn't bother to suggest she get it. I'm glad I didn't. It was Ginny Kauffman calling from Belle Ayre to say that I had not one, but two gentlemen waiting to see me.

Chapter 36

Dear Antiques Expert: A friend whose uncle lived in the Orient during the 1920 has inherited his collection of snuff bottles. He has no interest in keeping them. What would be the best way for him to sell them?

Snuff bottles became the rage in 18th-century China and Japan where snuff-taking was an upper-class social ritual. Small, attractive snuff bottles made a fashion statement much the way a pocketbook does today, and fine craftsmen made them in every imaginable material from jade and amber to glass and ivory. Many had silver and gold stoppers. These days fine snuff bottles sell for tens of thousands of dollars each, so I would recommend that your friend contact an international auction house to assess his collection. If they are of outstanding quality he may be looking at considerable money.

WHEN DEEP LAUGHTER greeted me the instant I opened the door of Belle Ayre, I froze. A male-bonding session between Southern-aristocrat, ex-priest turned thrift-shop-keeper Peter, and sophisticated Yankee business executive Matt, was not part of the bargain. I moved quietly down the hall and had almost made it to the steps when Ginny came bursting into the foyer from the kitchen.

"Sterling! I thought I heard you drive up."

I was trapped. I retraced my steps and stuck my head in the parlor door. The two men in my life rose to their feet.

Matt was even more handsome than I remembered.

And Peter? I'd never seen anyone look happier to see me.

"So . . . I see you two have met," I said. "Peter, Matt. Matt, Peter."

Matt stepped forward, leaned over, and bussed my cheek ever so lightly. "I'm afraid this job has been more than you, or I, bargained for. Peter here has been filling me in a little. A fine bunch this foundation's board turned out to be. I hope I haven't scared you away from other jobs."

I fought the temptation to touch my cheek.

"Let's say it's been a challenge," I said. "But you'll never believe what I have found out. We've got the thief, and guess what? He works for the security company."

Matt groaned. "Not another one of those. It's epidemic. We had one like that a few weeks ago in a house in Westchester County. Took a collection of snuff bottles if you can believe that. Thought they were *cute*." He smiled that smile of his and my heart skipped a beat.

"Turned out to be a couple of hundred thousand dollars worth of cute. Well, you can tell me all about it over dinner." Matt laughed jokingly. "Speaking of which, I know you want to freshen up before we go out. And Peter, you'll be joining us won't you?"

I avoided looking in Peter's direction to get his reaction. I was more concerned with how I looked. I must have been a wreck. Matt had as much as said so when he said I needed to freshen up.

"Yes, indeed," Peter said. "I'm looking forward to hearing 'the rest of the story,' as they say. And what's the situation with Dr. Fox? Have you heard more about him today, Sterling dear?"

Sterling *dear*? Where did that come from?

"Fox? Dr. Frank Fox?" Matt said.

"N . . . no, I haven't. I should have asked the police about him, but—"

"Police?"

"Yes, at the house—at Wynderly when they came to tell us about catching Emmett Cheatham—the burglar. Oh, it's complicated. I'll tell you all about it at dinner."

I looked from one to the other. Nothing had been said about dinner plans when Matt had said he was coming down. I was becoming more flustered by the moment. "I guess Ginny will have heard something about how Fox is doing."

"And she'll be able to call and change our reservations for dinner from two to three. I made them at Palladio—a reputedly wonderful restaurant at the Barboursville Vineyards. It's only about twenty minutes from here at the most. I hope you don't mind, Sterling. When I told my colleagues in Washington I was headed this way, they told me about it. Let's say we three meet here at," Matt Yardley checked his watch, "six ten sharp. I know it will be an early dinner, but after the day I've had, and it sounds as if yours has been worse than mine, Sterling. Is that all right with you, Peter?"

"Great. I've been meaning to get there myself."

"Good. Then we're set."

That's what you think, I said to myself.

Chapter 37

Dear Antiques Expert: On a recent trip to England we bought several antique copper pieces: a kettle, a couple of mugs and tankards, and a coffee urn. The dealer said these were popular in the 18th and 19th centuries. They are very colorful and attractive. Why don't we see early American copper antiques?

Copper has been used for making household objects since the fourth century BC. Because it is durable, but can also be hammered to a very thin thickness, copper is ideal for vessels used to carry or hold liquids, which are heavy. Copper was widely used in all civilizations to make mugs and pails and pots. But until the Western copper mines were discovered in the 1850s, copper was in short supply in America. Early American wares were primarily made of pewter, though those who could afford silver purchased items made from that precious metal.

PETER KEPT US entertained on the drive to Palladio with stories about the Barboursville ruins. A Christmas Day fire in 1884 had destroyed the Thomas Jefferson-designed home on the vineyard grounds. Now covered in vines, the evocative ruins remain a vestige of Virginia's past glory. But once we were seated at the candlelit table near the brick fireplace and our dinners ordered, the conversation turned to Wynderly.

"So tomorrow I'm actually going to get a chance to see the place," Matt said. "And some of the people I've been hearing about?"

"Michelle Hendrix will meet us there at nine thirty. She's the curator, remember. She'll probably show up around ten."

"And we think the mystery of who-done-it is cleared up," Matt continued. "That's a relief."

I explained how Emmett Cheatham had been identified as the burglar, but added my theory of how it had been done. "It was a makeshift security system to begin with. Michelle said the foundation had voted against incurring the expense of wiring the attic doors. Actually," I said, "I can understand their reasoning. They never *dreamed* anyone would scale the walls, either up or down, to gain access to the house, plus this is a very safe part of the country. Burglaries are next to unheard of around here."

"So the way you see it, this Cheatham just grabbed things up, slipped upstairs, lowered them down with a rigged-up pulley to some other guy waiting on a ledge or balcony?"

"I'll admit that one thing bothered me when I started figuring it out," I said. "Not only are the casement windows too small to crawl through, they can only be opened from the inside, which, of course, was one reason for thinking the robbery was an inside job. Plus, I'm sure the windows had been painted shut over the years." I paused, retracing the conversation I'd had with Michelle.

"So, how could the objects be slipped out of the attic, I

wondered. Then I realized that in the upper floors and attic there's the occasional French window that opens to a ridge or ledge." I couldn't help a playful smile. "Think Rapunzel. Better yet . . . Juliet."

When no one laughed I said, "Just kidding. The building code probably required them in case of fire. Those would still be operable."

I could tell Matt was dubious of my explanation.

"When you see the place, you'll understand," I said, dismissing his frown. "Think of a small-scale Windsor Castle combined with a miniature Mont Saint-Michel. There are turrets and protrusions everywhere. It would be easier than you think for someone to hide on a ledge or balcony, have things hoisted down to him and who knows . . . maybe even leave the things there to be gotten later."

"Is that what you think? That they came back to get them later, at night?"

"Night's a possibility, but not necessary for the theft. The place is deserted. The whole operation could have been done in broad daylight."

"And Cheatham would have had time to do this . . . to pick things out of various rooms in the house and get them up to the attic . . . and no one know about it? Where was the Hendrix woman all this time?"

"Trust me," I said. "This is rural Virginia—"

Matt looked around the room filled with well-heeled customers. "*This* is rural Virginia? Neither the setting, the menu, nor the people exactly fit my idea of 'rural.' "

Peter spoke up. "Well it is. Rural doesn't have to mean downtrodden or redneck. It's a shame it was dark on our drive and you couldn't see some of the houses along the way. Other than being older and more steeped in history, this region's little different from the countryside in Westchester County or Grosse Point or any other wealthy area."

Peter's usually mellow voice had a distinctively sharp edge to it. I couldn't decide if he was putting Matt down or taking up for rural Virginia.

Matt smiled. "Just teasing," he said. "You know the reputation the South has with us, ah, Yankees. Anyway, there's tomorrow. I'm sure Sterling will properly educate me during the daylight hours."

"Indeed I will," I said, doing my best to keep focused and sound composed. "And I have to agree with Peter. Think about Middleburg or the Inn at Little Washington. We're much more sophisticated than outsiders might imagine. Until they've come here, that is. But going back to Wynderly . . . What you have to understand is that after the house closed to tourists, it was rare for anyone other than Michelle to be there. At first I found her—"

I paused. I didn't want to reflect poorly on Michelle, or myself. I sighed and said, "Perplexing. Hard to read." Then with earnestness I said, "But now I've gotten to know her better, there's one thing I have *no* doubt about, Michelle's loyalty and love for Wynderly. And as far as the burglary goes," I said, "she knows she's under suspicion, and though now we know Emmett's the guilty one, she's still terribly worried. You see, Emmett is her cousin, which could cast aspersions on her. But it's clear that she had nothing to do with hiring the security company. That had been done years earlier. She didn't have any reason to distrust him. I don't think she even paid him any mind. Believe me, she's mortified by the whole situation."

Peter agreed. "Sterling's absolutely right. Why *should* she have distrusted him? But tell me, who do you think Cheatham's cohort was? Or, might there have been more than one accomplice?"

I gave Peter an appreciative smile before answering. I liked having an ally, especially a chivalrous one. "I don't know for sure, but there's this young wiry fellow. Billy . . . I don't remember his last name. I saw him with Emmett at the 7-Eleven one night—"

"Boy, you have been busy, haven't you," Matt said. "Perhaps I should begin to call you Madame Sleuth."

"As long as you don't call me Miss Marple," I said, laughing as visions of Hitchock's seductive heroines danced in my head—Grace Kelly, Ingrid Bergman, Eva Marie Saint . . . Any one of those would be fine.

"But the broken things? How do you explain those?" Matt asked.

"There I'm stumped," I admitted. "At first I thought it was a ploy to throw them off the scent. But thinking more about it, well, Emmett's bad temper seems pretty well known. If something made him mad . . ."

Then suddenly remembering Emmett's exchange with the 7-Eleven clerk about dreams of striking it rich, and Michelle's comment about some relative of his living in a big house, I rethought the situation.

"Or, maybe, and this is just my imagination running wild, I can ask Michelle more about this tomorrow . . . but there's the chance Emmett might have had some deep-seated grudge against Hoyt. Both families have been from around here for generations. Maybe something happened long ago . . . maybe not even to Emmett directly, but to someone in his family. This could have been his way of getting even." I leaned forward and dropped my voice. "You see, there's a whole lot to this story that I haven't told either of you."

Over the next three-quarters of an hour I told Matt and Peter about the attic and the diaries and the Kirklander appraisal, even the priest hole. I described how little clues had led to my conclusions about the dogs and the fakes and Hoyt's scheming. Even as I was speaking, more parts of the puzzle began coming together in my head. Like that peculiar notation on the very first receipt I had come upon that had started it all . . . the mention about the spoons that had descended in families in Saaz and been sold privately. I now realized that their "authentication" had been falsified and that they really were copies or fakes. It was probably one of Hoyt's early practice runs.

What I didn't tell Matt and Peter was Miss Mary Sophie's tale of Mazie's heartbreak. They were clearly more interested in learning the facts behind the burglary than in hearing one lonely woman's wrenching life story.

"But you haven't told Matt what happened to you last night, Sterling," Peter said.

Peter reached out and covered my hand with his and held it there. Then, looking Matt straight in the eye, Peter said, "That's the real reason why I rushed up here. I was worried about her. This lady's not only smart, she's quite courageous, and she has a conscience. She wants to do the right thing in every instance, even when her own safety is at risk."

I thought I was going to faint away.

"Oh, it was nothing," I said, only to immediately regret my words. This was my chance to shine. I thought again. Showering me with compliments wasn't Peter's usual way. Then again, not much about his behavior today had seemed like him. Was he staking out his territory? Perhaps so. Though that, too, seemed unlike him.

"No, I insist," Peter said and squeezed my hand encouragingly. "Tell him what happened last night."

"It was nothing," I repeated.

"You say that now." Peter laughed. "It was quite traumatic at the time. And, by the way, aren't you glad you didn't go to the police?"

"And I haven't even thanked you for your good advice," I said with heartfelt sincerity. "Now I *am* glad I didn't rush off to the police."

Matt's laugh interrupted what was turning into a private conversation. "Is somebody going to tell me what happened or not?"

Peter smiled his sweet smile . . . so different from Matt's sophisticated way. "Sterling?"

"Oh, OK," I said, and recounted how Emmett had run me off the road about this time last night. Then, as if to reassure myself, I carefully and slowly related exactly what the police officers knew about Fox's accident. "So that's what happened. You can understand why I was so upset when I first found out about Frank Fox's accident. Gosh, to think that just last night—"

Peter, who had sat comfortably back while I was talking, leaned forward, put his hand on my arm and broke into my sentence. "Matt. This afternoon, back at Belle Ayre, didn't you mention Fox?" he asked, adding, "Excuse me, I didn't mean to interrupt."

Matt Yardley looked from one of us to the other. Our eyes were fastened on him.

"Yes," he said slowly, "I did mention him. And after hearing all this tonight, especially your incident, Sterling . . ." He picked up his wineglass and swirled the last bit around before drinking it. He tried to sound casual, but there was an unfamiliar nervousness in his voice. "What I'm going to tell you calls for more wine."

Our waiter returned with three glasses of the vineyard's cabernet franc. "I don't think I fully explained why I was in Washington earlier today," Matt said.

"You said you had some appointments, I believe," I volunteered.

"Yes. As you can well imagine, Babson and Michael has numerous commercial and individual clients in the area. One has huge real estate holdings up and down the East Coast including several warehouses. A couple of weeks ago one of their warehouses in Florida had a suspicious fire. It probably didn't make the papers up here, but it was pretty big down in Miami."

"Miami?" Peter said. "I bet I know what's coming next."

"Well, I don't," I said.

Peter gave Matt a knowing look. "She may be smart, and shrewd, and a pretty good sleuth, but she's rather naive—in a good way."

I cast Peter the sternest look I could. It only egged him on.

"See," he said.

"It was arson, Sterling," Matt said. "It involved drugs and contraband and the usual stuff that you find temporarily stored in a port city until the cartel's network is in place to move it out. The thing that makes *this* situation so . . ." He spread his hands open and shook his head in disbelief. "So . . . hard to believe, is that among the containers that were saved, there were two from South America addressed to Dr. Frank Fox living in Albemarle County, Virginia. That, along with the Wynderly theft, is what brought me here . . . plus you, of course," he said, quickly adding, "I was eager to bring this case to a quick settlement even though the money isn't *that* big in the scheme of things. Most museums, even small, regional museums like Wynderly, have some pretty powerful people on their boards." He chuckled. "Let's put it this way, we like to keep everyone happy. But now you tell me Dr. Fox is on the Wynderly board?" His look bordered on astonishment.

"Oh yes, very much so."

"What, if I may ask, was in the containers?" Peter said.

Before Matt could answer I held up my hands for silence. "Could this naive woman take a guess?

"Vessels," I said. "Water vessels."

Peter looked at me querulously. Matt was so surprised that he thumped the table with the sides of his hands. "But how did you know?" he asked.

I smiled triumphantly. "It was just a guess . . . what you'd have to call an *educated* guess. You see," I said, "a couple of days ago Frank Fox asked me to appraise a collection of ancient vessels. He's a professor at a small college around here and his specialty is the hydrosphere—you know, water and the world." I made a big circle with my hands.

"Anyway, Professor Fox told me how some friend of his in the import business was making a gift to him of water vessels that had been used in ancient times. Fox, in turn, was going to set up an exhibition of the vessels showing water's importance to civilization and technology. He even mentioned setting up a foundation. But something didn't sound right. The idea seemed too obvious, too commonplace . . . not very scholarly or innovative." I paused and rethought the moment.

"Or maybe it was Fox himself," I said. "He's the nervous, twitchy type. I'm sure he was well intended, it's just that I couldn't see him persuading people to fund that sort of project. The way I figured it, Fox thought that if he put together an exhibit displaying the vessels he might get noticed by the University of Virginia. He had a friend, Victor. Victor, ah . . ."

"Shafer? The return address was some V. T. Shafer Enterprises."

"Yes, that's it. Victor Shafer."

"Well, using the vessels for an exhibit might have been what Dr. Fox told *you,*" Matt said. "The *truth* is, hidden inside the copper vessels in the containers addressed to him—drugs."

"But you mentioned South America, not Central America. And not Asia," Peter said.

"That was exactly my reaction," Matt replied. "Most drugs come in from Central Asia and Mexico and Central America. From South America, Peru's the prime candidate. But Brazil? Their drug exports mostly head to Europe.

"The thing is, who knows the cartel's plans once Fox received the shipment? At this stage of the game we have no idea if Fox was in on the scheme, or just being used. It'll be up to the law to determine whether he was knowingly involved."

I began slowly. "About the vessels, they were supposed to be antiques—"

"And they could have been," Matt said. "You wouldn't believe where drugs have been hidden. Heroin bricks sewn in the webbing of antique chairs. Packets of cocaine crammed inside hollowed-out cavities in picture frames. One of the best . . . if you could call it that . . . was a cloth tube concealing plastic bags of heroin hydrochloride stuffed inside a set of hammock ropes. The antique vessels make perfect sense."

"If I could interrupt," Peter said, "just how did they use them? You said copper. No stone or ceramic vessels?"

"No, these were all copper. Fake bottoms." He held up his thumb and first finger to show us.

"The drugs were wedged between a paper-thin false base and the real bottom like a sandwich. The whole section—the top piece, the packet, and the bottom—took up less than a quarter inch and appeared to be one piece of copper, of course. In fact, the two sheets of copper were sliced so thin the extra piece didn't add any discernable weight. Actually, though, customs had encountered that technique several times before. But here's what made customs suspicious of these so-called antique copper vessels."

Matt shifted his chair closer to the table. "First, the packages came from Brazil. When you think of true antique vessels you think of Africa or Mesopotamia or India, not Brazil. Second, *ancient* copper vessels from Brazil? That's another puzzler. Peter, you mentioned stone or porcelain. That's what you'd think of. Or even wood. As best I know, Brazil's not known for its copper. Chile and Canada and Zambia and Japan." He ticked the countries off. "Even Russia."

"I know, I know." In my excitement, I knocked over my water glass. "Do you remember *where* in Brazil the containers were shipped from?"

While Peter dabbed at the mess I'd made, Matt said, "Well they were shipped from Rio, of course. Let's see." He tapped his lips with his forefinger. "But the invoice was from a little town, some place I'd never heard of, of course. I do remember it was in, ah . . . what *do* they call the different regions in Brazil? States, provinces?"

"Federated states," I said.

"Yes. It was, ah, Minas Gerais. But the town . . ."

"Ouro Preto?" I caught my breath so rapidly I began to cough.

"Are you all right," they both asked at once.

"I'm fine. Everything keeps coming back to Ouro Preto. That's where Hoyt bought some of the Staffordshire spaniels, from antiques shops there, and São Paulo and Petrópolis. He spent a lot of time in Brazil with his tobacco business. And the stones, the rubellites—they're from the mines in Minas Gerais."

I waved my thoughts away with my hand. "But the name of the town I was *really* trying to think of is Miriana, right outside of Ouro Preto. I bet the packing invoices were from Miriana. On our trips to Brazil, Hank—my former husband—and I would always take a side trip to Ouro Preto for three or four days. It was like stepping back into the seventeenth and eighteenth centuries," I said, "especially the days we went out from Ouro Preto to the surrounding villages. Peter, remember I told you about the church in Miriana with the magnificent eighteenth-century German organ that was a gift from the king of Portugal—well, one time we stopped at a side-of-the-road crafts shop near Miriana, and I bought several charming copper pieces to take home for gifts. Little pitchers and bowls and boxes."

"So there must be *some* copper mines around there," Matt said. "I doubt if copper items would have been imported into a village like that to be sold. They'd sell their native crafts."

"Oh, there are all sorts of mines in Minas Gerais—and not just the gold and silver and gemstone mines . . ." I dangled the multicolored tourmaline bracelet Hank had bought for me there so they'd notice it. "There are industrial mines, too. There are definitely copper mines there. I remember watching the craftsmen making their wares. But you're right, Matt, there weren't many copper things. Most of the items were carved of soapstone or wood, or made of pottery."

Matt, who was making notes on a pad taken from his inside coat pocket, said, "And copper oxidizes so quickly, you can make a new piece look old by putting a few dings and dents in it and giving it a bath of saltwater. But back to the hydrosphere exhibit or foundation or whatever—that explains Fox's connection. And the way you describe him makes it sound as if he'd be the perfect patsy for a setup. Now, what we don't know is who's really at the other end. Shafer could have gotten roped into the scheme, or he could be one of the head honchos. But that's customs's problem—or ATF's. Not mine. All that aside . . ."

He lifted his glass in my direction. "Sterling Glass, you're pretty amazing."

I liked the way I felt, plus I'd had just enough wine to think that I was both smart and pretty.

"Are you the same guys who were calling me naive?" I

laughed. "You know what's really funny about all of this, though? I would never, ever, not in a thousand years have thought I'd use any of this information about Brazil . . . and certainly not to these purposes. Each trip was sort of a once-in-a-lifetime adventure. Who would have imagined how far the long arm of coincidence could reach?"

"Some people say coincidences are God's handiwork," Peter said. "But that aside, Matt, thinking about that Miami warehouse . . . Wonder what the chances are there might be some connection between that fire and Fox's accident? Think it might have been a way to wipe out the evidence at one end, and a potential witness for the prosecution at the other? It's a wild idea, but . . ."

"That thought's been rolling around in the back of my head, too," Matt said. "It's not as wild as it might seem. There have been countless incidences of . . . I guess 'retribution' is as nice a word as any for a gang hit. You can't put anything past drug smugglers. It's not beyond the realm of possibilities. They knew where Fox lived. It'll be interesting to see if the vessels he already has are still intact, or if they've been conveniently taken care of."

I slunk down in my chair.

For the second time at dinner Peter reached over and patted my hand. "It's all right, Sterling," he said. "From the time that each incident occurred, it's clear that your incident with Cheatham and Fox's accident had nothing to do with each other. Thank goodness they didn't. I'm awfully glad you weren't dragged into that mess."

"Me, too," I said to Peter. "Thank you again for your advice." I raised my wineglass and savored the last drop. "And thank you, Matt, for a lovely dinner."

"And look at all we've accomplished. Why, other than going over a few details tomorrow, I think we've done the bulk of the business tonight," he said as he signaled to our waiter.

Peter extended his hand toward Matt. "Please, let me . . ."

"Absolutely not," Matt said before Peter could finish. "I insist. Babson and Michael is *most* grateful."

Matt pushed his chair back to stand and Peter placed his napkin on the table, but I didn't move.

"I don't mean to put a damper on such a delightful night," I said, "but thinking about all we've said, it's as if Hoyt and Wynderly were just a preview to what was to come. First it was Hoyt with his counterfeiting and smuggling, though it seems to have been nothing but a game for him."

Thinking of Mazie, I felt like crying. Instead I said, "Now Fox. He was like a moth flirting with a flame, asking to get burned. Greed and ambition. And Emmett. Lord knows what *he* was up to." I laughed, but only for a second. "Speaking of which, who *knows* what the bank was doing in their connivance and manipulations? Force the close of the place so they could take it over—sell the house and the land? Sell the antiques?" I remembered Peggy Powers's insinuation that Frederick Graham's wife had her eyes on some of the pieces. "What's the world coming to . . . one big steal?"

Peter was the first to speak. "This is nothing new. Remember the Garden of Eden," he said.

"Oh, no. Not that *apple* again." Matt laughed.

Peter smiled and out of the corner of my eye, I thought I

caught a quick wink. "Can't get away from that apple, can we?" he said. "Even Hoyt and Mazie—"

"Huh?"

"The Delft plate, remember. That's the first piece you told me about," Peter said. "Actually, my point is that in Saint Paul's Letter to the Ephesians he wrote, 'We wrestle not against flesh and blood, but against spiritual wickedness in high places.'"

"Peter, you know me. I have to leave the Bible up to you," I said, "but one thing I *do* know. Though I can't vouch for their spiritual wickedness, with the exception of Emmett Cheatham, in this instance the evildoers were certainly people in high places."

"Which very often is the way it is," Matt said. "Like the situation at the Getty Museum . . ."

Peter laughed. "Sterling and I were talking about that a couple of days ago."

"Then you know that the grave robbers who *stole* the items seem to have gotten off relatively scot-free," Matt said. "But the art dealers who *sold* them and the Getty's curator who recommended *buying* them . . . *they're* the ones being raked over the coals."

A smile spread across his handsome face. "Know what's funny? It's not like this was my first insurance scam, but this one . . . When you put all the pieces together . . . it tops them all. Now every time I see an article about fakes and frauds and crooked art dealers all I'll be able to think of is Wynderly."

I couldn't help laughing. "Bogie and Bergman will always have Paris, while Matt and Peter and Sterling will always have Orange County, Virginia."

THE THREE OF US walked from the parking lot to the front door under the brightest stars I'd seen since camping along the Blue Ridge Parkway many years ago. Inside, we made our ways up the same staircase, along the same hallway, to our separate rooms. When we said good night we sounded like the Waltons whose homestead is in Schuyler, just down the way from Charlottesville.

"Good night, Sterling."

"Good night, Peter."

"Good night, Matt."

I closed my door, locked it, and slumped against it.

Damn, why'd they *both* have to be staying at Belle Ayre?

Chapter 38

Dear Antiques Expert: How often should I have my insurance appraisal updated?

Like the stock market, the antiques market fluctuates—sometimes just a little, but other times substantially. I recommend that you contact your appraiser after about five to seven years and ask that your appraisal be reviewed. A good appraisal should be so well documented that the appraiser won't have to return to your home, but can supply an update for any items whose values have changed significantly (either up or down). Your insurance agent will then have the new figures on record for your coverage.

I LEARNED QUITE a lot about Matt Yardley on the way to Wynderly that Saturday morning.

He really liked Peter, Matt said. That I could have done without. He'd been divorced twice . . . from the same woman. I was still trying to digest that tidbit of information when he explained that the second decree had come a few days after the first. But he'd laughed and said it had been a big mistake, that there had been some strange legal glitch. He'd been divorced for eight years. How *had* he escaped some other woman's clutches that long, I wondered, but didn't ask. He loved antiques and knew a lot about them, but had never taken the time to study them in the depth that I had. That gave me the perfect opening, but I bit my tongue to avoid sounding too eager by offering to teach him.

Despite Peter's attentiveness of last night, what guarantee did I have that it would continue once we were back in Leemont? Tracy DuMont's words rang in my head. "What's holding him back?" she had asked, only to follow it up by saying, "That minister fellow sounds like he doesn't quite get it." Yes, if given the opportunity, I'd be crazy not to give Matt a chance.

"Turn here," I said.

"Impressive acreage," he said. "Not a soul around, and not many on the road, either. I'm beginning to see what you mean about being able to pull off a crime in bright daylight. Even if there were a passerby, who'd think anything of seeing a security truck pull in or out of the driveway?"

"And there are other roads to Wynderly, back roads more twisty and less traveled than the ones we've taken. There's a pond down that way," I said, pointing. "And over there's a pagoda I haven't had a chance to see but I read about in one of Mazie's diaries . . . Oh, and I understand there's a summerhouse . . . as if they needed more room."

"Looks as if someone else beat us here," Matt said.

Parked right in the center of the driveway, so you had to pull onto the grass to get around it, was Tracy DuMont's Porsche—one of her fleet of cars.

"Oh my God," was all I could utter. "Pull around it and over on the side . . ."

About that time I saw Frederick Graham's 700 series BMW parked beside Michelle's car.

Matt laughed. "Glad I rented a Lexus."

I was in shock. "I don't know what they are doing here," I said.

Tracy met us at the door. "I wasn't about to sit back while the board does its usual namby-pamby poor-pitiful-us routine. It was something about seeing the boys from the bank starting to cart things out of here. After our supper, I did more thinking. I called Freddy, and he and I met yesterday. And then we learned about Emmett Cheatham's confession. I had Freddy call Michelle to let us in the house and here we are. Now he and I need to iron out some details, but it's fortuitous that you're here, Mr. Yardley." She smiled and looked coy.

"I've decided to buy Wynderly," Tracy said. "What I'll do with it, I can't say. But this I *do* know. Wynderly would go to the skunks in nothing flat if somebody didn't do something fast. I do have this one idea for the grounds, though. Mazie." Tracy DuMont held out both hands. "Mazie. Get it? I've been reading about how *mazes* have caught on all over the country. Iowa. Pennsylvania. There's even one on Plantation Road between Richmond and Williamsburg. I'm not talking about a formal boxwood maze like the one over there, the maze Hoyt had planted for her."

Our eyes followed her gesture. "No, I mean maize mazes . . . *corn* mazes. Over there in the pasture. They're becoming all the fad. A family adventure. A puzzle . . . but with a theme. Clues are posted all around and everyone has to find his way out. We'll call it Mazie's Maze of Maize."

We all carefully avoided eye contact with her and one another.

"And as for the house," she continued, "I've already spoken to Michelle. She's going to come to work for me."

Michelle glanced my way and swallowed hard.

"I'm sure I speak for Freddy Graham when I say I'm curious about how your company is going to settle the claim, Mr. Yardley," Tracy said.

Matt was accustomed to dealing with the likes of Tracy. He spelled out the procedure. "And," he concluded, "Ms. Glass has been exemplary in getting to the bottom of all this, down to figuring how the crime was committed. As soon as we have her report, the check will be cut. That will have to go to the foundation, of course. How you and Mr. Graham handle those particulars — "

"You'd better get that report ready in a hurry, Sterling," Tracy said. "Then I want you to come back and get to work here. You're for hire, I'm assuming. Michelle has admitted she doesn't know what she's doing. I can get someone else to teach her the ropes of running the place. And who better to teach her about the things . . . furniture, china, silver, paintings . . . than *you*. Deal?"

She didn't wait for my answer. "And then when you finish that, we can start on my house. I haven't had an appraisal made on my things for years. You're going to be busy for quite a while. And *you*, Mr. Yardley, I'll want to talk to you about insurance for Wynderly since you already hold the policy. We'll see how that goes. I have *other* houses, you know."

Her lack of subtlety was lost on no one. The old Tracy was back in full force. In just a few words she had sealed Wynderly's fate, tied up my life for at least the next month, and assured me of continued contact with Matt. I smiled and swallowed hard myself.

"It will be a pleasure doing business with you, Ms. DuMont. I think my presence here shows how anxious Babson and Michael is to bring about a fair settlement for Wynderly. I hate to rush, but now if you would excuse us," Matt said, taking my elbow, "I'm going to have to get back to D.C. to turn my car in and make my flight to New York."

He turned to me. "I fly out to Seattle on Sunday night." Then refocusing on Tracy he said, "A few clients there need personal attention. In the little time I have here I need to see the broken items left behind and . . ."

Matt Yardley broke into one of those smiles of his that made my heart flutter. His eyes swept the room. "And what better opportunity than to make a quick, preliminary run through Wynderly. Of course I'll be back to discuss this further with you, Ms. DuMont, but I agree, this meeting has been fortuitous—for all of us." He gave my arm a squeeze.

There was barely enough time to show Matt the workroom and main rooms of the house and still do a quick walk-through in the attic so he could see the Wyndfields' vast accumulation. Before I knew it, we were headed back to Belle Ayre so he could pack and I could get my car.

He was rounding one of the roller-coaster curves. "I've been thinking," he said. "I may make a trip of it when I come back to Wynderly. Take a couple extra days and drive down. You see, I've got a little sports car that would love these twisties." Matt took his eyes off the road long enough to give me a wink.

"Even if I fly, maybe you could meet me in Richmond or Charlottesville. We could rent a fun car."

"Spring's a beautiful time," I said, glancing up at the still-bare tree limbs bending over the road, hoping to hide the flush I felt spreading across my face.

At Belle Ayre, Matt left me talking to Ginny Kauffman to get the latest on Frank Fox while he retrieved his bags from his room.

Walking with Matt to his car I told him what I'd learned: that Fox had come out of the coma, but the doctors weren't allowing anyone to question him yet. Meanwhile the police were trying to piece together some sketchy information about another car that had been seen in the vicinity.

Matt heaved a heavy sigh. "Obviously our legal department is already working on the warehouse fire in Florida. Now with this connection—well, no reason for me to talk to the police here yet, though I'm afraid eventually they'll be calling on you once more is known about Fox and Shafer." He looked apologetic, though it wasn't his fault. "I'm sure that by Monday morning my secretary will have tracked me down in Seattle before the alarm's gone off. Oh, well." He checked the time. "But now I really *do* have to hit the road."

"Once I'm back in Leemont, I'll get the report right out to you." And it'll be a darn good report, I thought.

"I'm not sure when I'll be turning around to head back up here, but I imagine Tracy will see to it that it's pretty soon." I extended my hand for a friendly good-bye shake. "But you have a safe trip out west," I said.

Matt reached out, passed my hand by and took me by the

shoulders and looked me in the eyes. "And you, Sterling . . . *you* watch these roads late at night. Can't have anything happen to you. But we'll be in touch before then." With that he bent over and kissed me.

"Till then," he said and hopped into his car and drove off.

When he was out of sight I did what I had kept myself from doing yesterday. I touched the spot.

Chapter 39

Dear Antiques Expert: Among things I've uncovered in an old family trunk is a box of Victorian silver, all of it sterling. There are buttonhooks, a shoe buckle, clothes brushes, a little coin purse, and two or three card cases in different sizes and styles. Do these things have any value?

Though many charming Victorian sterling silver items like the ones you mention—buttonhooks, buckles, brushes, and such—are prized as mementoes of a past era, they're usually plentiful and aren't very valuable. But card cases are a different matter. They're attractive, practical, and great conversation pieces. Originally made for ladies' calling cards (a must in Victorian times), today they are perfect for carrying business cards. Cost-wise, cases decorated with a simple geometric or floral motif usually sell in the low hundreds. But more elaborate ones with scenes or historic places fall in the mid-to-high-hundred-dollar range.

THAT'S HOW PETER found me when he turned into the driveway. Standing on the grounds of Belle Ayre, my fingers touching my lips, my mind in a daze.

I pulled myself together. "Matt's gone," I said. "You just missed him. So, how's the auction going?"

"Good morning," Peter said and smiled.

"Is it *still* morning?" I asked, glad to have a chance to laugh. I don't know which was more surprising, Matt's kiss or Peter's driving up when he did.

"You've already gone to Wynderly and come back? I didn't realize Matt was leaving so early," Peter said. "Sorry I missed him. As for the auction, it's way out of my reach. I only managed to get a couple of Victorian smalls and a pair of neat botanical prints. With the New York contingent bidding against one another, they've got the really good stuff sewn up."

"Well, you're not going to believe all that happened at Wynderly," I said, finally having recovered sufficiently to remember back further than Matt's good-bye. "I can hardly wait to tell you."

Instead, Peter asked about my plans. I told him I wanted to run by Wynderly one last time before starting back to Leemont.

"How about this," he said. "We'll both get packed. While you're at Wynderly, I'm going to get on the road. Are you hungry?" he asked as an afterthought. "Me neither," he replied, seconding my quick shake of the head. "So I'll get back to Leemont before you do, probably by three thirty or four. Think you'll be back by five?"

I nodded. This time, yes.

"Good," he said. "Let's say you'll call me when you get there. I'll pick you up and we'll have a nice dinner at Loni's. I know how much you love their veal picatta. You've had quite a week, poor dear. I know you're weary. You can relax and tell me everything over dinner. How does that sound?"

I sighed all the way down to my toes. "Wonderful," I said.

Peter's sky blue eyes were smiling when he said "Grand. Just wish we only had one car. I'm going to miss you on that long, lonesome ride home. Guess I'll be able to make it till seven though. Will that give you enough time?"

"Unh-huh," I said weakly.

"Oh, and by the way, about the auction." He reached into his coat pocket. "When this came up, I couldn't resist. It made me think of you. It's a little gift to make up for all the troubles you've had to endure the last few days."

Peter handed me the prettiest sterling silver card case I'd seen in years. The embossed scene depicted a loving couple seated beneath a flowering cherry tree. There in the branches, love birds were cuddled close in a nest, and in the background was a quaint Victorian cottage.

I had to keep myself from throwing my arms around his neck.

"Peter! When I say I'm speechless you know I'm *truly* speechless. Thank you doesn't begin to say . . ."

"Turn it over," he said. He dropped his eyes.

On the opposite side, engraved in fancy script was the monogram *SGS*.

"What do you think the chances are that you'd ever find another calling card case with your initials on it," Peter asked, smiling shyly. "So you like it as much as I did. Good. There's one condition, though," he said. "I expect you to use it, not tuck it away in some drawer. It's perfect for an antiques appraiser's business cards."

How like a man, I thought, a little deflated. I turned it back over to the scene.

"And *you're* perfect for thinking of me. Thank you," was all I could say.

Peter's eyes met mine.

"And I liked the scene, too," he said.

I WAS HOPING everyone would still be at Wynderly. I needed to know how to be in touch with Tracy next week. Then I could hit the road, leaving my professional worries behind when I crossed the Orange County line for home.

When Wynderly's fate had been hanging by a thread, my head had been swimming with questions. Now many of my concerns would be resolved once Tracy, the foundation, and the bank had finalized their deal. The photos and receipts were of historical importance, of course. But what to do about Mazie's personal effects, her diaries and letters, especially those in my car? I would have to grapple long and hard with the moral dilemma presented by Miss Mary Sophie's plea that I be discreet and respectful of Mazie's memory. For that I would need to seek Peter's guidance. And the dogs and the stones therein . . .

Funny, but every time I thought about the dogs and their secret, lines of an old hymn Mother had loved played in my head. It seemed particularly appropriate to the moment:

> *While life's dark maze I tread,*
> *And griefs around me spread,*
> *Be Thou my guide.*

Yes, Peter was going to have to be my guide through the maze I had unintentionally walked into at Wynderly, a house whose walls really did have tales to tell.

AT WYNDERLY IT WAS business as usual. Frederick Graham was only as polite as the moment called for. Tracy pulled me aside long enough to make a typical Tracy DuMont comment. "Don't you hate annoyingly handsome men," she said, referring to Matt.

I didn't ask for her opinion of Peter. He clearly wasn't her type.

I was able to slip Michelle off by herself to tell her that I was looking forward to working with her and to assure her not to worry about the burglary any further.

It was thinking about Michelle that touched off one of those moments when, like the changing patterns of a kaleidoscope, images flash across our minds. For me it was the faces of the women I had met at Wynderly: Michelle, Miss Mary Sophie, Tracy, Mazie. No four women could have been much more different from one another. Yet, each had harbored secrets that had shaped their lives.

Years ago Mother had told me that every woman's soul was filled with secret chambers. That image had been vivid enough. But later, when I read Edith Wharton's story "The Fullness of Life," I had been shaken to my very being.

I have sometimes thought that a woman's nature is like a great house full of rooms: there is the hall, through which everyone passes in going in and out; the drawing-room, where one receives formal visits; the sitting-room, where the members of the family come and go as they list; but beyond that, far beyond, are other rooms, the handles of whose doors perhaps are never turned; no one knows the way to them, no one knows whither they lead; and in the innermost room, the

*holy of holies, the soul sits alone and waits for a footstep that
never comes.*

My own footsteps had invaded Mazie's holiest of holy
rooms. Now it was my soul that was sitting alone, waiting.

Leaving the parking lot I did two things I hadn't done in a
couple of days. First I plugged in my cell phone. As usual the
screen read "No Service Available," but this way it would be
ready once I got out of the boondocks. And I turned on the car
radio. I would have to settle for hearing Willie Nelson moan
about his outlaw ways, or the Abyssinian Baptist Choir prais-
ing God for all His goodness until I got further down the road.
I pushed the search button and listened to static crackling over
the airwaves while the tuner magically looked for a station.

I glanced into the rearview mirror for a parting glance of
Wynderly. Tracy in her mink and shearling coat, high heels,
and sunglasses was standing on the top step of the entrance,
hands on hips, giving Freddy Graham either instructions or a
bit of her mind, or both.

I couldn't help smiling.

At that very moment, the static ceased, and a station came
in. Joni Mitchell was despairing over how, too late, we learn
what we've lost. By then, we've paved paradise and put up a
parking lot.

The irony of the moment hit me like a wrecking ball.

But then, I thought, Wynderly was going to be saved. A
maze in the pasture was a lot better than a golf course around
the house. All that stuff in the attic would finally see the light
of day, as would the treasures hidden away in Mazie's secret room. Tracy loved antiques way too much to keep those

priceless pieces closeted. And I had a good feeling that given a chance, Michelle might even blossom. Yes, with a lighter heart, I was starting to look forward to returning to Orange.

I came to the end of the driveway and stopped. An old pickup truck was lumbering along. Had it not been for the thoughts playing over in my head, I would have gunned the motor and beat it on to the road. Instead, I sat and waited.

What a day I had had.

Smiling, I rummaged in my pocketbook until I found the silver card case Peter had given me. Holding it in the palm of one hand, I ran the fingers of my other hand over the raised decoration—the cottage, the lovers, the nesting birds. If only I could wish myself into such an idyllic setting. My heart raced. I was more anxious than ever to get home.

As the truck came inching along, I couldn't help noticing the white-haired man and gray-haired woman snuggling close in the cab of the truck. No wonder he was poking along. That old geezer was loving the moment.

I let out a loud sigh. Maybe I could still pass them.

I looked to my left. All clear. Then to my right. Emblazoned on the back of the pickup was a brand new bumper sticker. **Virginia** *is for lovers*♥.

That's the thing about life, Sterling, Mother said. *When it rains it pours.*

Dear—please let's go back
To that little provincial museum,
& through its little rooms again,

gray-green beads & various
other objects worthless
or unauthenticated

Please let's go back

—ELIZABETH BISHOP, "The Museum"

Author's Note and Acknowledgments

YES, THERE IS an Orange County, Virginia, just as there's an Orange County in California and North Carolina and five other states. I came to know Orange County's beautiful rolling hills and stately Georgian and Federal homes when living in Charlottesville and visiting my dear friend, Joe Rowe. I chose Orange County to be the setting for this book because I wanted a location where Wynderly would be totally out of place. Other than the kind of houses found there, the hauntingly beautiful Barboursville ruins, and the region's topography, the Orange County in *The Big Steal* is as fictitious as the story and its characters.

Speaking of places, as a child traveling with my parents, I toured many historic homes with hidden rooms and saw the Bannerman Castle ruins in the Hudson River. More recently, my husband and I visited the charming colonial Brazilian town of Ouro Preto, where the great American poet Elizabeth Bishop—whose unfinished poem "The Museum" is this book's epilogue—lived during the 1950s and 1960s. It was when visiting some of the galleries, shops, and roadside stands there that many of the ideas for *The Big Steal* began to form. Thus it is that experiences and memories come to play in the creation of a story.

A heartfelt thank-you to so many who provided encouragement and information, especially the librarians and booksellers who helped to promote Sterling's first adventure, *Stealing with Style*. My agent Jeanne Fredericks, editor Kathy Pories, and copy editor Bob Jones, and many friends at Algonquin deserve special recognition for their patience and wisdom, as does my daughter Joslin Hultzapple.

Thank you for your contributions, Gibson Worsham, Stephen N. Dennis, Jerry G. Keefer, Cynthia Price, Shawna Christos, Billy Jenkins, Wayne Oates, Annique Dunning, John Kukla, Susan Boaz, Nancy Evans, Bill Pillsbury, Carol Roper, Janella Smyth, Martha Steger, David B. Voelkel, Arthur J. Glaude, and my friends at James River Writers in Richmond and River City Writers in Danville. Thank you, Suzanne Savery at the Valentine Richmond History Center, Richard Lingner at the Isabella Stewart Gardner Museum, and the instructors at the Henrico County Citizens Police Academy. David Tulk of Madelena Samplers painstakingly explained technical details about Staffordshire dogs. Tracy Bryan at Virginia House and Deborah Knott de Aréchaga at Agecroft, in Richmond, and Melanie Leigh Mathewes and Kristin C. Law at Hermitage Foundation Museum in Norfolk, Virginia, provided invaluable information about hidden rooms and passageways. Supplementing my research on the early-twentieth-century American and Brazilian tobacco industry was Tobacco Merchants Association President Farrell Delman and his "strong right hand," Roberta Crosby. And thank you, Carol Foster, for sharing pictures of your father's years in Brazil after his graduation from Virginia Tech, and Roberto Ferreira de Novais and Magda Viera Novais, our Brazilian friends, for our magical time in Ouro Preto.

And to readers everywhere who treasure their antiques and the stories they hold, thank you.

A Quick and Easy Guide
to the Most Popular,
and Often Found, Antiques

When Sterling is in the homes of Miss Mary Sophie and Tracy DuMont she is surrounded by beautiful classical antiques like the ones you see when touring Mount Vernon, Monticello, and Williamsburg, or the wonderful eighteenth-century homes open to the public throughout the Mid-Atlantic and New England states. You may have seen this beautiful furniture, but not known exactly what to call various pieces you were looking at, and been timid about asking questions. You're not alone. Many people love antiques but feel intimidated by them. And if you don't know where to turn to learn more about these treasures, that may be because some dealers, museum curators, even collectors, prefer to keep their knowledge to themselves.

But you don't need privileged information to identify antiques. This brief layman's guide consists of two parts: a discussion of the terms "period" and "style," and illustrations of the most often found classical antiques.

Antiques can be fun and fascinating. Once you have some of the basics down, you may be ready to launch into a lifelong study that leads to wonderful discoveries and treasures—and keeps you from making mistakes. As Mabel Bason, the legendary Chapel Hill, North Carolina, antiques dealer told me when she was in her nineties, "I can learn something new about antiques every day."

Period vs. Style

Period antiques are pieces that were made during the time that the design originated, whereas pieces made at a later time to resemble those made earlier are distinguished from the older, original period pieces by the word "style."

So, Queen Anne *period* pieces were made in the early eighteenth century—in England from around 1702, when Queen Anne was crowned, until the end of her reign in 1714. But fashions then didn't change as quickly as they do today, especially across the ocean, and in America the Queen Anne period lasted till around 1750 or 1760.

Now fast forward: Pieces that look like Queen Anne period pieces but were made one or two hundred years later in the 1870s or 1950s, or even just last year, are properly called Queen Anne *style* or are said to be in the Queen Anne *style*.

A Pictorial Guide to the Classical Antique Periods

Most helpful to know when looking at antique pieces is which elements distinguish one design from another. For example, what is the difference between a Queen Anne chair (whether it was made in 1730 or 1930, in England or America) and, say, a Chippendale or a Hepplewhite chair? It really isn't that difficult.

A quick study of the following illustrations and explanations should help you begin to feel more comfortable around antiques connoisseurs and experts when they start talking about major categories of classical antiques—Queen Anne, Chippendale, Hepplewhite, and Sheraton.

Years ago, I overheard a crusty old dealer talking to a young couple shopping for a dining room table. Glancing down at the woman's shapely ankles, he said with a sly grin, "Start by looking at the legs." I don't know the outcome of their excursion, but as far as furniture goes, a piece's feet and legs can tell you a lot. Begin by looking there, then move upward to take in the entire piece. There you will see that the basic lines of the feet and legs are generally repeated.

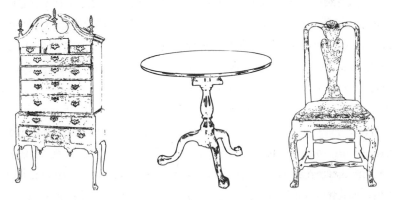

Queen Anne highboy
circa 1720–35

Queen Anne tilt-top table
circa 1750

Queen Anne chair
circa 1735–50

Queen Anne furniture dominated the first half of the eighteenth century, roughly until the mid-1750s. It is distinguished by its lovely curves and graceful lines. The legs, called cabriole legs, swell outward, as do the rounded feet. Those curvy lines are repeated at the top of the highboy and in the design of the drawer pulls, called escutcheons. Notice the round column of the tilt-top table and the curves of the vase-shaped back and arched crest rail of the chair back—these are characteristic of Queen Anne furniture. Keep the soft, flowing lines of these pieces in mind as you move into the Chippendale period, which followed Queen Anne.

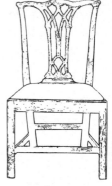

Chippendale chest
circa 1760

Chippendale dropleaf
table circa 1775

Chippendale chair
circa 1780

Chippendale (more commonly called Georgian in England, after the first four King Georges who ruled after Queen Anne on into the nineteenth century) was all the rage by the 1750s and remained so through the 1780s. Chippendale pieces are easily distinguished from Queen Anne furniture by their straighter, longer lines, which give them a heavier, bolder, and more solid look. Remembering to begin at the feet and legs, notice how the Queen Anne curvy lines have been replaced by angular lines. Moving your eye upward, you see each Chippendale piece has a totally different, more substantial feel to it. True, there are bends and scallops at the chair back, but they lack the sweep of those of the Queen Anne chair.

American furniture designed between 1785 and 1815 is given a broad name: Federal, so called in honor of the new federal form of government following our independence from England. But in England, the furniture of this era is known by the names of the designers who originated it: George Hepplewhite and Thomas Sheraton. Those names can also be used to distinguish differences among American Federal furniture pieces. Once again, by beginning with a piece's feet and legs, you can tell which pieces are Hepplewhite and which are Sheraton.

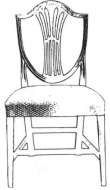

Hepplewhite chest
circa 1790

Hepplewhite dropleaf table
circa 1800

Hepplewhite chair
circa 1795–1810

Hepplewhite continued to use straight, angular lines, as had Chippendale, but in a more delicate way. Proportionally, Hepplewhite furniture is slimmer and often is inlaid with lighter colored woods. While a Chippendale desk or chest would be low to the floor, corresponding Hepplewhite pieces have taller, longer legs. To see this difference, compare the Chippendale chest with the Hepplewhite chest. Next compare the legs on the Chippendale and Hepplewhite dropleaf tables and chairs. The Chippendale legs are straight; the Hepplewhite legs are tapered, giving the pieces a lighter, airier appearance. Did you notice that the Hepplewhite chest has a slightly rounded, or bowed, front? This graceful touch combined with its taller, splayed outward feet makes it look freer, lighter.

Now compare the Hepplewhite inlaid and straight-lined pieces with the carved and rounded lines of the Sheraton period, which were made during the same 1785–1815 time frame.

Sheraton secretary/
bookcase, circa 1805

Sheraton console or
card table, circa 1800

Sheraton chair
circa 1810

While Hepplewhite legs are almost always square and tapered, Sheraton legs are generally round and often reeded, though sometimes plain. Many Sheraton legs also have a rounded ball or orb at the base of the leg. And while Hepplewhite pieces were often inlaid with lighter woods, carving was frequently used in the Sheraton pieces to add a design element to the basic lines. But because Hepplewhite and Sheraton furniture was being made simultaneously, often there is a combination of both design elements, as you see in the console or card table pictured above. Also note how the base of the secretary/bookcase has taller feet than those in the Chippendale chest. The eagle at top center (finial) is a common symbol of the Federal period.

That covers the "classical" antiques most often seen in eighteenth-century homes and museums, but antiques shops and malls and auction houses are filled with copies of the period pieces. Some of these, sadly, are fakes—pieces made purposely to deceive the public (and thus they are sold at high prices). But many are good, honest reproductions—pieces made "out of period" but in the "style" of an earlier design.

America's Centennial in 1876 came at the height of the Victorian era. But once the public saw so many exhibits of Colonial furniture, the old designs once again became popular. As a result, a huge Colonial Revival movement began. Once again Queen Anne, Chippendale, and Federal (Hepplewhite and Sheraton) designs were popular, and by the turn into the twentieth century, classical or Colonial styles dominated the home furnishing market, lasting until the 1950s when Modernism came in. As a result, much of the furniture found for sale today may look as if it were made in the eighteenth century but is actually Colonial Revival and not true *period* furniture.

Some of those later-made pieces were carefully crafted, either by individual craftsmen or small shops that turned out just a few pieces at a time, or by fine manufacturers who copied original pieces line for line. But many of the pieces made between 1910 and the 1930s took several design elements and combined them— the result being a mongrel. The two pieces illustrated below are examples of that era.

Colonial Revival chair
circa 1915

Colonial Revival chest of drawers
circa 1930

Looking first at the feet and legs of the chair, you see what look like rounded Sheraton legs. Yet the chair's back has a Queen Anne–style center splat, while the top or crest rail is straight, not arched at the sides, though the center has the same design that was present at the top (pediment) of the Queen Anne highboy.

The chest, on the other hand, has Queen Anne cabriole legs, while the drawer section has the heavier, straight lines associated with the Chippendale era, and the mirror perched on top is right out of the Victorian period—plus the bold herringbone veneer used on the drawers was a popular design element used in the 1920s and 1930s, but never in the eighteenth century. (Eighteenth-century tools couldn't cut pieces of veneer that large to glue onto the drawer fronts.)

When you are trying to date a piece that combines lots of design elements, remember that the piece cannot be any older than the most recent design incorporated in it. This means that, though the chair has some Queen Anne elements (1702–1750s), the Sheraton legs didn't come into fashion until the later 1780s. So this couldn't possibly be a Queen Anne chair—even though it was called that by the manufacturer. But could the chair date from the 1780s? No. The whole design is wrong for the eighteenth century.

The Three Major French Styles

Though French and Continental furnishings like many of those Sterling sees at Wynderly are not as popular in America as American and English designs, they are glamorous and quite elegant, and you should know that reproductions of eighteenth-century French period pieces have been made since the nineteenth century. Fine French period pieces usually are very costly.

The three most popular French styles found in shops, malls, and auction houses in America are Louis XV, Louis XVI, and French Provincial. To distinguish between the two very formal and highly decorative Louis periods, once again check out the feet and legs first. The two commodes shown below illustrate the difference perfectly. The curvy lines of the Louis XV legs and base are carried throughout the piece, as are the straighter lines of the Louis XVI commode. Louis XV and XVI pieces are often gilded, have gilt mounts, and are elaborately inlaid with different colors of woods (parquetry—geometric designs; marquetry—floral or scenic designs).

Louis XV commode
circa 1750–60

Louis XVI commode
circa 1785

French Provincial chest
circa 1780–1810

On the other hand, French Provincial pieces are just what the name implies—a simpler, toned-down rendering of the fancier or "citified" Louis XV and XVI designs. Without the gilding, fancy mounts, and elaborate inlay, the styles are more informal—appropriate for country living. So though the lines of French Provincial furniture can be curvy or straighter, instead of being made from expensive, highly finished woods, these more rustic pieces have a look all their own.

I hope this guide provides a helpful beginning step to understanding more about antique periods and fashions as well as fakes, and will leave you more confident and less timid about asking questions of those who are happy to share their knowledge with you.

Happy antiquing!

ROBERT M. SEXTON

EMYL JENKINS is a longtime antiques appraiser. She has worked at two auction houses and has written numerous books and articles on antiques, as well as a syndicated column. She is the author of *Emyl Jenkins' Appraisal Book*, *Emyl Jenkins' Southern Christmas*, *The Book of American Traditions*, *From Storebought to Homemade*, and *Stealing with Style*, among others. She lives in Richmond, Virginia.

Algonquin Readers Round Table Novels

Water for Elephants, a novel by Sara Gruen

As a young man, Jacob Jankowski is tossed by fate onto a rickety train, home to the Benzini Brothers Most Spectacular Show on Earth. Amid a world of freaks, grifters, and misfits, Jacob becomes involved with Marlena, the beautiful young equestrian star; her husband, a charismatic but twisted animal trainer; and Rosie, an untrainable elephant who is the great gray hope for this third-rate show. Now in his nineties, Jacob at long last reveals the story of their unlikely yet powerful bonds, ones that nearly shatter them all.

"[An] arresting new novel . . . With a showman's expert timing, [Gruen] saves a terrific revelation for the final pages, transforming a glimpse of Americana into an enchanting escapist fairy tale." —*The New York Times Book Review*

"Gritty, sensual and charged with dark secrets involving love, murder and a majestic, mute heroine." —*Parade*

AN ALGONQUIN READERS ROUND TABLE EDITION WITH READING GROUP GUIDE AND OTHER SPECIAL FEATURES • FICTION • ISBN-13: 978-1-56512-560-5

An Arsonist's Guide to Writers' Homes in New England, a novel by Brock Clarke

The past catches up to Sam Pulsifer, the hapless hero of this incendiary novel, when after spending ten years in prison for accidentally burning down Emily Dickinson's house, the homes of other famous New England writers go up in smoke. To prove his innocence, he sets out to uncover the identity of this literary-minded arsonist.

"Funny, profound . . . A seductive book with a payoff on every page." —*People*

"Wildly, unpredicatably funny . . . As cheerfully oddball as its title."
—*The New York Times*

AN ALGONQUIN READERS ROUND TABLE EDITION WITH READING GROUP GUIDE AND OTHER SPECIAL FEATURES • FICTION • ISBN-13: 978-1-56512-614-5

Saving the World, a novel by Julia Alvarez

While Alma Huebner is researching a new novel, she discovers the true story of Isabel Sendales y Gómez, who embarked on a courageous sea voyage to rescue the New World from smallpox. The author of *How the García Girls Lost Their Accents* and *In the Time of the Butterflies,* Alvarez captures the worlds of two women living two centuries apart but with surprisingly parallel fates.

"Fresh and unusual, and thought-provokingly sensitive." —*The Boston Globe*

"Engrossing, expertly paced." —*People*

AN ALGONQUIN READERS ROUND TABLE EDITION WITH READING GROUP GUIDE AND OTHER SPECIAL FEATURES • FICTION • ISBN-13: 978-1-56512-558-2

Breakfast with Buddha, a novel by Roland Merullo

When his sister tricks him into taking her guru, a crimson-robed monk, on a trip to their childhood home, Otto Ringling, a confirmed skeptic, is not amused. Six days on the road with an enigmatic holy man who answers every question with a riddle is not what he'd planned. But along the way, Otto is given the remarkable opportunity to see his world—and more important, his life—through someone else's eyes.

"Enlightenment meets *On the Road* in this witty, insightful novel."
—*The Boston Sunday Globe*

"A laugh-out-loud novel that's both comical and wise . . . balancing irreverence with insight." —*The Louisville Courier-Journal*

AN ALGONQUIN READERS ROUND TABLE EDITION WITH READING GROUP GUIDE
AND OTHER SPECIAL FEATURES • FICTION • ISBN 13: 978-1-56512-616-9

The Ghost at the Table, a novel by Suzanne Berne

When Frances arranges to host Thanksgiving at her idyllic New England farmhouse, she envisions a happy family reunion, one that will include her sister, Cynthia. But tension mounts between them as each struggles with a different version of the mysterious circumstances surrounding their mother's death twenty-five years earlier.

"Wholly engaging, the perfect spark for launching a rich conversation around your own table." —*The Washington Post Book World*

"A crash course in sibling rivalry." —*O: The Oprah Magazine*

AN ALGONQUIN READERS ROUND TABLE EDITION WITH READING GROUP GUIDE
AND OTHER SPECIAL FEATURES • FICTION • ISBN-13: 978-1-56512-579-7

Coal Black Horse, a novel by Robert Olmstead

When Robey Childs's mother has a premonition about her husband, who is away fighting in the Civil War, she sends her only son to find him and bring him home. At fourteen, Robey thinks he's off on a great adventure. But it takes the gift of a powerful and noble coal black horse to show him how to undertake the most important journey of his life.

"A remarkable creation." —*Chicago Tribune*

"Exciting . . . A grueling adventure." —*The New York Times Book Review*

AN ALGONQUIN READERS ROUND TABLE EDITION WITH READING GROUP GUIDE
AND OTHER SPECIAL FEATURES • FICTION • ISBN-13: 978-1-56512-601-5